Goodbye
to Budapest
A Novel of the
Hungarian Uprising

Margarita Morris

This book is a work of fiction and, except in the case of historical fact, any resemblance to actual persons, living or dead, is purely coincidental.

Margarita Morris has asserted her right under the Copyright, Designs and Patents Act 1988 to be identified as the author of this work.

http://margaritamorris.com

Cover design by www.bookscovered.co.uk

Published by Landmark Media, a division of Landmark Internet Ltd.

Copyright © 2019 Margarita Morris

ACKNOWLEDGEMENTS

Thanks to my editor, Steve, and my proofreader, Josie, for their invaluable comments and hard work.

PART ONE
OCTOBER 1952 - DECEMBER 1953

2

CHAPTER 1

The ringing of the doorbell invades her dreams.

Katalin wakes at once, alert and listening, but all she hears is the thudding of her own pulse in her temples. It's the dead hour of the night, long past midnight but hours before the grey light of dawn. She remembers going to bed early, tired after a long day of teaching, leaving her father in his favourite armchair reading a well-thumbed copy of Thomas Mann. A faint glow from the streetlights penetrates the curtains, bathing the room in dull sepia shades. Outside, the street is quiet.

Could she have dreamt the doorbell? There's always so much talk – whispered confidences, knowing looks – you can't help having these things on your mind.

'Did you hear about old Beke?'

'No, tell me.'

'They came for him in the middle of the night.'

'Dear God! How do you know this?'

'I saw his wife in the bread queue.'

'Shh! Here comes Piroska.'

You live in hope it will never happen to you. People talk of bell fright. The fear of the midnight bell. The terror induced by the ringing that wakes you in the hours of darkness, like a wolf in the forest. Katalin pulls the blanket up to her chin and listens, her jaw tense, alert with every fibre of her being.

The ringing of the bell splits the silence a second time, and this time it doesn't stop. This is no dream. Katalin sits up, shivering with cold or fright, she isn't sure which. Maybe it's not what she thinks it is. Maybe it's a neighbour come to ask for help. It could be old Maria from across the landing. Maria's husband, Milan, is a sick man. What if something has happened to him? But then why not wake József the caretaker? Katalin knows she is clutching at straws as she pulls on her dressing gown.

She opens her bedroom door and peers into the hallway of the apartment. Her father is already on his way to the front door, his tread slow and deliberate. Even in his threadbare gown he cuts a distinguished figure: tall and angular, neatly groomed grey hair, high forehead and intelligent professor's eyes. The bell is still ringing, its sound jarring. They'll wake the whole building if they carry on, but they don't care about such things.

'Papa?' She runs to his side, her eyes searching his face.

'Katalin, dear.' He lifts a hand to stroke her hair. The look of resignation in his eyes scares her more than the bell. With a sigh he turns the key in the lock and opens the door. The ringing stops abruptly.

Six men in uniform stand on the landing. It isn't Maria come to ask for help. It's the AVO. The feared and hated Secret Police. A new wave of terror passes through her. She puts a hand on the wall to steady herself. She feels exposed, standing there in her dressing gown and nightdress, barefoot. At the front of the group is a short, stocky man who resembles a bulldog with sagging jowls and a pudgy nose.

The door of the apartment opposite opens a crack. It's Maria come to see what all the commotion is about. The door closes in a hurry when she realises what is happening.

'Márton Bakos?' The bulldog addresses her father.

'Yes.'

'I have a warrant for your arrest. Stand aside.'

The bulldog stomps into the apartment, thrusting her father to one side. The reinforcements follow: a small army of five black-booted younger men, all of them taller than their boss and wearing fixed expressions. Behind them on the landing, hovers the scrawny figure of József the caretaker, stooped and unshaven. In his bony hands he clutches a set of keys, like a jailer doing the bidding of his masters. He smacks his lips together, taking in the sight of Katalin and her father, standing there in nothing but their nightclothes, blinking like frightened rabbits. Katalin scowls at him. He's the one who let the Secret Police into the building and brought them to their apartment. She notes that *he* isn't in his nightclothes, despite the lateness of the hour, but is wearing his usual brown trousers, grey shirt and old cardigan with the patched elbows. Did he know they were coming tonight?

The last ÁVO officer to enter the apartment looks familiar and Katalin realises with a jolt that she knows him. Tamás Kún. She hasn't seen him for years now, but they were in the same class at school. She remembers an awkward boy who didn't make friends easily. Tamás' blue uniform looks newer than the others'; the buttons shinier; the black boots not yet scuffed. She didn't know what had become of him, but now she does. A new recruit to the ranks of the Secret Police. She wonders what made him join. Tamás stares fixedly at the floor, refusing to catch her eye.

The two tallest officers, both broad-shouldered and strong, step forward and grip her father by the upper arms. He seems to shrink in size beside these two bullies. Fury rises up in her and she cries out, 'Let him go. He's innocent. He hasn't done anything wrong.'

The bulldog is surprisingly quick on his feet for a squat man carrying so much weight around his middle. Suddenly he's standing directly in front of her, his nose inches from hers. His breath smells of onions and cigarettes. 'I advise you to keep out of our way. Unless you also want to be arrested.'

'It's all right, Katalin,' says Papa. 'I'm sure this is all a misunderstanding and will be sorted out quickly.' She stares at him in dismay. How can he take this all so calmly? But that's the sort of man he is: even-tempered and sanguine. Katalin's instinct is to fight back, but in this situation, fighting would be useless and could do more harm than good.

'Gentlemen,' says Papa, 'do you mind if I dress myself before you take me away?'

The bulldog looks at his watch, as if time is pressing. 'Be quick!' The guards march her father to his bedroom.

Then the bulldog turns to the three remaining officers, including Tamás. 'You know what you have to do.' He indicates the apartment with a wave of his hand. 'Get on with it then!'

Like hounds let off a leash, they head into the living room and begin to search the apartment. Katalin watches them from the doorway, impotent fury burning inside her.

A blond youth who walks with a swagger like he owns the place, pulls books off the bookcase with complete disregard for their literary or sentimental value. Precious leather-bound volumes of European literature. Although a physicist by profession, her father speaks English and German and enjoys reading books in those languages. Charles Dickens and Thomas Mann are particular favourites. The volumes of Dickens he acquired at Oxford, England, before the war. The blond officer frowns at the unfamiliar titles. He holds each book open by its covers and then shakes it to see if anything falls out from between the pages. Nothing does, of course. Why would it? They aren't criminals or spies. The Hungarian titles he tosses unceremoniously onto the floor. The English and German ones, which he obviously can't read and no doubt suspects of being subversive, he places in a pile, presumably for further examination at AVO headquarters.

Tamás and a dark-haired officer pull the cushions off the couch and poke their fingers down behind the back of the frame. They roll back the rug to examine the floorboards, and shake out the folds of the heavy velvet curtains. What on earth are they searching for? It doesn't look as if they know either. They move to the piano. Katalin lets out an involuntary cry as the lid crashes open.

The piano belonged to her mother Eva. It's an old Bösendorfer upright from Vienna with an ornamental inlay on the front panel. It has a delicate tone and although Katalin doesn't play it half as well as Mama did, she likes to finger her way through some of Bach's easier pieces. When she hears Bach's complex harmonies, it's as if her mother is still there, beside her. It's a miracle the piano survived the war, when Mama didn't. But it might not survive this AVO search, they are being so brutal with it. They remove the lid and delve inside, causing the hammers to crash against the strings.

'Please be careful,' she says, wincing. They ignore her.

Tamás picks up the piano stool and tips it upside down. The lid flies open and Eva's much-loved copies of Bach, Beethoven and Brahms skitter across the floor. Tamás stoops down and shuffles through the pages, an uncomprehending look on his face, as if the staves of crotchets, quavers and semi-breves hold the clue to a secret language of espionage.

The blond officer has finished examining the books. He pushes past her on his way to the kitchen. There'll be nothing to find in the cupboards except pickled fruit ready for the winter, honey, salami, onions, bread and a large jar of paprika. She hears him pulling open the cutlery drawer and taking the lids off pans. A plate crashes to the floor.

In the living room, Tamás and his comrade have abandoned the piano. The dark-haired officer starts to lift paintings and photographs off the wall: scenes of Lake Balaton where they took family holidays before the war; a watercolour of the Mátra Mountains in north-eastern Hungary. He looks to see if there is anything stuck to the back of the frames.

Tamás turns his attention to a writing bureau, rifling through Papa's lecture notes, private letters and bills. He picks up a photograph album, the photographs held in place by adhesive corners which have dried with age. As he flicks the pages, photographs slip out and fly to the floor. Katalin sees one of her parents on their honeymoon in England and resists the urge to rush forward and retrieve it. She has precious few photographs of her mother. This one is of Márton and Eva in Oxford, standing in some cloisters in dappled sunlight. They are young newly-weds, arms around each other and very much in love. Tamás doesn't seem to have noticed it. But if she picks it up his suspicions will be aroused and he will probably take it off her.

The door to her father's bedroom opens and Papa reappears wearing a suit, shirt and tie, the way he always dresses for work when he's lecturing at the university or attending a committee meeting. The two AVO thugs still have hold of his upper arms.

'About time,' growls the bulldog. He has been pacing the hallway, like an animal deprived of exercise. 'Take him away!'

'Wait,' cries Katalin.

It's all happening so fast, she can't take it in. She runs to her father, throwing her arms around him, inhaling the familiar smell of his soap. She's too choked up to speak.

'Take care,' he whispers into her ear.

'Enough!' shouts the bulldog. 'We don't have time for sentimental nonsense.' He puts a firm hand on her shoulder and pulls her away. His touch revolts her and she wrenches herself free of his grasp.

The two men assigned to her father walk him to the door. József the caretaker, who has been standing outside like a sentinel all this time, moves aside to let them pass.

She doesn't have words to describe how she feels about him right now. He regards her with rheumy eyes and pursed lips.

They really are taking her father away. She follows them onto the landing and watches as they march him down the stairs.

József mutters something which Katalin doesn't catch, then follows the men down. At the turn of the stairs her father glances back up one last time, his face a mask, and then he is gone. Their footsteps echo in the stairwell, growing fainter as they reach the ground floor. She hears the creak and squeak of the heavy door. József never gets round to oiling the hinges. They'll be outside in a moment. She rushes back inside the apartment where the remaining officers are continuing with the search. Ignoring the bulldog standing in the hallway, she runs into the living room, stumbling over the chaos on the floor, and presses her palms and forehead against the cold glass of the window.

The men lead her father across the dimly-lit street towards two parked cars, black Russian Pobedas with long, curving bonnets. The driver of the first car jumps out, opens the rear door and the guards shove her father onto the back seat. The men climb in, one on either side to make sure he can't escape. The driver resumes his seat and the car swings away from the kerb, belching out a cloud of black exhaust. She slams her hand against the glass in frustration.

'Finished in here?' The bulldog strides into the living room. 'Go and search the bedrooms. And get a move on, can't you?'

Katalin spins round. It's not that she has anything to hide, but this search feels like a physical assault on her person. She follows them into the hallway, wishing she could tell them to stop. But it would be dangerous to provoke them. She remembers her father's last words to her. *Take care.*

The dark-haired officer joins the blond one in her father's room and Tamás makes his way down the hallway to her own room. The bulldog is instructing the men in her father's room, telling them to be extra thorough. Katalin takes the opportunity to slip past him and follow Tamás. She stands just inside the doorway and watches as he peers under her bed, slides his hand under the mattress, pulls her clothes from the wardrobe and then moves to the antique chest of drawers that used to belong to her grandmother.

'What are you looking for?'

He ignores her question and pulls open the top drawer, the one that holds her underwear. As soon as he sees what the drawer contains he slams it shut, his face as red as a beetroot. He's still as awkward as he was as a teenager.

After that, he doesn't bother with the other drawers but turns instead to the window seat where her violin lies in its case. Her heart skips a beat when she sees him walking towards her most precious possession. She fears he'll take his anger at his own awkwardness out on the violin. Should she risk reminding him that they were at school together? Whilst never friends, surely a shared past will mean something to him?

He has his fingers on the clasp of the violin case. Katalin peers into the hallway. The bulldog is in the bathroom. She hears the toilet flushing. She steps back into the room and closes the bedroom door.

'Tamás.'

He swings round at the sound of his name. 'Don't talk to me! I'm here to do a job.'

'Please don't touch my violin.' She holds his gaze with hers, staring hard into his frosty blue eyes. It's a battle of wills to see who will blink first.

She wins.

The bulldog is back, stomping up and down the hallway shouting at his men to get a move on if they know what's good for them. At the sound of his voice Tamás jumps.

'I think you'd better say this room is finished, don't you? You don't want to get into trouble with your boss.' She's playing with fire, but can't help herself.

Tamás pushes past her and out of the room. Her pulse is hammering hard in her ears and for a moment or two she feels dizzy. She sits down heavily on the bed and tries to calm her breathing which is coming in short bursts.

In the hallway the bulldog is shouting orders; they are preparing to leave. She creeps back to the hallway and watches as the men box up items to take away for examination, mostly papers and books.

Finally they leave, carrying the boxes out of the apartment to the waiting car.

Within seconds Katalin is shaking all over, her brief moment of victory over Tamás forgotten. It's the shock of what has just happened. She wishes her friend Róza were here now. With her medical training, Róza would know what to do for the best. Katalin collapses on the sofa amid the wreckage of the living room and curls herself into a ball.

You live in hope it will never happen to you. And then it does.

CHAPTER 2

You officious, jumped-up little toad, thinks Zoltán. He bites his tongue to stop himself from saying the words out loud.

Csaba Elek, the Party Secretary at the factory, is reading aloud from the Party newspaper *Szabad Nép, A Free People*. His voice is a sanctimonious drawl that makes Zoltán want to roll the paper up and stuff it down his scrawny neck.

The triumph of socialism over the evils of capitalism...Soaring productivity levels...The rewards of communism...

Zoltán has heard it all before a thousand times. Repetition doesn't make any of it true.

He's standing shoulder-to-shoulder with his co-workers half an hour before the working day is due to start. Everyone is expected to come in early for the compulsory morning reading of the Party line of the day. It's a form of brainwashing before people have had a chance to properly wake up.

Gazing down at them from the wall behind Csaba Elek is a portrait of *Our Wise Leader Rákosi*. Fat and bald, the bloated face of Stalin's best pupil appears to sit directly on his shoulders, with no neck in between. The eyes under the thick eyebrows are cold, the half-smile on the lips artificial.

Zoltán has long thought that if the workers could have half an hour extra in bed, or time for some breakfast and a coffee, then they might be more productive at their work. Instead they have to stand here like lemons, whilst Csaba Elek tells them that productivity has tripled, nay quadrupled, in the factories in recent months thanks to the economic wizardry of Erno Gerő and his miraculous Five Year Plan.

Zoltán catches Sándor's eye and the other man stifles a yawn which makes Zoltán want to yawn too. Yawns are catching like that. As is laughing. Both are frowned upon severely by the Party officials who sit on the platform, scanning the assembled workers, noting absences and indiscretions. Both are taken as signs of disrespect towards the Party. And disrespect is a punishable offence.

'...and this is all thanks to our great leader, Mátyás Rákosi.' Csaba Elek's voice rises to an emotional climax at the mention of Rákosi's name. If this were an opera, thinks Zoltán, now would be the moment for an impassioned aria or a stirring chorus. Instead the assembled factory workers dutifully break out into thunderous applause. This happens whenever Stalin or Rákosi are mentioned by name. You have to demonstrate the appropriate level of enthusiasm, or risk being a marked man. The Party officials are on their feet, clapping along with everyone else, but mostly they are watching for anyone lacking sufficient fervour. Zoltán joins in. He can do without the hassle of being labelled a troublemaker.

After a moment or two the applause becomes a rhythmic clapping that is almost hypnotic. It's tiring to keep this up for minutes on end, but no one dares be the first to stop.

The old man standing in front of Zoltán, a veteran of the First World War who lost half his right leg fighting the Russians, sways on his one good foot and his wooden peg leg. He looks as if he might keel over and then those around him would topple like dominoes. Zoltán risks the wrath of the Party Secretary and stops clapping so he can put a steadying hand on the old man's shoulder. Surely this can't go on for much longer, can it?

He's tired himself today. He didn't get much sleep last night. He was reading late, a favourite pastime of his, when he heard the sound of car engines in the street. In a country where few people own a car, the sound of a throbbing engine, particularly after midnight, usually means only one thing. He turned off the light and stood to one side of the window frame so that he was hidden from view and watched as two black Pobedas pulled up outside. Six AVO men got out of the cars and went into the building opposite, let in by that miserable old caretaker, József. Then a few minutes later the lights went on in the Bakos' apartment and Zoltán's worst fears were proved right. They'd come for Márton Bakos. *Her* father.

When the AVO men brought Márton Bakos out into the street he saw her, with her forehead pressed against the window, a look of desperation on her face. He wanted to call out to her, offer some comfort, but there was nothing he could do. If he'd interfered they'd have come for him too and he'd be no good to her locked up in some AVO cell. He would have to find some other way to lend his support.

Eventually the Party Secretary gives the sign for the clapping to stop. The workers drop their hands to their sides, the sense of relief palpable. The reading is over for today.

From the platform Csaba Elek glares at him. He must have noticed him stop clapping before the others. He has blotted his copybook, which was never perfect to begin with. Zoltán stares back defiantly.

'Thanks, son,' whispers the old man. 'Don't know what came over me there. Felt a bit faint.' He limps off to his workstation, his wooden leg tapping on the floor. He should be taking it easy, thinks Zoltán. Not working in this factory twelve hours a day until he drops dead.

Csaba Elek carefully folds the newspaper and tucks it under his arm as if it's a sacred text. He'll go to his office now and write up his daily report: who was missing, who wasn't paying attention, who stopped clapping before the order to cease had been given. Zoltán has no doubt his name will be on it. With a sigh, he turns away and finds Sándor by his side.

'Hey, Zoltán, you all right? You look a bit rough today if you don't mind me saying.' Sándor lays a hand on his friend's shoulder. The two of them are like brothers. After a shared childhood on neighbouring vineyards north of Budapest, they enlisted for the labour battalions together in '44. With hundreds of others they were shipped off to Transylvania to build the Árpád Line, a chain of trenches and fortresses in the Carpathian Mountains intended to ward off the Russian advance. Their defensive efforts may have been ultimately futile, but their childhood bond grew all the stronger.

'Late night,' says Zoltán. Now is not the time to go into details, even with Sándor. Too many listening ears.

'Oh yes?' asks Sándor raising an eyebrow. He always has an eye for a pretty girl.

'It's not what you're thinking.' Although he wouldn't have stayed by the window keeping watch for anyone else.

*

Katalin wakes with a start. She's grown cold and stiff, curled up on the sofa. She hadn't expected to sleep and her neck is painful from lying at an awkward angle. She sits up, rubbing her eyes. A cold, grey light bathes the room. All around her the floor is strewn with books, papers and photographs. The sight of all this chaos brings back the events of last night with such frightening clarity that she looks behind her in case they are still there, lurking. The hated Secret Police. But they have gone, and they have taken her father with them.

Fear turns to rage.

How dare they barge in like that and arrest her Papa. What possible reason could they have for doing such a thing? She and her father live quietly, minding their own business, trying not to ruffle feathers, but still the Secret Police have violated their lives, and her father is now goodness knows where. She'll never forget the sight of him being manhandled into the back of the black Pobeda and driven off. A thought strikes her. What if that is the last time she ever sees him? People disappear and never come back. You hear such stories, but you try not to think about them. You keep your head down and try not to draw attention to yourself. But someone drew attention to her father and now he's been taken. She chokes back a sob. No, she mustn't think like this. She must try to stay strong, for his sake.

She gets to her feet, careful not to step on precious photographs and books. Many of them now bear the imprint of AVO boots. She would like to start tidying up straight away, restore order and remove all traces of those men, but there isn't time now. She has to go to work. Piroska Benke, the school secretary, will mark her file if she's late. The woman is a bureaucratic machine, keeping detailed reports on all the pupils and members of staff. She guards her office more securely than the Catholic Church guards the treasures of the Vatican. And the headmaster, György Boda, is always looking for any excuse to find fault. *How can we expect the children to learn punctuality and the correct forms of behaviour if we do not set an example ourselves?* Besides, she has to pay the rent on the apartment. She doesn't expect that her father's salary will be paid now that he has been arrested.

She steps across the living room and pulls the door closed behind her, telling herself she'll deal with it later. In the kitchen she is confronted with yet more mess: a ripped open loaf of bread; unscrewed jars, their contents spilt; pots and pans taken from the cupboards and left on the worktop; a smashed plate on the floor. It's from a set of her grandmother's crockery with a blue flower design. They've always taken good care of things. The communists would say the design was bourgeois but Katalin has always thought it rather pretty.

There's no hope of mending the plate. She picks up the broken shards and places them carefully in the bin. Then she tears a hunk of bread off the damaged loaf. She finds a pat of butter that hasn't been touched and spreads it on the bread, forcing herself to chew and swallow. She doesn't want it, but she can't teach all day on an empty stomach. She must keep her strength up for the day ahead, and the days after that. Her father rebuilt his life one day at a time after the war and she must now do the same. She washes the bread down with a cup of strong black tea. Then she goes to her bedroom and finds a clean skirt and blouse. For a moment she looks at her violin case, remembering her small victory over Tamás. She'd like to take the violin with her but she has no need of it today. It's safer here. She puts on her coat and leaves the apartment, taking care to make sure the door is locked behind her.

She makes her way down to the ground floor, annoyed to see that József the caretaker is up already, sweeping the front steps in his slippers. Did he rise early on purpose to observe her? She hoped not to encounter him today of all days. She is suspicious of the role he played last night in letting the AVO into the building. She steps nimbly around his broom, keen to avoid being drawn into conversation.

'Good morning, Miss Bakos.' The old man's voice is thin and squeaky. Katalin recoils at the whiff of Pálinka – plum brandy – on his breath.

'Good morning, József.' She holds her head high, determined not to be intimidated by him. But a caretaker wields considerable power over the tenants in his building. It wouldn't surprise her to learn he's an informer. She must be careful. *Take care.*

'Bad business about your father.' He smacks his lips together.

Katalin narrows her eyes, picking her words with care. 'I'm sure it's all a misunderstanding and will be sorted out soon enough. If you'll excuse me, I must be on my way.'

He returns to his sweeping with a shake of his head. Katalin walks on, feeling his eyes on her back, but not daring to turn around.

The streets are busy with people hurrying to work, no one catching anyone else's eye. There's a queue at the tram stop and another one at the bakery, snaking around the corner. Although Katalin feels marked out, no one pays her any attention. Everyone has their own problems to keep them occupied. Most people know someone who has been arrested. They're not interested in one more.

There's a chill wind to the early October day. The cold air clears her head and she finds she's able to think better. Last night shouldn't have come as such a shock, she realises, because the signs have been there for a while. Her father is a physicist who teaches at the Technical University in Buda. A few months ago he was asked to sit on a committee on atomic energy and had been attending meetings at the Central Research Institute for Physics in Csillebérc, Budapest's 12th district.

'It's all part of the Five Year Plan,' he told her on one of their walks through the City Park. 'Gerő hopes nuclear power will bolster the economy by providing cheap electricity for the factories.'

'I thought you were sceptical about Gerő's Five Year Plan.'

'Yes, but that doesn't mean I don't want to see it succeed. It would be good for Hungary if it worked.'

'I suppose it's an honour to have been chosen to sit on the committee.'

'You don't refuse such a request.'

But for weeks now her father has suspected that his letters are steamed open and resealed before he receives them. When he uses the telephone at work there's a click on the line. Father and daughter have always talked openly to one another, but recently they have avoided discussing politics in the apartment in case of bugs. They play the radio at a high volume to mask their private conversations. Hungarian gypsy music is effective at drowning out their voices and is approved by the authorities, unlike American jazz which is seen as subversive. Recent walks in the park or to the cemetery to visit her mother's grave have been marred because her father feels there is someone following them. If travel were permitted they might have gone to Oxford, a place he always talks about with such fondness. As it is, they've had to stay in Hungary. She has sensed a growing pessimism in him lately, as if he knew it was only a matter of time before the Secret Police came for him. And now they have.

The question is, what is she going to do about it? People say you mustn't make a fuss, otherwise they'll come for you too. But she can't do nothing. If there's no news in a couple of days, then she'll go and see her father's friend and colleague, Professor Károly Novák. She's known Professor Novák ever since she was a little girl. He and his wife, Ilona, have always been good friends to her father. Yes, that's what she'll do.

At the school gates she hears the sound of running footsteps behind her. It's Tibor, the ten-year-old who lives with his mother in the apartment above hers. He's chewing on a piece of bread, his backpack bouncing on his back. He's growing fast. His trousers are too short for him, and his wrists are sticking out of his jacket sleeves.

'Careful you don't trip, Tibor,' she says, pointing at his shoe lace which has come undone, if it was ever tied in the first place.

He gives her a mischievous grin, stuffs the chunk of bread in his mouth, and bends down to tie his lace. He's a good kid, if a little boisterous. He runs ahead of her into the playground to join his friends. Katalin envies him his carefree attitude and wonders how long it will last. Then she takes a deep breath before going into the school.

*

How many times, in the space of an hour, can you walk up and down a cell that measures three yards by four? Márton Bakos has already lost count. It only takes him a couple of strides to get from one side to the other.

For now he's given up pacing and is standing in the freezing cell, shivering from a combination of cold and fear. The cell has a wooden plank for a bed, with no mattress, no pillow and no blankets. Above the plank is a tiny window covered in iron bars. The window opens into an air shaft which is letting in a cold draught. In the middle of winter it will be unbearable. A naked bulb on the white-washed wall glares permanently. There is no off-switch in the cell.

He has no idea what time it is, but thinks it must be late morning. He's been here hours already.

He doesn't know how long he'll be able to stand this. He's not a young man anymore and he feels older than his fifty-five years. The war aged him. It aged everyone it didn't kill. And the subsequent years of Soviet occupation have left him disheartened. Communism has not delivered the brighter future it promised and instead people lead lives of deprivation and fear. But he must not give way to despair yet. Without hope the body soon gives up too.

When the doorbell woke him last night, it was hardly a surprise. There had been warning signs – letters opened and inexpertly resealed; the telltale click of a listening device on the telephone line; that creeping sensation on the back of his neck that told him he was being followed. It was only a matter of time. If he could have done something about it, he would have. But you can't just run away. That only makes you look even more suspicious. Besides, they can always find you, wherever you go.

Not that he's done anything wrong. At least he doesn't think he has. In this country you don't have to commit a crime to find yourself on the wrong side of the law. Someone will have denounced him, maybe in an attempt to further their own standing with the Party. He doesn't want to think who that might be. He'd rather not know. His only thought is for Katalin. She mustn't try to find out any information, or she'll put herself in danger. That was what he really meant when he said, 'Take care.' He hopes she understood him.

He's at 60 Andrássy Avenue. He recognised the place immediately, although they drove him in through a side entrance into the inner courtyard. This grand building, in the Italianate style, has the power to strike terror into the hearts of ordinary Hungarian citizens. During the war it was home to the fascist Arrow Cross Party. Now it's the headquarters of the equally reviled communist Secret Police, the AVO. Different regime, same methods.

You hear rumours about what lies behind the building's elegant façade, but only now has he discovered for himself the truth of those rumours.

On arrival, they took him to a room on the first floor where a young officer with a supercilious air was sitting behind a desk. The officer regarded him with a mixture of boredom and disgust. Márton stood tall and tried to retain his dignity. It's how he was brought up, to be unfailingly polite. He spoke to confirm his name.

'Hand over your shoelaces and tie,' said the officer. The request surprised him but he tried not to let it show. He did as he was asked. It seems he mustn't be allowed to kill himself. If they want him dead, that's their prerogative, not his. After the way they arrested him, barging into his home in the middle of the night, he didn't expect to be treated like royalty. But he wasn't going to give this arrogant upstart the satisfaction of showing that his manner offended him.

'And your watch.'

Márton undid the leather strap and laid the watch on the desk next to his tie and shoelaces. It had been a present from Eva on their first wedding anniversary. He wished that he'd left it at home but he never went anywhere without it and had put it on without thinking.

It was on the tip of his tongue to ask why he had been brought here, but the officer gave the order for the guards to take him away and he was brutally shoved out of the room.

They took him to a staircase which led down to the cellars. Every fibre in his being recoiled at the thought of descending into that unknown dungeon. But with a rifle butt jabbing him in the small of his back, what other choice did he have? They were trying to intimidate him and he was determined not to let them. He placed a foot on the first step and took a deep breath. He had the feeling he was descending into hell, except that he had always imagined hell to be hot and dark, and this cellar was cold and damp and lit with a harsh electric light. At the bottom, the air was rank with a concoction of disinfectant, body odour, blocked drains, and other unidentifiable stenches. He tried to breathe through his mouth.

The guards marched him down a corridor. At the end they threw him into a tiny cubicle and slammed the thick wooden door, sliding the heavy steel bolt into place.

His first reaction was one of panic. He's never liked confined spaces, especially underground. He ran to the door and banged his fists on it.

'There's been some mistake. Let me out. I'm innocent.' His words echoed uselessly.

A small rectangular spy hole in the door banged open.

'Shut up!' yelled one of the guards. The hole banged shut again.

After that the spy hole was opened and shut every five minutes. The whole cellar reverberated to the sound of spy holes banging open and closed, like a hellish percussive symphony designed to rattle the nerves.

If their intention is, indeed, to rattle his nerves then they are succeeding. He tried sleeping last night but couldn't get comfortable on the wooden plank and the glare from the light bulb kept him awake. He turned to face the wall but the spy hole banged open and the guard shouted at him to lie on his back. He did as he was told. He tried putting his hands under his head as a makeshift pillow. The spy hole banged again.

'Arms flat on the plank. Palms upwards!'

Reluctantly he obeyed.

But sleep eluded him. Now he's given up lying on the hard plank. He prefers to stand or sit. All he can think of is his daughter, Katalin. She's a strong, resourceful girl. But he fears she will try to do something about his arrest, and that could land her in trouble too. Whatever tortures the AVO have in store for him, he will bear them better if he knows that she is safe and getting on with her life.

Down the corridor a door opens and orders are shouted.

'Move!'

Then other doors open and slam shut. He listens, trying to make sense of what is happening.

It seems the prisoners are being taken out of their cells one at a time. He waits his turn, trepidation mounting in his breast. His cell is at at the end of the corridor so he'll be the last one let out.

Eventually the door to his cell is opened and two armed guards order him out. It's a relief to step out of the tiny cell, but he doesn't know where they are taking him.

They march him down the corridor to a trough filled with scummy water.

'Wash!'

He recoils from the filthy water. How is he supposed to wash himself in that? One of the guards jabs him in the back with his rifle butt. Márton starts to unbutton his shirt.

Reluctantly he splashes water over his face and torso. The only available towel is threadbare and already wet from previous use. It smells of other bodies. He dries himself as best he can and puts his shirt back on. Then they take him to a toilet. One of the guards stands in the door whilst Márton does his business. Afterwards they return him to his cell and lock the door.

So this is the morning routine, he thinks. It is degrading and dehumanising. But it's all part of the act. Don't let them intimidate you.

When all the prisoners have washed and used the bathroom, the corridor falls silent. Now what? After what feels like an age, he is startled by a loud, metallic clatter. The prisoners are again let out one at a time to fetch their breakfast. Tepid soup in a metal bowl and a piece of damp bread. He takes the food back to his cell and eats it. The bread tastes like cardboard. He forces it down, telling himself he must keep his strength up for whatever lies ahead. His only wish is to be allowed home to his daughter.

*

After registration, the whole school gathers outside for the weekly march around the playground singing songs in praise of Comrades Rákosi, Stalin, Lenin and Marx – gods whom the children have been taught to worship. The large red flag on top of the building flutters in the breeze, adding a sense of ceremony to the occasion.

Katalin leads her own class of six-year-olds – the youngest children – to join the others, having first checked that all her charges are wearing the compulsory red neckerchiefs. She keeps a few spare in her desk just in case. She doesn't want the children to get into trouble over something so trivial. Their mothers have more pressing things to think about. But Piroska Benke, the school secretary, would notice if a child wasn't wearing a neckerchief and would make a formal complaint to the parents. The family might be accused of being anti-communist.

The children are excited because they get to play drums or shake tambourines and the younger ones at least enjoy marching, lifting their legs with exaggerated movements, their backs ramrod straight and their tiny chests puffed out. For now they stand and wait, the little ones fidgety but expectant, the older ones showing signs of boredom.

György Boda, the headmaster, climbs onto a raised platform and gives the signal. The whole school erupts into a rousing song about people working hard for themselves and building a better future free from bourgeois oppression. Katalin is sure most of the children have no idea what half the words mean.

The front row of children leads the march and the others follow behind. Some of them are out of step at first and there's almost a pile-up in Katalin's class because some of the boys are trying to go too fast. But under the stern eyes of the headmaster and the school secretary, they quickly fall into a steady rhythm.

The children will be in a good mood for the rest of the day. But as Katalin listens to their piping voices, the lyrics proclaiming the dream of socialism sound hollow to her ears. Many of these children are too skinny because there's always a shortage of bread and meat in the shops; their clothes are hand-me-downs, patched and darned to last another winter; they will return home to fathers and mothers exhausted from long hours in the factories or queueing for food.

And what will she return home to? An empty apartment. Tears well in her eyes. Standing a few feet away, Piroska Benke frowns at her and Katalin realises she has been failing to sing. She swallows the lump in her throat and does her best to join in with the chorus.

When the children have sung and marched to three songs, the headmaster makes a short speech about how they must all be good communists. Then the children file back inside, their cheeks pink from the exercise and the cold air. As he walks past with his classmates, Katalin notices that Tibor's shoe lace is undone again.

The rest of the morning Katalin is too busy to worry about her own troubles. The children take up all her time and energy with their constant demands for attention. She collects up the borrowed neckerchiefs and puts them back in her drawer for next week. Then she tells the children to take out their number books. The marching has tired them and they labour over their sums, yawning with open mouths, faces screwed up in concentration, pencils scratching on the thin paper. Katalin walks up and down the rows of desks, helping with an addition here, a subtraction there, studiously ignoring the portrait of *Our Wise Leader Rákosi* who gazes down on her classroom from the wall behind her desk. She tells the children to put their number books away ten minutes earlier than usual and calls them to gather around for story time. They sit cross-legged at her feet, eager to be entertained. What child doesn't enjoy a story? But the text is a Party-approved tale about the benefits of collective farming. One or two of the youngest ones lie down at the back of the group and fall asleep. Who can blame them? She wishes she could read them something more exciting. Her father used to tell her the story of St George and the Dragon at bedtime. The patron saint of England, the country that sounded like a paradise to her childish ears. Has her father been arrested because of his English contacts?

'Miss, can I go to the toilet please?'

Katalin is jolted back to the present moment by the voice of Katya, a little girl with her hair in two tightly plaited braids.

'Yes, of course,' says Katalin.

Katya gets up and runs to the door.

Then there's the inevitable clamour of raised voices. 'Miss, Miss, me too. I need the toilet too.'

'All right, but you can't all go at once. You must line up and take your turn. And remember to wash your hands.'

By the time they have all trooped off in pairs − a maximum of two girls and two boys at any one time − it's time to start getting them ready to go home. Their mothers will be coming to collect them at one o'clock, having spent most of their precious mornings queueing for bread and other essentials.

Katalin takes her class outside and waits with them as each child is collected. Then she goes back inside to tidy up and prepare for the next day. In the corridor she encounters Piroska Benke, the school secretary and Party afficionado bearing down on her, clipboard in hand. Katalin tries and fails to reach her classroom before Piroska Benke accosts her.

'Miss Bakos, I must speak to you.'

'Shall we go into my classroom?'

'Here will do perfectly,' says the secretary, standing her ground. 'Miss Bakos, there have been complaints from the other teachers that you allow the children in your class to run around the corridors during lessons.'

Katalin has no idea what Piroska Benke is talking about, but then she realises it's because she allowed them to use the bathroom. 'They are only little children,' she says. 'Once they've decided they need the toilet, it becomes a matter of urgency for them.'

'Nevertheless,' says Piroska, 'you must teach them self-control and discipline. It's what the Party expects.'

'Of course,' says Katalin. She forces herself to smile at Piroska, but inside she's seething. Party this, Party that. Piroska Benke is a walking encyclopedia on Party directives and policies. Piroska regards her with narrowed eyes, mistrustful of Katalin's smile. Katalin is sure Piroska would like nothing better than to report her to the authorities for failing to teach proper socialist values.

'From now on I will ensure that the children in my class behave with the appropriate level of self-control,' she says. Anything to get Piroska Benke off her back.

Piroska gives a curt nod and marches off.

Katalin returns to her classroom and shuts the door with more force than is strictly necessary. She's exhausted from the events of last night. With a sigh, she starts to walk around the classroom, picking up dropped pencils and pieces of paper, straightening the desks and chairs, and wiping the blackboard clean. Then she puts on her coat and heads for the door before anyone else can detain her. She already does extra hours as part of the group tasked with implementing special measures to keep the school hygienic and healthy so as to avoid unnecessary absences through illness – one of the many Party policies overseen by Piroska Benke. She doesn't want to spend her spare time analysing statistics or discussing ways to rearrange the contents of the stationery cupboard for greater productivity benefits.

But outside the school gates she hesitates. She has no desire to go straight home to the empty apartment. On an impulse, she takes a detour to her favourite café where the jovial proprietor, Feri, is busy behind the counter, serving his speciality strong black coffee to workers and students. A radio behind the counter is playing traditional Hungarian gypsy music, violins and an accordion.

'And what can I get you today, mademoiselle?' asks a beaming Feri. He told her once that he visited Paris in the twenties and fell in love with Parisian café culture. It amuses him to sprinkle French words into his speech. It's a dangerous habit, but he does it nonetheless.

'Just a coffee, and a slice of ginger cake, please.' Feri makes the best ginger cake in Budapest.

He cuts her a generous slice and sets the order down in front of her. 'Voilà.'

Katalin pays and finds a free table near the window. She's so worn out, the coffee and cake will give her a boost before she goes home to face the chaos of the apartment. She bites into the cake. It's perfectly moist and spicy, just how she likes it. The rich, pungent aroma of the coffee wafts up to her nostrils. How her father would enjoy being here with her now. A lump forms in her throat and she takes a sip of the too-hot coffee to mask her distress. She mustn't break down in public. To distract herself she picks up a copy of *Szabad Nép, A Free People,* which someone has left behind on the next-door table. The front page of the Party newspaper informs her that industrial productivity in Hungary is growing at exponential rates, the country's technological advances are the envy of the civilised world, and it's all thanks to their great leader, Rákosi, and their Soviet masters in Russia. All propaganda and lies. But you can't say that out loud or the Secret Police will come for you, like they came for her father. Did Márton Bakos speak out of turn about the authorities? She can't believe he would have been so careless. She jumps at the touch of a hand on her shoulder.

'Katalin, I was hoping I'd find you here. Sorry, did I startle you?'

She breathes out a sigh of relief. It's her best friend Róza. Not the AVO come to arrest her for subversive thoughts. She folds up the newspaper and puts it away. 'Sorry, I was miles away. Come and sit down.'

'Just let me get a coffee and a slice of cake. I've been on my feet all day and I'm done in.' Róza was at school with Katalin. Now she is a medical student and puts in long days at the hospital. 'Is that the ginger cake? I think I'll have the same.' She goes to the counter and comes back with a coffee and slice of cake. 'Oh my God, this cake is so good. I'll have to ask Feri for the recipe.' She wipes the crumbs from the corner of her mouth and licks her fingertips. Then she looks more closely at Katalin and frowns. 'What's the matter? You look terrible, if you don't mind me saying.'

Katalin shakes her head and chokes back a tear. Róza puts her cake down and takes hold of Katalin's hand. She waits for Katalin to speak, her medical training evident in her calm demeanour.

'They came for him last night.' Katalin keeps her voice

low. Fortunately the gypsy music is loud enough to mask her words so that only Róza can hear them. They lean their heads close together.

'Who? Not your father?'

Katalin nods.

'Oh my God, I'm so sorry. I had no idea. You should have called me.'

'It was the middle of the night.'

'That's how those bastards work.'

'They searched the apartment too. Made a terrible mess.'

'What were they looking for?'

'Who knows? Evidence, I suppose.'

'But what's he supposed to have done?'

Katalin shrugs. Both of them know that Márton Bakos doesn't need to have done anything. People denounce their neighbours and colleagues on the slightest pretext, often to avoid being arrested themselves. Cook a special meal for a loved one? Be careful when disposing of chicken bones or egg shells in case a neighbour with a grudge accuses you of capitalistic hoarding. Wear a new shirt to work? Watch out in case a colleague suspects you of being in the pay of American agents. How else could you afford new clothes?

'Do you want to stay at my place?' asks Róza. 'You can sleep on the couch.'

Katalin is touched by the kindness of the offer. As the daughter of someone who has been arrested, Katalin is tainted herself. But Róza wouldn't think like that. Katalin is tempted to accept, but Róza shares a cramped apartment with other medical students. There simply wouldn't be room and she doesn't want to impose. Her father may be gone a while.

'Thank you,' she says, 'but I should go home and tidy up the mess.'

'Of course, but if you ever change your mind…'

Katalin smiles, grateful to have at least one friend in

this cruel world. She looks at her watch. She's already stayed longer than she intended and she's so tired. 'I should be going.'

'I'll walk with you as far as the corner.'

The two friends walk along the darkening streets. Weary-looking people are making their way home. A tram stops just ahead of them and disgorges dozens of grey-faced workers returning from factories and offices.

'You won't believe who was part of the AVO team last night,' says Katalin, suddenly remembering.

'No, who?'

'Tamás Kún.'

'What, Tamás from school?'

'That's him.'

'Gosh, I'd forgotten all about him. I haven't seen him for years, not since we left school. I never thought he'd join the Secret Police, although to be honest I didn't know what he would end up doing. He was a bit of a nobody at school.'

'Well, he's found a career for himself now.'

'Did he recognise you?'

'Yes. I think I annoyed him by telling him not to open my violin case during the search.'

Róza draws in her breath sharply. 'Take care, won't you? You don't want to fall out with people like that.' They've reached the corner of Király Street where they will go their separate ways.

Róza squeezes Katalin's hand then draws her into an embrace. *Take care.* Those were her father's last words to her before they took him away. She's always careful. It's the only way to be in this country.

'Let me know what happens,' says Róza. 'And remember, you're always welcome to come and stay.' Then she disappears down the street and Katalin heads home alone.

She pushes open the heavy outer door to the apartment building as quietly as she can. She doesn't want to alert

31

József to her return. But he appears immediately, carrying some rubbish for the bins in the courtyard. He nods his head at her as he shuffles past. Katalin could have sworn he was waiting for her. Maybe he writes a report for the AVO on what time she leaves and returns each day. She must be careful who she brings to the apartment. She runs up the stairs and lets herself in.

She knows at once from the stillness of the air that no one has been here since she left to go to work that morning. Papa has not returned. Of course, he hasn't. She closes the door behind her and leans against it. She did try not to get her hopes up, but still she couldn't help wondering if she'd walk in and find him reading in his favourite armchair. *All a big misunderstanding, Katalin dear. Once I'd had a chance to explain myself, they apologised for dragging me in during the middle of the night. They're not such bad chaps after all, you know. Just doing their jobs.*

It's a minute before she has the will to move away from the front door. She's going to have to get used to this, coming home to an empty apartment. But she can't leave it looking like this. If her father should, by a miracle, come home and find his beloved books scattered over the floor it would break his heart.

She changes into some old trousers and a shirt and ties her hair out of the way. Then she opens the door to the living room. She flinches at the sight of the mess. It's even worse than she remembered. There's nothing for it but to get stuck in.

She tackles the books first, smoothing out the crumpled pages and arranging the titles on the bookcase in alphabetical order of the author's name, just the way her father likes. There are glaring gaps where the English and German titles used to be.

She turns her attention to the music from the piano stool. As far as she knows, the AVO didn't take any of the music with them, which is something to be grateful for. Her mother, Eva, loved Bach's *Goldberg Variations* and

Beethoven's sonatas – *The Moonlight* and *Appassionata* were her favourites – and would sit at the piano for hours filling the apartment with beautiful sounds. As Katalin gathers the sheet music together, she comes across a piece which isn't piano music. It's a Mozart aria from *The Marriage of Figaro*, the Countess's lament *Dove Sono* – *Where are the beautiful moments of sweetness and pleasure?* – and Katalin remembers a time, long ago, when Ilona Novák, wife of her father's colleague Károly Novák, stood right where Katalin is standing now and sang that aria with her pure, clear voice whilst Eva accompanied her on the piano. It was a long time ago, before the war, and Katalin couldn't have been more than nine or ten. But now she thinks about it, that must have been the last time the Nováks came here. Why didn't Ilona come back for her music? Why was it never returned? She leaves it on top of the piano, thinking she can take it with her when she calls on Professor Novák.

She quickly tidies what's left of the papers on the desk, then kneels down and picks up the photographs that fell from the photo album. She finds the one of her parents on their honeymoon in Oxford, glad that she didn't draw Tamás's attention to it last night. She looks at the smiling couple. Her father has a full head of hair and her mother's hair is dark and wavy. It turned grey during the war. Her parents were so young when this photograph was taken. Young and full of hope, before the war destroyed so many lives. She props the photo up next to a vase on a side table so that she can look at it. Other photos, she slots back into the album.

She's about to put the album away when she spots a photograph that has half slid under the couch. She stoops to pick it up. When she turns it over she gasps. It's an old photograph of herself and her childhood friend Liesl Weinberg, taken on the occasion of Liesl's eighth birthday.

She hasn't thought of Liesl in a long while because the memory is too painful. She has buried it deep inside her.

But seeing the photograph after all these years, she can't stop the memories flooding back.

Playing in Liesl's apartment upstairs where Tibor and his mother now live. Listening to Liesl's father playing the violin – haunting, sad, slow melodies. Liesl's grandfather reading a book with strange squiggles that Katalin couldn't understand. The yellow star that Liesl and her family were forced to wear during the war. The forced move to the ghetto; the deportations by train. And then, in the final months of the war, the shooting of Jews on the banks of the Danube by the fascist Arrow Cross Party, their bodies pushed into the icy waters and carried downstream by the current.

Katalin is crying hard now. Crying for the friend she lost during the war. Crying for the father who has been arrested. She was too young to save Liesl, but can she save her father?

*

'Zoltán Dobos! Sándor Maier!' Csaba Elek is scurrying across the factory floor towards them, a clipboard in his left hand, a pen in his right. He looks like a zealous ferret.

'What does he want now?' breathes Zoltán, laying down his tools. The Party Secretary has been hanging around all day like a bad smell. It's already six o'clock and Zoltán is hoping to leave on time for once. He wants to get back to Király Street and see if Katalin Bakos is all right. See if she's still there, at least.

'A meeting has been called,' says Csaba Elek, puffing himself up with importance. 'You two have been selected to attend.'

'What's it about?' asks Zoltán, keeping his voice level so as not to betray his frustration. He can sense Sándor's disappointment. He was planning to go on a date.

'We are setting up a committee to look into productivity levels and ways in which we can increase them in accordance with the Five Year Plan.' Csaba sounds like he's parroting a dictum from on high.

This is the first Zoltán has heard of any such committee, although meetings like this are a regular occurrence. Last month he had to participate in a movement fighting for the care of tools and their repair. A completely pointless activity in Zoltán's opinion. And as for Comrade Gerő's Five Year Plan, it has brought nothing but sky-high inflation and food shortages. This is Csaba's way of punishing him for being the first to stop clapping when Rákosi's name was mentioned at this morning's reading. Never mind that he was doing a good deed by helping the old man stay on his feet. Csaba is one of those people who needs to boost his ego by demonstrating his power and authority. Zoltán has come to realise that underneath all the spouting of dogma, Csaba Elek lacks confidence. Still, he can make trouble for people, and right now Zoltán is lucky that his punishment isn't anything worse. He nods his head and says in his most sincere voice, 'That sounds like a wonderful idea, Csaba Elek. We'll be delighted to attend, won't we Sándor?'

'Ab-so-lute-ly,' says Sándor, articulating every syllable with exaggerated enthusiasm. Zoltán tries not to laugh. One of these days Sándor is going to go too far.

Csaba Elek looks momentarily disconcerted. Maybe he was hoping for some opposition from them. It would have given him an excuse to report them.

'Please, lead the way,' says Zoltán.

Csaba Elek turns on his heel and almost trots towards the meeting room.

'Prick,' says Zoltán under his breath. He wouldn't dare express such opinions to anyone other than Sándor.

The meeting drags on as Zoltán knew it would. There are a dozen of them there, including Csaba who takes the minutes. Nonsensical suggestions are put forward, such as doing a day's work each month with materials saved from the previous month. But everyone shows their enthusiasm for these suggestions by nodding their heads vigorously. It's important to express your support. Zoltán thinks of Márton Bakos and how he was unceremoniously bundled into the black Pobeda last night. He's sure Professor Bakos hadn't done anything wrong.

It's gone eight o'clock by the time the meeting wraps up. They've achieved nothing of any practical use as far as Zoltán can see, but Csaba Elek looks pleased with himself. He'll go away now and type up the minutes. Tomorrow the decisions of this meeting will become factory policy and everyone will have to work harder.

'Thought we were never going to get out of there,' says Sándor once they are finally outside. He rushes off in the hope that his date will still be waiting for him in the bar where he should have been two hours ago. Some chance.

Zoltán catches a tram back to Király Street. By the time he arrives outside her building, the light is off in her apartment. He hopes it's because she's gone to bed early, exhausted from being woken up in the middle of the night, and not because she's disappeared. He climbs the stairs to his own loft apartment, sits down in his reading chair and picks up the book he was reading last night. But for a long time he doesn't open it. He just gazes out of the window into the darkness.

*

When the last customers have left for the night, Feri locks the door of the café and pulls down the shutters. This is his favourite time of day. He sweeps the floor and straightens the tables and chairs, all the while humming along to the gypsy music that continues to play from the radio behind the counter.

When he has finished tidying up, he pours himself a small glass of Pálinka. Then he switches off the radio and goes to a private room at the back of the café where he has another, secret radio, hidden behind a pile of books.

He puts the glass on a small wooden table and sits down in his favourite armchair that he's had since before the war. It's the only piece of furniture he managed to save when the building he was living in was hit by German shellfire. This secret radio he acquired after the war. Now, late at night when he has an hour to himself before going to bed, he switches on the radio, which is tuned to the wave-length for *Radio Free Europe*. He hopes there won't be too much disturbance on the channel tonight. The Hungarian authorities are always trying to stop people from listening to this US-sponsored station broadcast out of Munich. The Soviets do their best to jam the signal whenever they can. Satisfied that the hiss and crackle of static is not too bad, he settles back with his Pálinka, closes his eyes, and listens to news from beyond the borders of Hungary.

Hungarians, take up arms against your Soviet oppressors. The United States will support you if you do.

Feri sips his drink and dreams of a better world. A world where he can listen to whatever radio station he likes without fear of being arrested. Is that too much to ask for?

CHAPTER 3

Early the following morning Tamás Kún arrives for work at the headquarters of the Secret Police on Andrássy Avenue.

Smartly dressed in his blue uniform and shiny black boots, he mounts the steps with a feeling of pride. The uniform gives him a sense of identity, unlike the faceless masses who queue for the trams in their drab gabardines, berets and headscarves. Factory workers, office workers, whatever. He despises their mundane lives precisely because their fate would have been his if he hadn't been accepted into the ranks of the AVO. His teachers didn't think he would amount to much. Well, he's shown them now. If he felt so inclined he could make up some reason for denouncing every last one of them.

'If your father could see you now,' his widowed mother said the first time he came home in his new uniform. She gazed fondly at the photograph of his father in his war uniform which has pride of place on the mantelpiece. Growing up, Tamás feared his father's bullying nature and unpredictable temper, but now he's the one who wears the uniform and has nothing to fear.

Instead, people fear him. Like the woman on her way

to the shops this morning who stopped on the street corner to let him pass ahead of her. It gives him a sense of power. And goodness knows, he's never had that before. The taste is sweet.

The deference shown to him by the woman this morning has boosted his confidence which, admittedly, took a slight knock the other night at the arrest of Márton Bakos. But Tamás was excited to be taking part in an actual arrest, to see at first hand how these things are done. Tamás's boss is not an easy man to please. Vajda has a habit of barking orders that make you tremble. He was keen to show his boss that he's a valuable member of the team, someone to be trusted with important tasks.

At first that snivelling caretaker didn't want to let them into the building and complained about being woken up in the middle of the night, even though the old man was wearing his day-time clothes. But Vajda intimidated him into letting them in and taking them to the apartment, even insisting that the man stand and watch the arrest, making him complicit. That was his punishment for being obstructive. Tamás took all this in, watching and learning.

It was all going so well up until the moment they trooped into the apartment. But then he recognised Katalin and his confidence deserted him like a fleeing traitor. He didn't realise it was *her* father they were coming to arrest. He and Katalin were at school together, in the same class, although never friends. Tamás didn't have many friends at school. The other children found him too serious and teased him. He found them childish. If he had been allowed to do his job in peace and get out of there, everything would have been fine. But she had to go and humiliate him. He should have opened the violin case, he should have done his job properly. The case almost certainly contained incriminating documents, otherwise why would she stop him from opening it? If Vajda finds out he capitulated so easily, he'll have Tamás thrown out of the Secret Police, or worse. He can't afford to lose this job. He has himself and his mother to support.

He pushes open the door to the office he shares with half a dozen other low-ranking AVO men. The air is already heavy with the fug of cigarette smoke and male sweat. The windows overlook the inner courtyard which never seems to get any fresh air. Tamás's desk is squashed in the corner, beside a gunmetal filing cabinet, almost as an afterthought.

Gábor, the blond officer who carried out such a thorough search of Márton Bakos's bookcase, is perched on the edge of his window-facing desk, one black-booted foot on a chair, telling a rude joke to his comrades. Gábor is a couple of years older than Tamás and likes to boast about his alleged sexual conquests, although they only have his word for them. He's the sort of person Tamás would have kept his distance from at school, but he has a grudging respect for him now. Gábor wouldn't let Katalin walk all over him. He worries that Gábor suspects him of being weak. He's determined to prove him wrong.

The laughter breaks off as Tamás walks over to his desk, giving him the uneasy feeling in the pit of his stomach that he was part of Gábor's joke.

'Just the man I was waiting for,' says Gábor, swaggering over towards him. 'The boss wants to see us.'

'He does?' Tamás prefers to avoid Vajda first thing in the morning. Vajda is not a morning person. With his thickset neck and sagging jowls that hang off his face like excess lard, he resembles a hippopotamus with a hangover. But he's the one in charge, the one Tamás must look to for praise and advancement. He follows Gábor down the corridor.

Vajda is sitting at his big mahogany desk, with a view across Andrássy Avenue, signing documents. Arrest warrants, confessions, top-secret memos. He doesn't even bother to pretend to read them, just scrawls his signature and adds each one to a growing pile on his desk next to a marble bust of Stalin.

'The arrest of Márton Bakos,' says Vajda without preamble when the two officers are standing before him, 'was a good job.' Usually Vajda likes to take the credit for successful night raids. Tamás wonders, not without a glimmer of hope, if for once Vajda is about to say that Márton Bakos has been convicted on the basis of evidence unearthed by Tamás and Gábor in their search of the living room at the Bakos's apartment.

'But the girl,' continues Vajda, 'strikes me as suspicious.' He puffs out his cheeks and eyes Gábor and Tamás with narrowed eyes.

Tamás's hope is extinguished as effectively as if it had been drowned in the Danube. Has Vajda somehow found out about his failure to open the violin case?

Vajda turns to Tamás. 'You didn't find anything in her room?'

He forces himself to look Vajda in the eye. 'No, comrade.'

'And you did a thorough search?'

'I did.' He feels himself breaking out in a cold sweat. He would never be able to stand the interrogations the prisoners have to endure.

'I'm putting her under surveillance,' says Vajda. 'But for now you're both on cellar duty. Keep on eye on Márton Bakos for me and if he asks about his daughter let me know immediately.'

'Yes, comrade,' Tamás and Gábor say at the same time.

As they leave Vajda's office, Tamás silently breathes a sigh of relief. His secret is safe for now.

'You got the plum job the other night, you lucky bastard,' says Gábor as they descend into the fetid air of the cellars.

'What do you mean?' asks Tamás. He doesn't like Gábor's insinuating tone.

'Searching the girl's bedroom.' Gábor smirks. 'I bet you enjoyed yourself going through the bitch's underwear.'

'I gave the whole room a thorough search, not just her

clothes.' He hopes Gábor doesn't notice him blushing in the artificial light.

'I'd have given *her* a good going over if it was me,' says Gábor, leering. 'Know what I mean?'

Tamás never knows how to respond to Gábor's provocative comments and is glad when they reach the bottom of the stairs.

He shivers in the cold, damp air. It always takes him a while to acclimatise to the stale smell in the cellars. The two guards who've been on duty all night look relieved that their replacements have shown up and they can ascend back to ground level.

'All right,' says Gábor. 'You take that corridor, I'll take this one.' Gábor has chosen the section with the fewest prisoners in it, the lazy sod.

Tamás merely nods his agreement. He's just glad to get away from Gábor and his lewd talk. He adjusts the rifle on his shoulder and starts to patrol the corridor.

If he's honest with himself, this is a job he loathes. But someone has to do it. If he proves his worth in this stinking place then maybe Vajda will promote him to bigger and better things, like writing the confessions that the prisoners are forced to sign. He thinks he'd be good at that.

He bangs open the first spy hole with more force than is strictly necessary and peers into the dingy cell. It gives him a moment's pleasure to see the occupant of the cell jump like a startled rabbit. The ones who have been here the longest no longer jump at the banging of the spy holes. They've grown accustomed to it, or they're too weak from cold, hunger and tiredness to care anymore. He slams the spy hole shut and makes his way down the corridor, banging the spy holes open and closed. In each cell a wretched prisoner sits shivering. They must be guilty of the most horrendous crimes, otherwise why would the Party arrest them and lock them up in such hideous conditions? This is what Tamás tells himself when he's doing this godforsaken job.

He comes to the last cell in the corridor and opens the spy hole. Sitting on the edge of the wooden plank is Márton Bakos. He hasn't been here long but already the experience has changed him. He's unshaven and looks as if he hasn't slept. If Katalin could see her father now, she wouldn't be so cocksure of herself. But Márton Bakos doesn't react like the other prisoners. Instead he merely looks at Tamás with a puzzled expression. Maybe the fool doesn't understand the reason for his arrest. Tamás stares back with the most hateful look he can muster, just like he's been trained to do. But Márton Bakos doesn't blink and look away. Tamás is unnerved by this. He slams the spy hole shut with so much force that his hand slips and he grazes his knuckles on the rough wall. Damn and blast. He's got hours of this to put up with.

*

Márton keeps looking at his left wrist, at the place where his watch used to be, forgetting it's no longer there. Punctuality has always been important to him. What did his colleagues think when he failed to turn up for work yesterday? *It's not like Professor Bakos to be late. I wonder what's keeping him? You don't think...?* And what about his students at the University? He pictures them sitting in the lecture theatre, waiting for him to show up, getting bored, giving up, going for a cigarette and a coffee. Speculating as to what might have happened. Will his friend and colleague Professor Károly Novák take on his teaching workload? He can't help feeling that he's letting people down, being arrested like this.

The only time he's been allowed out of his cell since yesterday was for the morning routine of washing in the cold, scummy water and using the toilet in the presence of one of the ÁVO guards. Breakfast was another piece of stale bread. He maybe managed an hour of sleep last night but it wasn't enough. He feels groggy and unable to focus but there's too much banging for him to rest now. In this place, time is measured not by minutes and hours, but by the number of heartbeats between the banging of the spy holes. He's counted to seven hundred so far.

Bang! The spy hole in the door slams open and Márton sees a young face glaring at him. It's one of the lads in the team that arrested him. He looks vaguely familiar. Márton scans his face, trying to place him. A former student perhaps? Or was he at school with Katalin? He's the right sort of age. The boy attempts to give him a look of loathing and contempt which merely looks comical on his youthful features. As a teacher Márton's instinct is to reach out and ask what the matter is. He's well liked by his students and has helped many a young person through a crisis. In Márton's book no one is irredeemable. But the lad slams the spy hole shut and Márton hears him cursing. He must have hurt his hand on the wall.

He drops his head into his hands, closes his eyes, and tries to think. They're bound to question him at some point so it's best to be prepared. He thinks back to his work in recent weeks. There's been nothing out of the ordinary at the university. But a few months ago he was asked to sit on a committee looking into the possibility of building a nuclear reactor. It wasn't a request he could refuse without falling foul of the authorities. There aren't that many scientists in Budapest who could have taken his place, so he agreed, even though it meant doubling his workload. Katalin was concerned about him doing too much, but he told her not to worry. But they were watching him. He didn't like it, but assumed this was routine for those involved in government work.

There was that matter the previous month of the report from the Russian scientists regarding the uranium enrichment process. When Márton checked the figures he discovered a serious error in one of their calculations. Naturally, as a scientist concerned with producing accurate work, he corrected the error and asked Professor Novák to confirm that his revised calculations were correct. What was he supposed to do? Leave the error unchallenged? That would have been unthinkable in something so safety-critical. He was only doing his job, a job that the authorities asked him to do. He passed the corrected report back to the Russians and even received an acknowledgement from them. But the Russians can be touchy about having their errors pointed out to them. Could his arrest have anything to do with that?

There are also things in his past that mark him as suspicious. As a post-doctoral student he spent time in Oxford. He has nothing but fond memories of his time in England, where he developed a taste for warm beer but never quite grasped the subtleties of cricket. He learned from some of the pre-eminent scientists in his field, and he lapped up the cultural and intellectual life of the university. He thrived in the medieval college dining halls and the atmosphere of open, vigorous debate. How can he make these people in the Secret Police understand that just because he spent time in England when he was younger, doesn't mean he isn't a loyal Hungarian? He's only ever wanted the best for his country. After the injustices of years under the fascist dictator Horthy, and then the brutality of the Arrow Cross Party during the war, he thought the communist leaders wanted the best too. Now he's not so sure.

The cell door bangs open and Márton jumps to his feet in anticipation that they are finally going to explain the reason for his arrest. He's ready to put his case and defend himself. The sooner they can get started, the better. But the two guards who enter the cell close the door behind them and Márton realises with a sinking heart that he isn't going anywhere. They've only come to take his fingerprints.

He rolls his thumb and fingers on the ink pad as instructed and then on a piece of white card.

'Hold this under your chin.' One of the guards gives him a wooden number plate. The other produces a small camera from a pocket and photographs him, first from the front and then in profile. Like a common criminal. He's unshaven and has hardly slept. He must look like everyone's idea of a felon.

The guards leave and Márton is once again left on his own. How much longer can this go on? He lies down on the plank and closes his eyes. The light from the naked bulb prevents him from sleeping.

*

Katalin has been awake since the first grey light of dawn, unable to sleep. Her dreams were haunted by visions of her father in a prison cell. What are they doing to him? If only there was some way for her to find out what is going on. She dresses, eats the last of the bread – she'll have to call in at the baker's later today – and leaves for school. The children, at least, have the power to distract her from her own thoughts.

Piroska Benke is already outside her classroom, waiting for her. Does the woman have a home to go to, or does she crawl into a corner of her office each night, like a spider?

'There you are,' says Piroska as if Katalin is late, when in fact she's early. 'The headmaster wants to see you in his office.'

'Now?' asks Katalin. 'What about my class? The children will be arriving soon.' She likes to be there to greet them when they arrive. They are still very young and some of them don't like saying goodbye to their mothers.

'I will watch your class,' says Piroska, although she sounds as if she'd rather be harvesting turnips in a muddy field.

Katalin walks to the headmaster's office with a sense of foreboding. György Boda doesn't normally communicate directly with the staff, preferring to use Piroska Benke as his messenger. She knocks on the door.

'Come in.' The voice is gravelly from years of smoking Russian cigarettes.

'You wanted to see me, sir?'

'Sit down.' The headmaster indicates a chair on the other side of his desk. György Boda is in his fifties with a receding hairline and a cleft chin. The obligatory portrait of *Our Wise Leader Rákosi* oversees the meeting from the wall behind the headmaster's desk.

Katalin sits upright with her hands clasped in her lap. Is she about to be fired because her father's been arrested? She'll defend her father with her dying breath if she has to.

'Do you know Tibor Nadas?'

'I'm sorry?' The headmaster's question has caught her unawares.

'Tibor Nadas. How well do you know him?'

'I know who you mean, sir. But he's not in my class. He's older.' Katalin pictures the ten-year-old who always runs around with his shoe laces undone.

'But you live in the same apartment block, do you not?'

'Yes.' Katalin is wary now, for Tibor's sake as well as her own. His mother, Petra, is someone Katalin counts as a friend.

'I want you to keep an eye on him. Report anything suspicious.'

Katalin's stomach lurches. The headmaster is asking her to spy on her neighbours. He wants her to become part of the loathsome system that resulted in her father's arrest. 'Such as?'

'Do I have to spell it out to you?' asks György Boda, frowning. 'Western influences. Does his family listen to *Radio Free Europe* or *Voice of America*? Are there unexplained extravagances? That sort of thing.'

Katalin thinks of Tibor's clothes which are too small for him. His widowed mother can hardly be accused of having too much money. His father was killed in the war.

Petra takes in sewing.

'Why Tibor?'

'The boy is a disruptive influence. He must be getting his ideas from somewhere. We can't allow subversive ideas to spread in a school environment.'

'I see.' Although she doesn't see at all. György Boda is not a man to argue with. 'Is that all, sir?'

The headmaster dismisses her with a curt nod.

Katalin leaves the office, her heart thumping. She understands this task is as much a test of her own loyalty as it is about Tibor. When she returns to her classroom, Piroska Benke has the children sitting on their hands in total silence, looking miserable. No doubt she is punishing the whole class for some minor infraction of one child. Katalin would have handled the situation differently. She will have a job to engage them in their lessons now.

In the morning break, she dashes over to the baker's. She joins the end of the queue, mostly women in headscarves with string shopping bags over their arms. She hopes this won't take too long. She needs to get back for her next lesson. But if she leaves it until school has finished, the baker will have sold out.

A tap on her shoulder. In her agitated state, Katalin jumps, emitting a small squeak. The women in front of her turn their heads, their faces full of suspicion. No one draws attention to themselves if they can help it.

It's Petra Nadas, Tibor's mother.

'I thought it was you,' says Petra, without a trace of self-consciousness. 'How are things after, you know...?'

When Katalin doesn't reply immediately, Petra rushes on. 'We heard what happened.'

I'll bet you did, thinks Katalin. The ringing of the doorbell must have woken everyone in the building, if not half the street. Goodness knows what József has been telling people. And Maria, the old woman who lives opposite, is a terrible gossip.

'If you need anything,' says Petra, 'you know where to

find us.'

'Thank you,' says Katalin, touched.

'Anyway, I must be off,' says Petra. 'I'm baking a cake for Tibor's birthday. Don't tell him. It's meant to be a surprise.'

'That's nice,' says Katalin. 'He'll like that.' She glances in Petra's shopping bag and sees sugar and butter and eggs. This is precisely the sort of thing that the Party would consider an extravagance. It's the sort of thing György Boda would want her to report. Katalin has no intention of doing any such thing. Knowing Petra, she'll be going without essentials herself in order to afford this treat for her son. The queue shuffles forwards and Katalin looks anxiously at her watch.

*

Márton comes to with a jolt. Despite the bright light, he must have nodded off. But a noise in the corridor has woken him up. He listens with a sense of dread to the sound of some poor devil being dragged back to their cell in pain. Booted feet. Shouted orders. A whimpering cry. And then the cell door being slammed shut. My God, what do they do to people here?

He rubs his eyes which are sore and prickly from the incessant light. How he craves just five minutes of total darkness. And silence. He doesn't know how long he slept for. It's impossible to know in this artificially lit dungeon what time of day it is. He sits up, stretches and stands. His muscles are stiff and sore from the wooden plank. And he's cold from lying in the draught from the air shaft. He rubs his hands and arms to try and bring some life back into them. His fingertips are stained black from the fingerprinting session earlier.

Bang! The never-ending opening and closing of the spy holes goes on and on. Don't the guards get bored doing that all day? He wants to shout at them to shut up, but then he remembers the cries of the man in pain. But really, it's enough to drive a man crazy, never mind being cooped up in this stinking pit. And there's a gnawing hunger eating him from the inside. It must be hours since breakfast.

He hears a clattering of metal pots in the corridor and almost weeps with relief. One by one the prisoners are let out to fetch a bowl of watery soup and a piece of stale bread. Márton carries his bowl back to his cell, careful not to spill a drop. He dips the stale bread into the thin liquid and starts to eat, forcing himself to chew slowly to make the meal last longer. When he's finished the bread he licks the inside of the bowl with his tongue. It's nowhere near enough to satisfy his hunger, but that's all he's going to get until the morning.

He doesn't expect anything else to happen this evening, so after his meagre dinner he lies back down on the wooden plank. He's still tired. To block out the noises in the cellar he tries to fill his mind with memories of Katalin playing the violin. How does the opening of Mendelssohn's violin concerto go? If he can just hear the melody in his head...

The cell door crashes open and a guard shouts at him.

'On your feet!'

Márton blinks his eyes open. There are two of them standing there, rifles in hand. The young lad from earlier must have gone off duty. These two are older and look like hardened criminals. Márton recognises the type. During the war such men signed up for the Arrow Cross Party and persecuted the Jews. When the fascists were defeated and the communists gained power, they were the first to switch their allegiances.

'I said, on your feet!'

The guard makes a threatening move towards him. Márton scrambles to his feet.

'Out!'

Warily he steps into the corridor.

'Hands behind your back! Walk!'

Without his shoelaces, his shoes flap with each step, slowing him down.

'Get a move on, can't you?'

He tries to increase his speed, but it's not possible in shoes that threaten to fall off his feet. He feels the rifle butt jammed into his back.

They make their way, him faltering, the guards getting impatient, up staircases and along corridors. At least he's out of the stinking cellars, walking on a carpeted floor, no longer shivering with the cold. It's pathetic how grateful he feels.

The guards deliver him to a comfortably furnished office. Sitting behind a mahogany desk in a leather chair is the man who led the arrest, the bully who tried to intimidate Katalin. His hands rest on his paunch and his flabby face glows red, as if he's just enjoyed a good meal with a fine wine. The scent of cigar smoke hangs in the air.

'Sit down.' Red-face points a stubby finger at a straight-backed, wooden chair placed about five feet away from the desk.

Márton sits down and places his hands on his knees. Now that he's out of the stinking cellars, he can't help but be aware of his own stench, emanating from his filthy body. He's still wearing the shirt and suit he came in, a poor choice of clothes in retrospect, but how was he to know? The guards who brought him up from the cellars stand to one side. He can see their rifles in his peripheral vision.

Red-face reaches across his desk to a lamp standing next to a bust of Stalin. He flicks a switch on the lamp and, without warning, turns the light full into Márton's face. The bright, white light is blinding and Márton blinks, his eyes watering. He can no longer see the man's ugly features, but that is little consolation. His eyes are already sore from lack of sleep and the bulb that shines incessantly in his cell. This piercing light is going to give him a headache if he's not careful. He tries to soften his focus and gaze somewhere off to the left.

'Tell me about your life,' says his interrogator. 'Start with your childhood.' He makes it sound as if they are two old pals reminiscing over a glass of Pálinka.

Márton wasn't expecting this. He expected to be questioned about his work, maybe his friends and acquaintances. What does his childhood have to do with anything? Still, if that's what he wants to hear.

He starts to speak about his family. He has no idea how far back he should go, so he starts with his paternal grandfather. He was a landowner in north-eastern Hungary near the Mátra Mountains. Nothing unusual in that, he thinks, but maybe not such a good start for his case. One of the first acts of the government after the war was land reform. The arable land that his forebears had farmed for generations was seized and redistributed. Are they going to accuse him of being a bourgeois capitalist because of his grandfather? He glosses over much of his childhood, not wishing to spoil happy memories, and moves on to describe how his father moved to Budapest to train as an engineer at the Technical University. Red-face gives no response to any of the information that Márton provides. Since Márton can't see his face behind the blinding light, his interrogator could be asleep for all he knows.

After he has been speaking for about half an hour, Red-face interrupts him. 'Why are you here, Bakos?'

The question surprises him. It's a good question and one he would like answered. But how is he supposed to answer it himself? Is he his own accuser? The opening line of Franz Kafka's novel *The Trial* suddenly comes to mind. *Someone must have slandered Josef K because, without having done anything wrong, one morning he was arrested.* Maybe he'll wake up from this nightmare and discover that he's turned into a giant beetle. Anything would be preferable to being kept in that stinking cell.

'I repeat, why are you here?'

He squints into the bright white light and says, 'I would

like to know that myself. There must have been a mistake. If you can tell me what I am accused of, then I'm sure we can clear this up.'

Red-face slaps his hand down on the desk, causing him to jump. 'There is no mistake!'

Of course, he thinks wryly, the Party never makes a mistake. It is inviolable. 'I'm sorry, I didn't mean...'

Red-face interrupts him. 'We know what we know. But it is your job to tell us what you have done. This is how we work. If you admit your mistakes we shall say that you slipped. Now tell me, why are you here?'

Márton tries to make sense of the twisted logic. It's like being made to play a cruel parlour game where no one will explain to him what the rules are. The only thing he can be fairly sure about is that he is going to lose.

'I have done nothing wrong, as far as I am aware.' He's so tired, he just wants to get out of this room and lie down on his wooden plank. It must be well past midnight by now.

From the exasperated grunting sounds coming from behind the desk, Márton takes it that Red-face is not satisfied with this response. He addresses the guards.

'Take him to a typewriter. He will write his autobiography until four in the morning. Then take him back to his cell but do not permit him to sleep.' Red-face moves to stand in front of the desk, his wide girth mercifully blocking out most of the light from the desk lamp. Still, a white glow shines around his features like a parody of a halo. 'You will have plenty of time to think about what you have told me because you are not going to sleep. Do you understand?'

'Yes.' What can he tell him in writing that he hasn't already told him verbally? It seems like a pointless exercise.

One of the guards takes him to a small windowless room with a typewriter on a wooden desk and orders him to start typing. There's a pile of paper on the desk beside the typewriter. He's going to be here a long time. With a heavy heart, Márton lifts his fingers to the keys and starts to type.

CHAPTER 4

Still no news. It's the third day since Papa's arrest and Katalin has heard nothing. He told her to take care, and by that she understands that she shouldn't kick up a fuss with the authorities. That never does anyone any good. But she can't sit around doing nothing, it's driving her crazy.

Her childhood friend Liesl has been haunting her dreams. They are playing together in the forest, a game of hide-and-seek. Katalin closes her eyes and counts slowly down from ten. When she opens her eyes Liesl is in the jaws of a big, black wolf, her body limp and bloody. She wakes in a cold sweat, her heart thumping. *Oh Liesl,* she thinks, *I let you down. I couldn't save you from those Arrow Cross thugs.* She imagines Liesl's thin body sinking to the bottom of the Danube and she wipes away a tear. No, this time she must act.

After work she catches a tram that will take her across the River Danube from Pest on the east side of the city to Buda in the west. She is going to call on Professor Károly Novák, Papa's colleague and long-standing friend at the Technical University. She takes the lost Mozart aria in her bag, thinking she can return it to Ilona. It's a reminder of happier times.

The tram is packed and there is nowhere to sit down. Katalin holds onto a pole and sways in time with those around her. An old woman in a black headscarf clutches a loaf of bread under one arm, a look of defiance on her weathered face. Katalin closes her eyes and lets herself be carried along by the gentle rocking movement. She remembers a tram ride to Buda before the war with her mother when they took a picnic to the top of Gellért Hill. Katalin was amazed at how far she could see, the whole of Pest laid out before her, the Danube snaking its way between the two halves of the city like a giant silver serpent.

A squeal of brakes and her eyes fly open. Are they already in Buda? No, it's just the stop on Margaret Island in the middle of the Danube. The bridges have all been rebuilt since they were destroyed by the retreating Germans at the end of the war. She peers out of the window at Castle Hill in Buda, the jagged remains of the Royal Palace just visible against the darkening sky. The last stronghold of the Germans, the Palace was reduced to rubble by the advancing Red Army. She has heard there are plans to renovate it. The tram doors close and they are moving again. This time she keeps her eyes open. She mustn't miss her stop.

It's years since she's been to the Novák's house, but she's sure she remembers the way. She has a mental image of Professor Novák as a jolly man who enjoys his food and recounts amusing anecdotes around the dinner table. She pictures his wife, Ilona, a raven-haired beauty and an opera singer. Before the war there were parties at the Novák's house or her parents' apartment. Ilona would entertain everyone with her beautiful clear voice, singing arias from Mozart and Puccini. Katalin was allowed to stay up late if she behaved herself and didn't get in the way. It was a musical education to be cherished.

She disembarks in the heart of Buda. It's quieter here than in Pest, the atmosphere more modest and homely.

Houses with steeply pitched red-tiled roofs line the hilly, cobbled streets. Accordion music drifts from an upstairs window. A cat darts across the road and slinks into a courtyard.

As she makes her way up a leafy hill she mentally rehearses what she's going to say to Professor Novák. He won't be able to intervene directly with the authorities. He would be sure to get himself arrested if he did. But could he act as a character witness for her father? She has no idea how these things work. She experiences a moment of doubt, thinking she shouldn't have come, that her visit won't do any good. But she's here now isn't she? She might as well see it through. At the very least he might know something about why her father was arrested.

She stops outside an ivy-clad house with blue shutters. A small car is parked in the drive. She doesn't remember the Nováks owning a car, but maybe they've acquired one somehow. She's sure this is the right place though. Lights are on in the downstairs rooms, so someone is at home. She walks up the garden path and rings the doorbell.

The door is opened by a middle-aged woman wearing a black dress. Her grey hair is tied up in a severe bun. 'Yes?'

Katalin hesitates. This woman is certainly not Ilona, unless she's aged badly. It must be twelve or thirteen years since she last saw the Nováks. The woman looks at her expectantly but doesn't smile or offer any form of encouragement.

'I'm sorry, I thought this was Professor Novák's house. I must have been mistaken.'

'This is Professor Novák's house,' says the woman briskly. 'Is he expecting you?'

'No, but if he's at home I'd be very grateful for five minutes of his time.'

'What name shall I give?'

'Katalin Bakos. Professor Novák works with my father, Professor Márton Bakos.'

'Wait here a moment, please.'

The woman leaves Katalin standing in the hallway whilst she bustles off with an air of being terribly busy. She must be the housekeeper, thinks Katalin. She didn't know the Nováks had a housekeeper, although now she thinks about it, she doesn't suppose Ilona prepared all the food for those parties herself. There must have been someone else slaving away in the kitchen. She looks around. An oil painting of the Mátra Mountains hangs on one wall, a scene of Lake Balaton on another. A modern telephone stands on a side table beneath a mirror with an ornamental frame. Sounds filter through a closed door: voices, laughter, a tinkle of glass and cutlery. She's chosen an inconvenient time to call. She smells roast chicken and her stomach rumbles. She should have eaten before coming here.

A door opens and the woman reappears followed by Professor Novák. He's wiping his mouth with a napkin. It's definitely him, but he's put on weight since she last saw him and his hair has thinned.

'This is the young lady,' says the housekeeper. She stands very erect, her hands crossed in front of her.

'I see, well, er...' The professor scratches his head and looks momentarily alarmed, before appearing to collect himself. 'Thank you, Erzsébet.' He dismisses her with a wave of his hand. She's clearly reluctant to leave, but turns and walks through a door. Katalin glimpses a well-equipped kitchen. She imagines the housekeeper listening at the keyhole. Professor Novák is probably thinking the same thing, because he hurriedly ushers Katalin into another room and closes the door before she has a chance to say anything. They're in a book-lined study at the front of the house. He doesn't invite her to sit, but stands with his arms folded, regarding her with a frown on his face.

'I'm sorry I've interrupted your dinner,' she says. 'I could come back another time.'

'No, no, you mustn't do that.' He flaps the napkin impatiently. 'But you're here now. What can I do for you?'

Does he really have to ask?

'It's about Papa. The AVO took him away two nights ago.'

Professor Novák presses his fingers into his forehead as if he has suddenly developed a severe headache. 'Yes, I know.'

'Well, it's just that, I've had no news about where he's being held or how long the AVO are going to keep him under arrest. I wondered if you knew anything. Do you know where he is?'

He looks her directly in the eye. 'Does anyone else know you're here?'

'No.'

'Good.' He goes to the window and closes the curtains.

'Do you have any idea why he's been arrested? Does his arrest have anything to do with his work?' It's a bold question, but one that Katalin is determined to ask. 'Is it to do with the nuclear programme?'

Professor Novák gives her a sharp look. 'What do you know about that?'

'Nothing really, just that there's talk of building a nuclear reactor at Csillebérc. Papa said it was for research into atomic energy.'

'He shouldn't have discussed his work with you.'

'He didn't go into details. I wouldn't have understood them if he had.'

Katalin is frustrated with the way the conversation is going. They're getting off topic. She's not interested in the nuclear programme, only in what might have happened to her father.

'I just want to know where he is and what is happening to him.'

She can feel a lump starting to form in her throat. She grits her jaw, determined not to cry.

Professor Novák seems to deflate and the fight goes out of him. He drops his hands to his sides and a look of sorrow passes across his face. Or is it regret?

'Listen,' he says, 'your father is a good man. I'm sorry about what has happened to him, truly I am. But I can't help you. You'll just have to be patient. His arrest must have been a high-level political decision. It's probably best to let things take their natural course.'

'So there's nothing I can do?'

'There is nothing anyone can do.' He throws his hands up in despair. 'I would like to see your father released as much as you, but you know how things work in this country.' Beads of sweat have sprung up on his brow and he dabs at his face with his napkin.

He's afraid, she thinks. Afraid that if he gets involved they'll come for him too. It was a mistake to come here.

Behind Professor Novák the door opens and Katalin hears Ilona's crystal clear voice. 'There you are darling. We wondered what had happened to you. Erzsébet is about to serve dessert. You mustn't keep the guests waiting.'

Professor Novák moves aside, revealing Ilona to Katalin's view. Her long hair is still dark with only a hint of grey at the temples. She's lost none of her Slavic good looks – the almond-shaped eyes fringed by thick lashes, the high cheekbones and the full lips, painted a shade of deep pink. When she sees who her husband's visitor is, the smile freezes on her lips.

'Do you remember Katalin Bakos?' Professor Novák asks his wife. 'Márton's daughter. It must be years since you've seen her.'

'I remember,' says Ilona. Her pure soprano voice is cold and brittle. She turns to face Katalin. 'What are you doing here?'

'I thought your husband might be able to help…'

Ilona cuts her off. 'You should never have come to this house. What were you thinking of?'

Katalin doesn't know what to say. Even if the Nováks couldn't offer help, she had at least expected some sympathy. What has happened to those years of friendship? Professor Novák stares at the carpet and shuffles his feet. Ilona glares at her, stony-faced. Katalin reaches into her bag and takes out the copy of the Mozart aria which Ilona left in the apartment all those years ago. It might remind this brittle woman of old friendships – *beautiful moments of sweetness and pleasure.*

'I think this is yours.'

Ilona looks as if she's been stung and refuses to take the music, crossing her arms.

Katalin shrugs and drops the music onto a side table. She should leave before Ilona picks up the phone in the hallway and denounces her. Something must have happened to sour relations between Ilona and Katalin's parents which is why she never returned for the music and doesn't want it now.

'I'm sorry I interrupted your dinner,' says Katalin. 'Please don't keep your guests waiting on my account.'

The Nováks refuse to look her in the eye as she crosses the hallway – Erzsébet is hovering in the kitchen doorway – pulls open the front door and walks out.

She hurries down the street and doesn't look back. It's not until she's well out of sight that she pauses for breath. Her heart is pounding with a mixture of fury and fear. Mostly fear. But they were frightened too, she thinks. That's why they won't help me.

A cold drizzle is starting to fall and she hasn't brought an umbrella with her. The people she passes all have their faces down and their collars turned up against the inclement weather. It's still some way to the tram stop. Katalin picks up her pace, keen to get home.

After a few minutes she becomes aware of the sound of a car engine behind her, crawling in a low gear. She expects it to overtake her but it doesn't. She glances behind and sees a black Pobeda, like the one that took Papa away. Her heart skips a beat. Is it the bulldog and his men? Are they following her? The tram stop is just up ahead, about two hundred yards away. A tram is already there, waiting, the small queue of people climbing aboard.

She breaks into a run and the car accelerates behind her. The last person in the queue, an elderly lady laden with shopping bags, starts to board the tram. *Please take your time*, thinks Katalin. But the old woman is surprisingly quick on her feet and hops on board. Katalin sprints the last few yards, but the tram moves away from the stop just as she reaches the last carriage. She doubles over, hands on her knees, gasping for breath.

As she straightens up, the car drives past the tram stop and then accelerates away. She is sure it was following her. She huddles under the shelter and waits for the next tram to come along. After about fifteen minutes she hears the clatter of the rails as it trundles into view. She finds an empty seat and sits shivering as she crosses the Danube back into Pest. All she wants to do now is get home and be safe. But what if the men in the black car are waiting for her? Maybe she should go to Róza's place instead. But didn't Róza say she was working late at the hospital tonight? Katalin is so tired, she can't remember. She doesn't want to risk going all the way to Róza's to find she's not there.

When she gets back the street is empty. There are no parked cars waiting outside her building. She starts to relax. As she climbs the stairs she decides that she'll heat up some soup then have an early night. At the turn in the stairs she freezes. A man is standing outside the door to her apartment, ringing the bell.

*

Ilona fixes a smiles to her face and returns to their dinner guests – a Party official and his wife. Like the Countess in *The Marriage of Figaro* she will remain outwardly calm and dignified. She hopes her acting skills are good enough to carry her through the rest of the evening. But inwardly, she's a jagged mass of nerves. How dare Katalin turn up unannounced like that and put them all at risk? It was a foolish and selfish thing to do. The girl should have had better sense. Opposite her, at the other end of the table, her husband looks badly shaken by their unexpected visitor. He would probably have tried to help Katalin if she hadn't intervened in time, and then where would they be? She takes a large mouthful of wine and apologises for the interruption, dismissing it as one of the neighbours calling about some trivial matter. Whilst Erzsébet serves dessert – crème caramel followed by cheese – she smiles at the couple and turns to the husband.

'You were just telling us about Gerő's Five Year Plan for transforming the Hungarian Economy. Do please continue. It's such a fascinating topic.'

The Party official – a pallid man who looks as if he doesn't get enough sunshine – wipes his mouth with his napkin and picks up where he left off. His wife – a rather dour woman – nods her head at every other sentence. Ilona smiles and nods and does her best to appear interested, but she's no longer listening to the production figures of the factories, if she ever was.

The housekeeper appears in the doorway to announce that coffee is served in the lounge, thankfully bringing the lecture to an end. Ilona rises to her feet a little too quickly. 'Shall we?'

As she ushers their guests through to the other room, she gives Károly a hard stare, warning him to pull himself together. Once in the lounge, she notices the Mozart aria left by Katalin on a side table. *Dove Sono – Where are the beautiful moments of sweetness and pleasure?* She scoops it up and slides it under a copy of the Party newspaper, *A Free People.* She hasn't sung that aria for so many years. The memories it evokes are too painful. She doesn't want to be reminded of those times. She has made her choice and she must live with the consequences.

*

Katalin's instinct is to turn and run, but it's too late. He's already seen her. She stands frozen at the turn of the stairs, clutching the banister. The low-wattage bulb on the wall behind him is casting his face in shadow, but she sees a tall figure in a long trench coat. He's wearing a beret set at a crooked angle. Not your typical AVO dress code, but you can't be too careful. He could be in plain clothes.

He takes a couple of steps down the stairs.

'Who are you?' she asks, stepping backwards. 'What do you want?' Her heart is beating fast and her limbs are tensed, ready to take flight.

He stops on the third step from the top and holds his palms up in a gesture of reassurance. 'I'm sorry, I didn't mean to frighten you. My name is Zoltán Dobos. I live in the building opposite.' He points across the street. 'I'm a friend of your father's.'

A friend of her father's? Has Papa ever mentioned a Zoltán Dobos? Katalin thinks not. She's suspicious but intrigued.

'How do you know my father?'

'Fair question.' His tone is friendly and reasonable, not at all offended. He walks down a couple more steps towards her. 'But we can't talk here.' He gives a significant nod in the direction of József's door and holds his right hand up to his ear. He's right that the building has ears. 'Is there somewhere we could go? A café maybe?'

He's stepped into a pool of light and she can see him more clearly now. Dark eyes, well-defined cheekbones, a strong-set jaw and a straight brow that almost meets in the middle, giving him a serious look. His complexion is olive-skinned, like the peasants who work all day in the fields. He looks older than her, but by how much it's hard to tell, maybe no more than a couple of years. The trench coat looks like something left over from the war. She notices it's fraying at the hem.

'There is a café that stays open late,' she says.

'Feri's place? I know it well. Shall we?' He descends the

last few steps and joins her on the landing. He's tall, she only comes up to his shoulder, but his manner is entirely unthreatening. Rather he seems to be leaving it to her to make the decision. She could say no and she feels sure he would simply go away. But something tells her he would be sad if she did. And besides, she's curious. He says he knows her father. Maybe he can tell her something useful, unlike Professor Novák. She'll feel safe at Feri's.

She nods, and his face breaks into a broad smile, lighting up his stern features and making him look younger.

Outside, he lights a cigarette and offers her one which she politely declines. They walk to the café in silence through the darkening streets. She has to hurry to keep up with his longer stride. The way he walks, it's as if he owns the pavement.

The café is empty, save for two old men playing chess. Feri is humming along to the radio, polishing glasses behind the bar. He smiles when he sees the two young people approach the counter.

'Mademoiselle, Monsieur, what can I get you?'

They order two coffees and two pastries and sit down at a corner table, out of earshot of the chess players. Katalin is ravenous after her visit to Professor Novák. She tucks in to her pastry which is flavoured with cinnamon and nutmeg.

'I saw what happened to your father the other night,' says Zoltán, stirring his coffee.

'You did?' She is surprised he is telling her this. Most people prefer not to admit to seeing anything. If you don't see or hear what happens to your neighbours, you can't be held responsible for them. It's easier and safer that way.

He nods. 'Like I said, I live directly opposite.'

'I've not seen you before.' She is certain she would remember him if she had. He's not conventionally good-looking but he's the sort of man who would stand out in a crowd. He's taken off the beret and his hair is dark and springy. The hands that pick up the pastry are strong and a little roughened, as if he does manual labour.

'I've only been there three months. I leave for work early and get back late most nights.'

'You must have been up very late if you saw the AVO arrest Papa.' She sips her coffee and waits for him to explain himself further.

'I like to read when everyone else is asleep. I was sitting by the window when I heard the cars in the square. I saw they were Russian Pobedas. That usually means only one thing. Only the Secret Police call at such unsociable times.'

Katalin nods. 'I was in bed. The doorbell terrified me. At first I thought it was just a bad dream, but then it rang again and wouldn't stop.' She shudders at the memory. At the time she felt so vulnerable and alone, she had no idea someone else was watching events unfold. A thought occurs to her – was he spying on them? But she doesn't believe he had sinister intentions. He wouldn't admit to it so freely if he was spying for the AVO. Everyone hates informers.

'What were you reading?' she asks.

'Thomas Mann's *The Magic Mountain*. In fact your father lent it to me.'

'He did?' The AVO took away the rest of her father's German books. She's pleased they didn't take this one. 'It's one of his favourites,' she says.

He smiles, remembering. 'We got chatting one day here in this café about books. He saw I was reading *Crime and Punishment* and he asked me what I thought of it. He was reading *Anna Karenina*. He offered to lend me some Thomas Mann. I'll return it soon. I've nearly finished it.'

'It is all true,' says Feri who is wiping down the nearby tables. 'Those two always have their heads in a book.'

Katalin laughs. She has no worries about Feri overhearing their conversation and she can well believe what she is hearing. Her father often reads in cafés and likes nothing more than a literary discussion. She imagines

Zoltán Dobos and Márton Bakos getting on very well.

Feri moves off to chat to the elderly chess players and she is once again alone with this strange man whom she has only just met. Suddenly she feels shy and picks at crumbs on her plate, not sure what to say. There's so much she'd like to tell him, but where to start?

Zoltán breaks the awkward silence that has fallen between them. 'The reason I came over this evening is because I wanted to make sure you were all right. I'd have come sooner, but work got in the way.'

'Thank you,' she says. 'I'm glad you did.' She is touched by this act of kindness. She has a sudden urge to tell him everything that's on her mind.

'The worst thing,' she blurts out, 'is that I don't know where they've taken him or what's going to happen to him.'

'They've probably taken him to the Secret Police headquarters on Andrássy Avenue, but you can't just march in there and demand to know. They'd lock you up too.'

'Then what am I supposed to do?'

'Be patient. I know that's not what you want to hear, but you don't have any other choice.'

'I went to see my father's colleague today in Buda.'

'And I'm guessing from the look on your face that it wasn't a successful trip.'

'Far from it.'

'The thing is,' says Zoltán, 'people are scared. It's the only way the Party can stay in power, by making people afraid of them. It's not that people don't want to help, but they have to think about themselves and their own families first.'

He speaks calmly and openly. It's a brave thing to do, thinks Katalin, criticising the Party in public. Feri can be trusted, but what if one of those old chess players overhears? What if one of them is an AVO informer?

'You don't seem afraid,' she says. She realises that this

is what marks Zoltán out as different. He walks tall, both literally and metaphorically. She's never met anyone quite like him before.

'I try to believe what Roosevelt said, that the only thing we have to fear is fear itself.'

'And do you?'

'Most of the time.' He laughs. 'Well, at least some of it.'

There's a draught of cold air as the two chess players open the door and walk out into the dark street. It's grown late. She could sit here all evening, talking to Zoltán, finding out what else he reads late at night. She wants to ask him about his work, his family, where he's come from. So many questions. But Feri has turned the radio off as if he's trying to give them a gentle hint that it's time to be leaving.

'We should go,' she says. 'Thank you for coming to find me.'

'My pleasure. I'll return *The Magic Mountain* in a couple of days.'

She smiles at the prospect of seeing him again. Maybe he'd like to borrow more books, the ones the AVO didn't take with them.

They bid Feri goodnight and walk back to Király Street. There are no cars following them and she feels safe in Zoltán's presence.

He walks her to the door of her building where they pause on the pavement. There's a moment's awkwardness when she doesn't know what to say to him but she doesn't want him to leave just yet.

He takes her hand in both of his and says, 'If you ever need me, I'm just over there, on the top floor.' He points to the building opposite.

'Thank you.'

'Well, goodnight then.'

'Yes, good night.'

He still has hold of her hand. 'Would you like to have lunch with me on Saturday afternoon? I know a place that does good food.'

'Yes, I'd like that very much.'

'That's wonderful. I'll come for you at midday.'

He gives her hand a gentle squeeze and then he's striding across the square, his trench coat flapping behind him. Katalin lets herself into the building and runs up the stairs. She feels lighter than she's done since the AVO arrested Papa. That night she sleeps soundly without waking.

*

Sleep is the thing Márton desires above all else. For the second night in a row, he is sitting in front of a typewriter, typing his life story. Apparently yesterday's effort was not good enough and, like a naughty schoolboy, he is being made to do it all again.

His back is stiff and sore, his buttocks are numb and his fingers are starting to cramp up. It's an old typewriter and the mechanism is recalcitrant at best. The words on the paper swim in front of his eyes, blurring and reshaping themselves into meaningless squiggles. His head nods forwards, his neck muscles unwilling to hold it up straight a moment longer. The guard on duty prods him in the back with his rifle butt and orders him to keep typing. He's starting to run out of things to write.

He can't imagine what relevance his childhood has to his present predicament. Nevertheless, he does as he's asked and fills pages with stories of growing up in eastern Hungary. Once he starts to type the memories flood back: the acres of arable land handed down through his family from one generation to another; picking apples in the orchard; fishing in the river; plentiful harvests; good wine. The peasants who worked on the land were treated well. It was a time of abundance and plenty, unlike now. He grew up free to roam the hills and forests, to explore and discover. That was how he became a scientist, through his love of nature. His father saw that he wasn't cut out to be a landowner and encouraged him with his education. He went to university and studied physics. His parents were proud of him. But they died in the war. In some ways it was a blessing. It would have broken their hearts to see their land divided up and redistributed in the government's land reform programme. He had a good childhood but it would be better for him now if he'd been born a peasant. The Party professes to love peasants and factory workers, although Márton has long doubted that is truly the case.

And now he must write about his time in England. He remembers wisteria-clad quadrangles, medieval college dining halls, summer walks in Christ Church Meadow, punting on the river Cherwell, lively debate, stimulating lectures and above all a thirst for knowledge and the freedom to discuss ideas openly and without fear. There's no getting away from the fact that this was one of the happiest periods of his life. But he must play all of this down as he types his life story for the AVO. England is the imperialist enemy now. That is how the high-ups in Hungary see things. And they are the ones holding him prisoner. He skims over his Oxford days, trying to make out that the time spent there was not so important to him after all.

He hits the keys of the typewriter, making more and more spelling mistakes as he struggles to stay awake. He's sure that much of what he's writing is gibberish, but if he pauses for a moment the guard will prod him in the back with his rifle.

Finally, when he's filled twenty pages with stories about his life, the guard tells him to get up. He staggers to his feet, his knee joints clicking. He has no idea what time it is, but it must be early morning. He lets himself be led back to his cell like a lamb. All he wants is to lie down on the wooden plank which has now assumed the desirability of a feather mattress. But there's a note pinned to his cell door. The prisoner is not allowed to sleep.

He stands in his cell, shivering with cold and swaying on his feet as his eyelids close. Is it possible to sleep standing up?

CHAPTER 5

'You did what?' Róza looks horrified. She puts down her coffee and stares at Katalin across the table. They are sharing a slice of apple and cinnamon pie at Feri's. Its sweet and spicy texture crumbles in the mouth. The radio is playing the usual stream of Party-approved folk music and Feri is humming along to the tunes as he walks around clearing the tables.

'I went to see Professor Károly Novák. I thought he might know something about Papa's arrest.'

Róza shakes her head. 'You shouldn't have taken the risk. You might have been followed.'

Katalin doesn't say anything about the car in Buda. It would only confirm Róza's worst fears. 'You don't know what it's like, this not knowing.'

Róza gives her a sympathetic look. 'So did Professor Novák tell you anything?'

'No, nothing. But the worst thing was when his wife appeared.' Katalin still can't reconcile the Ilona of last night with the woman she remembers from all those years ago, the one who sang Mozart so beautifully in her parents' apartment. 'She made it plain that I wasn't welcome in their house. She couldn't get me out of there fast enough.'

Róza taps the table with her finger. 'They know something, then. Or at least she does. Which is precisely why you mustn't talk to them. They're dangerous.'

'But they were such good friends of my parents.'

'Even so.'

They fall silent. Outside, darkness has fallen and a gentle rain patters against the window. She can't understand why people her parents once trusted would turn her away so cruelly. Unlike Zoltán who went out of his way to find her and offer his support. A man in a trench coat is crossing the road, weaving between the trams. Katalin's heart somersaults in expectation. She's been thinking about Zoltán all day, unable to get him out of her mind. She squints into the night, but it's not him. She swallows her disappointment.

'What is it?' asks Róza. 'Did you see someone you know?'

Róza doesn't miss a thing. Katalin feels herself starting to redden. She wasn't going to say anything about Zoltán until she'd got to know him a bit better, but Róza will pester her until she spills the beans.

Katalin stirs her coffee with one of Feri's little silver spoons. 'When I arrived home last night there was a man standing on the landing outside my apartment. He was ringing the bell.'

'Good grief, you must have been terrified after what happened to your father!'

'I was at first. But it wasn't the AVO.'

'So who was it?'

'His name is Zoltán Dobos. He lives across the street. He's only a year or two older than us, but he says he's a friend of Papa's. They got to know each other talking about books. He saw what happened the night when the AVO came to arrest Papa, and he came over to make sure I was all right.'

Katalin can see the disbelief on her friend's face and it

disappoints her. She wants Róza to like Zoltán, not mistrust him.

'Are you sure he is who he says he is?' asks Róza, lowering her voice. 'You can't be too careful. He might be an informer.'

'No, I don't think so.'

'What makes you so sure?'

How can she explain? Is she putting too much faith in a shared love of books? No, there has to be more to it than that. In the end she says, 'He wasn't afraid to speak his mind. Not many people are brave enough to do that.' When Róza continues to look sceptical, Katalin adds, 'Anyway, I'm meeting him for lunch on Saturday.' She enjoys the look of astonishment on her friend's face.

*

'What is this pile of waffle?' The red-faced officer holds up the pages that Márton has typed. He flicks through the sheets with his tobacco-stained fingers, scowling at the densely packed prose.

'That is my life story,' says Márton. He's so exhausted he doesn't have the will to argue. 'It's what you asked for.' He doubts the man has read it. He doesn't look as if he has the patience to read a child's story book, let alone dozens of pages of autobiography.

It's late evening and Márton is back in the upstairs office, sitting on the hard wooden chair opposite the man whose name he has discovered, from overhearing the guards talking, is Vajda. He's had no proper sleep for the last forty-eight hours. Every time he's nodded off for ten minutes, the spy hole has banged open and the guard on duty has shouted at him to wake up. He's relieved that Vajda hasn't turned on the interrogation lamp, but on the other hand it means he can see the cold-hearted ruthlessness in the man's eyes.

Vajda takes the top sheet of paper, scrunches it into a

ball and tosses it across the room. 'Lies! All of it lies!' He continues to scrunch up sheet after sheet and throw them around the room, like a child having a tantrum, until the floor is littered with Márton's life story.

Márton sits tight, clenching his fists. He wasn't expecting Vajda to praise his literary efforts, but he riles at being called a liar. Every word he has written is the truth.

When Vajda has finished playing ball he leans across the desk and points a stubby finger at Márton. 'What have you got to say for yourself?'

'I told the truth,' says Márton, forcing himself to look Vajda square in the eye.

'Bollocks!' Vajda's jowls wobble and spittle flies from his mouth.

'What else would you have me write?'

'What about your spying activities?'

'What on earth are you talking about?'

Vajda sits back in his comfortable chair. 'You spent time at Oxford. You have friends in the west. You shared our nuclear plans with them.'

So that's what they think of him, is it? Despite the fug of exhaustion clouding his brain, He is incensed by this slur on his integrity. 'That's an outrageous lie. It's true that I have some personal friends in England, but I have never passed on to them anything relating to my work.'

'I don't believe you.'

And there you have it, thinks Márton. How can he prove that he hasn't done something if the AVO are determined to argue that he must have done it?

'You will spend another night typing your life story,' says Vajda with menace. 'And this time I advise you to think more carefully about what you write.'

*

Katalin's neighbour Petra Nadas has invited her upstairs for a slice of Tibor's leftover birthday cake.

'Sorry there's not much,' says Petra, passing her a small piece of chocolate sponge with a strawberry jam filling. 'Tibor's already eaten most of it himself. You wouldn't believe how much a growing boy eats.' She sighs and wipes her forehead with the back of her hand. 'He's at his friend Géza's house so we should have half an hour of peace and quiet before he gets home.'

She clears piles of sewing and mending off the two armchairs so they can sit down.

'This is delicious,' says Katalin, taking a bite of the cake. The ingredients must have cost Petra a small fortune. 'Did he enjoy his birthday?'

'Oh yes,' says Petra, licking crumbs off her fingers. 'But now that he's eleven he's going to be even more of a handful. I can just see it.'

'He's a good kid though,' says Katalin.

Petra smiles indulgently. 'Yes, but his head is so full of wild ideas.'

Katalin looks down at her plate as she recalls the headmaster's words. *We can't allow subversive ideas to spread in a school environment.*

She glances around the room. It's sparsely furnished with a couple of worn armchairs, a table on which sits Petra's sewing machine, and an old dresser for plates. A single framed photograph of Petra's late husband sits on the mantelpiece in his uniform before he went off to war. There are no books and there's no radio. Tibor isn't getting his ideas from *Voice of America*, that's for sure.

'Tibor was very sorry to hear about your father,' says Petra.

'That's kind of him. I didn't know he knew Papa.'

'He's always liked Márton,' continues Petra. 'Ever since Márton gave him those comics.'

'What comics?' asks Katalin, confused.

'I'm sorry, I thought you knew.' She shifts in her chair. 'Your father had them from a friend of his in England – American comics they are – and Márton gave them to

Tibor because he thought he'd enjoy them. They're in English of course, but Márton translated them for him. Tibor likes the pictures though. Especially the ones about a man who is so strong he can lift cars and jump vast distances. Let me show you.'

She disappears and comes back with half a dozen magazines featuring a man engaged in extraordinary feats of strength and bravery. The main character wears a tight-fitting blue outfit with a red letter 'S' emblazoned on his muscular chest. A red cape billows out behind him. The images are dynamic and skillfully drawn, depicting a world full of excitement and adventure. A world of heroes, so different to the fearful one they inhabit. It's obvious why these comics would appeal to an eleven-year-old boy. This is clearly where Tibor gets his wild ideas. But what is harmless fun for an American child would be viewed as subversive by the Hungarian authorities. Márton took a terrible risk giving these comics to Tibor. If the AVO found them, Petra would be arrested and Tibor would be sent to a state-run orphanage. Such a place doesn't bear thinking about.

'He must keep these hidden,' Katalin says, passing the comics back to Petra. 'You wouldn't want them to fall into the wrong hands.'

Petra bites her lip, nodding. 'I know. But there's so little to entertain a child with. What can you do?'

*

Clack, clack, clack. The prisoner hits the typewriter keys with a rhythmic monotony. Tamás can see that Márton Bakos is dog-tired. His head keeps lolling on his shoulders, his eyes are bloodshot and puffy, and his fingers are trembling with cold and exhaustion. This is the third night running that he's been made to stay up and type his life story, and he hasn't been allowed to sleep properly during the day. Tamás wouldn't be able to stand it himself, he knows that much.

Last night Gábor stood guard whilst Márton Bakos typed. 'You'll have to prod the bastard every five minutes,' Gábor advised him this morning. 'It's the only way to keep him going. Lazy sod.'

'Right,' said Tamás. 'I'll make sure he doesn't stop.'

Gábor grinned and slapped him on the shoulder. 'We'll make a decent AVO officer out of you yet.'

For the last two hours Tamás has been carrying out his orders dutifully, prodding Márton in the small of the back with his rifle butt every time it looks like he's going to fall asleep. But, really, what's the point? The chap can hardly keep his eyes open. And the clacking of the typewriter is getting on Tamás's nerves. Half an hour of peace and quiet would do them both good. But can he take the risk?

It's two in the morning. He's got another couple of hours of this to go before he can take the prisoner back to his cell.

Márton's head lolls forward once more.

Sod it, think Tamás. Instead of jabbing Márton in the back with his rifle, he puts a hand on the man's shoulder. 'Shut your eyes for half an hour. But don't tell anyone or we'll both be in trouble.'

Márton regards him with bleary eyes. Then he leans forward and rests his head on his folded arms. Within seconds he's snoring gently.

For a moment, Tamás frets. What is he doing? If his boss were to come along now, he'd be fired on the spot. Or worse, he'd be arrested and questioned as a traitor. But Vajda went home to his comfortable bed hours ago. All right for some, thinks Tamás.

It's eerily quiet now the typewriter has fallen silent. Tamás stands by the door and listens.

After half an hour he hears footsteps in the corridor.

'Wake up,' he hisses, shaking Márton by the shoulders.

Márton groans and opens his eyes.

'Start typing!'

Dutifully he starts plucking at the keys and the footsteps pass by. Tamás breathes a sigh of relief. He also feels a sense of power. It's up to him if and when Márton Bakos sleeps. Márton is in his debt.

*

What to wear? She can't wear the cream blouse because she's worn it all week to school and it needs washing, and the navy one is missing a button but she doesn't have any navy thread in her sewing box. But then Katalin feels a stab of guilt. Her father has been gone for days and didn't take any spare clothes with him. He'll still be wearing the suit and shirt he went in if they haven't given him anything else. She would take him a change of clothes if they would let her see him, but from what she's heard of the regime at 60 Andrássy Avenue, she knows that's impossible.

She takes a green blouse from its hanger and puts it on. The cuffs are a little frayed, but that doesn't matter. It's only lunch, she tells herself. It's not as if they're going to the Café New York or anything.

But what about her hair? Should she put it up or keep it down? She tries pinning it up, they way her mother used to. It makes her look older, more sophisticated, but the pins refuse to stay in place and slide out after a minute or two. Frustrated, she gives up and pulls a brush through her unruly locks.

A quick ring on the doorbell makes her jump. She can't hear it now without being reminded of that night the AVO arrested her father. But this ring was light to the touch and only lasted a second, almost apologetic. She opens the door and finds Zoltán on the landing, wearing the same trench coat he had on when she first saw him, his beret set at a crooked angle. He has a book in his hands.

'I finished it last night,' he says, holding out Thomas Mann's *The Magic Mountain*.

As she takes the book from him her fingers brush

against his and she feels a tingling down her spine. 'Did you enjoy it?' she asks.

'Very much.' He gives her a quizzical smile and she realises that she should invite him in.

'Sorry, come in. I just need to put my shoes on. I won't be a minute.'

His tall frame seems to fill the narrow hallway and Katalin becomes conscious of the tight space and their proximity to one another. Suddenly she can't remember where she left her shoes.

She drops the book on the sofa in the living room, then hunts for her shoes which seem to have miraculously vanished since she took them off last night.

'Are you looking for these?' asks Zoltán, holding up a pair of brown shoes.

Katalin blushes. 'Thank you.' She slides her feet into them and then they're ready to go.

As they walk down the stairs József is sweeping the hallway. Zoltán greets him with a cheery *hello* which József acknowledges with a grunt. Katalin can feel the caretaker's eyes on her as they leave the building.

They catch a tram to the outskirts of the City Park. Zoltán says he knows a place that serves cheap food in plentiful quantities.

The restaurant is unfussy with plain white table clothes and only one option on the menu – a spicy meat stew. It's the first hot meal Katalin has eaten since her father was arrested. As she spears a chunk of beef on her fork, she wonders if it's wrong to be enjoying herself when he is probably being held in some dank cell on a starvation diet. The guilt must show on her face because Zoltán says, 'You have to look after yourself. One day your father will come home and he won't want to find you wasted away.'

'Do you really think they'll let him?' she asks. It's the question she hasn't dared put to herself.

'It's too soon to give up hope.'

She knows he's right, but she still feels guilty.

Zoltán asks her about her work at the school and is understanding when she complains about Piroska Benke, the school secretary. He tells her about his factory and does an hilarious impersonation of the Party secretary, Csaba Elek, reading aloud from the Party newspaper. Katalin starts to relax.

After they've eaten, Zoltán suggests a walk in the park and she readily agrees. It's a fine day, one of the last good days they'll have before winter sets in, and the park is busy with people making the most of the opportunity. Zoltán offers his arm, and she falls into step with him, enjoying the sunshine. A football rolls into their path and he kicks it back to a group of boys who are playing on the grass. She can almost believe she lives in a normal country.

But then they come across Stalin.

He's impossible to miss. The giant bronze statue towers over them, glinting in the late afternoon sun, reminding Katalin that life is far from normal. She looks up at Stalin's head with its scrolls of wavy bronze hair, but the statue appears to lurch against the scudding clouds and she has to look away, feeling dizzy.

She's always found the scale of this statue difficult to comprehend. The dictator's knee-high boots alone are six feet or more. He is posing as an orator with one hand across his chest as if he is about to impart words of wisdom. The base of the massive limestone plinth is decorated with relief sculptures of grateful Hungarians paying homage to their overlord and master. *Thank you for liberating us from Nazi Germany. Thank you for showing us the true path to happiness and prosperity. Thank you for being such a wise and omnipotent leader.*

This is the man who gave Rákosi lessons in how to be a tyrant. The AVO is fashioned on the Soviet model for a Secret Police. Stalin has assumed the magnitude of a mythical deity, his place assured for all eternity. What would it take to topple such a god? The idea alone is heretical.

Katalin shivers as the sun disappears behind a cloud, and Zoltán offers to take her home.

They stop outside the entrance to her building and it seems only natural to invite him in for a coffee, despite what the caretaker may think if he's hanging around.

She invites Zoltán to make himself comfortable in the living room whilst she flusters around in the kitchen, rinsing out two mugs. She didn't do the washing up this morning because she spent so much time trying to decide what to wear. And to be honest, she's let things go a bit since her father's arrest. She just doesn't have the energy any more. She forgot to ask Zoltán how he takes his coffee. She's nearly out of sugar. She sniffs the cream and hastily pours it down the sink.

'Just black for me. No sugar.'

She spins around to find him leaning against the door frame, a faint smile playing about his lips. How long has he been standing there watching her?

'Okay,' she says. 'I can do black coffee.' She fills two mugs and passes one to him. She's conscious of the general clutter in the kitchen and the smell of sour cream in the sink.

In the living room she has tidied up the mess left by the AVO but she's still aware of a lingering sense of their presence, a smell she hasn't been able to eradicate. When she's got time she's going to polish all the surfaces with beeswax.

Zoltán wanders over to the piano, lifts the lid and plays a few notes with his left hand. 'Do you play?'

'Very badly,' she says. 'My mother was the pianist in the family.'

'Is this her?' He's noticed the photograph of her parents which is still propped on the side table where she left it.

'Yes,' she says. 'It was taken when they were on their honeymoon in England. What about your family? Are your parents still alive?' He's only told her about his current life, nothing about where he came from.

'They died in the war,' he says.

'I'm sorry.'

'They were originally from Transylvania. But after the Treaty of Trianon the borders were redrawn and their part of Hungary became Romanian. They crossed the border to live in what was left of Hungary, leaving their families behind. I never knew my grandparents.' He puts the photograph of Katalin's parents back on the side table. Then he looks at her with an expression full of heartfelt emotion. 'I would like to live in a world without borders.'

'So would I.'

He holds out his arms to her and Katalin falls into them without hesitation. As her lips meet his, she feels hope for the future.

CHAPTER 6

For seven long nights Márton types his life story. He doesn't think there is anything new to say, but with each retelling more and more details come back to him: catching trout in the river with his father as a child, foraging for mushrooms in the forest, his mother's stews, the thrill of arriving in Budapest as a student, lectures in Oxford. And then years later, meeting his future wife at a party, taking her out to the Café New York on her birthday, the siege of Budapest and the devastating news that his wife had been caught in the crossfire between the Germans and the Soviets. Of Katalin he tries to write as little as possible. He doesn't want her mixed up in all this trouble.

He hasn't been taken to Vajda yet to have his words thrown back at him.

He barely sleeps all week. If Gábor is supervising one of the typing sessions then there is no mercy. He has to keep typing, no matter how tired he is. If he starts to nod off, which he does frequently, Gábor jabs him in the back with his rifle butt. But if Tamás is on duty, he lets Márton have half an hour's kip here and there. Márton understands that being the one to set the rules bolsters the boy's fragile ego, but he isn't complaining. Sleep is sleep and he'll grab whatever scraps are offered to him. He repays Tamás by typing extra hard when he's awake. It seems only fair.

He spends his days in his cell, most of the time not allowed to even sit or lie down. He has developed the ability to sleep on his feet. The banging of the spy holes and the screams of other prisoners punctuate his dreams.

He is swaying on the balls of his feet, eyes closed. He anticipates that any minute now the cell door will open and he'll be taken back to the typewriter room. He doesn't know what else he can tell them. At least he is permitted to sit whilst typing.

Footsteps in the corridor. The bolt slides across. He braces himself for another night of wordsmithing. The door opens and his heart sinks at the sight of Gábor. He was hoping for Tamás. He stumbles out into the corridor, so tired he can barely see where he's going. No matter. He could find his way to the typewriter room blindfolded if he had to. But at the turn in the corridor Gábor jabs him in the back and says, 'This way.'

He is taken to Vajda's office.

Vajda is sitting behind his desk with his hands resting on his belly which appears to have grown even bigger since Márton last saw him. Márton on the other hand is growing thinner by the day. He's still wearing the same suit he was wearing when they brought him in but the trousers are getting loose around the waist. If he'd worn a belt they would have taken it off him.

'Sit!' Vajda points at the familiar wooden chair.

Márton collapses onto the chair. He expects to see piles of paper on Vajda's desk – his output from a solid week of mindless typing. But apart from the telephone, the interrogation lamp and the bust of Stalin, the desk is quite bare. If Vajda produces those dozens of pages and starts screwing them up into balls Márton thinks he might just lose it. How far could he throw Stalin's bust in his fragile state?

But Vajda opens a drawer in his desk and pulls out a single sheet of typed paper. He also takes a fountain pen from the drawer and unscrews the lid.

'This is your confession.' He slides the sheet of paper across the desk towards Márton. 'You are required to sign here.' He points at the bottom of the page with a stubby index finger.

'My confession?' Despite his exhaustion, Márton is not aware that he has confessed to anything, although he has been falsely accused of spying.

'Yes, your confession. Now sign it.'

'May I read what I am being asked to sign?' They've done their best to bring him to a point of near physical collapse, but he still has a shred of dignity inside him. Even Vajda can't expect him to sign a document without reading it first.

Vajda harrumphs as if Márton's request is quite out of order, but he makes no formal objection. Márton leans forward, picks up the piece of paper and reads the opening line.

I, the undersigned, freely confess to my crimes of betrayal and treason against the Party and the State.

But as he reads and re-reads the document, he is filled with incredulity and then anger. He has to resist the overwhelming urge to screw the confession into a ball and aim it squarely at Vajda's fat head. If this is Vajda's work, then he has concocted a fiction of accusations and lies worthy of the most far-fetched spy novel. How is he supposed to have smuggled nuclear secrets out of the country to his friends in England? The confession isn't clear on that point. Reading on, he learns to his amazement that he intends to sabotage the Party's efforts to build a fair and just society based on Marxist-Leninist principles, he has no respect for Comrades Stalin or Rákosi (well that much is true at least) and he is also guilty of hating the working class, having come from a family of feudal landowners. This apparently makes him a fascist swine.

'I will not sign this concoction of lies.' Márton returns the piece of paper to the desk with a self-control that makes him proud.

Vajda looks affronted and a muscle starts to twitch in his flabby jowls. 'Lies?! You have the audacity to accuse the Party of lying?' Spittle sprays the surface of the desk.

'All I'm saying is that this confession is not true. Therefore I will not sign it.'

'You are making a grave mistake.'

Márton wonders for a moment if he is indeed making a mistake. Will Vajda accuse him of worse crimes if he refuses to sign this confession? But still, he can't bring himself to admit to spying and hating the working class. 'This confession is not true,' he repeats. The words are starting to sound hollow.

'But this' – Vajda waves the document in the air – 'is the truth as we see it.'

So that's it, thinks Márton. The Party is always right. The Party must always be proved to be infallible. It is the duty of every worker to bow down before the superiority of the Party. What can one individual do against the might of the Party? It would take the whole society to rise up against the power of the State, but such a thing is unthinkable. The whole society merely consists of individuals who are frightened for their own survival. But still, someone has to make a stand.

'I will not sign.'

'Too bad for you.' Vajda sounds almost satisfied that he has refused. What new tortures does he have in store for him now? He rings a bell on his desk and Gábor reappears. Vajda whispers something to him and the corners of Gábor's mouth turn upwards in a sly grin.

'On your feet.' Gábor takes him by the arm and pulls

him roughly to his feet.

He walks Márton to a whitewashed room and orders him to stand facing the wall. 'Closer.'

Márton shuffles forwards a couple of inches.

'Move closer,' barks Gábor.

Márton moves closer still, until his nose is no more than an inch from the white wall.

'Stand still. If you move, I will kick you.'

Márton takes the threat seriously.

*

Mid-morning Piroska Benke appears at the classroom door to summon Katalin to György Boda's office. With a martyred expression she says that she, Piroska Benke – school secretary and Party official with far more important things to do – will watch the children for half an hour.

'Be good for Miss Benke,' Katalin tells her class. They're doing their morning sums. Some of them struggle without extra help, which is unlikely to be forthcoming from the school administrator. Their faces fall and she pities them, but there's nothing to be done.

She suspects she's being called to give account of her spying activities on Petra and Tibor. As she walks down the corridor, she mentally rehearses what she's going to say. She will not betray her friends.

She knocks on the headmaster's door and he calls her into his office.

'Take a seat, Miss Bakos.'

He's friendlier today, perhaps hoping to get more information out of her if he makes the interview sound more like an informal chat.

'Coffee?'

'No thank you,' says Katalin. 'I don't want to be away from my class for too long.'

He sits back in his chair. 'In that case, tell me what you've discovered about Tibor Nadas.'

She takes a deep breath. 'There's really nothing to report. He lives alone with his mother. They don't own a radio so he's not listening to foreign stations. There are no books in the apartment.' Katalin has decided that comics don't count as proper books.

'Then how do you account for his behaviour? He is not like the other children. He initiates games of daring. He doesn't respect authority.'

'I think there's a perfectly harmless explanation,' says Katalin. 'His father died in the war, a true Hungarian patriot. I think Tibor feels a responsibility as the man of the house, so to speak, to look after his mother. He's an imaginative child, and in his case he sees himself as a hero, someone that his soldier father would have been proud of. I'm sure there's nothing more to it than that.'

'Hmm,' says György Boda, stroking his moustache. He doesn't look convinced.

You must have been a child once, thinks Katalin, although it's hard to imagine this man running around in short trousers. Don't all children want to have fun and games? Instead they have to learn Party songs and march around the playground like good socialists.

'I will be keeping a close eye on that boy,' says the headmaster, 'and if I find that you have been covering for him in any way, it will not look good for you.'

Katalin is dismissed. When she arrives back at her classroom the children are all sitting with their fingers on lips. No one looks happy.

*

Who would have thought that a white wall could be a thing of such horror? The AVO certainly know all the worst psychological tricks to play.

Márton can't focus on the wall. He's standing way too close to it. If he sways on his feet, which he does almost constantly, his nose grazes the rough surface. When sleep overpowers him, he bangs his forehead against it. Dents, smudges and imperfections in the wall blur in front of him, assuming the shapes of faces glimpsed in clouds. His mind plays tricks on him, conjuring up crowds of spectators that mock him, animals that threaten to kill him and swirling waters that threaten to drown him.

He still has enough sense left to know that he's hallucinating, but there is nothing he can do to stop it. He blinks to try and make the images go away. How close is he to madness? If this carries on, he could lose his mind and become like one of those poor souls who sit in their cells whimpering all day.

His feet have gone numb and lost all sense of contact with the stone floor. As his mind spins out of control, his body has the sensation of floating. He imagines floating out through the walls and floors, rising above the streets of Budapest. He's high above the Danube now, following the river as it flows eastwards towards Romania and the Black Sea.

He must have fallen asleep again because he loses his balance and topples forwards, banging his forehead against the wall. A sharp kick from a steel-capped boot to the back of his leg makes him cry out in pain.

'Stand still. What did I tell you? If you move, I will kick you.'

Márton resumes his position facing the wall. The movement, however brief, has restored some feeling to his feet. Good job, he thinks, that they took his shoe laces off him when he arrived. His feet have now swollen so much that his shoes pinch him.

The swirling shapes on the wall assume monstrous proportions. Sinister, contorted faces leap out from spy holes. Malevolent grins, evil stares. He closes his eyes, trying to shut out the vile visions. He loses his balance again and this time a rifle butt is jabbed into his kidneys.

He feels sick and dizzy. Fainting would be a relief. He's been here for hours already. He suspects there are still many hours left to go.

*

This is the right street. The closely packed apartment houses, the narrow street which rarely gets the sun. Katalin remembers coming here once with Róza to deliver some school books when Tamás was off sick with a severe case of tonsillitis. The teacher chose her and Róza for the task because he said he could trust them. Tamás was a sickly child, always off with something or other. But that must have been, what, ten, twelve years ago now and she hasn't been back here since. She still can't believe that Tamás Kún is an ÁVO officer.

Róza advised her against this plan, telling her it was foolish at best, dangerous at worst. But Zoltán said that Tamás has more to lose than she does. He failed to search her room thoroughly and dereliction of duty is a serious offence in the Secret Police. He could be accused of treason. Zoltán thinks Katalin's plan is worth a shot.

He offered to come with her, but she thought it would be better if she came on her own. She doesn't want to get Zoltán into trouble. They've grown close in the past week. He's taught her how to feel again.

She finds the building, still smoke-blackened and pockmarked from bullet wounds inflicted during the war. The entrance door stands open, the paint peeling. Leaves have blown inside.

An old woman, the caretaker Katalin assumes, is sitting on a chair in the hallway, knitting. Her knitting needles don't pause in their clicking as she looks Katalin up and down.

'Good morning,' says Katalin. 'I'm looking for Tamás Kún. Does he live here?'

The old woman makes a phlegmy sound in her throat. 'Third floor.' She nods towards the stairs. 'The lift's not working.'

Katalin climbs the dimly lit stairs. A smell of boiled cabbage lingers in the stairwell. Somewhere in the building a baby is crying.

The light on the third floor is broken and the landing is cast in shadow. She takes a deep breath and knocks on the only door. There's no bell.

The woman who opens the door is a good few inches shorter than her. And she's greyer than Katalin remembers. The apron she's wearing over her brown dress is stained with grease spots. She looks at Katalin with suspicion as if she doesn't get many visitors and those she does are not welcome.

'I'm sorry to disturb you, Mrs Kún, but is Tamás in?'

'He's working.' She starts to close the door.

'Will he be home soon?'

'What do you want him for?'

'I think he might be able to help me. Please, Mrs Kún. It's important.'

Mrs Kún glances down the stairwell as if she's afraid of eavesdroppers. Katalin expects the neighbours don't take too kindly to having an AVO officer living in their block. 'Keep your voice down. You'd better come in.'

'Thank you.'

The apartment is dingy. Everything is old and worn, from the threadbare carpet to the patched armchairs and mis-matched cushions. There are no books. In the centre of the mantelpiece is a framed photograph of a man in uniform who looks like an older version of Tamás. His father presumably.

'He should be home soon,' says Mrs Kún.

'I don't mind waiting.'

'Well, have a seat then.' Mrs Kún grudgingly indicates one of the armchairs as if aware that it won't be comfortable.

Katalin perches on the edge of the chair. She'd dearly love to ask Mrs Kún what made Tamás join the AVO, but the older woman has made it very clear that she doesn't want to talk. Instead she says, 'Don't let me disturb you. Please carry on with whatever you were doing.'

Mrs Kún nods and goes into the kitchen. Through the thin partition walls Katalin can hear her busily clattering about with pots and pans. She hopes this visit will prove more fruitful than her visit to Professor Novák and his wife.

The minutes tick by and she wonders if Tamás is ever going to appear. Then suddenly she hears the front door opening and closing.

'I'm home, Mother.'

Mrs Kún goes into the hallway. Katalin can just make out the sound of frantic whispering. Then Tamás appears in the doorway to the living room. He's clearly surprised and embarrassed to see her there. Katalin jumps to her feet.

'What you are doing here?' he asks. Mrs Kún is hovering behind him, wringing her hands.

'I'm sorry to intrude, but I wanted to ask you about my father.'

'I can't tell you anything. You must go.' He's less threatening without his jacket and his boots. She remembers the boy who was sick with tonsillitis.

'Please, Tamás, I'm begging you. You were there the night they arrested him. You must know where he is and what is happening to him.'

He stares past her, saying nothing. How to get through to him?

She turns and picks up the photograph on the mantelpiece. 'Is this your father?'

Tamás leaps across the room and snatches the photograph from her hands. 'Don't touch that!'

'I'm sorry,' she says, startled by the ferocity of his response. Now you know what it feels like to have your privacy invaded, she thinks.

He puts the photograph back into place, adjusting it until he's satisfied.

The man in the photograph looks like a bully, but he's still Tamás's father and Katalin understands that Tamás must crave the man's approval, even though he's dead.

'I suppose your father would be proud to see you in the uniform of the Secret Police,' she ventures. Tamás still has his back to her but she notices his shoulders tensing. 'He'd want to know that you were doing the job to the best of your ability. Doing a thorough job. Not cutting corners.'

Tamás spins around, his face blazing red. Katalin takes a step back, expecting him to shout at her to get out. She shouldn't have reminded him of his failure to search her room.

'All right! I'll tell you. He's at the AVO headquarters on Andrássy Avenue. He's being questioned.' The fight seems to go out of him.

She wants to ask what her father is being interrogated about, but she senses she's only going to be granted a certain number of questions. Instead she asks, 'And how is he?'

Tamás frowns then says, 'Quiet.'

What does that mean? That he's alive but refusing to talk? Or that they've battered the life out of him until he can't speak?

'And what will happen to him?'

'If he does the sensible thing and signs the confession, he'll be tried and sentenced. But if he refuses to sign –' Tamás lets the sentence hang.

'What do you mean *signs the confession?* He hasn't done anything wrong. He's got nothing to confess!' She can only assume this so-called confession is a pack of lies which is why her father has refused to sign it.

Tamás shrugs, confirming her suspicions. How can he bear to work for these people? Katalin has one last request before she goes. She reaches into her pocket and pulls out a folded piece of paper. This is a lot to ask. If he's found out, it would land him in serious trouble. And the consequences for her could be disastrous. She almost doesn't do it, but then she says, 'Will you give him this?'

Tamás looks horrified.

'Please?'

He snatches the piece of paper from her hand and stuffs it into his trouser pocket. 'You have to leave now.'

'Thank you,' whispers Katalin. Even though she loathes everything that Tamás stands for, she appreciates the enormous risk he's taking on her behalf. She has no idea if he'll pass on the message to her father, but at least she knows Márton is still alive. Tamás could report her for what she's done, but somehow she doesn't think he will. He would only compromise himself.

On her way out she smiles at Mrs Kún. The smile is not returned.

*

When Márton eventually collapses in front of the white wall, the guards drag him back to his cell, semi-conscious and muttering gibberish. He falls onto his plank bed but the images which have played out on the wall are impregnated in his mind's eye, running on an eternal loop. He groans out loud, trying to make them go away. He is only barely conscious of the fact that now he is one of those whimpering madmen.

But he isn't allowed to lie there for long. It soon turns out that the AVO have something else planned for him. Still feverish from his hallucinations, they drag him to a cell with two inches of cold water covering the concrete floor and throw him inside so that he falls on his knees, soaking his trousers.

Drip, drip, drip. Márton crouches in the cell, shivering uncontrollably. The dank walls are running with water, and drops fall at irregular intervals from the ceiling onto his head. The cold is so bone-chilling that it numbs his mind as well as his body. Only the jerks of cramping leg muscles and the castanet-like chattering of his teeth remind him he is still alive.

He's never been so cold in his life, not even during the harshest winters of the war. He hugs himself tight and rubs his arms in a vain attempt to warm up. He could lie face down and drown himself. Maybe it would be for the best.

*

Tamás is back on cellar duty, patrolling the underground corridors at AVO headquarters. From the grand façade of the building you'd never guess there was such a loathsome place hidden underneath. He takes his frustration out on the prisoners, banging the spy holes open and shut with as much noise as he can make. Today he's in a particularly bad mood.

Katalin Bakos's visit, two days ago, has unnerved him more than he cares to admit. He can't understand the boldness of the girl, calmly sitting in his living room, waiting for him to come home. His mother was clearly terrified of her. He didn't even know that she knew where he lived. Children from school never came home to play. But then he remembers two girls bringing him some work when he was off sick. Was that Katalin and her friend Róza? He thinks it might have been.

What makes him angry is that Katalin Bakos has again exposed his weaknesses. He should have opened the violin case when he searched her room. He should have thrown her out of his apartment and refused to speak to her. And he should certainly have not taken the note which is currently burning a hole in his trouser pocket. He should have destroyed it, but he didn't. Another sign of weakness.

He's not weak!

To prove it he bangs open a spy hole and shouts at the prisoner inside to get his lazy arse off the wooden plank. What does he think this is, a holiday?

The truth is, Tamás would like nothing better than to lie down and take a nap but he can't, so he sure as hell isn't going to let anyone else have a rest.

He hasn't slept properly for the last couple of nights, worrying about Katalin's stupid note. He has to get rid of it quickly, before someone like Gábor finds it. The thought makes his stomach churn.

He comes to the end of the corridor and pauses outside Márton's cell door. If only Márton wasn't still here. If the fool had only signed the confession he would be on his way to trial and a proper prison by now, instead of suffering the torture of the white wall and the wet cell, Tamás's idea of hell.

He glances down the corridor. There are no other guards in sight. Gábor is off somewhere beating the living daylights out of a prisoner who has so far refused to co-operate with anything. He'll co-operate when Gábor has finished with him.

Tamás bangs open Márton's spy hole and sees him sitting there, staring into space. He looks like a lost child, abandoned and neglected. He doesn't even react to the spy hole being opened. The last forty-eight hours have all but finished him off. Probably turned him into a lunatic.

'On your feet,' shouts Tamás.

No response.

'Didn't you hear what I just said?'

Márton staggers to his feet and gazes at him with dead eyes.

Tamás looks back down the corridor, terrified at what he's about to do. Then he lets forth a torrent of abuse, whilst at the same time reaching into his pocket, throwing the note into the cell and then slamming the spy hole shut with a force that surprises even him. There he's done it.

*

Márton barely hears the insults that Tamás throws at him. He has heard far worse since being brought here. When he lived in England he learnt the saying *Sticks and stones may break my bones, but words will never harm me.* He's not sure he entirely agrees with that, but he's too tired to care.

Hours standing in front of the white wall watching the darkest projections of his mind followed by hours kneeling in cold water have weakened him to a point he didn't think possible. He's lost so much weight because he doesn't have the appetite for the grey water that passes as soup in this place. When Tamás shouts at him to stand up, he does so because it's easier to obey than to try to resist. He doesn't have the mental energy for resistance anymore.

The boy is certainly surpassing himself in his stream of invective today. But then in the middle of this torrent of abuse, Márton sees something white fluttering to the floor of his cell. He thinks at first that a moth or butterfly has somehow found its way into this underground cesspit and experiences a fleeting moment of wonder. But if it ever was a living creature, it's now dead. It lies on the floor by his feet, motionless. The spy hole bangs shut and Tamás's footsteps recede down the corridor. Still Márton stands still, listening to the beating of his heart, expecting the door to fly open any moment. After a minute of silence, he bends down to look more closely at the object by his feet and realises it's a piece of paper. He picks it up with shaking fingers and unfolds it. It's only small, no more than a couple of inches square.

Tiny writing covers the paper. At first his tired eyes can't focus and his brain is too addled to make any sense of what he's seeing. But gradually the writing starts to form itself into words and the words acquire meaning. With a surge of joy he realises that the note is from Katalin, telling him that she's all right and that she hopes he is too. Tears spring to his eyes, blurring his vision. She took a risk giving this note to Tamás, but the boy has delivered it and won't want to get himself into trouble. Márton understands, too, that he must destroy the note immediately otherwise the consequences for himself, Tamás and Katalin would be severe.

After reading the note once more, and holding the precious piece of paper to his lips, he tears it into tiny shreds and lets the pieces fall through a grate in the corner of the room, one at a time, like snowflakes. He would have liked to keep that piece of paper and treasure it forever and already he feels its loss. But it's given him hope, knowing that Katalin is safe. And hope gives him strength to endure.

*

This time, when Vajda slides the confession across the table, Márton picks up the pen and signs his name in a shaky scrawl at the bottom of the page.

I, the undersigned, freely confess to my crimes of betrayal and treason against the Party and the State.

There, he's done it. He's confessed to being a spy and an enemy of the working class. He hopes Vajda is satisfied. It pains Márton – the seeker of facts and scientific truth – to put his name to this pile of lies, but he has come to realise that things will only go worse for him if he doesn't sign. It's simply a matter of survival.

'There, that wasn't so hard, was it?' Vajda smiles at Márton for the first time in their acquaintance. It does nothing to improve his bulldog features, only serving to emphasise his wobbly jowls. He rings the bell on his desk and a guard appears. Márton is disappointed to see it isn't Tamás, but Gábor.

Vajda gives Gábor his orders. Gábor looks furious that Márton has finally co-operated. No doubt he was anticipating another session in front of the white wall or something worse. He manacles Márton's hands and takes him outside to a waiting car. After so long stuck underground in the stinking cellars, the cold, fresh air slaps Márton on the face. He gulps in large lungfuls of air and stares in wonder at the cloud-filled sky before Gábor shoves him into the back of the car. He has no idea where they are taking him, but at least it's not back to his cell.

It's a short drive from Andrássy Avenue to the Marko Street jail. Half an hour after leaving AVO headquarters, Márton finds himself in a prison cell with a table, a chair, a straw mattress and blankets. Compared to where he's just come from, this feels like a luxury hotel.

That evening he receives a visitor. Vajda enters the cell and sits down heavily on the chair. He puts a sheaf of papers on the table.

'This,' he says, pointing at the pile of paper, 'is the script for your trial. You need to learn it.'

Márton feels as if he's been punched in the chest. His trial is to be a show trial, a worthless acting out of lies. They are not interested in the truth. They have already condemned him. After all, like an idiot he signed the confession.

Vajda leans forwards and narrows his eyes. 'If you deviate from this script, the judge will stop the trial. The result for you will be months of torture. It's your choice, but I would advise you to learn the script.' He stands up. 'I'll come back in a few days and we can practise.'

Left on his own, Márton picks up the script and starts to read through it. Here are the judge's questions and Márton's pre-prepared responses. He mouths the words silently to himself, repeating them until he has them word perfect.

Three days later, the trial goes exactly as expected. The judge – the sort of stony-faced hardliner who spent the war years in Moscow learning how to be a good communist – asks the questions that Márton knew he would ask. Márton gives the required responses. There are a dozen prisoners on trial at the same time, men who look worn down by their ordeal. They too sound as if they are reciting by rote.

Members of the Secret Police play the role of defence

lawyers. Márton doesn't know why they bother with this charade when everyone knows the whole procedure is nothing but a piece of theatre. His designated defence lawyer stands up and says that no one should be surprised that Márton turned out the way he did given that his ancestors were all imperialist swine. It's not much of a defence, but what can you expect?

When all the cases have been heard, the court withdraws to reach its considered verdicts. In a proper judicial process it should take many hours, even days, to consider the cases of so many men. But the judge and his lackeys return after only twenty minutes, the verdicts obviously already decided. Márton supposes they just went outside for a cigarette. One by one the men stand to hear their fate.

When it's Márton's turn to stand, his legs shake so much he doesn't think they will hold him up.

The verdict is guilty. Then the judge delivers Márton's sentence in a voice devoid of emotion. 'In the interests of the security of the People's Republic and in view of your foreign espionage connections, you are sentenced to twenty-five years of hard labour.'

Twenty-five years? For crimes he hasn't committed? My God, he'll be dead before they let him out.

His legs buckle under him and he clutches the table for support.

CHAPTER 7

Tamás thinks he will be happier at work now that Márton Bakos has left Andrássy Avenue. He prefers it when the prisoners held in the underground cells are nameless individuals with no connection to himself. His first thought on hearing that Márton is to be tried and sent to a labour camp is one of relief. He will no longer be reminded on a daily basis of how he failed to search Katalin's room properly, and she will no longer be able to ask him to pass on messages. Everything can go back to normal and he can carry on trying to prove himself.

But it isn't working out like that. At first he can't place the unfamiliar sensation that he feels. But he's coming to realise that he misses the prisoner who occupied the cell at the end of the corridor. He has to admit that Márton Bakos impressed him with his quiet dignity. The man never got angry, despite the deprivations and humiliations he suffered. When he was asked to type his life story, night after night, he did so even though he could barely sit up straight and keep his eyes open. And he showed gratitude for the snatches of sleep that Tamás allowed him.

Tamás finds himself wondering what it would have been like to have had a father like that, instead of the unpredictable, short-tempered man who could be loving one minute and drunk and violent the next. Tamás and his mother lived in fear of his erratic mood swings. When he died on the Eastern Front, Tamás was both relieved and devastated.

He's supposed to be patrolling the underground corridors, but he enters Márton's vacated cell and sits down for a moment on the hard wooden plank. He just wants to feel Márton's presence one last time. And then it comes to him that there is one small thing he could do. He could find Katalin and tell her where her father is now. Not that he cares about Katalin – she's caused him no end of trouble. But he would do it for Márton's sake.

He hears Gábor's angry voice at the other end of the corridor, shouting at one of the prisoners that he's a filthy swine. Tamás jumps to his feet and leaves the cell. Soon it will be occupied by someone else. The arrests never stop.

*

The condemned men are taken outside to a yard. A couple of shiny Black Marias are parked in the centre of the yard, their engines idling. A line of about thirty or so men are already standing with their noses to the wall, their hands clasped behind their backs. They are filthy, ragged and half-starved. Márton notices that some of them have difficulty standing up straight, as if their bodies have been broken by torture. AVO guards are walking up and down behind the men, ordering them not to turn around or look sideways. Márton is reminded forcibly of the hours he spent standing in front of the white wall and the terrifying visions that tormented his mind. He almost loses his nerve when he is suddenly pushed into position next to a large man in a dirty blue shirt and torn trousers.

'Stand there!'

His nose is an inch from the stone wall. He can smell his neighbour, a mixture of sweat and grime, and hear the man's heavy breathing, but he dare not look. Out of the corner of his eye he sees the man tilt his head in Márton's direction.

'No turning around,' shouts an AVO officer behind them. 'No looking!' Márton hears the familiar sound of a rifle butt being jabbed into his neighbour's kidneys. He's felt that excruciating pain himself countless times when being taken to see Vajda or during those interminable nights sitting in front of the typewriter, and he winces in sympathy. The man grunts and puts his hands out against the wall to stop himself from hitting his head as he lurches forwards.

'Hands behind your back!'

Márton stands stock still, listening to the booted footsteps moving away. Only when they have gone some distance does he risk a quick glance to his left. He takes in a man who must have been strong once, but whose clothes now hang off him, as his own clothes do. The man is sporting vivid yellow and brown bruises on his cheek where he's been kicked or beaten. Márton catches the man's bloodshot eye and in that split second a bond is formed between them: you've been through hell too; we're in the same boat; we have to stick together, us prisoners. Then they both turn to face the wall as more men are added to the line.

Márton closes his eyes and tries to shut out the tramp of boots, the bellowed orders and the yells of those being hit for failing to stand up straight without moving. He shivers in his worn suit and old shirt. The man who has appeared on his right has a hacking cough. He spits on the ground and Márton sees drops of blood in his spittle.

Finally, the officer in charge gives the orders for the men to be herded into the Black Marias.

'About bloody time,' mutters Márton's neighbour in the blue shirt.

The men turn away from the wall and shuffle across the yard to the open doors of the waiting lorries. Márton's feet have gone numb and he can barely feel them.

'Hurry up, you lazy sods!'

'We haven't got all day!'

'Get a move on, old man!'

After keeping the men standing in front of the wall for ages, the AVO guards are now impatient to be rid of them, using their rifle butts to beat them into line.

The man with the cough stumbles behind Márton and clutches at his jacket.

'Sorry,' he wheezes.

'No problem,' says Márton.

'No talking!' bellows an AVO officer in Márton's ear.

An old man at the front of the line has trouble climbing the steps into the Black Maria. Two AVO guards take him by the arms and throw him into the lorry. The man cries out in pain.

'Dear God,' mutters Márton's neighbour.

After that, the guards push the men up the steps, paying no heed as they stumble and fall. Márton lurches into the dark interior and immediately trips over the feet of someone who has fallen on the floor. He bumps heads with someone else and feels an elbow poke him in the ribs. It's chaos. Some of the men are laughing hysterically, others are cursing and grunting.

'Watch out you oaf. That's my leg you trod on.'

'Shouldn't have left it lying around.'

Unable to stand up, Márton crawls to a space on the edge and sits down, drawing his knees up to his chest so that he's less likely to get in anyone's way. The air in the lorry is already fetid with the smell of unwashed bodies, sour breath and the lingering stench of damp cells.

A man lands next to him and Márton recognises his blue-shirted companion from the yard, the man who took a beating for turning to look at him.

'All right there?' asks the man.

'Just about.'

'At least they can't stop us talking in here.'

'There is that.'

When the last man has been squeezed in, the guards slam the rear doors shut. Márton hears a bolt being driven home on the outside. And then the vehicle lurches forwards and the men topple into each others' laps. By the end of this journey they're going to be well acquainted with each other, he thinks.

*

The Black Maria rumbles along the road, its engine coughing and spluttering every time it brakes or accelerates. A fine piece of Soviet engineering, thinks Márton, as the vehicle lurches round a corner and he's thrown against his neighbour for the umpteenth time.

As his eyes adjust to the gloom, he is able to make out faces. They are a rag-tag bunch of old and young. Age-wise, he's somewhere in the middle. What they all have in common is they're half-starved, unshaven, dirty and smelly.

'Béla Toth,' says the man in the blue shirt sitting next to him. He extends a roughened hand which Márton clasps in the cramped space.

'Márton Bakos. How do you do?'

'Pleased to meet you,' says Béla. They haven't forgotten how to be civil to one another. It seems more important than ever in these inhumane conditions. 'So what story did they make up about you?' Béla asks the question casually as if they're two old friends having a drink in a bar. Márton appreciates that Béla assumes his conviction is based on lies.

'Well apart from being a saboteur and hating the working class...'

'Goes without saying.'

'It would appear I was endangering the People's Republic because of my overseas connections.'

Béla nods his understanding. 'They thought you were a

spy.'

'What about you?' asks Márton.

'Me? Oh, I was chief engineer in a gun factory. We got a big order to supply weapons to Russia, but the Soviet design was faulty. If we'd made the guns according to their specifications, they wouldn't have shot in a straight line. So I corrected the error. But I made the mistake of telling my boss and the Ministry in Moscow what I'd done.'

'But you were doing the right thing, surely?' Márton thinks of his own work, correcting the calculations for the enrichment of uranium.

Béla scoffs. 'The AVO didn't see it like that. They pointed out something I'd missed.'

'Which was what?'

'Their argument was that the Soviet Union might have been planning to give the guns to the Hungarian army.'

'But you'd still want them to shoot straight, wouldn't you?'

'Ah, wait for it. It gets better. You see apparently I was planning an attack against the Soviet Union with a conspiracy of Hungarian army officers. Naturally, *we* wouldn't want guns that didn't shoot in a straight line, so correcting the error was for our benefit, and not in the interests of the Soviets. The faulty design was deliberate and I should have left it as it was. You can't really argue with that, can you?'

Talking in his deadpan way, Béla makes the story sound funnier than it is, and those sitting nearby can't help themselves from laughing. He's attracted quite an audience.

After that a few more men volunteer their tales of midnight arrests, absurd allegations and cruel injustices.

'I am a respected scientist in my field,' says one. 'I was arrested on my way to a conference in Czechoslovakia. They said I was planning to escape to West Germany and from there to America. But I would never leave my family behind in Hungary.'

'I was a lawyer and they arrested me for fascist crimes I never committed. They confiscated my library of books. They are ignorant swine, the whole lot of them.'

'I was a meteorologist,' says one man who introduces himself as Horváth. He's quietly spoken, with round, wire-rimmed glasses that give him a studious look. 'When I forecast a cold wind blowing in from the east, dispersing the milder weather from the west, I was accused of being anti-Russian.'

'Don't you know they never have bad weather in Russia?' quips a voice. 'The sun shines out of Stalin's arse.' This rouses a chorus of raucous laughter.

Márton notices a young man who is listening avidly to the conversation, but not joining in. His eyes flit from one speaker to another, wide with disbelief. He looks no more than nineteen or twenty. He should be at university studying, thinks Márton, or out enjoying himself with friends.

'What about you, lad?' he asks, drawing him into the conversation.

The young man blushes as all those sitting nearby turn to look at him. 'I didn't do anything wrong, honestly.'

'Neither did the rest of us,' says Béla.

The young man stares at his feet and says in a voice that's barely audible, 'I was in the tavern with some friends. They were singing forbidden songs. I wasn't joining in though. I'd gone outside to see the barman's daughter, Hanna.'

'Bit of a looker, was she?' asks a voice.

'Shut up you oaf,' says Béla. 'Let the boy speak.'

'The others all got off with a warning for singing banned songs. But I think the barman made out I was the ringleader because he found me kissing his daughter.'

'Bad luck, son,' says Béla. 'What's your name?'

'András.'

'You stick with us, lad. We'll be all right if we stick together.'

The lorry judders to a halt. They can't have gone that far. The engine is switched off and an expectant silence falls over the prisoners.

They hear the bolt being slid back, then the doors are wrenched open and everyone is ordered out. Márton looks around trying to work out where they are, then he hears men muttering the name Kistarcsa. It's a small town some fifteen or so miles east of Budapest and the site of a concentration camp during the war.

The men are shepherded into a long, white-painted building and then taken to a narrow room with bunk beds crammed along the walls. The windows have been painted over with whitewash, casting the room in a permanent gloom.

Béla throws himself down on the nearest bunk bed. 'Wake me up if anything happens.' Within seconds he's snoring softly. Horváth, the meteorologist and predictor of easterly winds, takes the bunk above Béla's. Márton and András take the next pair of beds.

In the fading light, Márton lies on the lower bunk, thinking of Katalin. It's possible that he'll never see her again. Up above he can hear András sobbing quietly.

*

It's already growing dark when Katalin makes her way home after a day at work. Piroska Benke has kept the staff late on a bureaucratic form-filling exercise. No doubt Zoltán will also have been kept late at the factory, attending one of Csaba Elek's interminable meetings. A steady rain is falling, the water collecting in the gutters at the side of the road. People hurry past, heads down, not looking.

Since she spoke to Tamás and gave him the note for her father, she has heard nothing. Sometimes she worries that she may have put her father into more danger by trying to make contact. That's if Tamás actually handed it over. Maybe he just destroyed it.

As she approaches her building, a figure steps out of a doorway. It's a man, muffled up against the cold and wet. He has a thick scarf around his neck, covering the bottom half of his face. She doesn't think he's anything to do with her, until he puts out a hand to stop her. She looks around in alarm, expecting to see a black Pobeda car crawling along the street, but there is none.

'Katalin.'

She jumps at the mention of her name. She knows that voice.

The man lowers the scarf a fraction. 'It's me, Tamás.'

'My God, Tamás. What are you doing here? You frightened the life out of me.'

'I have news.'

'About Papa?'

He nods and looks over his shoulder, his eyes darting up and down the street.

She can't believe it. She's wanted to hear something for so long, and now she feels nervous about what Tamás might tell her. 'Come inside,' she says. 'Out of the rain.'

'No, I can't stay. I just wanted to tell you that father has been sent to a labour camp.'

Katalin balks at the news, imagining all sorts of horrors. 'Where? In Hungary? He hasn't been sent to the Soviet Union has he?'

'I don't know.'

'What was the charge?'

Tamás shrugs. 'Does it matter?'

'But what was his sentence? Five years? Ten years? Fifteen?'

'I'm sorry, I don't know that either.'

Katalin clutches at her throat, the rain streaming down her face. She wants to prise information out of Tamás, but she believes him when he says he doesn't know any details. He starts to move away from her, clearly keen to leave.

'Wait,' she says, putting out a hand to draw him back.

'Why have you come to tell me this?'

He hesitates, biting his lower lip, then he says, 'Your father is a good man.'

Then he pulls the scarf back over his mouth and hurries away.

Katalin watches him go. He's the last contact with Papa and now he's gone.

*

They're in a state of limbo. It seems that Kistarcsa is merely an internment camp and not their final destination, but no one knows how long they will stay here or where they will be sent afterwards. Márton and the other men spend their days cooped up in the gloom of the dormitory with its whitewashed windows, talking. At least they're no longer being held in solitary cells. Speculation about their future is rife. Will it be the gulags of Siberia where they will freeze to death in the harsh winter? Horváth, the meteorologist, has them all worried with the news that winter temperatures in Irkutsk can fall as low as fifty below freezing. Béla makes a joke out of it, but Márton notices the fear in András's eyes whenever the gulags are mentioned. He draws the boy aside and chats to him about other things – physics and chemistry are mutual subjects of interest. Márton doesn't want to think about the gulags either.

Márton appreciates the company of the other men. For the most part they are educated – intellectuals and skilled professionals. He has come to realise that the Party doesn't like people who think too much. He feels a special bond with Béla and Horváth, and a fatherly concern for András.

But there are thirty of them crammed into the airless dormitory so it's not surprising that sometimes tensions run high. There's always someone who snores too loudly, someone who farts, someone who grinds their teeth at night. Then there are the nightmares that wake them up in the dead of night: the indignities and tortures suffered at the hands of the AVO, the terrors and fears, the memories of loved ones and the hopelessness of their situations. Frayed nerves and lack of sleep lead to stresses that threaten to escalate into violence. Béla has stepped in on more than one occasion. He does so now when voices are raised at the far end of the dormitory. Miklós, a former factory foreman, is arguing with his neighbour.

'Hey, fellers, take it easy.' With his calm but authoritative manner, Béla has assumed the role of group leader. Every group needs a leader, it seems, and he's their man.

'Who put you in charge?' asks Miklós, turning on him. The dormitory falls silent and holds its collective breath.

'No one,' says Béla. 'If you don't like it, say so. We can take a vote on it. I'm all in favour of democracy. I'm just trying to keep the peace around here.'

No one stands up for Miklós. After a moment, Béla walks away and lies down on his bunk. Miklós returns to his own bunk and sits fuming.

It's the inactivity, thinks Márton, and the boredom. We're all going quietly stir-crazy stuck here.

He seeks out András and they pick up a conversation they've been having about the solar system. It helps to pass the time, although it reminds Márton of everything he's left behind.

*

After two weeks stuck at Kistarcsa – it feels more like two months – the guards wake them early one day and order everyone outside to the yard. Márton estimates there must be hundreds of men here. Some of them have been here much longer than his own intake, their hair grown long, their faces resigned.

'What's going on?' asks András. 'Are they taking us somewhere?'

'I don't know,' says Márton.

'I don't want to go to Siberia. I'll throw myself from the train.'

'Now, now,' says Béla. 'Just stay calm.'

The guards load them into trucks and they are driven to Kistarcsa train station. The train waiting on the platform has ten windowless freight cars, a couple of passenger cars up front and a locomotive belching clouds of black smoke. The men huddle on the platform, surrounded by armed AVO guards.

Márton thinks of the transportation of Jews during the war and his skin prickles with icy fear. The Jews never came home. He can see from the looks on their faces that Béla and Horváth are having the same morbid thoughts. He tries not to let his own fear show for András's sake, but the boy is already ashen with terror.

The officer in charge gives the order and the guards herd the prisoners into the freight cars like cattle, cramming as many as they can into each compartment. The car smells of disinfectant, but there's a lingering odour of blood, urine and vomit that has impregnated the wooden floor and walls. When the doors close, it's dark inside. There is no room to sit.

There's a grinding of metal on metal, and the train starts to lumber out of the station. Márton presses his eye up against a crack in the wooden slats and watches as Kistarcsa slides away.

The train picks up speed and then trundles along for an hour or so. Speculation about their destination mounts as they head east. It looks as if their worst fears are coming true. It's the Siberian gulags after all. They'll never see their beloved Hungary again. Márton regrets not asking Tamás to take a message to Katalin, but it's too late now.

Suddenly the train grinds to a halt. They haven't gone that far, must still be inside Hungary's borders.

'Where are we?' asks András. 'Are we getting out?'

'Let me take a look,' says Béla. He turns around in the

cramped space and presses his eye up between the wooden slats. 'Can't see a whole lot, but I reckon we're in Hatvan.'

Hatvan is a small town some thirty miles east of Budapest. What now? Silence falls on the carriage as they listen for sounds of movement outside on the platform. Anything that will give them a clue as to what's going on. But no doors open and no one leaves the train. The AVO guards remain in their carriage up front, no doubt sitting with their feet up and smoking cigarettes.

'I wish they'd get a bloody move on,' says Miklós. 'Never could stand hanging around like this.'

'Cool it,' says Béla. 'We'll get where we're going soon enough and then you'll wish we hadn't arrived.'

Suddenly the train jolts forwards. Everyone starts to talk at once.

'Quiet,' says Béla, holding up a finger. The voices drop. 'Listen.'

Márton can't hear anything except the clicking of points as the train crosses the tracks.

'We're changing onto a branch line,' says Béla, speaking with the authority of someone who knows these kind of things. 'We're not going to the Soviet Union after all.'

'Well thank God for that,' says Horváth.

'Where are we going then?' asks András.

'I reckon we're heading into the Mátra Mountains,' says Béla. 'Time for a bit of shut-eye.' He leans against the corner of the carriage, folds his arms and lets his head drop forwards. Márton envies him his ability to fall asleep, wherever they are.

Lulled by the rhythm of the train, Márton closes his eyes and recalls images of the Mátra Mountains in his mind's eye. The name is enough to take him back to his childhood. It's a beautiful and ancient landscape. He has happy memories of trekking through the wooded hillsides and vineyards with his father, the distant peaks blue in the hazy summer sun, the smell of pine resin, birdsong in the air. But in the winter the mountains are cold and covered in snow. He almost wishes they were going to Siberia after all. Whatever is waiting for them in the mountains, it won't be good. He doesn't want his childhood memories to be sullied.

He must have nodded off because he's jerked awake when the train comes to a halt. Béla is already peering through the slats.

Doors slam, booted feet tramp and voices shout orders. It sounds as if there's a small army out there to greet them. This is it then, thinks Márton. This is our destination, wherever we are.

The door clangs open and a cool, evening light floods the carriage.

'Out. Now!' shouts an AVO officer.

The men shuffle off the train. They are stiff from standing so long in a cramped space. As he clambers down, Márton blinks in the light of the setting sun and looks around him. They are on a small station platform. The air is heavy with the scents of late autumn. A sign on the side of a one-storey building informs him that they are in Recsk. He doesn't know the place. From the look of the small, dilapidated station building, it's nothing more than a village. A nondescript sort of place quietly minding its own business until the government decided to set up a labour camp on its doorstep. He wonders what the villagers make of all this. If they've got any sense, they keep out of the way.

The prisoners crowd onto the platform which is barely big enough to contain them all. A hundred or more armed AVO men and soldiers point their submachine guns at them, just in case anyone thinks of making a run for it. No one does.

A lieutenant pushes his way through the armed guards and stands there scowling at the raggedy group of prisoners. He goes up to an old man and pushes him in the chest so that he nearly falls over. His neighbours catch him just in time and prop him up. 'What's the use of that?'

shouts the lieutenant, pointing at the old man. 'I need workers here, not geriatrics.'

The old man coughs and straightens himself up, obviously keen to prove that he can stand without help. Márton has doubts about how long the poor fellow is going to last out here.

'Right, get going,' shouts the lieutenant. 'You're not here to enjoy the scenery.'

The guards leap into action and start to order everyone towards the exit, knocking them into line with the butts of their weapons. There are no lorries to transport them. They are to walk to the camp, it seems.

Márton falls into step alongside Béla, András and Horváth. They are near the front. Behind them the line stretches back further and further as the old and infirm struggle to keep up. They can hear the guards shouting abuse at the slow coaches. As if they've all had the same thought, those at the front of the line slow their pace so that the stragglers have a chance to catch up. They're going to have to stick together in this place.

As the path climbs out of the village, Márton notes that the landscape is just as beautiful as he remembered it. The distant hills resemble a Japanese painting in shades of blue and green. The leaves on the trees are coppery yellow and fiery red. If he dies out here, at least he'll have returned to his childhood roots.

They turn a corner and he comes face to face with a sight that destroys his memories in one blast. The lush forest has been ravaged. Trees that had stood for centuries have been cut down to create a huge quarry in the mountainside, an ugly scar on the face of the earth. When Márton looks down he sees that the grey-blue andesite rock is dotted with drops of scarlet.

CHAPTER 8

The wind whips through Márton's torn shirt, cooling the sweat on his emaciated body. They've been given old army uniforms to wear, full of holes. With an aching back and stiff shoulders, he bends to pick up the rear handles of the stretcher loaded to breaking point with rock hewn from the mountainside. With a similar effort, Béla lifts the front of the stretcher. Together they make their precarious way down the steep slope, their feet sliding on bits of loose gravel.

Márton's hands are raw with blisters. He needs to watch they don't turn septic, but there's no soap to wash with, never mind medical supplies. He's wrapped them in rags for now. As they descend, he does his best to keep up with Béla's longer stride. They can't afford to drop their load, or the guard will beat them for slacking. Their job is to carry the rock down the mountainside to the breakers working at the bottom. Where the ancient forest used to stand is now a stone quarry.

'Idiots,' muttered Béla to Márton on their first day at the quarry. 'Look at that slope. It's too steep. There'll be a landslide one day, you mark my words.'

Márton suspects Béla is right. Béla has an instinct for

things like this, plus he's a trained engineer.

They've been here for two weeks, but it feels more like a lifetime. There are hundreds in the camp, but Márton has been put into barracks with the men he was with at Kistarcsa. Béla, Horváth and András are his family now.

He has learned from long-standing inhabitants of the camp that they will not be allowed to write to their families or receive any letters or parcels. It's a devastating blow. He feels as if he's been exiled from his life, his previous existence erased. The men here are nobodies. Individual identity is obliterated in the dirty old army uniforms they are forced to wear. Not that his suit and shirt were in any fit state to be worn, but they were the last remnants of his old life. Sometimes he dreams that he can't remember who he is anymore. He wakes from those dreams in a cold sweat and it takes him a moment to orientate himself. Then he hears the snores and nighttime mutterings of the other men in the dormitory, and a black despair washes over him. If it weren't for the companionship of the others, he dreads to think what he might have done to himself by now.

It's astonishing how quickly they've adapted to a new routine. They sleep alongside their fellow prisoners in a dormitory ripe with the smell of unwashed bodies and sour breath. They rise at dawn, queue for the toilets, consume barley-coffee for breakfast and then, under armed guard, trudge up to the quarry to start the day's work, their arms and back still aching from the previous day and the day before that. The old and infirm have been given jobs in the carpenter's shop or the tailor's and shoemaker's where the guards have their suits pressed and their boots re-soled. But everyone else spends their days labouring in the quarry. Lunch and dinner are served on the hillside from the camp kitchen: watery soup and vegetables. A couple of times a week, if they're lucky, there are tiny bits of horse meat in the soup, otherwise there's no protein. How is a man expected to smash rocks all day long on a diet that would barely keep a child alive? They are growing dangerously thin. And the weather is turning cold. There'll be snow soon.

On their long walks to and from the quarry each day, Horváth explains to him the different cloud formations and what they mean for the weather. Cumulonimbus clouds at the end of the day are welcome because they provide the men with the means to wash themselves. But increasingly the mountains are shrouded in a thick, grey nimbostratus which blocks the view and slowly drenches everyone in a permanent drizzle.

As Márton follows Béla down the slope, their ninth trip of the day so far, he has a view of the camp on the opposite hillside. The barracks are surrounded by a double barbed-wire fence with a strip of no man's land in between. Beyond the fence are watchtowers manned by armed guards. Then there's another double barbed-wire fence and more watchtowers around the camp as a whole. You'd be crazy to try and escape. You wouldn't stand a chance. So instead they spend twelve hours a day hewing, carrying and breaking the rock. In the evenings they line up on the hillside whilst the guards run up and down, counting them. It's dark by the time the counting has finished. Exhausted and starving, they stumble down the slope, tripping over logs and tree stumps. The guards beat anyone who falls behind. If your boot gets stuck in the mud, you leave it until the morning. It will still be there, filled with rainwater.

When they're out of earshot of the guards, Béla chats to Márton about his family and his life in Budapest. A bit of conversation helps to take their minds off their blistered hands, painful muscles and rumbling stomachs.

'I said to my wife, if anything happens to me, you have to get out of Budapest. Go and stay with your parents in the country. They're less likely to come after you there.'

'It's good she's got somewhere to go,' says Márton, thinking of Katalin stuck in Budapest.

'She's a resourceful woman,' says Béla proudly. 'She'll do the right thing. It's the little girl, see. We were scared that if we both got arrested she'd be sent to an orphanage. She's only two.'

Márton can't see his face, but he can hear from the crack in Béla's voice that he's on the verge of tears. Béla coughs and spits to bring his emotions under control. If the other men see this softer side to him it will undermine his position as leader.

'All right,' says Béla, 'on the count of three. One, two, three!' They tip the contents of the stretcher onto the growing pile of rocks. The tension in Márton's arms releases and his muscles throb with relief at letting go of the weight. You could build a palace with all this stone, he thinks.

He spots András stooped over a boulder, swinging a sledgehammer. The boy has the job of breaking the rocks into smaller pieces. Béla showed him a good technique to use, but András isn't cut out for this type of work. None of them are, to be honest, but András especially. The boy should be in a library reading books or in a science lab doing experiments, not out here working himself into the ground. In the evenings he's noticed a glazed look in the lad's eyes which is more than just physical exhaustion. Márton would like to stop for a moment and chat to him, but there's a guard with a submachine gun standing close by. Without a word, Márton and Béla pick up the empty stretcher and head back up the slope to fetch more rock. They've got another three hours to go.

*

It's Katalin's birthday and Zoltán has insisted on throwing a party, inviting Róza and Sándor. Under the circumstances, Katalin would have let the day pass unnoticed, but now that they are gathered around Zoltán's tiny dining table, eating his speciality goulash, she's pleased he persuaded her. She's glad to finally meet Sándor, Zoltán's childhood friend about whom she's heard so much, and to introduce Róza to Zoltán. Hopefully now Róza will stop having doubts about him.

'More wine?' asks Sándor, uncorking a second bottle of red. He refills everyone's glasses then lifts his in the air. 'Compliments to the chef! This is the best goulash ever, Zoltán my friend.'

'You're drunk,' says Zoltán, drinking from his own glass, but Katalin can see he's pleased with the praise.

'Just enjoying myself,' says Sándor, smiling at Katalin and Róza. His gaze rests on Róza for a moment or two, and Róza smiles back, her face flushed, and not just from the wine, thinks Katalin.

For dessert Zoltán unveils a selection of delicious looking cakes and pastries which he admits to buying from Feri's café.

'Too much choice,' says Sándor, trying to decide between an almond slice, a chocolate cake and an apple tart.

'Good job we don't have democratic elections in this country,' jokes Zoltán. 'You'd never be able to make up your mind.'

'Now there you're wrong,' retorts Sándor, opting for the almond slice. 'I'd vote for whoever promised to abolish the daily reading from the Party newspaper.' This gets a laugh. 'And especially if they throw the Russians out.'

A moment of silence falls on the party. 'Do you think the Russians will ever leave?' asks Róza, leaning forward, her eyes bright.

'Not of their own accord,' says Sándor.

'Then how?'

'One day the people will say, enough is enough. Hungarians will wake up and realise that they want their country back. And when that day comes I'm going to be out there doing everything I can to make it happen.'

Zoltán puts an arm around Katalin and whispers in her ear. 'There'll be no stopping him now. He's quite a firebrand once he gets going.'

Katalin sips her wine and listens with fascination to the exchange between Sándor and Róza. Sándor is full of revolutionary talk and ideas about free speech and workers' rights. It's inspiring stuff. Róza in particular seems to be lapping up every word. Katalin rests her head on Zoltán's shoulder and smiles to herself. The government can lock people up and send them to labour camps, but it can't stop them from thinking and dreaming. She hopes her father is still able to dream, wherever he is.

*

The days turn to weeks and the weeks into months. Winter comes to the mountains bringing its entourage of freezing rain, snow, sleet, ice and death. Márton sees men drop dead through exhaustion, cold and starvation. At first it's just the odd one or two: old men who might not have had long left anyway. But in recent weeks the numbers have been increasing alarmingly. Men in middle age simply keel over and die, their uniforms and boots redistributed amongst the survivors.

Márton has learnt to notice in advance the signs of impending death: the pallid complexion, the vacant eyes, the somnambulistic walk. When they go like that, it's only a matter of time. Two or three days at the most. He's pointed the signs out to Béla, Horváth and András so they can watch out for each other.

He and Béla are loading their stretcher with yet more rocks to carry down to the breakers. Their blistered hands are blue with the cold. They're in danger of frostbite. Márton can see how his friend has grown thin and grey. When he bends over to pick up the rocks, bony shoulder blades protrude from underneath the worn army uniform. Márton supposes he must look the same, but he hasn't seen himself in a mirror in ages. He'd rather not know.

When the guard on duty turns his back and walks a short distance away, Béla beckons Márton close.

'I have an idea,' he says in a voice barely above a whisper. The howling wind will ensure that the guard hears nothing. Dark, heavy clouds have been gathering since the morning. They don't need Horváth the meteorologist to tell them that a storm from the east is on its way.

'For what?' asks Márton.

'Escaping.'

Márton thinks Béla must have gone mad. He looks at his friend closely, but all he sees in the haggard face is a steely glint in the eyes. 'How?' he asks.

Béla looks towards the guard, but he's lit a cigarette and shows no sign of turning round. 'There's an old man in the carpenter's shop who says he can help. He's going to carve a replica submachine gun out of wood.'

'A wooden gun?' Now Márton really does think that Béla is deluded.

Béla nods, his expression serious. 'He'll use tin on the bits that should be steel. He's a skilled craftsman. He says it'll look like the real thing when he's finished.'

'And then what?' asks Márton. 'You can't shoot the guards with a replica weapon, no matter how convincing it looks.'

'I don't plan to shoot anyone,' says Béla. 'I've come to know a couple of the old fellers who work in the tailor's and shoemaker's. When the gun's ready, I'll dress up as a guard and pretend to march a group of us out of the barracks on a Sunday.' In the week there's a roll call at noon, but on Sundays they are only counted before being locked in for the night.

Márton shakes his head in disbelief. Who does Béla think he's kidding? Isn't it better to just accept things as they are?

The guard tosses his cigarette stub away and starts to walk back towards them. They fall silent, pick up the stretcher laden with rocks and start to make their way down the mountainside. Béla whistles a tune as he walks, an old Hungarian folk melody.

Béla's idea has got Márton thinking. It would be a hazardous thing to do. But if it worked? If it meant he could see Katalin again?

They meet Horváth and Miklós, carrying their empty stretcher back up the mountainside.

'All right fellers?' says Béla. His idea of escaping seems to have made him cheerful.

Miklós nods and grunts in reply, but Horváth doesn't even seem to be aware of their presence. He puts one foot in front of the other like a dead man walking. Dear God, thinks Márton, please not Horváth. He was fine yesterday. He'll make a point of talking to him this evening when they're back at the barracks. You've only got to look at Béla to see the importance of maintaining a positive mental outlook.

They've barely gone another twenty yards down the slope when there's a rumbling like thunder. Márton isn't in the least surprised. From the dense mass of clouds obscuring the mountain tops, a storm has been on the cards for some time. But the rumbling crescendos, growing in intensity like timpani in an orchestra.

They turn and see a sight that freezes Márton's blood. A cloud of dust is making its way down the mountainside. It can mean only one thing – a landslide. As they stand rooted to the spot, the cloud expands as the loose rocks in its core dislodge smaller stones and debris. Just as Béla said when they first arrived here, the slope is too steep and the ground has become unstable. They are standing in the path of a deadly avalanche.

He and Béla drop the handles of their stretcher, scattering rocks, and stumble to the side out of the way. Miklós and Horváth, further up the path, are much closer to the accelerating landslide which resembles a river in full flow. Márton sees Miklós drop his end of the stretcher and dive for cover behind a rocky outcrop. But Horváth, the meteorologist, stands still as if mesmerised by this force of nature hurtling towards him. Instead of running to safety, he kneels on the ground, brings his hands together and bends his head in prayer. The rocks hurtling towards him must have a combined weight of several tons. One minute Horváth is kneeling on the ground, the next he vanishes in the cloud of rock and dust. The torrent continues its slide down the mountain, oblivious of the destruction it has caused. As the ground levels out, the rocks pile up in a massive heap which will take days to clear.

Márton falls to his knees, retching, his empty stomach bringing up a foul yellow bile. The sight of his friend being crushed beneath the landslide is too much for him. Horváth was a good man. He didn't deserve this. None of them deserve this. Béla is already staggering back up the hill, dragging the empty stretcher behind him. With sorrow in his soul, and limbs that feel like lead, Márton follows him. Miklós emerges, shaken but unscathed, from behind his hiding place. They stare at the bloodied remains of Horváth, his body crushed, his smashed face unrecognisable.

'Why didn't the idiot run?' asks Miklós. 'He could have saved himself.'

'It was already too late for him,' says Márton.

The guard who was patrolling the top of the mountain comes running down. 'Don't just look at him,' he shouts. 'Pick him up and take him back to the camp.'

With shaking hands, Márton helps Béla and Miklós lift Horváth's broken body onto the stretcher. Then they begin the long trek back to the camp. Horváth's half-starved body weighs almost nothing, yet it is the heaviest load Márton has ever carried.

*

The feelings of optimism engendered by Sándor at

Katalin's birthday party are soon squashed when she arrives at work one morning to be told by Piroska Benke that the headmaster wishes to see her in his office.

Leaving the children once more in the dubious care of the school secretary, Katalin makes her way down the corridor with a feeling of foreboding in her heart. If György Boda is expecting her to have more to report on the subject of Tibor and his wayward ways then he's going to be sorely disappointed. She knocks on the door and the headmaster bids her enter.

'Please, take a seat.' His neutral tone of voice gives nothing away.

She sits on the wooden chair indicated, clutching her hands in her lap. Rákosi gazes down at her from the wall. She avoids meeting those loathsome eyes and focuses instead on the books in the bookcase, mostly works of Lenin and Marx.

'Miss Bakos, it has come to my attention that you keep a number of red neckerchiefs in your desk drawer and that some of the children in your class wear them during our weekly marches in honour of our great leaders.'

For a moment Katalin is flummoxed. How can he know about the spare neckerchiefs she keeps in case the children forget to bring theirs in? The children would certainly never tell him, they're terrified of the headmaster. And then she thinks of Piroska Benke supervising the children whilst she has been in these meetings. The school secretary has no interest whatsoever in the children and probably spends the time spying on the contents of Katalin's desk. She wishes now she'd had the sense to take the offending items home with her.

'I know how important it is for the children to be properly attired for the occasion,' she says in her defence. 'I wouldn't want any of them to get into trouble.'

'Their parents are supposed to provide them with neckerchiefs from home. Failure to do so shows a lack of support for the Party.'

'With all due respect, sir,' says Katalin, 'many of these parents are working long hours in factories. I'm sure they mean no disrespect, but they have enough to do in the mornings bringing their children to school and getting themselves to work on time.'

'That is not my concern,' says György Boda. 'From now on, all children must wear their own neckerchiefs and failure to do so will result in appropriate action being taken against the parents. Is that clear?'

'Yes,' says Katalin.

'Good. You may return to your class now.'

Katalin escapes into the corridor and closes the headmaster's door behind her, resisting the overwhelming urge to slam it shut. She wants to scream at the petty, nonsensical rules imposed on her and the children.

When she arrives back at the classroom, Piroska Benke gives her a self-satisfied smile on her way out. Katalin slides open her desk drawer to find that her supply of spare neckerchiefs has vanished. The children will be marching around the playground tomorrow morning. She'll have to remind them to bring in neckerchiefs tomorrow, but some of them will forget or maybe don't even own one. Where can she find a new supply at such short notice?

*

Weeks drift by with a mind-numbing monotony, and there's no more talk of escaping from the labour camp. Maybe it was just a dream of Béla's after all, something to rouse the spirits and give them hope. But Horváth's death has cast a black cloud over the dormitory. Like an impenetrable fog of stratus, thinks Márton. If Horváth's death was simply a tragic accident, it would be bad enough, but it's the way he resigned himself to his fate, seemed to welcome it even. What's to stop any of them from just throwing themselves off the mountainside? There are enough sheer drops to choose from.

The weather turns even colder, if that's possible. Márton thinks of Horváth's prediction of a cold blast from the east that got him arrested in the first place. The wind that rips across the mountains feels as if it's come directly from Siberia, bringing Stalin's regards with it. It claws its way into their skin and freezes their bones. Men are falling ill. At night Márton hears András coughing, a chesty, repetitive cough that shakes the bunk bed they share. It doesn't sound good. The boy has grown weaker in recent days and there's a glazed look in his eyes that Márton doesn't like one bit.

Márton and Béla are trudging down the mountain with their load of rocks when Béla suddenly announces that everything is ready for this Sunday. The escape plan is going ahead in two days' time.

'I thought the whole thing was off,' says Márton. 'You haven't mentioned it since the day...' His voice trails off. He was going to say, the day Horváth died.

'I trust you,' says Béla. 'But I didn't want to risk word getting out. The fewer people who know, the safer for all concerned.'

'Of course.' There are those who report to the guards in exchange for favours, like extra rations and less work. There are informers even here.

Béla explains that the escape party will consist of himself, Márton, András and the old man Lovas from the carpenter's shop, the one who has carved a replica weapon. Any more would be too risky.

'Are you sure this is going to work?' asks Márton.

'What's the alternative? We're working ourselves into the grave here. We have to try this before we drop dead from exhaustion or just lose the will to live.'

Márton thinks of András. Last night's coughing fit was particularly bad. The boy is hardly getting any sleep which isn't helping his situation. This morning he looks like an old man. At the bottom of the slope they tip the rocks from the stretcher onto the growing pile. András is swinging a mallet at a large rock, but his strokes are so feeble that he's having no effect. He looks at them out of eyes that seem to have shrunk in his head. It's almost as if he doesn't recognise them. If anyone deserves a shot at freedom it's András. He will die if he stays here much longer. They have to give Béla's plan a go. If they succeed, Márton can find Katalin and take her somewhere safe. But if they fail? No, he can't allow himself to think of that. Béla has shown himself to be resourceful and sensible. They have to give it their best.

Márton barely sleeps on Saturday night. He can hear András tossing and turning in the top bunk. His cough is getting steadily worse, a dry hacking cough that is painful to listen to. At least Béla is snoring soundly.

Sunday dawns cold and grey. The clouds are dense and heavy, presaging snow. Márton hardly dares look András and Béla in the eye for fear of giving them away. He notices that András is trembling as his fingers fumble over the buttons on his uniform. Without saying a word to each other, they traipse outside to the yard for their morning mug of barley-coffee. When Márton looks around for Béla, he's already disappeared.

Márton shuffles around, trying to keep warm. Since Horváth's death more good men have succumbed to the harsh conditions and the mood in the camp is at an all-time low. The guards only make the remaining men work even harder, and hatred for the AVO has increased beyond measure.

'Here comes one of the filthy bastards now,' mutters Miklós, as a uniformed guard marches across the yard towards them. Miklós turns away and Márton almost does too, thinking that this guard will be looking for men to clean the toilets or something. If he assigns Márton and András to the task then Béla's plan won't get off the ground. But as the guard comes nearer, he realises with a shock that it's Béla dressed in a uniform stolen from the tailor's. He knew this was part of the plan, but he hadn't expected Béla to look so convincing. He's wearing the cap pulled down low over his eyes and carrying the replica submachine gun tucked under his arm. If you don't look too closely, it's surprisingly realistic. Márton tries not to stare at Béla in case it encourages the other men to stare too, but everyone else is determinedly ignoring the approaching guard, the sight of the uniform enough to strike fear into their hearts. Márton's own heart is beating furiously. Beside him András looks pale as a ghost, his hands trembling. Lovas, the old man from the carpenter's who carved the wooden weapon, is walking in front of Béla, his head hanging down, looking contrite. Béla is shouting random abuse at him to make the pair of them look more convincing.

Béla stops by the men eating breakfast and looks around as if deciding who to pick on. Those not in on the secret keep their eyes downcast. They're so accustomed to avoiding eye contact with the guards they don't look close enough to realise it's Béla in disguise. Márton tries to appear relaxed even though his nerves are on edge. One false step and the consequences will be dire. Béla suddenly turns on him and András.

'You two, drop your bowls now!'

He has warned them he will do this, but it's still unnerving to be shouted at by someone you trust. If he's such a good actor, what's to say this whole ploy isn't an elaborate trick to catch would-be defectors? But Márton refuses to let the idea take hold. This is Béla, his friend.

'You're wanted in the quarry for an extra shift.'

He and András obey wearily, careful not to appear too eager. András's cough is working in their favour because the boy is so debilitated by it, all his movements are slow and lethargic.

Béla manhandles them into line behind Lovas and shouts at them to get moving. Márton hears sighs of relief amongst the remaining men that they haven't been picked to do extra labour by this particularly aggressive guard. If only they knew.

Two soldiers are manning the gate, chatting to each other, their breath misting in the cold air. The weapons slung over their shoulders are not replicas, thinks Márton, as his stomach lurches. This is the moment of truth. They will either get away with their ruse or be shot on the spot. He experiences a sudden moment of clarity at the realisation that his life could be over in the next few seconds. Everyone and everything he has ever truly loved flashes before him: Eva, Katalin, Oxford, books, music. Everything that makes life worth living. So real, and yet so fragile.

When the soldiers see Béla and his men approaching they stand to attention. Márton focuses on their black, shiny boots, not daring to look them in the eye. Béla's uniform has fooled them so far. They might just get away with this if the guards don't look too closely at Béla's face. But none of the guards see the prisoners as individuals anyway. To them, they are just one faceless mass.

'Open the gates,' orders Béla.

'You're early today,' remarks one of the guards, his tone challenging. 'We weren't told to expect anyone leaving early.' He sounds like a real pedant, a stickler for the rules. Despite the cold, Márton feels himself sweating.

'Yeah, I know,' says Béla in a bored voice. 'But I've got orders from the top. These lazy bastards have been given extra work. Caught them slacking yesterday.' He jabs András in the back with his replica weapon.

Don't overdo it, thinks Márton.

'Well, in that case,' says the other guard, 'make sure you work them extra hard.'

'Don't worry, I intend to.'

The pedantic guard turns to the big metal gate and begins the laborious process of unlocking it, turning the key and sliding back the heavy steel bolts. It seems to take forever. Márton imagines the men in the watchtowers spying on this performance, their weapons at the ready. Could it be possible that these two guards are only co-operating because they've guessed the truth and they want to enjoy the spectacle of seeing the escapees gunned down by their comrades? His mind is a jumble of conflicting thoughts and emotions. He is only vaguely aware of András and Lovas standing either side of him. And then, suddenly the gate is wide open. He blinks at the sight of the open space in front of him, even though he has gone this way every day on his way to the quarry. But that has always been in a mass of men and now it is just the four of them about to walk through the gate. He has to resist the urge to run. Béla has warned them they must behave like they always do, and not get over-excited.

'Out!' shouts Béla and they stumble forward.

As he crosses the threshold Márton feels a heady sense of relief. He's crossed the boundary of the camp and he's still breathing. Keep walking, he tells himself, just keep walking.

He hasn't gone more than three or four yards before he realises with a shock that András is no longer by his side. Where is he? Slowly, so as not to draw attention to himself, he turns his head to look.

András is still inside the perimeter fence, doubled over, a spasm of coughing holding him prisoner.

'You're not going to get any useful work out of this one,' says the guard who opened the gate. 'I'd leave him behind if I were you.'

Márton wants to shout that they can't leave András behind, but that would give the game away. No prisoner would ever insist on a fellow prisoner being sent to work in the quarry, especially not one in András's enfeebled state.

'Bah,' says Béla to the guard. 'Don't let him fool you. It's all an act to get out of doing any real work.' He goes right up to Andras and shouts, 'Get a bloody move on, you lazy sod!' He shoves András so hard that the boy flies through the gate, stumbles and falls to his knees.

'Get on your feet!' Béla gives him a kick up the backside for good measure. The guards inside laugh as they close the gate and lock it.

Béla leads his co-conspirators in silence towards the quarry.

*

As soon as the four men are out of sight of the watchtowers, they change direction and quickly disappear into the forest. As a child Márton was warned not to stray too far into the trees for fear of becoming lost, but now the forest is a place of refuge, welcoming them into its dense mass of trunks. Even their footsteps are smothered on the thick carpet of fallen leaves and rotting vegetation. When he looks back he can no longer see the watchtowers.

'We bloody did it!' shouts Béla, full of triumph. He thrusts the fake weapon in the air.

'Not so loud,' cautions Márton. 'They might still hear us.'

'Come on,' says Lovas. 'We should get as far away as we can as quickly as possible.'

András leans against a tree for support, his breathing ragged. But at least he has lost that glazed look he's had for weeks now. You can't save everyone, thinks Márton, but if you can save just one…

The plan is to head north towards the Czechoslovak frontier, a distance of roughly ten miles. If all goes well they will reach the border by nightfall. Once there, they will turn west towards Austria. Béla has talked of getting their story broadcast on western radio or printed in western newspapers. *Radio Free Europe* is always encouraging the Hungarians to stand up to their Soviet oppressors, but people in the West don't know the half of it.

After the initial exhilaration of their miraculous escape

has worn off, they fall into single file, silently picking a path through the undergrowth. Béla takes the lead, followed by the old man Lovas, then András. Márton brings up the rear, trying not to think about the gnawing hunger in his stomach, his aching limbs from months of heavy lifting, and his leaking boots. He tries to take his mind off his physical aches and pains by focusing on the heady sense of freedom. He inhales the rich scent of pine resin and remembers how he used to forage for mushrooms as a child. His grandfather taught him which ones were safe to eat and which ones were poisonous. He keeps an eye out for anything edible, but it's the wrong time of year. It's too cold and the ground beneath their feet is iron-hard.

They plod on for a couple of hours before they stop to rest. Their pace has been painfully slow at times, but Béla reckons they've done about four miles. They're well away from the camp and can afford a quick breather. Márton, Béla and Lovas lean against tree trunks, but András lies down on the ground and closes his eyes. His face is flushed and sweat is beading on his brow, running in tiny rivulets down his temples. Márton leans forwards and touches the boy's forehead. It's burning. It's a miracle he's kept going for as long as he has.

'He's got a fever,' says Márton. 'He won't be able to carry on much longer.'

'We need food and shelter,' says Lovas. 'We'll never make the border tonight.'

Márton fears the old man is right. They might have trekked ten miles when they were all strong and fit, but in their present condition such a distance now seems wildly over-optimistic.

'So what do you suggest?' he asks, looking at his companions.

Béla stands up and walks a short distance. 'The forest can't go on for much further. There must be a farm somewhere nearby. Dressed like this' – he indicates his stolen AVO uniform – 'I could always intimidate a local farmer into giving us food, but I'd rather not do that sort of thing.'

'We can't just go knocking on doors,' says Lovas, 'in case the inhabitants are in the pay of the Secret Police.'

Márton feels something close to despair. Have they escaped from the labour camp only to die of hunger in the middle of nowhere? A sound in the forest makes him look up.

'What's that?'

He can see from the look of alarm on the other men's faces that they heard it too.

'Ssh,' says Béla.

There is nothing for a moment except the rustle of the wind in the trees. Then they hear it again. A snapping sound, like footsteps on twigs.

'Someone's coming,' hisses Béla under his breath. 'We need to hide.'

Béla puts his hands under András's shoulders and Márton takes the boy's feet. Together they haul him behind a fallen tree. Then they lie on the ground and try to camouflage themselves with fallen branches and leaves. Márton's heart is hammering against his bony ribcage. It must be the guards come to hunt them down. But why aren't they making more noise with their thick-soled boots and their vicious guard dogs? These sounds are light, as if a lone person is moving around.

Through the canopy of brushwood, Márton sees a small, stooped figure come into view. It's an old woman, dressed head to foot in black, her head covered in a grey scarf. In her arms she's carrying a bundle of sticks. She stops near the place where the four men were sitting a moment ago and looks around. Her face is weathered and lined, like old, cracked leather. But her eyes are sharp and watchful. She knows someone has been there. Someone has disturbed her forest.

Márton glances across at Béla and they exchange a look

of understanding. This old woman could save them. Or she could report them to the Secret Police. But without her help, András might not survive. It's a risk they have to take.

'Madam.' Béla scrambles to his feet, throwing off sticks and leaves, some of which still cling to his uniform, giving him a wild, untamed appearance.

The old woman drops her bundle of sticks in fright, emitting an ear-piercing shriek. Márton expects her to flee at the sight of Béla's uniform, but she stands her ground. 'You can't arrest me! I've done nothing wrong. I mind my own business and don't bother anyone.' Her voice is high and cracked and Márton notices that half her teeth are missing. Despite her diminutive size, she looks ready to fly at Béla and attack him.

Béla tosses the replica weapon aside and holds his hands up in supplication. 'No, madam. I'm sorry I frightened you.' He bends down and starts to pick up her sticks. 'I'm not a member of the Secret Police. I'm an escaped prisoner from the labour camp at Recsk. There are four of us. We need your help. One of our group is sick.' He gives her back her bundle of sticks.

Márton and Lovas emerge from their hiding places. András rolls over and groans. They must look a sorry state, thinks Márton, in their ragged army uniforms, covered in leaves and bits of moss, like wild creatures.

The old woman scrutinises Márton and Lovas, making up her mind about them. Her reaction when she thought Béla was a member of the Secret Police bodes well. It would appear she is no supporter of the political regime.

'Where's the sick one?' she asks.

'Through here,' says Márton, showing her András lying on the ground.

She bends down and lays a knobbly hand on András's forehead. 'Fever,' she says matter-of-factly. 'Can you carry him?'

Béla holds András under the shoulders and Márton

walks in front holding his ankles. After the stretchers of rock they've been carrying down the mountainside, András is a featherweight. Lovas walks in front with the old woman, helping her collect more sticks on the way.

Half an hour later they arrive at a small, stone cottage on the edge of the forest. Next to the cottage there's a ramshackle wooden barn with a corrugated iron roof and a small chicken run in which half a dozen scrawny birds are pecking at the dirt.

'We're half a mile from the village here,' says the old woman. 'No one will bother us.' She points at András. 'Bring him into the cottage. We'll make him comfortable.'

They find themselves in a low-ceilinged single room with a stone floor and whitewashed walls. There's a wooden table and a couple of wooden chairs. One corner of the cottage, presumably where she sleeps, is curtained off.

'Put him down there.' She points to a woven rug on the floor in front of the hearth. Then she disappears behind the curtain and returns with a blanket. 'I'll treat the fever with my herbal remedies until he's better. What's his name?'

'András,' says Márton. 'He's only a boy.'

The old woman nods her understanding. 'The rest of you can sleep in the loft in the barn. I'll show you where.'

On the ground floor of the barn is a cow who regards them with lazy indifference and goes back to chewing the cud. 'There's plenty of space up there.' She points to a wooden ladder. 'And hay to keep you warm.'

'We are very grateful to you, Madam...' says Béla.

'Call me Dorottya.' There's a distant look in her eyes, as if she's thinking of something else. 'My husband was arrested back in 1949,' she says. 'I haven't seen him since. He's probably dead now. But if he did escape I like to think that someone would look after him. Make yourselves comfortable. I'll cook some potatoes for you.'

She returns later with a bowlful of hot potatoes and a

jug of fresh milk. It's the best meal that Márton has had in a long while. As they tuck into their food, he imagines what is happening back at the camp right now. The guards will be running up and down the lines of men, counting and re-counting. *Why are there four men missing? We must have mis-counted. Count them again!* The camp commander will be barking orders. But at some point they are going to have to admit that some men have actually escaped, despite all their tight security, weapons and barbed wire. They have been fooled and they will not be happy about it. He feels a pang of guilt for his fellow prisoners left behind who will have to endure the endless re-counting before they are allowed to return to their barracks. He hopes the guards don't take their anger out on the other prisoners, but he supposes that is inevitable.

*

For two nights in a row, Dorottya sits beside András, applying cold compresses to his forehead. During the day she treats the fever with a mixture of elderflower and chamomile from her store cupboard. She naps herself whenever he's resting quietly. But tonight is the worst of it. His temperature has risen to fever pitch and in his delirium he tosses and turns, moaning out loud and calling for a girl named Hanna, whoever she is. Probably his sweetheart before he was arrested. What are the chances that she's waiting for him to return? Dorottya dips her cloth into the bowl of cold water, wrings it out and presses it firmly over his head.

'There, there,' she says. 'Quiet now. It's going to be all right.'

He reminds her of the son she once had. The son she lost to the war. She doesn't know why András and the other men were sent to the labour camp at Recsk and she doesn't care. She assumes they are political prisoners, but she's not interested in politics. She's lived long enough to remember the days of the Austro-Hungarian Empire, two world wars, fascism and communism, and she doesn't have time for any of it. She has lived her life surviving on the land and bartering with her neighbours in the nearby village. A jar of honey in return for a string of onions. Eggs in return for flour. She collects mushrooms in the forest and dries them so they will keep through the winter. She picks wild strawberries and blackberries and turns them into preserves. So long as she has her cow, and her chickens, and her patch of land she can manage. She knows she doesn't have long left for this world herself, but if she can make András better and see these men on their way then she will have done something worthwhile.

The men return her hospitality by doing jobs for her during the day. Béla mends her roof where the rain drips through; Lovas uses his carpentry skills to carve a bowl and wooden spoons out of an old log; and Márton reinforces the chicken run so that the foxes can't get in.

The fever reaches a peak in the early hours of the morning. As András drops in and out of consciousness, his eyes rolling in their sockets, Dorottya fears for his life. She works tirelessly, applying cold compresses to his head, chest and feet, doing everything she can to bring his temperature down. Just before dawn the fever breaks and András lies still, his breathing returned to normal. She sits with him for another twenty minutes, but the danger is past now. As the birds begin their morning chorus, she crawls into her own bed for a couple of hours sleep.

The next day András is able to sit up and eat some potato soup, always a good sign in Dorottya's book. A young man like that should have a healthy appetite.

Márton comes into the cottage to enquire about the boy's health as he has done every day since they arrived.

'He's over the worst,' she tells him. 'He's sleeping now. He needs a few more days to build his strength up, then I expect you'll want to be on your way.' The guards at the camp must be looking for them and could arrive here at any time. Still, Dorottya will be sorry to see the men go. Especially András who she has developed a soft spot for.

'We thought we could go into the forest and collect more firewood for you,' says Márton.

'Thank you, that would be very kind.'

She watches the men set off and then she starts her daily chores, milking the cow and collecting eggs from the chickens.

She's peeling potatoes at the kitchen table when a knock on the door makes her jump. She isn't expecting any visitors.

'Dorottya, are you in there?'

She sighs. It's Anika from the village. The woman is a dreadful gossip but harmless enough. Still, she doesn't want Anika to see András sleeping in front of the fire. Anika won't be able to keep her mouth shut.

Anika raps on the door a second time. 'I have your jar of honey here.'

András stirs awake and sits up. He must have heard the knocking. He looks at the door and she can see the fear in his eyes.

'Quickly,' she whispers. 'Behind the curtain.'

He nods his understanding and crawls to the space behind the curtain where her own bed is. She goes to unbolt the door.

'Ah, there you are,' says Anika, stepping uninvited into the cottage. She's carrying a jar of honey from the bees she and her husband keep. Dorottya will give her half a dozen eggs in exchange. That's the agreement they have.

Anika is a big woman – it's all the honey she eats – and seems to fill half the available space. She puts the jar on the table and stands looking around. She's clearly not in any hurry to leave.

'I'll fetch your eggs,' says Dorottya. She takes six freshly laid eggs from a straw-lined basket and places them in a bowl. She has already given the biggest eggs to the men this morning in return for all their hard work.

'Have you heard the news?' asks Anika.

'I haven't heard anything.' There's no radio in the cottage. Dorottya prefers it that way.

'There's been a break-out from the camp in Recsk.' Anika is slightly breathless telling her this, as if it's the most thrilling thing to have happened in their neck of the woods for years.

'Is that so?' Dorottya tucks a cloth around the eggs so that they won't break.

Anika nods her head. 'Of course, you're so isolated out here, Dorottya, you don't get to hear what's going on. But I thought I should warn you. The escaped prisoners could be dangerous.'

'I'm perfectly safe here. Here are your eggs.' She holds out the bowl, hoping Anika will just take it and leave but she suspects the real reason for Anika's visit is to gossip about the escaped prisoners. Anika will be hoping for some information she can pass on to her husband and the rest of the village.

Anika takes the bowl but makes no move to leave. 'Is that mint and lavender I can smell in here?' she asks, wrinkling her nose.

Dorottya has been infusing mint and lavender leaves in boiling water to help soothe András. The aroma is calming.

'Yes,' she says. 'I find it relaxing.'

'I noticed on the way in that you've mended the chicken run,' says Anika. 'My husband could have done it for you.'

'I managed,' says Dorottya. Anika's husband is always promising to do things and never getting round to them.

Anika's eyes flit to the rug in front of the hearth where András was lying only moments ago. There's a kink in it. Then her eyes dart to the curtained-off area. Dorottya wills András to stay silent and not cough. His cough is much better than it was, but sometimes it still catches him out.

She moves towards the door, hoping that Anika will take the hint and leave. 'I'm sorry I can't ask you to stay for tea, but I'm rather busy.'

'Of course,' says Anika. 'Don't let me keep you. Goodbye.' She looks around the cottage once more and then takes her leave.

Anika knows, thinks Dorottya, or at least she suspects, and that's just as bad. Tomorrow, the men must leave. It's not safe for them here anymore.

*

That night Márton lies awake, unable to sleep. When they returned from from the forest with enough firewood to keep Dorottya warm for months, she told them about Anika's visit.

'I've known her for years but I wouldn't trust her as far as I can throw her,' she told them.

'Then we'll be on our way,' Béla said. 'We don't want to put you in any more danger.'

They turned in early and Béla was soon snoring gently. Lovas nodded off too. It seems that Márton is the only one who can't sleep.

It's clear to him that they can't possibly make it all the way to Austria on foot. There isn't going to be a Dorottya every twenty miles willing to give them food and shelter. They will need to find some form of transportation. But how are they going to do that without giving themselves away? And they need to get out of these wretched old army uniforms.

He must have drifted off to sleep at some point because he's suddenly awoken by the sound of dogs barking. He sits up, looking around. In the grey light of dawn he can see that Lovas is also awake, looking around in alarm. Only Béla continues to snore, the dreamless sleep of the innocent.

'Béla, wake up!' Márton leans over and gives him a gentle shake.

'What the…?' He comes to with a grunting sound.

The barking is coming closer. It sounds like three or four large dogs, the sort you wouldn't want to meet in a dark alley. A flapping and clucking starts up in the chicken run and they hear the cow getting to its feet and letting out a long bellow. The dogs are in the yard now and there are stomping boots and men's voices.

Silently, Béla points to an old tarpaulin that's lying in the corner of the loft. Moving as quietly as they can, they crawl underneath and lie flat. If they keep as still and quiet as possible then maybe the guards won't find them. But they'll find András in the cottage, thinks Márton. He feels responsible for the boy as if he was his own son. He can't let them take András. The boy has his whole life ahead of him, whereas Márton has already lived over half of his.

Suddenly the cow starts stamping its feet and lowing in distress. The men and dogs have entered the barn and are now standing directly beneath where the men are hiding. Scenting their prey, the dogs are going berserk, their barks reverberating like gunshots.

'Search up there!' orders a voice.

Márton holds his breath as he hears footsteps on the ladder. On one side of him, Béla is rigid like a statue, but on the other side, Lovas is trembling. At least the dogs can't climb the ladder, otherwise they'd be found out in no time. There's a thump on the floorboards as the man hauls himself into the loft. Then the unmistakable tread of heavy boots – the regulation boots worn by members of the Secret Police. The boots recede for a moment whilst the guard explores the other end of the barn. But then the boots come closer. Márton can practically smell the polished leather. His heart is thudding so hard he's sure the guard must be able to hear it.

Suddenly the tarpaulin is ripped from above their heads and the game is over. The guard calls out to his superior that he's found the prisoners, but the words die in his throat as Béla rises like a Colossus and shoves him backwards towards the hatch opening. For a moment they tussle, but Béla is the taller of the two and the guard can't see where he's putting his feet. With a grunt, Béla gives him one last push and the guard falls through the opening and lands on the ground with a thud.

For a fraction of a second, even the dogs are stunned into silence. And then all hell breaks loose. A stream of bullets are fired into the loft, peppering Béla who is still standing near the opening. Márton watches in horror as his friend's body goes limp and topples through the hatch like a sack of corn.

'No!' shouts Márton, but he can hardly hear himself over the noise of the snarling dogs, and the terrified cow, and the angry voices. He collapses on the floor in shock and horror.

Another guard appears at the top of the ladder. 'If you two don't want to end up dead like your friend, then you better surrender yourselves now.'

Márton is heartbroken. Béla was a true friend. It was his cunning and bravery that enabled them to escape in the first place. If it hadn't been for András's illness, they would have been far from here by now. But he can't blame András for this. It's not the boy's fault he fell ill.

Márton and Lovas climb down the ladder and are seized by the guards. The guard who fell first is sitting up, rubbing his head and arms. He'll be bruised and have concussion, thinks Márton, but otherwise he'll be all right. Béla, on the other hand, is lying sprawled in a heap, blood from his many wounds pooling on the floor of the barn.

There are four guards in total and four big, black dogs, growling and baring their teeth. Márton and Lovas are chained together by their wrists and marched into the yard. Dorottya and András are also there, having been brought out of the cottage. András, although over the worst of his illness, looks utterly defeated. But the diminutive Dorottya has a look of defiance on her face.

When the guards try to put chains on her, she kicks and spits at them. 'You can kill me,' she shrieks, 'but you're not taking me to one of your blasted camps.'

'Fine,' says the one in charge. 'If that's what you want, it will make our lives easier.' He lifts his gun and shoots her in the head. She crumples to the ground like a rag doll.

The sight is too much for András who falls to his knees and vomits.

'On your feet,' shouts the guard. 'Now.'

András is chained to Márton and Lovas and then the three men are shoved into a truck and driven back to the camp.

At the sight of the barbed wire fence, Márton wants to fall to the ground and weep. For three glorious days they were free. And now they have been brought back to this hellhole. There is no further hope of escape now. He sees a line of fellow prisoners on their way to the quarry, looking even more wretched and ragged than he remembered them. Márton, Lovas and András are taken to the camp commander. He gives them a lecture on how they have shown themselves unworthy of socialist re-education and will be sorely punished.

'You will spend the next two weeks locked in solitary confinement and will spend two hours each night in short chains.'

They are taken to the prison block and each put into a tiny cell. It reminds Márton of the cell he occupied at Andrássy Avenue when he was first arrested. That night he learns what is meant by 'short chains'. The guards bind his wrists to his ankles, pulling the rope so tight that it cuts deep into his flesh, restricting the circulation. It's agony to sit hunched in this position for more than ten minutes. He weeps with the pain. He'll be like this for two hours.

CHAPTER 9

The months pass. Katalin is often surprised when she
realises how much time has gone by since her father's
arrest. She thinks about him constantly, but Zoltán tells
her that her father would want her to carry on with her
life, not spend it moping. Still, it's hard. Whenever she
hears a favourite piece of music, she thinks how much her
father would have enjoyed listening to it. When she looks
at his books on the bookshelf, she can't help picturing him
in his reading chair, absorbed in the pages of a novel.
When she goes to Feri's café, he gives her an extra large
slice of cake, in honour of her Papa.

She hasn't seen Tamás since he came to tell her that her
father was being sent to a labour camp. That was before
Christmas, before the winter brought the bone-penetrating
cold and the long, dark nights. Throughout the winter she
can't bear to think of her father in some remote camp
goodness knows where, being made to do slave labour.
Her only hope is that he has made friends amongst the
other prisoners. If he is still alive. In moments of despair,
Zoltán holds her tight and tells her that she mustn't give
up hope.

And then, almost imperceptibly, winter releases its grip

on the city and people re-emerge as if from a siege. The days lengthen, the last pockets of snow melt, and the flower sellers reappear on the street corners. Róza will soon be qualified as a doctor; Petra complains that Tibor is growing out of all his clothes; Zoltán continues to put in long hours at the factory and has read his way through most of her father's books; Csaba Elek delivers the daily lecture from *A Free People*; Feri is a little greyer but still makes the best cakes and coffee; József shuffles around in his patched cardigan, watching everyone's comings and goings from the building. Katalin continues to teach at the school, the children march and sing on a regular basis, and Piroska Benke, the school secretary, keeps her attendance records immaculate.

And then in March, when the first buds of spring are starting to sprout, something so shocking happens that life comes to a juddering halt. The trams and buses grind to a stop; schools and offices are closed; shop owners pull down the shutters; factory workers clock out early. People assume expressions of stunned disbelief. Some seem to be genuinely grief-stricken. For Stalin, the leader of the communist world, has died.

'Actually *dead*?' The woman in front of Katalin in the bread queue is full of disbelief, as if Stalin was somehow immune from mortality.

'It can't be true,' says her friend.

'My husband heard it from official sources,' says a third woman, full of the self-importance of those in the know.

'But what will happen to us now?'

Katalin holds her tongue. Do these women know what they are saying? Stalin was a monster, yet they are talking about him as if he was a god. Or is it just a trick to catch out people who are not sufficiently grieved by the news? She puts on a doleful face and tries not to smile.

That evening she and Zoltán join the crowds at the City Park, not because they mourn Stalin's passing, but because they understand that this is a momentous occasion in their country's future. What it will mean, no one yet knows. But it is impossible for it to mean nothing.

There are more people in the park than on a summer's afternoon. Crowds throng the foot of Stalin's giant statue, moving silently, each lost in their own thoughts, not daring to say what they are really thinking, even now. On the edge of the square AVO officers stand, watching.

An eerie quiet has descended on the city. Everything has changed, but in some ways nothing has changed. Mátyás Rákosi, General Secretary of the Hungarian Communist Party, is still alive and well, and as dangerous as ever. The vast network of agents, spies and Secret Police is still in place. You still have to be careful.

Katalin and Zoltán meander amongst the crowds, arm-in-arm, silently observing the spectacle. Some people have brought candles with them. They place them reverentially on the steps of the marble plinth, lighting them with matches. The flames flicker in the breeze. Many of them blow out, but there are always more candles to replace them. It looks like a Catholic shrine. Just as long as Stalin doesn't rise from the dead, they'll be all right. Even Katalin can't quite get used to the idea that he's finally gone. He seemed so indestructible when he was alive. They all thought he would live forever. She cranes her neck to look up at the bronze statue. It's so tall that the head is lost in the darkening gloom. Only the six-foot-high boots are properly visible. What will happen to the statue now? Will it become a temple to the god Stalin?

She doesn't want to be here anymore, surrounded by strangers whose grief, she thinks, is largely put on for show. 'Let's go home,' she says to Zoltán.

He nods his head in agreement. They turn their backs on the giant statue and start to weave their way back through the crowds which are growing by the minute.

*

At Recsk, the guards do their best to keep the prisoners isolated from the outside world but nevertheless, by the end of March 1953, a rumour starts to filter around the camp that Stalin is dead. For the first time in months, Márton sees a flicker of hope in the eyes of his fellow prisoners. And slowly, things start to change.

The old camp commander who put Márton, András and Lovas into isolation after they were recaptured, is replaced by a new man who introduces a shorter working day and gives them Sunday off. The food improves, ever so slightly, and the men grow a little stronger. And then one day in June, on his way back from returning some tools to the tool shed, Márton sees a newspaper which a guard has left lying on top of a woodpile. The guards never used to be so careless. Looking around to make sure no one is watching, He grabs the paper in a state of high excitement. Words are food for the soul and for months he's been starving.

The totally unexpected news is that Imre Nagy has been made Prime Minister. Márton rereads the article to make sure he's understood correctly. But it's there in black and white: since the death of Stalin – a momentous event in itself – Moscow have put Nagy, the moderate, in place of Rákosi, the hard-liner, at the top of the Hungarian tree. This is news indeed!

He folds the newspaper, tucks it inside his shirt and walks as fast as he can to the barracks to show the others.

The newspaper is passed from hand to hand. Every man wants to read the news for himself.

'But what does this mean for us?' asks András.

It's a good question, and one that Márton doesn't know the answer to. But the change of leadership at the top must be a good sign. He feels the stirrings of real hope.

A couple of weeks later, a group of ten men are released from the camp. They are ordinary criminals who have never expressed much interest in politics. After that, ten or twenty a day are released.

By September the numbers remaining have dwindled to a mere twenty men, Márton and András among them. Their release must surely be a matter of time now.

And then eventually, on a warm autumn day, they're standing in line to receive a shave from the camp barber. Afterwards they go to the warehouse where the guards issue each of them with an old suit and a pair of shoes which have seen better days. The commander gives each of them a judge's order placing them under police surveillance and threatens that they will be imprisoned for ten years if they speak about their imprisonment and the conditions in the labour camp.

'I advise you,' he says, 'to tell your families that you have been on a study trip in the Soviet Union.'

The irony of the situation is not lost on Márton. In some ways the whole experience has been one long study trip. He has learnt, at first hand, of the brutalities of Soviet communism. It's a lesson he's never going to forget.

At the gate, he turns back one last time and looks at the barracks standing deserted against the mountainside. Then he takes András by the arm and says, 'Come on, son. We're going home.'

*

Katalin reheats some soup in a pan and cuts herself a slice of bread. She's been on her feet most of the day, teaching, and doesn't have the energy to cook anything more complicated. Besides, since she's been living on her own, cooking doesn't seem worth the trouble. She's expecting Zoltán to call round later but not yet. Often he works twelve or fourteen hours a day, by the time he's attended the compulsory early morning collective newspaper reading, the lunchtime Marxist seminars, the after-work trade-union meetings, the factory committee meetings and the various campaigns such as the movement to increase productivity through the introduction of labour competitions. By the time he arrives home, he's usually exhausted.

She stirs the soup. It's just starting to bubble, so she turns off the heat and pours the steaming liquid into a bowl. She's about to sit down when the doorbell rings. It can't be Zoltán already. It's probably Petra returning the cake tin Katalin lent her. She hopes it isn't József the caretaker. She goes to answer the door.

Two men stand on the threshold. An old man and a younger one. They're both wearing shabby suits that hang off their lean frames. The older man lifts his face to hers and she lets out a cry of recognition.

'Papa!'

She throws her arms around him, feeling how thin and shrunken he is under his borrowed clothes. He staggers slightly under her embrace and she steps back, tears in her eyes. She's been hoping for almost a year that her father would come home, but she always pictured him as he was when the AVO took him away: tall, upright, dignified and smart. The man who has come back to her is sunken, dirty, thin and shabby. But it's her father, and when she looks in his eyes she sees that inside it's still the same man.

'Come inside.' She takes him by the hand and draws him into the apartment.

'Let me introduce my friend,' says Márton, indicating the younger man who has retreated into the shadows. 'This is András. He has nowhere else to go. I've told him he can stay with us for the moment.'

'Of course,' says Katalin, taking András's hand. 'You're very welcome.'

*

The wedding is to be a simple affair. Róza has been helping Katalin to alter a dress that used to belong to Katalin's mother. It's the floral cotton dress Eva is wearing in the photo taken in Oxford on her honeymoon.

The evening before the wedding, Róza brings the altered dress round to Katalin's apartment for a fitting. Márton and András have been instructed to take Zoltán to Feri's café for at least an hour so they won't be disturbed.

'You're so slim, I've put some darts in the back to take it in at the waist,' says Róza, smoothing her hands over the fabric. 'How does that feel?'

'It's perfect,' says Katalin. 'You're so clever with a needle and thread. I could never do anything like that.' Looking at herself in the mirror, she feels as if her mother is there with her, giving her blessing to the marriage. Zoltán proposed a month after Márton's return, once things had settled down a little. They're all still adjusting to the changes in their lives, but the wedding has given them something to focus on, something to look forward to.

'Yes, well I've had enough practice sewing up cuts and wounds at the hospital,' says Róza with a grim smile.

Katalin pulls a face.

'Don't worry, I didn't use a hospital needle on your dress.'

'I should hope not!'

'Now, what are we going to do with your hair?'

'What can we do with it?' Katalin has always envied Róza her thick red hair that is so easy to style into any shape.

Róza rolls her eyes. 'Really, Katalin, you weren't going to walk down the aisle with it just hanging down, were you? What if it's a windy day? It'll blow all over the place. Now stand in front of this mirror.' She moves behind Katalin and takes her long hair in her hands, deftly twisting it. Then she pulls hair grips and pins from her pocket and starts pinning the twisted knot of hair into place.

'Ouch, careful where you're sticking that,' says Katalin as a hair pin grazes her scalp. 'I hope you're more careful with your patients.'

'Sorry, but you have to suffer for the sake of beauty.' She sticks a couple more pins in and says, 'How does that look?'

Katalin tilts her head in front of the mirror, turning first one way and then another. She's impressed. She never thought that putting her hair up would make such a difference. Her neck looks longer, and more elegant. The line of her jaw is more defined. She looks more like Eva.

'I like it,' she says. 'But you'll have to do it for me tomorrow. I won't be able to do it myself.'

'Of course I'll do your hair for you,' says Róza. 'It will be my pleasure.'

'Thank you,' says Katalin, embracing her friend. 'You're the best. Now help me out of this dress before the men come home.'

She hopes the wedding will be a new start for everyone. Zoltán will move into the apartment she shares with her father because it's larger than his own place. They'll be able to care for Márton together, who is still recovering from the effects of his imprisonment. Who knows, maybe one day they will have a child of their own. It's something to hope for the future.

The wedding day itself dawns cold and bright. Róza arrives at the apartment early to help Katalin dress. She's managed to find some winter flowers to weave into Katalin's twisted hair.

Her father has put on his best suit, the one he didn't wear when he was arrested. It's too big for him but he's put a belt in the trousers to keep them up. He's in the living room, gazing at the photo of his wife and himself on their honeymoon in Oxford.

When he looks up, she can see the surprise in his eyes. Wearing her mother's dress, she does look like Eva did when she was younger. He takes a handkerchief from his breast pocket and dabs at his eyes. Then he straightens himself up and walks towards her. For the first time since his return, he looks like his former self.

'Katalin, my dear, you look beautiful.' He kisses her on the cheek.

A car pulls up outside and toots its horn.

Róza runs to look out of the window. 'Sándor's here,' she says. 'It's time to leave.'

Katalin takes her father's arm and together they descend to the ground floor. Sándor is waiting for them beside the open door of a car he has borrowed for the occasion. She and her father sit in the back and Róza joins Sándor in the front.

It's only a short drive to the nearby church. The priest is waiting by the open door when Sándor pulls up outside.

'Good luck,' says Róza, giving her hand a squeeze.

Sándor and Róza go inside whilst Katalin and her father exchange a few words with the priest, an elderly man in a long cassock.

'If you're ready?' asks the priest.

'Yes,' says Katalin. 'I'm ready.'

The priest enters the church and gives a nod to the organist who starts playing Mendelssohn's wedding march.

As Katalin and her father walk down the aisle, Zoltán turns to her and smiles. She's never seen him looking so smart and handsome and her heart fills with joy.

Afterwards, they all gather at Feri's for a private party. He has pushed the tables together to make one long table and he has baked a special cake for the occasion. Katalin and Zoltán sit in the middle of the table, surrounded by their family and friends. Sándor has his arm around Róza and she is smiling and laughing at his jokes. András and her father are deep in conversation. Petra is wiping a smear of chocolate off Tibor's face whilst he tells her to stop fussing.

In the middle of dessert, Feri stands up and taps his spoon on his wine glass. 'Ahem, mesdames, messieurs, if I could have your attention please? Thank you. I wish to propose a toast to the happy couple. To Katalin and Zoltán, may they live long and happy lives, in freedom and prosperity!'

As everyone raises their glasses, Katalin looks at the

smiling faces of her family and friends. She vows she will do everything she can to keep them safe in the future. She won't let them be separated again.

PART TWO
OCTOBER 1956

CHAPTER 10

Monday, 22 October 1956

The cry of an infant invades her dreams.

With a mother's instinct, Katalin is awake at once, pushing back the bed covers and feeling her way across the cold floor to the cot at the foot of their bed. Little Eva is six months old and has only recently started sleeping through the night. But with military precision she wakes at five thirty every morning demanding to be fed. Katalin scoops the baby into her arms, breathing in her warm, biscuity smell and pops her little finger into the tiny mouth to silence the squawks before she wakes her two-year-old brother, Lajos, who is still fast asleep in a camp bed on the other side of the room. Zoltán is stirring now too, sitting up and rubbing his eyes. A grey light filters through the curtains and outside the first trams of the day trundle past.

Katalin takes her daughter into the kitchen and straps her into her high chair. She needs to hurry and get some food into the child before the crying wakes the whole building. There are six of them living in the apartment now. Katalin, Zoltán and the children sleep in what used to be her parents' room and Márton has moved into what was Katalin's room. András sleeps in the former spare room. It's a bit crowded at times, especially when they have to queue for the single bathroom, but they're lucky they have the place to themselves, with so many people forced to live in communal apartments with strangers. Katalin tears off a chunk of bread and passes it to Eva who starts to gnaw at it with her half dozen tiny teeth. The crying stops and Katalin breathes a sigh of relief as she warms some milk in a pan.

She turns at the sound of footsteps in the hallway. Her father appears in the kitchen in his dressing gown.

'I hope Eva didn't wake you,' she says.

'I was awake anyway,' says Márton. Since his release from the labour camp at Recsk, he doesn't sleep well. She hears him moving about the apartment late at night or in the early hours of the morning as if he can't exorcise the ghosts of his imprisonment. She has tried to get him to talk about his experience as a prisoner, but he just shakes his head and turns away. He hasn't been allowed to return to his old job at the university, but he says he wouldn't have the heart for it now. Sometimes he asks her to play the violin for him and he listens with his eyes closed. It seems to soothe him and she's glad to do it.

She pours the warm milk into a bottle and passes it to her daughter. 'Shall I make us some coffee?'

'Yes please, love.' He sits down at the table, patting his granddaughter on the head. Only the children have the power to cheer him up these days.

For the next half hour the apartment is bustling with life as everyone gets ready for their day. Zoltán appears with Lajos and makes the little boy some breakfast. Katalin gets herself ready for work. András eats a slice of bread and leaves for a lecture at the university where he's studying engineering. Márton says he'll go and visit Feri at the café later.

When Zoltán has left for the factory, Katalin takes the children upstairs to Petra's, along with bottles of milk and spare nappies for Eva. She pays Petra a small allowance to look after the children whilst she's teaching at the school, but Petra says she loves to do it anyway.

On her way up the stairs, Katalin passes Tibor coming down. He's shot up, and at thirteen – nearly fourteen, he often reminds her – is now taller than she is.

'Morning, Miss,' he says, grinning. He's at the high school now, but he hasn't lost any of his cheeky charm. She can't help glancing at his shoe laces to see if they're done up. She wonders if he still has his collection of American comics and hopes he remembers to keep them hidden. Things have changed, but you can't be too careful.

Petra holds the door open to let them in. Lajos runs into Petra's apartment as if it were his own home.

'Aren't you getting a big girl?' says Petra as she takes Eva in her arms.

'I'll try not to be late,' says Katalin. Piroska Benke, the school secretary, has called a meeting tonight to discuss efficiency and productivity quotas. What that has to do with education and the welfare of children, Katalin can't begin to imagine.

'Don't worry,' says Petra. 'We'll be fine here.'

'Be good,' Katalin calls to her son. She pecks Eva on the cheek and then heads off to work.

*

Zoltán suppresses a yawn as he listens to the nasal voice of Csaba Elek droning on from that day's copy of *A Free People*. The factory workers still have to gather half an hour before the official start of their shift for the daily reading. It's the same old Party propaganda that Zoltán has heard thousands of times before.

On the wall behind the Party Secretary, portraits of Erno Gerő and András Hegediüs, the latest General Secretary of the Party and Prime Minister respectively, look down imperiously at the assembled workers. It amuses Zoltán to see Csaba Elek trying to keep up with the changing faces at the top. When Nagy, the reformer, was deposed, Csaba Elek wasted no time in hanging the new portraits as if he feared imprisonment for not being up to date with the powers-that-be. The period of relative liberty when Nagy took over as Prime Minister in June '53, and which resulted in the freeing of prisoners – including Zoltán's father-in-law – from the labour camps, came to an abrupt end in April '55 when Nagy was suddenly expelled from the Party, presumably for having gone too far with his reforms. Nagy was lucky not to be executed. Instead he retired to his house in the country to enjoy life, and who can blame him? Meanwhile the puppet masters in Moscow appointed Hegedüs as Prime Minister, but real power still lay with Rákosi as General Secretary of the Party. And now, even Rákosi has been replaced with another hardliner, the infamous Erno Gerő of the failed Five Year Plan. Hungary's politicians are selected according to the whims of the Kremlin.

Zoltán is frustrated at the way things seem to have taken a backward step. He remembers only too well the brief period of excitement seven months ago when the news broke in Hungary that the new Soviet leader Khrushchev had denounced Stalin at the Twentieth Party Congress.

Khrushchev spoke of the great harm caused by limitless power in the hands of one person and claimed that Stalin made up the term *enemy of the people* which led directly to the repression of anyone who disagreed with him. Confessions had been extracted by torture, and high-ranking Russians were now having their convictions overturned and were being rehabilitated posthumously. Even Stalin's reputation as a military genius is now in tatters because according to Khrushchev he failed to heed warnings in '41 that the Germans were about to invade the Soviet Union. The Red Army was woefully under-resourced, no preparations were put in place and once war was underway Stalin planned operations on a globe instead of a detailed map, if you can believe it.

Incendiary stuff indeed, Zoltán thought at the time. But in Budapest, Stalin's statue still stands tall in the City Park, a reminder to everyone of his godlike status.

Csaba Elek's reading comes to an end and the workers break into a round of applause. Zoltán joins Sándor at their workstation and another day begins.

*

It's mid-morning and Márton Bakos is making his way along Erzsébet Boulevard, past the grand turn-of-the-century buildings that hark back to a more refined age. He could have taken the tram as Katalin told him to, but he's in no hurry to arrive at his destination. Besides, walking gives him the illusion of freedom. He can almost imagine himself in Paris. Well, maybe not quite. He mustn't be late though. There would no doubt be a penalty for lateness.

Since his release he has tried to live a quiet life, doing his best to go unnoticed. At first he felt self-conscious whenever he left the apartment, convinced that his suffering must be plain for all to see. But then he came to realise that no one was paying him any attention – other people have enough problems of their own. These days he takes comfort in the simple pleasures of life – time with his family and grandchildren, chatting to Feri in the café, and taking a walk along the Danube when the weather permits.

When he arrives at his destination, he pauses a moment to straighten his tie and smooth back his thinning hair. Then, with a deep breath, he pushes open the door to the Café New York and steps inside. He used to come here with Eva, before the war, for special occasions. Anniversaries, birthdays, that sort of thing. But that was ten years ago and now he shies away from such ostentatious venues.

When the university declined to take him back

following his release from the labour camp, Zoltán offered to help find him work at the factory, but he declined the offer with thanks. Instead he helps Feri out occasionally at the café, somewhere he feels far more at home than in this elaborate place with its scrolling marble pillars and gold leaf embellishment.

A black-clad waiter steps forwards, looking him up and down. 'May I help you, sir?' The tone is peremptory, as if he thinks Márton may have stumbled in here by mistake.

'I'm here to meet someone.' Márton can see the man he's come to meet already seated at a table, pouring himself a coffee from a silver pot.

The waiter nods and stands aside.

As Márton approaches the table, the man looks up and gestures to the seat opposite. As a condition of his freedom, Márton is required to meet on a weekly basis with an AVO agent called Colonel Szabó. Tall and thin, the colonel is the polar opposite of Márton's previous nemesis, Vajda. Szabó cuts a cadaverous figure, with his hooded eyes, sunken cheekbones and prominent Roman nose. He always arranges their meetings in the most showy café in Budapest, a trait which Márton finds hard to reconcile with the man's supposed communist principles. Amid the lavish architecture and the clink of cutlery on fine china, Márton has to account for his days whilst the colonel takes notes in his black book. Márton supposes he goes back to Andrássy Avenue and writes up their conversations in Márton's file, which must be getting rather thick by now.

'Coffee?'

'Thank you,' says Márton.

Szabó clicks his long fingers and orders coffee for Márton. Then he takes out his notebook and unscrews the lid on his fountain pen. He turns to a clean page and says, 'So, what have you been doing this week?'

It's humiliating to have to report all his comings and goings to the AVO. When he was freed from the labour camp three years ago, he thought freedom meant freedom. He should have known better. The AVO have been keeping a close eye on him ever since his return.

'I help out at Feri's café most days.'

The waiter places a coffee pot on the table and Márton pours himself a cup.

Szabó writes in his notebook in a spiky script. 'Who visited the café last week?'

'No one in particular. Just the regulars.' He's not going to start naming people like Zoltán, his son-in-law, or Sándor who often pop into the café. And he's certainly not going to tell Szabó that tonight he plans to accompany his son-in-law to a meeting of the Petőfi Circle, a popular debating group for anti-Rákosi intellectuals. He has no doubt that if Szabó wants to find out these things, he has the means to do so.

Szabó lights a cigarette, inhales deeply, and blows a thin stream of smoke towards the ceiling. 'What radio station does Feri listen to?' He regards Márton with his deep-set eyes.

This is a new question that Szabó hasn't asked before.

'He always plays gypsy music in the café,' says Márton truthfully. Szabó is watching him intently. Márton takes a sip of the bitter coffee to calm his nerves. He's not about to admit to this man that he and Feri often enjoy a glass of Pálinka in the evenings when Feri tunes in his secret radio in the back room and they listen to *Voice of America* or *Radio Free Europe*. Feri still has dreams of one day going to Paris and opening a café there. Márton would like to see Oxford again. It's their dreams that keep these two old friends going.

Next, Colonel Szabó moves on to Márton's reading material. Szabó, who seems to regard himself as something of an intellectual has assigned Márton the collected works of Joseph Stalin, a writer whose contribution to world literature Márton has yet to appreciate. Reading, which used to be one of life's greatest pleasures, has become a dreaded slog. Fortunately, he is a fast reader and possesses a good memory so he is able to spout a few select phrases on the subject of dialectical materialism. Szabó listens attentively, nodding his head from time to time.

The scientist in Márton would like to ask Szabó a simple question. If communism is ethically superior to capitalism, as Marxist philosophers claim, why does it need to be imposed through fear and tyranny? And if the Five Year Plan is the solution to the country's economic problems, why do so many people have so little? But he knows that such questions could put him back in prison. Communism does not tolerate dissent.

He must have said enough in support of Stalin's arguments because Szabó clicks his fingers for the waiter to bring the bill. 'Same time, same place next week,' he says to Márton.

'Yes,' says Márton, getting up to leave.

He hurries out of the Café New York and exhales a sigh of relief that the meeting is over for another week.

*

Tamás Kún scuttles into the hall and sits down at the back. Out of his AVO uniform he feels insignificant and vulnerable, but Vajda has sent him on an undercover mission to infiltrate a secret meeting of radicals. If he wore his uniform everyone else would leave. He fidgets in his seat, watching the room fill with people, mostly young students but some older ones too. There must be a couple of thousand people here at least.

He recalls the first meeting Vajda sent him to, back in May. There were just a few dozen nerdy intellectuals at that meeting. The title of the debate was *The Twentieth Soviet Party Congress and the Problems of the Hungarian Political Economy*. Over the course of the evening it turned into a bitter attack on Rákosi's policies: his economic policies, his agricultural policies and the latest Five Year Plan. Some of the speakers became so hostile that Tamás fled before the end for fear of being recognised and lynched.

Then during June audiences grew to a thousand or more. He infiltrated one meeting where the speakers accused the regime of perverting history and someone dared to criticise the Treaty of Trianon. At another meeting, which largely went over Tamás's head, the main speaker railed against Hungarian Marxism and advocated the study of non-Marxist philosophers such as Plato, Hegel and Schopenhauer. At other gatherings people have been openly hostile to Stalin and Stalinists, debated Hungary's natural resources, proposed the revival of Hungary's musical life, and condemned the inadequate compensation for confiscated property. It makes Tamás's head spin.

He feels like a fish out of water amongst all these intellectuals with their fine language and their high ideals, going on about freedom, humanism – whatever that means – and national independence, for goodness' sake. The Petőfi Circle was nothing much to worry about until Comrade Khrushchev made that ridiculous speech at the start of the year – he must have been off his head on vodka – and now the whole world is jumping on the free speech bandwagon, saying whatever they think. It's starting to get out of hand. Tamás can't understand why the Party doesn't just ban the Petőfi Circle, but Gábor, who seems to understand these things better, says it is all part of a grand plan to let the opposition fully reveal itself so that it can be more effectively destroyed. At the start of July *A Free People* published a Hungarian Central Committee resolution denouncing the Petőfi Circle, and meetings were suspended. But then in the summer Rákosi was replaced with Erno Gerő, and in September the Petőfi Circle meetings resumed, as popular as ever.

The hall is packed now and there is standing room only. From their clothes Tamás can see that many of the people here are factory workers. The influence of the

Petőfi Circle is spreading beyond the intellectuals. As the last few people squeeze into the hall, he feels his stomach lurch. Someone he never expected to see again has just walked in. Márton Bakos. He's older and greyer than when Tamás last saw him, but it's unmistakably him. He's in the company of two younger men, one of whom is wearing a long greatcoat and a beret perched at an angle. Tamás hunches in his seat, keeping his head down. He doesn't want Márton to see him here.

Tamás has no idea what tonight's debate is about – he barely hears a word. At the first opportunity he slips out before anyone recognises him. He'll have to make up tonight's report. He suspects Vajda doesn't read them anyway.

*

'Are you coming to the meeting this afternoon?'

András looks up to see Anna slipping into the seat opposite him in the canteen. She's clutching her leather satchel to her chest and she gives him a smile that lights up her pretty, oval face and her bright blue eyes. He's met her a few times at lectures at the Technical University where they're both studying engineering but hasn't yet plucked up the courage to ask her out. The last time he kissed a girl he found himself arrested and sent to a labour camp on charges of subversion. But he'd like to get to know Anna better. He'd like that very much.

'What's the meeting about?' He usually keeps away from political meetings at the university. The so-called questions are mostly pre-arranged slogans about how wonderful the regime is. After his experience at Recsk, he just tries to keep his head down and get on with his studies. With his record, the ÁVO could come for him again at any time.

'Some students from Szeged are going to be there,' says Anna, tucking a stray blond curl behind her ear. 'They've left the Union of Working Youth and have reinstated the United Organisation of Hungarian University and College Students, or whatever it's called. They should get themselves a snappier name in my opinion. Anyway, they've got some radical ideas they want to present, apparently.'

András digests what she's just told him. 'You mean they've left the *communist* student union and returned to the *democratic* student union banned by Rákosi?' It all sounds highly unlikely.

Anna nods her head, smiling. 'Yes, that's a much more succinct way of putting it. So are you coming? Everyone's going to be there.'

András's curiosity gets the better of him. Or maybe it's more to do with Anna and the attraction she holds for him. 'Go on, then.' And why not, he thinks? If Márton Bakos is brave enough to attend meetings of the Petőfi Circle, it won't hurt to go along to a meeting at the university. Especially if *everyone* is going.

By the time they arrive, the atrium is already packed with students, the air buzzing with the hum of excited voices.

'Normally there's only a few dozen here,' Anna shouts into his ear. 'Or a couple of hundred at the most. This is a fantastic turnout.' She's standing so close to him he can smell the rose scented soap on her skin. He's glad he came even if the meeting turns out to be the usual Party propaganda.

But she's right about the turnout. There must be a couple of thousand here already. All the seats are taken, some students are perched on window ledges, others are standing shoulder to shoulder. It's the sort of crowd an academic lecturer can only dream of. In spite of his earlier scepticism, a thrill of excitement goes through him. Anna could well be right, maybe this is the start of something big. The AVO can't arrest this many people. There has to be safety in such a large crowd.

'Let's try and get to the front,' says Anna. She takes hold of his hand and starts to weave her way through the dense mass of bodies. He does his best to keep up, apologising to everyone he passes for pushing through. His heart is pounding, more from Anna's touch than from being in such a large crowd.

Eventually they reach the front of the podium where the student organisers are hastily discussing last minute points on the agenda. Anna leans close and gives him a quick kiss on the cheek. He wants to kiss her back, but one of the student leaders steps up to the lectern and calls the meeting to order. A hush soon settles on the crowd and the meeting is under way.

Everyone listens with rapt attention to two students from Szeged in the south of Hungary who have come to talk about their decision to leave the party-controlled student union and reinstate the old democratic organisation. Their bravery in taking a stand is warmly applauded and it doesn't take long for the Budapest students to decide to do likewise. For the first time in his life András glimpses the possibility of real change. It just requires enough people to come together and the freedom to voice their opinions.

The student chairing the meeting takes a question from the centre of the floor and everyone falls silent to hear what is being said.

'Why are Soviet troops still occupying Hungary?'

A stunned silence follows the question. Someone has dared to voice the unthinkable. Disbanding a student union and setting up another is one thing, but freeing Hungary of Soviet control? Is that really possible? András can see the habitual suspicion in people's eyes. Is the questioner laying a trap? Are they going to be denounced for demanding that the Soviets leave?

But then a wave of sound starts to build across the hall as voices chant in unison, 'Russians go home! Russians go home!'

András finds himself chanting along with everyone else, caught up in the swell of fervour that is sweeping across the hall. The positive energy generated by the chanting is like a surge of electricity, empowering the crowd. Beside him, Anna chants as loudly as anyone, her pure clear voice ringing out. He's so glad he came now. He wouldn't miss this for the world.

After a few minutes, the chanting gives way to a friendly chaos with everyone talking over everyone else. The chairman does his best to restore order, and then a young man stands up and calls for a demonstration on the streets the next day.

'We should show our sympathy and solidarity with the Polish workers in Poznan who have been brave enough to demonstrate.'

'Yes,' cries a voice from the crowd. 'We must demonstrate. That's the only way the government will listen to us.'

Shouts of agreement fill the hall. The students don't just want talk, they want action.

'But the demonstration has to be about more than just solidarity with Poland,' shouts Anna. 'What do *we* want for our country?'

After that the suggestions come thick and fast: the removal of Soviet troops from Hungary; free elections; a minimum living wage; freedom of the press and the right to free speech; the release of political prisoners; the removal of the giant statue of Stalin from the City Park. The list goes on and on. András's head is spinning trying to take it all in. Can they really just go on a march and ask for these things without some terrible consequences? He desperately wants it to be true.

It's gone midnight by the time the students have agreed on a list of sixteen demands. 'We need volunteers to type these up,' says the student organiser. Anna's hand shoots up and so does András's.

An hour later, when they have typed up dozens of

posters, András suggests that they break into the room housing the Roneo duplicating machine. That way, they'll be able to run off hundreds of copies.

It's the early hours of the morning when he and Anna join dozens of other students distributing the posters all over the city. They stick them to trees, street lights, shop fronts and buildings. The posters set out the students' sixteen demands and call for a mass demonstration tomorrow afternoon. When they've finished András takes Anna in his arms and kisses her properly for the first time. The future is suddenly bright with possibility.

CHAPTER 11

Tuesday, 23 October 1956

'Hurry up and finish your bread,' says Katalin to her son. Two-year-olds can be infuriatingly slow sometimes, especially when you need to leave for work promptly. Lajos looks at her with his big, doleful eyes that have the power to melt her heart. But this morning she needs to be firm with him or she's going to be late and Piroska Benke will mark her file. From her high chair, little Eva bangs her empty bottle and squawks in delight.

'Come on, young lady, let's get you changed,' says Katalin, lifting Eva out of the chair and taking her to the bathroom.

By some miracle – after a whirlwind of eating, dressing, washing and teeth cleaning – they're all ready to leave fifteen minutes later. Zoltán left for work half an hour ago. There's no sign this morning of András. Even her father seems to be having a lie in for once, which will do him good.

She closes the door behind her and takes the children upstairs to Petra's. After a quick handover – she would like to stay and chat but there just isn't time – she hurries down the stairs. József the caretaker is sweeping autumn leaves from the doorway and muttering something about all the litter flying around this morning. Katalin squeezes past him, murmuring a quick 'Good morning.' And then she's off down the street before he has time to reply.

She's hasn't gone far before she realises that she's the only person walking quickly. Usually people are in too much of a hurry to dawdle. There are trams to catch, early morning meetings to attend, queues to join if you want to get the best cuts of meat before the butcher sells out. But today people are huddled around trees and lamp posts and shop fronts, not seeming to care that they're going to be late.

Katalin is torn between wanting to know what's going on and getting to work on time. Can she spare a minute? She approaches a group gathered at a tram stop and peers around heads to see what all the fuss is about. Someone at the front is reading out a list of demands about democratic elections and freedom of speech amongst other things. There's talk of a march this afternoon. Fine sentiments indeed, but she feels uneasy. After what happened to her father she knows you have to be careful what you get mixed up in.

Whatever is going on, it won't last, no matter how much she would like it to. The government will put a stop to it and the consequences for the instigators will be severe. And now she really is going to have to get her skates on if she's not going to be late. The children will be marching around the schoolyard in twenty minutes singing songs in praise of communism.

*

Márton is astonished to find that he's slept in. Usually his demons wake him in the early hours of the morning. He dreams he's heard the ringing of the doorbell, or he's been told to type out his life story for the hundredth time and he's run out of things to write. He's crouching in two inches of water and his wrists are tied to his ankles so that his muscles cramp up. He wakes in a cold sweat of fear so he paces the apartment, unable even to find solace in his beloved books. But last night he slept soundly and he feels so much better for it. He puts it down to Zoltán persuading him to go along to the Petőfi Circle meeting. It's done him good to know there is a real appetite out there for political change, that people are not afraid to stand up and criticise the regime.

The apartment is already empty. His daughter and son-in-law will be at work. András will be at the university, most likely. Feeling in the mood for some company and conversation, Márton dons his hat, picks up his stick and sets off in the direction of Feri's café. It's a crisp autumn day, the sun shining out of a cloudless sky. He'll fortify himself with a coffee and a pastry and then maybe take a little walk. He's doing himself no good sitting at home all the time. Life has to go on.

He doesn't get more than fifty yards down the street when he becomes aware that there are groups of people congregating around lamp posts and trees. There's a buzz in the air, as if something is afoot. A car toots its horn. People laugh and cheer.

What on earth is going on? He joins a group of people clustered around a shop window and tries to see what they are looking at. The window is plastered in sheets of paper covered in typed writing but he's not close enough to read what it says.

'What is this?' he asks the man standing next to him.

'It's the students,' says the man. 'They've printed a list of demands for the government. Sixteen in total. Who'd have believed it?'

Who indeed, thinks Márton, this is quite extraordinary. He needs to get closer and see for himself.

Those at the front make way and he is able to move forward and read the list of points for himself. It's a detailed list and in his excitement he skims the page, picking out the highlights. Amongst other things the students are asking for the immediate evacuation of all Soviet troops, a new government under the direction of Imre Nagy, free and secret elections, a reorganisation of the economy, a minimum living wage, a review of all political trials, freedom of the press, the removal of Stalin's statue and the replacement of foreign emblems with the old Hungarian arms of Kossuth.

Márton can hardly take it all in but his scientific mind immediately starts to analyse the situation. The students' demands are extensive and radical. They would require a complete overhaul of Hungarian life and politics. This is revolutionary talk. How he wishes he was still a student and could have taken part in the debate that led to this extraordinary document. The eternal optimism of the young to change the world!

He moves away from the window so that others can take their turn. Feeling energised by what he has read he walks with a brisker step to Feri's.

Feri is doing a lively trade this morning. 'What can I get you, *mon ami?*' He beams at Márton from behind the counter.

'A coffee please, and I think I'll have one of your almond tarts.'

'I take it you have heard the news?' asks Feri, pouring a pot of coffee.

'I read one of the posters on my way here. Quite extraordinary.'

'Indeed.' Feri places an extra large slice of almond tart onto a plate. 'And this afternoon there is to be a march.'

'A demonstration? Will the authorities allow that?'

'Just let them try and stop us,' says a familiar voice behind Márton. He turns to see András in the company of a pretty female student with blonde hair and bright blue eyes. 'There are no lectures today. All the students will be out marching.' The girl nods her head, her smile lighting up her whole face.

'I will close the café this afternoon,' says Feri. 'I don't want to miss something like this.'

'Then I'll join you,' says Márton, taking a bite of his almond tart. He feels years younger already.

*

Not a lot of work is being done at the factory today. Everyone is too distracted by the posters they picked up on their way into work this morning. Even Csaba Elek's reading from *A Free People* was less self-assured than usual and the applause less enthusiastic, petering out after just a minute or two. Sándor dared to yawn and look at his watch as if he was bored.

As a result of all this distraction, productivity levels, which have never been as high as the management likes to claim, plummet to a new all-time low. They definitely won't hit their unachievable targets for the month, but they wouldn't have done anyway. So much for the Five Year Plan. Csaba Elek must be having palpitations, thinks Zoltán with glee.

Instead of focusing on their work, the employees are all talking about the students' sixteen demands, especially the one about earning a living wage. They're all struggling to feed and clothe their families on the pittance they earn. One brave soul has pinned one of the posters to the factory noticeboard, obscuring a schedule of committee meetings and Party directives, thereby risking the wrath of the Party Secretary. But nobody cares anymore what Csaba Elek thinks. There's talk of walking out early so they can join the march and lend their support to the students.

'Are you up for it?' asks Sándor, his eyes alight with excitement.

'You bet I am,' grins Zoltán. 'This could be it – the start of the revolution.'

*

'Hush, everyone. Listen.' Feri turns up the volume on the radio behind the counter. Márton pauses in the conversation he is having with András to listen to the announcement.

In the interests of public order, The Ministry of the Interior has banned all public gatherings in Budapest until further notice.

A storm of protest amongst the café's clientele drowns out the broadcaster's next words.

'They can't do that,' says András. 'The march has to go ahead.'

Márton admires the boy's spirit, how much he's grown in confidence since those days at Recsk. Anna seems to have worked wonders on him. 'They are probably too late to stop the demonstration now anyway.'

'Then we still go?' asks Feri.

'Why not?' says Márton.

'Then we shall all have another slice of cake, on the house,' says Feri. 'We must keep our strength up for the long walk ahead.'

A further announcement on the radio an hour later informs them that the demonstration will be allowed to proceed after all. A cheer goes up and everyone prepares to leave.

Márton, Feri, András and Anna join the crowds gathered around the statue of the poet Petőfi overlooking the Danube. There must be thousands of people here, and not an AVO officer in sight. Some people are carrying small posies of white flowers as a sign of peace. The Hungarian people have seen enough bloodshed in their history. This is to be a peaceful demonstration.

Márton feels tears spring to his eyes as a young actor from the Budapest National Theatre reads aloud Petőfi's poem.

Arise Hungarians.
Magyars, rise, your country calls you!
…

And then they're off, walking along the banks of the Danube, the crowd swelling with every passing minute. Márton and Feri link arms, two old friends who've survived both world wars and who just want their country to be free. András and Anna are holding hands, two young people radiant with the glow of love and the excitement of the demonstration which they have helped to bring about. They all join their voices with those of their fellow citizens. They proclaim their solidarity with the brave Polish people who have led the way in standing up to their Soviet oppressors. They demand the right to self-determination.

As the crowd moves across Margaret Bridge towards Buda there are shouts for Erno Gerő – architect of the Five Year Plan which was supposed to transform the Hungarian economy, and now leader of the Party – to be thrown into the Danube. People wave Hungarian flags with a gaping hole in the middle where the Soviet star has been cut out. There are cries of *Russians go home!*

Onward they march until they arrive at the statue of General Bem, the national hero of Poland and Hungary, in Bem Square, joining forces with another large crowd from the Technological University in Buda. Márton hasn't walked so far in years, but instead of feeling exhausted – like he did when he had to carry rocks down the mountainside at Recsk – he feels reinvigorated. The hope of the crowd has infected him and given his ageing body new life. His dear friend Feri is fired up with optimism. If only Béla were here to witness this, how he would have loved it.

At the statue of General Bem the students' sixteen demands are read out once more and then there are calls for the demonstrators to go to Parliament Square. Márton will keep going as long as he has breath in his lungs and blood in his veins.

*

When school is over for the day, Tibor and his best friend Géza have no intention of just going home. How could they? The city is alive and no one is afraid anymore, especially not a pair of fourteen-year-old boys, going on fifteen, as they like to remind everyone.

They explore the streets, enjoying the spectacle. They can't remember the last time they had so much fun. They join a crowd watching in awe as a firefighter climbs an extra-long ladder to remove the five-pointed Russian star from the top of a public building. Coming across a Russian bookshop that specialises in the writings of Stalin, Lenin and Marx, they find the windows smashed and the shelves bare. The books have been piled high in the street and set alight in a gigantic bonfire. Hundreds of thousands of words of communist propaganda and rhetoric are turning to ash and blowing away in the wind.

Moving on, they find themselves caught up in a groundswell of people heading towards the City Park. There is talk of toppling Stalin's giant statue.

'We've got to see this,' says Tibor, his eyes wide. His mum will no doubt give him an earful for being late home, but she'll understand when he tells her where he's been. He wants to do something that will make her proud and prove that he's not a child anymore.

'You bet,' says Géza, playfully punching him on the arm.

The crowd heading towards the park is so huge that people are walking in the road, blocking a convoy of trucks from getting through.

The driver of the front truck leans out of his cab. 'Hey, what's the big deal? Where's everyone going?'

'To the statue,' shouts Tibor. 'We're going to pull it

down.'

The truck driver pulls a face at Tibor and Géza. 'Are you kidding?'

'Absolutely not,' says Tibor.

The driver considers his response then seems to come to a decision. 'All right then, hop in the back. I'm going that way.'

People crowd into the backs of the trucks and the drivers take them to the City Park.

A huge crowd has already gathered around the giant bronze statue of Stalin. But they have not come here to pay their respects, like they did on the day that Stalin's death was announced. They have come here to destroy this icon of communist power and oppression. There's just one problem – the statue is enormous. Even climbing up it would require a feat of superhuman strength and agility, never mind pulling it down.

The driver who gave Tibor and Géza a lift introduces himself as Péter. 'I have some steel cables in my truck,' he says. 'The problem will be getting up to the statue to attach them.'

'I've got some rope,' says another truck driver. 'We could throw a rope lasso around the neck and climb up that way.'

'I'm good at climbing,' volunteers Tibor. He expects the adults there to dismiss his offer, but no one does. They're serious about bringing this statue down and they'll take all the help they can get.

It takes a whole team of them using ladders and standing on shoulders, but they eventually manage to secure a rope round Stalin's neck. The spectators cheer.

'Think you can manage to get this steel cable up there?' Péter asks Tibor.

'Sure,' says Tibor. When he was little he dreamt of flying around Stalin's statue, one arm outstretched, like the images of his hero Superman in the comics which his mum told him to keep hidden. He might not be able to fly, but it's still a dream come true to climb the statue as if it were a mountain waiting to be conquered. Stalin used to be the one with all the superpowers, but now he's just a grotesque lump of metal.

Tibor loops the steel cable around his shoulder and climbs one of the ladders to the top of Stalin's six-foot-high right boot. At the top of the ladder he reaches for the length of rope and secures it around his middle. Then, grasping the rope in both hands, he puts one foot against Stalin's leg and starts to hoist himself upwards. He's young and strong and it feels fantastic to be doing something so daring. When he reaches Stalin's right arm, which is folded across his chest, he levers himself up so that he's standing on the dictator's forearm. Don't look down, he tells himself. You can do this. Just a bit further and he's standing on Stalin's shoulder. He loops the steel cable around the massive neck, then makes his way back down to the cheers of the crowd.

Géza slaps him on the back. 'You did it.'

Only when Tibor looks back up at the statue and realises how far he climbed does he start to laugh. When more cables have been looped around the statue, the ends of the cables are tied to the backs of the trucks.

'Everyone stand back,' shouts Péter.

The truck drivers climb into their cabs and, on the count of three, they all press their accelerator pedals. Exhaust fumes belch, wheels spin and rubber tyres burn, but the statue doesn't budge.

'We need more weight,' shouts one of the drivers. 'Everyone get in the trucks.'

Tibor, Géza and dozens of other people scramble on board to provide human ballast. But still nothing happens.

And then the cables start to snap one by one.

'It's not working,' cries Tibor in frustration. He feels as if the statue is mocking them. They're like ants trying to bring down a mighty oak tree. There has to be another way.

Then some factory workers arrive in a van and they've brought bottles of gas and blowtorches with them. Right, thinks Tibor, now we're talking. He stands back as the workers set about blasting Stalin's knees, just above the top of his boots. Sparks fly as the intense blue flame cuts into the bronze.

'That should do it,' shouts one of the workers. 'Now get the trucks again.'

This time when the truck drivers hit the accelerator pedals, they actually start to move forwards.

'It's coming down! It's coming down!' shouts Tibor.

And sure enough, there's a creaking and cracking sound and the giant statue totters on the brink.

'Run!' shouts Tibor.

Everyone scatters in different directions, laughing and cheering, as the giant figure falls to the ground in a great crash. The crowd roars in delight.

Tibor wipes the sweat from his brow and leans forwards, his hands on his knees. They did it. They actually did it. The mighty god has been toppled. He looks up at the stone plinth where a pair of empty bronze boots still stand. Their owner will never wear them again.

*

'Where do you think you're going?'

Zoltán and Sándor turn to face Csaba Elek who is trotting down the corridor after them, looking flustered. He can't be having a good day, thinks Zoltán.

'Haven't you heard? There's a revolution going on,' says Zoltán. He almost feels sorry for the Party Secretary whose world is crumbling before his eyes.

'But the working day is not yet over,' protests Csaba Elek, making a point of looking at his watch.

'Dear me, how inconsiderate of the revolutionaries not to wait until the end of the factory shift,' says Sándor.

'Your absence from work will be noted in your file and

reported to the authorities.'

'I tell you what,' says Zoltán, his moment of sympathy rapidly running out, 'why don't you take my file and stick it up your arse?' He gives the stunned secretary a playful slap on the cheek, then turns and walks out of the factory followed by Sándor.

'That was brave,' says Sándor when they're outside.

'He's had it coming a long time,' says Zoltán.

They catch a tram back to the centre of Budapest where they find the city in uproar. People are out on the streets in their thousands, Soviet stars are being pulled off the top of public buildings, shops are daubed with the slogan *Russians go home!* It's better than Zoltán could have imagined.

'Where to?' asks Sándor.

A group of students walk past shouting that they're going to the radio station to get their demands broadcast to the nation.

'Shall we?' asks Zoltán.

'Why not?' says Sándor.

*

Márton and his companions walk with the crowds heading back across the river to Pest. It's dusk by the time the thousands of demonstrators are gathered in Parliament Square gazing up at the ornate, Gothic building that houses their government. Márton can only guess at the political turmoil that must be going on inside that building right now. Gerő could never have anticipated something like this when he let the march go ahead. If the man's got any sense he'll resign before the mob comes for him.

The crowd wants Imre Nagy as the country's leader. They chant his name, calling for him to be reinstated. He's still a communist, of course, but at least he's a moderate. Someone who will listen to reason.

The crowd is swelling all the time as more and more

people pack into the square, the mass of bodies offering some protection against the chill night air. They chant, they sing, and they wait. They'll wait all night if they have to. No one shows any inclination to go home.

But it seems that the Party has other ideas.

Suddenly all the lights are turned off and the square is plunged into darkness. The singing and the chanting turns into boos and jeers.

'They're trying to make us leave,' shouts a voice.

'We won't leave,' shouts another.

'Don't go.'

'Stay where you are.'

'Everyone keep calm.'

And then a beautiful thing happens. A man standing in front of Márton rolls up the newspaper he has been carrying, takes a cigarette lighter from his pocket and lights the edge of the paper, holding the makeshift torch high above his head. One by one more people follow suit, setting light to newspapers and leaflets, whatever they have to hand. Márton and Feri both light their copies of the students' sixteen demands. Within a minute the square is filled with a sea of flickering lights and Márton looks around in wonder. It's a sight to bring a tear to his eye. The singing and the chanting resumes, as fervent as ever.

After a few minutes, the street lights in the square are turned back on. The politicians have obviously got the message that this crowd isn't going anywhere. A shout of triumph goes up. It's a small victory against the bullying tactics of the Party, but it's a victory all the same. The shouts for Imre Nagy intensify.

Eventually, the man himself appears on the balcony, his chubby features and round, wire-rimmed spectacles making him look like an overgrown schoolboy. He blinks at the crowd as if he can't quite believe what he is seeing and hearing. He holds up a hand and the crowd falls silent. This is the moment they have been waiting for.

'Comrades,' begins their would-be leader.

Márton's heart sinks. Nagy has made a tactical error. The crowd groans and jeers. The language of Soviet socialism has no place in the new Hungary. Words like *comrade* and *collectivisation* have become poisoned by association.

'We are not comrades!' the crowd yells back, asserting its right to individual choice.

Nagy holds up a hand, acknowledging his mistake, and tries again. 'Young Hungarians, with your enthusiasm you will pave the way for democratic socialism...'

That's more like it, thinks Márton. Nagy is clearly someone who is able to adapt to a changing situation, and that is what this country needs right now.

Nagy keeps his speech short but it seems to satisfy the crowd which breaks out into a spontaneous rendition of the Hungarian National Anthem.

'Glad you came?' asks Feri when the singing dies down.

'I wouldn't have missed this for the world,' says Márton.

*

By the time Zoltán and Sándor arrive at the radio station, the narrow cobbled streets are already thronged with thousands of people. Zoltán has never seen anything like it. The energy, excitement and determination of the crowd is contagious. He's dreamt of participating in something like this for years. And now it's finally happening.

'Come on,' he says to Sándor. 'We have to get closer.'

They weave their way through the crowds until they are within sight of the main building: an ornate four-storey house with cherubs on the roof, a balcony above a wide portico and a huge oak front door. Nearby are various studios and storage depots. Armed AVO officers are standing guard outside the main building, looking wary, but not pointing their weapons at anyone. The demonstrators are simply calling for a microphone so they can broadcast their demands over the airwaves. Zoltán and Sándor join their voices to the rest.

The figure of a woman appears behind a net curtain at a first-floor window.

'That's the director of Budapest Radio,' someone shouts. 'She's the one who has the power to let us have a microphone or not.'

'We'll stay here until she gives us one.'

Spurred on by the appearance of the radio director, the crowd keeps chanting. After another ten or fifteen minutes there are shouts of 'Stand back!' and 'Make way!'

The crowd parts to let through a radio van which has been dispatched from one of the depots.

This is it, thinks Zoltán. The demands of the crowd are actually going to be met. If it was that easy, why didn't they demand something like this sooner? But he knows why. Because they've been living in fear, and not without reason. But not anymore.

A hush falls on the crowd. From an open window on the opposite side of the street, strains of gypsy violin music drift across the air.

A female radio announcer climbs onto the roof of the van and informs the crowd through a loud hailer that the director of Budapest Radio has agreed to broadcast the students' demands. She holds up one of the typed posters listing the sixteen points as if to prove the director's good faith. A cheer goes up from the crowd and then there are calls for silence. The broadcast is about to begin. One of the technical crew passes her a microphone and gives her a signal. She clears her throat and begins to read aloud.

'We demand the immediate evacuation of all Soviet troops...'

The woman is reading out the third or fourth demand when a murmur of discontent arises in the crowd.

'This is a hoax!' shouts an angry voice, interrupting the announcer mid-sentence.

Caught off guard, she pauses and scans the crowd,

looking for the source of the interruption. Zoltán sees indignation, but also fear in her eyes.

'They're not broadcasting,' shouts the same angry voice. 'Listen.' The violin music coming from the open window across the street has changed to that of an accordion. 'They're still broadcasting gypsy music. She's not broadcasting our demands.'

How quickly the mood of the crowd changes. Hope turns to anger. Joy turns to fury.

'Liar!'

'Cheat!'

Zoltán feels a crushing sense of disappointment. Why couldn't the radio director have done what she said she was going to to do? Did she really think she could fool this crowd with a hoax and everyone would be happy and go home to bed? Is she really that stupid?

'Bastards!' shouts Sándor, his fist in the air.

The female announcer drops the microphone and jumps down from the van as angry protesters swarm forward. Zoltán is shoved out of the way as two students drag the driver from his seat. One of the students climbs into the van and starts the ignition. Everyone jumps back as he revs the engine and then reverses at high speed into the big oak doors of the radio building.

The armed AVO officers are no longer simply observing the crowd, they are holding their Kalashnikovs at the ready. This is going to turn nasty very quickly.

'Are you going to shoot your fellow Hungarians?' shout the protesters nearest the AVO. 'Shame on you!'

The student who has commandeered the van drives forward a few feet, then once again reverses into the door but the old oak holds fast.

Something whizzes past Zoltán's ear and he realises that people are throwing stones at the windows of the radio building. Glass shatters.

'What the…' Sándor ducks down and brings his hand to the back of his head. His palm comes away bloody.

Someone with a lousy aim has accidentally caught him on the back of the head.

'We should go,' says Zoltán. He doesn't like the look of those AVO men who are getting jumpy, itching to fire into the crowd.

'Not bloody likely!'

'But you're hurt.' Concussion most likely, thinks Zoltán. Róza would know.

'I'm fine. This is the only way they'll listen.' Sándor picks up the stone that hit him and lobs it at the building, shattering a window on the second floor.

What the hell, thinks Zoltán. He too picks up a stone and throws it. He's angry at the way things have turned out. But what revolution in history was ever entirely peaceful?

He bends down to look for another stone and sees a canister rolling towards him along the cobbles. Suddenly he can't see a thing. A cloud of acrid smoke pours from the canister, making his eyes water and sting. He stumbles backwards, choking on the noxious fumes. He hears shouts of 'Tear gas!' and 'AVO inside the building!'

Panic starts to rise up inside him. He mustn't lose Sándor who needs medical assistance, whatever he might say. But he can't see a damn thing and he can barely breathe. He doubles over, coughing and trying, in vain, to spit out the foul taste that is filling his mouth and burning his throat. In their haste to run away, people crash into him. He loses his balance and falls to the ground. He struggles back to his feet but immediately yelps in shock as a jet of freezing cold water hits him full on, soaking him to the skin.

The AVO are spraying jets of water from the upper storey windows of the radio building in an effort to disperse the crowds. But at least the water is clearing the poisoned air.

The crack of gunfire echoes around the narrow street. Fuck, thinks Zoltán, first the tear gas, then the water jets and now they're shooting us.

A girl, no more than sixteen or seventeen, staggers towards him, her clothes sodden, her wet hair plastered to her head. Her eyes are wide with fear. Instinctively Zoltán reaches out a hand to her. She shouldn't be here in this chaos. She should be at home with her family. He'll offer to escort her home, make sure she gets there safely.

He calls to her and their eyes meet. A burst of machine-gun fire. Her body goes rigid, her head flies backwards and she crumples to the ground. A crimson stain spreads across her chest.

'No!' shouts Zoltán. He drops to his knees beside her and presses his hands to the wound in a vain effort to stop the bleeding. Her blood washes over his hands, staining the sleeves and front of his coat. 'Hold on,' he shouts. 'An ambulance will be here soon.' He has no idea if it's true. The battle is raging around him but he no longer sees or hears anything.

The girl looks at him as if she wants to say something, and then her eyes close and her head flops to the side. The rise and fall of her chest ceases. Zoltán can't believe that she's just died and he doesn't even know her name.

A hand on his shoulder spins him round. It's Sándor. 'Hungarian soldiers from the barracks are on our side and they're handing out weapons to anyone who wants one. We have to arm ourselves.' He points in the direction of a Hungarian army truck surrounded by scores of outstretched hands, eagerly grabbing hold of rifles and submachine guns.

'Arm ourselves?' Zoltán is incredulous. 'A weapon did *this!*' He points at the body of the dead girl.

'I know,' says Sándor. 'Which is why we have to fight back. Come on.'

Sándor pulls him away and together they stumble over falling bodies, slipping on the wet cobblestones. Armed protesters surge past on their way to fight the AVO. Sándor grabs two rifles from a soldier who's handing them out like lollipops and passes one to Zoltán.

'I'm going home,' says Zoltán. He can't get the image of the dead girl out of his mind.

*

'I swear to God I will give that boy such a hiding when he comes home, he won't know what's hit him.' Petra is standing at the window in Katalin's apartment watching the street, worry etched on her face.

Katalin hugs Eva to her. Lajos has his arms around her leg, sensing that something is not right with the world. At least her children are too young to get caught up in what's going on today. But Tibor is fourteen – nearly fifteen she reminds herself – and Katalin can't say she's surprised that he didn't come straight home after school today. What teenage boy hasn't dreamt of being a hero?

'I'm sure he's fine,' she says, trying to reassure Petra. 'He's a smart boy. He won't do anything silly.'

'I wouldn't be so sure,' says Petra, pulling a face. They both know Tibor has a mind of his own and is prone to wild ideas.

But Katalin has her own worries too. Márton and Zoltán have also not yet returned home. She went to look for them at Feri's but found the café closed, its shutters drawn. It's dark outside now, but still the streets are alive with protesters. The distant sound of gunfire makes them both jump. It sounds as if things are getting violent.

Then Petra lets out a cry of relief. 'It's Tibor. I can see him!'

'I told you he'd be fine,' says Katalin, pleased for her friend. The happiness is written all over Petra's face, but by the time she steps onto the landing to intercept her son on his way up the stairs she has resumed the role of stern matriarch. Katalin watches from the doorway. She's curious to hear what Tibor has been up to.

Tibor runs up the stairs two at a time but stops short

when he sees Petra standing at the top, arms akimbo, glaring at him.

'And where the hell do you think you've been, young man?'

'Aw, Mum, it was amazing. We went to the statue and some men gave us a lift in their trucks and I climbed Stalin's statue and then some men got their blowtorches out and we pulled the statue down and smashed it to pieces on the ground and...'

'Enough! Upstairs now! I've been worried sick about you.'

'You didn't have to worry, Mum, I was fine. And you should have seen...'

'I said upstairs!'

Katalin catches Tibor's eye as he follows his mother up to the top floor. He has the grace to look sheepish and she gives him an encouraging smile. Petra will soon calm down now that he's back safe and sound. The question is whether she can keep him safe.

Katalin is about to close the door when she hears voices and footsteps on the stairs. It's her father and András. Thank God they're home safe.

'Papa. I've been so worried about you,' she says as the two men reach the landing. She realises she sounds just like Petra scolding her son. She ushers them into the apartment and closes the door. 'You didn't go on the march, did you?'

'We most certainly did,' says her father, taking off his coat and hanging it up. 'Tell her András, she won't believe me.'

András nods enthusiastically. 'We walked with the protesters all the way to Bem Square in Buda and then back to Parliament Square where we heard Imre Nagy make a speech.'

'Goodness,' says Katalin. She would never have thought her father had the physical strength for such a trek, not since his return from the camp. But in fact, now she looks at him more closely, he looks better than she's seen him in ages. More alive. As if he's found a new purpose to live. He scoops little Eva into his arms and gives her a kiss.

'There's some bread and salami in the kitchen,' she says. 'Help yourselves whilst I put the children to bed, and then you can tell me all about it.' Zoltán is still not back and she prays to God that he'll be home soon. Its her duty to keep her family safe, just as Petra's job is to keep Tibor safe. She puts the children to bed – they've stayed up much later than normal today – and joins her father and András in the kitchen where they are demolishing the food she left out.

Between mouthfuls they tell her about the march and the demonstration in Parliament Square.

'They're calling it a revolution,' says Márton.

'Do you think this really is the start of change?' Katalin hardly dares hope, after all these years.

'I think it could be.' He takes her hand and gives it a squeeze.

The apartment door crashes open and she runs into the hallway. Zoltán and Sándor are standing there soaking wet and covered in grime. The side of Sándor's face is streaked with blood and there are blood stains on Zoltán's coat. They are both carrying rifles. Where the hell did they get those from?

'Oh my God!' If Tibor had come home in this state – and carrying a weapon! – then Petra would have had something to worry about. 'Whatever happened to you two?' She rushes into her husband's arms and hugs him tight.

'Things turned nasty at the radio station,' says Zoltán. 'Can you help Sándor? He's been hurt.'

'Get out of these wet clothes,' says Katalin. 'Then come into the kitchen.'

Ten minutes later she is washing the congealed blood out of Sándor's hair with a cloth and a bowl of warm water.

'You should get a doctor to take a look at that,' she says.

'I'll be fine,' insists Sándor. 'It's just a cut from a stone. There were others with far worse injuries than this.'

Katalin looks at Zoltán, but he's staring into the middle distance with a glazed look on his face. She wonders what he saw at the radio station that is haunting him so.

'Sit still and let me put a bandage on you,' she says to Sándor.

She finds a length of gauze bandage in the first aid box and wraps it inexpertly around his head, fixing it in place with a safety pin. Róza would know how to do this sort of thing properly, but if what Sándor says is true, Róza will be dealing with worse cases at the hospital right now.

When Sándor is bandaged up, Katalin pours everyone a glass of Pálinka which they've had in the cupboard for years and hardly ever touch. It's been such a momentous day that it seems to call for something a little stronger than coffee.

As the smooth, sweet liquid hits her throat, she says a silent prayer of thanks that everyone is home safe. But what the next few days will bring, nobody knows.

CHAPTER 12

Wednesday, 24 October 1956

Katalin stirs at the sound of distant rumbling, like thunder. It's still dark outside and the children are both fast asleep. She doesn't want to get up yet. Last night, they fell into bed late, having drunk more of the Pálinka than they'd intended. Sándor went to sleep on the sofa in the living room. She rolls over, wanting to snuggle up close to Zoltán, to breathe in his scent and feel safe in his arms. But his side of the bed is empty.

Now she's properly awake and she sits up, whispering his name in the dark. There's no reply.

The rumbling is getting louder and she doesn't think it can be thunder after all. Thunder comes in short bursts, but this sound is continuous. Suddenly she knows. She's heard that sound before, during the war. She sees herself as a little girl, watching the arrival of the Red Army and her mother telling her it's going to be all right. But of course, it wasn't all right. And now she's a mother herself with a family to care for. And the tanks are returning to the streets of Budapest.

She slips out of bed and pulls on a dressing gown. In

the living room Márton, Zoltán, Sándor and András are huddled around the radio, their faces drawn. The clock on the mantelpiece says it's half past four.

Counter-revolutionary, fascist and reactionary elements have attacked our public buildings and AVO organisation in an attempt to overturn the forces of law and order. To restore law and order, all meetings, assemblies and demonstrations are forbidden. The AVO organisation will enforce the law rigorously. This is an announcement of the Hungarian People's Advisory Board.

'We're not fascists!' cries Sándor. 'How dare they make those accusations!' His bandage has slipped off overnight, exposing a patch of dried blood on his hair.

Soviet soldiers are risking their lives to protect the citizens of Budapest and the whole nation. Welcome our Soviet friends and allies!

Márton turns off the radio with a shake of his head and a look of indescribable disappointment in his eyes.

'The authorities are lying,' says Zoltán. 'The Russians aren't here to protect us. They're here to destroy the revolution.'

'But...' Katalin has so many questions she doesn't know where to start. *What can you do about it? Where's this all going to end? What's going to happen to me and the children if you are killed fighting?*

'We have to stand up to the Russians,' says Sándor. 'And this time we're going to win.'

A look passes between the three younger men as if they've already decided on their course of action.

'What are you going to do?' asks Katalin. Her mouth is dry and there's a tight knot of fear in the pit of her stomach.

Zoltán takes her hands in his. 'What started yesterday is the beginning of real change. But we shouldn't have expected it to be so easy. It's going to take more than just a march and toppling a statue. We can't give up now.'

She nods her head, unable to speak. She wants to tell Zoltán to stay at home, let other people risk their lives fighting for freedom, but every mother and wife in the city will be thinking the same thing. And then where would they be? Back to square one.

He strokes her hair. 'Stay here with your father and the children. I'm doing this for us and for our children's future.' He kisses her on the lips. 'I love you.'

'I love you, too.'

*

Armed with the rifles they acquired at the radio station the previous evening, Zoltán and Sándor set off in search of a group they can join. On the grand sweep of Erzsébet Boulevard, signs of yesterday's demonstration are everywhere. The elegant nineteenth-century façades are daubed in red paint with the words *Russians Out!* The charred remains of bonfires to burn Soviet books smoulder in the breeze. Hungarian flags with the Soviet star cut out of the centre flutter from windows. But the mood of joyous liberation has been replaced with a palpable sense of fear and expectation. Pockets of armed men and women cluster on street corners, preparing to defend their city to the death.

'Soviet tanks coming!' A cry goes up that the enemy is on its way. In fact Zoltán can feel their approach in the vibrations of the cobbles under his feet, although he can't yet see them.

'Over here,' shouts Sándor, grabbing Zoltán's arm and pulling him into the porticoed entrance of a building. All around them, armed civilians take cover in doorways and behind trees, holding their weapons at the ready. Zoltán hears a click as Sándor releases the safety catch on his rifle. Across the street, upstairs windows are flung open and youngsters lean out holding bottles with rags hanging out of the tops.

They are getting closer now, their caterpillar tracks making a racket on the cobblestones, setting every fibre of Zoltán's being vibrating. He peers out from their hiding place and sees a convoy of three Russian tanks rounding the bend in the boulevard. They are coming straight down the middle of the road, big, ugly and faceless, their guns swivelling left and right, ready to fire.

Suddenly all hell breaks out as those in the upstairs windows lob their lighted bottles of petrol at the tanks and those on the ground fire their weapons. Exploding Molotov cocktails quickly engulf the tanks in balls of flame, but the Russians are not defeated yet. The front tank aims its gun at the building where Zoltán and Sándor are taking cover.

'Run!' yells Zoltán.

The two friends sprint down the street just as an explosion behind them blows the front off the building. A shower of masonry and glass crashes to the ground, missing them by inches.

'Bloody hell,' says Sándor once they're clear of the danger zone. 'That was close.'

Zoltán doesn't have words to describe what he's just experienced. When he turns and looks back up the road, he sees bodies lying where once civilians stood. The only consolation is that the tanks are now blazing infernos and the Russians inside will never fire on Hungarians again.

As they continue on down the road, it becomes clear to him that if they are going to have any chance of succeeding against the Russians, they need to organise themselves into strong fighting units with a strategy. They can't simply wander the streets in twos and threes, hoping to pick off a Red Army tank here and there.

At the junction between József Boulevard and Üllői Avenue an armoured vehicle is driving cautiously. Hungarians hiding in doorways open fire on the vehicle on top of which is mounted a machine gun. The vehicle skids to a halt as its tyres burst and the driver slumps in his seat, blood running from a bullet wound to his temple. One of the freedom fighters runs from a doorway and tosses a bottle at the stranded vehicle. Zoltán smells petrol fumes at once. Everyone holds their breath, waiting for something to happen. Two other Russians inside the vehicle must know that if they so much as try to escape, someone will shoot them dead.

Then an old man totters out from behind one of the large advertising cylinders that line the pavement. He's wearing an old coat that reaches almost to his ankles. With shuffling steps he approaches the petrol-doused vehicle, takes a box of matches from his coat pocket and strikes a flame. Quite calmly, he tosses the lit match into the petrol which ignites in an instant, sending up a wall of flame around the vehicle and its doomed occupants. The old man turns and walks calmly back to the advertising cylinder as the crowd erupts with shouts of 'Long live freedom!' and 'Russians go home!'

The Russians flee from their burning vehicle and a hail of gunfire finishes them off.

'Save the machine gun!' shouts a man's voice. The Russians are dead but the machine gun is valuable. They shouldn't let it go to waste.

People run towards the burning vehicle, trying to put the fire out with their coats. It's a dangerous thing to do.

'Get the sand!' shouts Zoltán, pointing to the large boxes of sand used to grit the icy roads in the winter.

Leading the way, he takes off his trench coat which is still damp and blood-stained from the night before and uses it like a sack to scoop up armfuls of sand. Others follow his example and do likewise. Soon the flames are doused and the prized machine gun is lifted from the roof of the burnt-out vehicle. They also find ten submachine guns, a couple of pistols and boxes of ammunition. A small treasure trove of weaponry which they can use in the fight.

'Good idea about the sand,' says the man who first shouted that they should save the machine gun. He holds out a hand. 'The name's Bandi.'

Zoltán shakes his hand and introduces himself and Sándor.

'Come and join our group,' says Bandi. 'We need people like you.'

*

András can't help feeling as if he's partially to blame for the violence that has broken out across the city. He was part of the student meeting that organised the march, he helped type up the posters and he roamed the streets late at night, sticking them on trees and lamp posts, encouraging his fellow citizens to rise up against the government. And now look what has happened. When Zoltán and Sándor came home last night covered in blood, he felt sick to the pit of his stomach. He doesn't want anything bad to happen to his new friends. He doesn't want to lose them the way he lost people at Recsk – Horváth crushed by the rock, or Béla shot by the guard. He pours his heart out to Anna when they meet that morning at the university.

'It's normal to feel the way you're feeling,' she says, taking his hand in hers and stroking the side of his face. 'I wouldn't love you if you didn't feel like this.'

'But I don't think I can kill anyone,' says András, wondering what sort of a freedom fighter that makes him. On the other side of the hall student volunteers are arming themselves with weapons from a nearby barracks. The mood amongst them is ebullient and defiant. 'If that's what it's going to take to make the revolution successful, then I'm useless here.'

'You're not useless. I feel exactly the same way as you about using a gun. But there's something else we can do.

They're setting up a first aid centre at the Práter Street School near the Corvin cinema. They need people to look after the wounded and also cook food for the freedom fighters. I've said I'll help out. Will you come with me?'

'Of course,' says András, relieved that there's something useful he can do. But mostly he's just happy to be with Anna and know that she's all right. He'll do anything to keep her safe.

*

Everything that Ilona Novák has worked so hard to achieve is going to be destroyed: their nice house; their comfortable life; their good standing with the Party; her husband's job as a university professor. She's afraid, and who can blame her?

Woken at dawn by the thunder of Russian tanks entering the city, she and her husband, Károly, listened to the radio broadcasts with a growing sense of dread. Talk of counter-revolutionaries and a breakdown in law and order frightens Ilona. She's always found that the best way to get on in this society is to co-operate with those in power. It makes for an easier life. But now it seems as if everyone else in Budapest is hell-bent on causing as much trouble as possible. If there's one thing Ilona knows, it's that it won't end well.

'We have to leave,' she tells her husband who has been sunk in despair since the student-led protest yesterday. 'We should get out of Budapest, at least for the time being. Things will calm down in a few days now that the Russians are here.' She has an unwavering faith in the ability of the Russians to put things right. They defeated the Nazis in the war. Surely they can stamp out a local skirmish?

'But where would we go?' asks her husband.

'We could go to my sister's in Magyaróvár.' They haven't spoken for months – not since their father's funeral – but surely her sister will understand this is an emergency?

'If you think that's for the best, dear,' says Károly wearily.

'I do.'

They spend the next half hour packing suitcases. Should she take her fur coat? It's only October now. Surely they won't be gone that long. They'll be back home before the winter snows come.

They load the luggage into the car and set off.

'We'll have to fill up,' says Károly before they've reached the end of the road. 'The tank's nearly empty.'

Ilona wants to scream in frustration. Her husband should have foreseen a situation like this and kept the tank full as a precaution.

They turn onto the main road but their progress is painfully slow due to the large number of armed insurgents – Ilona refuses to call them freedom fighters – roaming the streets, dozens of burnt-out vehicles and an abandoned tank. At the first petrol station they come to, she is astonished to see that the pumps are being guarded by teenagers carrying weapons.

'This is disgraceful,' she mutters. 'They should be in school. Where are their mothers?'

When Károly stops to ask if he can fill up his car, a spotty youth, who can't be more than thirteen years old, tells him that the fuel is to be used for Molotov cocktails only. The same thing happens at the next petrol station they try. Ilona is becoming increasingly anxious. She's not used to not getting her own way.

At Móricz Zsigmond Square they are forced to turn around because the square is barricaded by a roadblock made from cobblestones ripped from the road. Rebels bang on the car and tell them it's not safe to be driving around. They should join the revolution or go home.

'This is hopeless,' says Károly. 'We'll have to go back.'

Ilona bites back an angry comment. They'll just have to sit tight and pray that the Russians restore order soon.

Katalin takes the children upstairs to Petra's. Tibor, who has been grounded, is sulking in the corner of the living room.

'He's driving me up the wall,' says Petra under her breath. 'Keeps saying he wants to be a freedom fighter and that he should be out there doing his bit. I've told him he's too young, but he doesn't want to listen to me. What do I know? I'm just his mother, after all.'

Katalin gives her a sympathetic smile. At least Lajos and little Eva are too young to get involved. But her heart lurches at the thought of Zoltán out there. Where is he? What's he doing? She hasn't heard from him all day. Much as she likes Sándor, she worries that his recklessness will lead them both into trouble. She tries not to let the children see how scared she is. But her first duty is to look after her family, which means making sure they have something to eat. She things of her own mother during the war, risking her life to put food on the table. When Katalin checked the cupboards that morning she was appalled to see how bare they were.

'I'm going to the shops,' she says. 'Can you mind the children for half an hour, please?'

'You can't go out there,' says Petra, grabbing her hand. She looks as if she wants to say more, but stops herself with a glance at Lajos who is looking at them both with a frown. He knows something bad is going on.

'I'll be careful,' says Katalin. 'And we have to eat. I'll buy some food for you too.'

Petra nods, thankful. 'I'll give you some money.'

Outside, Katalin walks quickly, keeping close to the shelter of the buildings. Other women with shopping bags are out too, scurrying like mice, darting from one street corner to another. The air is thick with the smell of gunfire and burning fuel. Sporadic shots, like firecrackers, ring out. She turns a corner and stops abruptly at the sight of a dead

Russian lying on the pavement, his face and hands burnt to a crisp. The body has been covered in white lime powder to stop the spread of infection, like a sprinkling of snow. It's a shock to see something so horrific close up, but she walks determinedly on, telling herself that her mother must have seen similar things and worse during the war and always returned home with a smile on her face.

She goes to the butcher's first but the counter is bare save for a handful of shrivelled salami sausages.

'There were no deliveries today,' the butcher's wife tells her. 'This is all I've got.'

'I'll take two,' says Katalin, remembering the food shortages they suffered during the war. She hopes it won't get as bad as that, but best to be prepared.

The baker sells her the last loaf. It's already going stale.

On her way back, she makes a short detour to Feri's café. All the tables are occupied by people with weapons, openly discussing politics and the new free Hungary they are fighting for. Behind the counter, Feri looks like a young man again. There's a smile on his face and a bounce in his step.

'What can I get you, Madame?' he asks, beaming at her.

'Just a coffee please.'

'On the house,' says Feri, pouring her a cup of his speciality brew. *'Vive la révolution!'*

*

Zoltán and Sándor are now members of a group based at the Corvin cinema and calling themselves the Corvin Circle. Dozens more ordinary Hungarians turned freedom fighters are joining them all the time.

The squat rectangular building with a flight of steps leading up to a curved front entrance is the perfect headquarters from which to plan their line of attack. Surrounded by a semi-circular sweep of buildings five to six storeys tall, the cinema can only be accessed by narrow alleyways which a tank can't enter. The buildings surrounding the cinema also happen to be situated on the junction of Üllői Avenue and József Boulevard, a major intersection – the perfect spot from which to ambush and destroy enemy tanks. A school in nearby Práter Street is being used as a canteen and first aid station for minor casualties. More serious cases are taken to the hospital.

At the fuel pumps at the petrol station behind the cinema, students and children, some as young as ten or eleven, are busy filling empty bottles with petrol. The Molotov cocktails are a simple but effective weapon against tanks.

Rifle in hand, Zoltán is now stationed at an open fourth floor window on József Boulevard, overlooking the junction with Üllői Avenue. A row of Molotov cocktails is lined up at his feet, the bottles stoppered with a rag doused in Russian vodka. He'd like a cigarette to calm his nerves but with all this flammable liquid around, that would be a bad idea. Half a dozen other freedom fighters, including Sándor, are located at adjacent windows. There is nothing to do but wait.

In the space of twenty-fours hours he has gone from being a simple factory worker, husband and father to being a freedom fighter, armed with a weapon, waiting for his chance to take on the enemy. Apart from Sándor and Bandi, he doesn't know the names of any of those he's fighting alongside, whether they have wives or children, what they do for a living. But none of that matters here. What matters is that they are united in a single cause – to evict the Russians from their country and to take control of their own futures. He thinks of Katalin, his son Lajos and little Eva. The children are too young to understand any of this, but it's them he's fighting for.

A shout goes up from the street where lookout scouts have been roaming. A Russian tank is coming from the direction of Boráros Square.

In an instant the atmosphere in the room changes to

nervous anticipation. Zoltán feels his heart beating against his ribs like a caged animal trying to escape. Beads of sweat form on his brow.

He feels the approach of the tank before he sees it. The floorboards vibrate and the window panes rattle. Every nerve in his body hums with the rumbling of the caterpillar tracks on the road's surface.

And then the tank comes into view, like a giant, deadly insect, armour-plated and invincible. As it makes its cumbersome way across the intersection, it swivels its gun from left to right, firing randomly.

Zoltán sees the barrel of the tank's gun pointing directly at their building and shouts, 'Take cover.' Everyone ducks down as the tank fires, hitting the floor above them. Lumps of plaster fall from the ceiling, creating a dust storm.

He crawls back to the window and sees the tank preparing to attack the building opposite. He grabs the nearest Molotov cocktail and lights the vodka-soaked rag. Then he lobs it as hard as he can at the tank. It falls short and explodes in a ball of flame. Everyone starts throwing petrol bombs from all the neighbouring windows in a desperate bid to bring the monster to its knees. The bottles explode on the tank's turret and outer casing, engulfing it in flames and smoke, but, like a creature with supernatural powers, the tank refuses to die. Its gun is still manoeuvring, preparing to shoot another round.

'Aim for the cooling vents of the engine compartment,' shouts Sándor. 'At the back, see there?' He points. 'The trick is to make the engine catch fire.'

Zoltán throws another bottle, and this time it hits the exact spot Sándor indicated. The bottle explodes and seconds later the tank's engine ignites, sending up a blazing inferno that forces him back from the window. The air fills with thick black smoke, making it difficult to breathe.

'Tank's on fire! Tank's on fire!' The shout goes up that the inside of the tank is burning. It'll be like a furnace in there. 'Serves them right!'

What has he done? Zoltán recoils in horror when he imagines the Russian soldiers inside that tank, men with mothers and wives and children, and now they are being incinerated inside their metal prison. He collapses on his knees, shaking in shock.

Strong arms pull him to his feet and drag him back to the window. 'Look!' shouts Sándor.

The Russians are trying to escape from their fiery pit. As they pour out of the hatch and make a run for it, freedom fighters in the street shoot them down.

Afterwards, when the ambulance crews arrive to pick up the Hungarians wounded in the battle, they leave the dead Russians lying in the road where they fell.

*

'I need more bandages,' calls Róza, 'and get me more anaesthetic and painkillers. Whatever you can find.' The young nurse on duty rushes off to fulfil her request. The hospital has just received yet another batch of casualties who are being carried in on stretchers. The most serious cases – those with limbs blown off – are rushed into the operating theatres. Those with bullet wounds and burns line the corridors, their moans and cries pitiful to hear.

'I don't know where we're going to put them all,' complains Magda, the hospital administrator, frantically turning over sheets of paper attached to her clipboard. 'We're running out of beds, and as for the morgue it's already full up. What are those men doing in the corridor?' She frowns at three young men slumped against the wall, still holding rifles in their hands. The middle one has blood pouring from a cut to his head whilst his friends do their best to prop him up. They have slipped through Magda's system, their names not on her list. She normally runs the hospital with a precision that makes the Kremlin look like a bunch of sloppy amateurs, but her system is breaking down in the face of the chaos that has erupted on the streets.

Róza doesn't have time for Magda and her bureaucracy. All that matters is trying to save as many lives as she can. She's been swabbing wounds, extracting bullets, stitching torn flesh and administering drugs ever since the first casualties from the radio station were brought in last night. She didn't go home but caught a few hours sleep at the hospital in the hours before dawn. Now the fighting has escalated beyond anything she thought possible and she has heard harrowing accounts of death and destruction from those still able to string a sentence together. The dead are taken straight to the morgue.

This isn't what she had in mind when she chose to study medicine – working in a war zone.

The nurse that she sent off a minute ago is back with a couple of boxes of supplies. She's pink-cheeked and out of breath from having run up and down the stairs, the lifts being out of order. 'We're running low on bandages and medicine,' she says. 'This was all I could find.'

Róza grits her teeth. 'Well done. Now come and help me with these men.' Most of the young fighters who've been brought to the hospital just want to have their injuries patched up as quickly as possible so they can get back to fighting the Russians. But still the wounded and the dying keep coming. Róza feels as if she's trying to hold back the tide.

CHAPTER 13

Thursday, 25 October 1956

Tamás has never seen so many people crammed into one place, and it's a terrifying sight. A seething mass of humanity, singing and chanting and waving banners.

Alerted by the authorities that a demonstration was amassing in Parliament Square the AVO have been ordered to man the roof of the Ministry of Agriculture, opposite the Parliament building. Tamás doesn't have much of a head for heights and almost wishes he was back underground, patrolling the cellars at Andrássy Avenue. He'd always hoped for promotion to a desk job, but that dream never materialised. Now, from his dizzying vantage point he watches the swarms of demonstrators flooding into the square. Counter-revolutionaries, he's been told to call them. Whatever they are, they're an unstoppable wave, surging from all directions, with their slogans and flags and their pent up resentments. There's no sign of them stopping. Tamás knows how to induce fear in someone who's cowering in a dank, underground cell. But now he's the one who's afraid to the pit of his stomach. His submachine gun shakes in his sweaty palms. Gábor is standing next to him, muttering insults under his breath. If only Gábor would shut up and go away. Vajda – God help us – is giving the orders. For now they've been told to watch and wait. Tamás prays it won't come to anything worse.

The march two days ago took him completely by surprise. Where has this sudden surge of energy and defiance come from? He never imagined that the views expressed so brazenly at the Petőfi Circle meetings would amount to anything tangible. The population, which is normally so subdued and downtrodden, has suddenly sprung to life like a caged tiger let out into the wild. The tearing of the Soviet star from flags seems to him sacrilegious.

Yesterday he welcomed the sight of the Soviet tanks rolling into the city. The Soviets will know how to restore order. The Hungarian government doesn't seem to have a clue.

But Soviet tanks are lined up in front of the Parliament building and they're not doing anything to disperse the crowds. More tanks are lumbering into the square. He watches one which has come to a halt about fifty yards from the Ministry of Agriculture. Unbelievably some of the demonstrators are actually climbing onto the tank. The tank hatch opens and a Russian soldier pops his head out. He appears to be having a conversation with the Hungarians sitting on top of his tank. They all learn Russian in school, although Tamás was never very good at it. Then the marchers tie Hungarian flags to the radio antenna of the tank and punch their fists into the air in a sign of triumph. Tamás finds this all very confusing. Whose side are the Russians on now?

The crowds in the square are shouting that they want Erno Gerő to be removed from office. Gerő of the Five Year Plan that was going to transform Hungary into a country of heavy industry and prosperity. The Five Year Plan now lies in ruins and the liberal Imre Nagy has been made Prime Minister. No wonder the uprising is being allowed to proceed unhindered.

Impatient as ever, Vajda has obviously decided to take matters into his own hands. He picks up a loud hailer and moves to the front of the roof. Tamás feels a deep sense of foreboding. Vajda is not the man to disperse a crowd calmly.

'This is the police,' bellows Vajda into the loud hailer.

The calls for Gerő's removal from office continue unabated.

'I repeat, this is the police,' yells Vajda.

The chanting gradually dies down and Vajda seizes the moment. 'This is an illegal demonstration. You must disperse immediately. I repeat, this demonstration is unauthorised.'

Vajda has certainly attracted the demonstrators' attention now. Thousands of people are looking up at the rooftop of the Ministry of Agriculture and Tamás feels horribly exposed in his blue uniform against the terracotta roof tiles.

Vajda's announcement is greeted with jeers. 'This is a peaceful demonstration,' shout the protesters. 'We are unarmed.'

'This demonstration is illegal,' bellows Vajda. 'You are ordered to disperse immediately!'

The announcement has the effect of tossing a lighted match onto a pile of dry kindling. Voices which were singing songs of freedom a moment ago, now erupt with hate-filled slogans.

'Murderers! Assassins! Torturers! Down with the AVO!' This lot are no longer afraid to say what they think. They have the advantage of numbers.

'I repeat...'

Tamás wishes the fool would shut up. He's only making matters worse, incensing the people. But Vajda continues to bellow into his loud hailer, his bulldog neck and flabby cheeks bulging with the effort.

'Murderers! Pigs! Kill the AVO!'

The words ring in Tamás' ears and the truth dawns on him that these thousands of people want him dead. He clutches his submachine gun with trembling hands. Beside him Gábor stamps his feet as if he's itching to respond to the taunts.

With his diplomatic efforts in tatters, Vajda flings down the loud hailer and turns to his men.

'Right, you know what you have to do. You are here to defend socialism. You are here to defend the workers of this country against these counter-revolutionary scumbags. I expect every one of you to do your duty. Engage your weapons. Fire!'

Almost before Vajda has finished giving the order, Gábor lifts his submachine gun and lets off a round of ammunition. The other officers soon follow his example and a hailstorm of bullets rains down onto the crowd. Only Tamás stands frozen to the spot, his hands and arms refusing to co-operate. Down below, the chants turn into screams. Tamás wants to turn and run but there's nowhere to go. Behind him is the pitch of the roof and the way to his left and right is blocked by his comrades.

Suddenly Vajda is behind him. Tamás can smell his sweat and his stale breath. 'Shoot boy! Your job is to shoot!' Vajda nudges his arm so that he almost loses his balance. Tamás fears that if he doesn't obey, Vajda will not hesitate to topple him from the roof into the crowds below. He lifts his weapon, closes his eyes, and shoots blindly into the mass of screaming people.

*

When the shooting starts Katalin and her father are trapped, penned in by the thousands crammed into the square: old and young, men and women, factory and office workers, university students and schoolchildren.

That morning she agreed to accompany Márton on

what was supposed to be a peaceful demonstration, hoping to see and hear for herself Imre Nagy, the newly appointed Prime Minister.

But their songs of freedom have turned into screams of terror. Shots are ringing out, ricocheting off the surrounding buildings, and the crowd is panicking, yelling, crying.

Katalin grabs her father's arm. 'We have to get away before this becomes a massacre.'

'Which way?'

Everybody is running, pushing and shoving in all directions. She sees a young man staggering towards her, clutching his stomach. Blood is pouring through his fingers. His eyes lock with hers. 'Help me,' he gasps.

Despite the danger they're in, she can't abandon this young man to his fate as he stumbles and falls at her feet. She and Márton both kneel in the boy's blood and do their best to comfort him. He can't be more than fifteen or sixteen, just a kid really.

'What's your name?' she asks.

He looks at her with imploring eyes and tries to speak, but only a croak comes out.

'It's all right, son,' says Márton, stroking the boy's forehead. 'You're very brave.'

The young man closes his eyes and takes his last breath.

Katalin wants to scream with the senselessness of it all. She's never been this close to a dead body before, except the Russian soldier yesterday, but he had already taken on the unreal aspect of something not entirely human. This nameless young man is still so real, his body still warm. He's someone's son, maybe someone's boyfriend or brother. And he died here, shot by the Secret Police, by his own people. She wishes she knew his name, where he was from. She'd like to be able to tell his mother that her son died for a good cause.

But the shooting has started up again, or maybe she just didn't notice it continuing whilst she watched the young man die. She comes to her senses.

'Papa, we have to go. The ambulances are arriving. They'll take him away.'

Márton is still kneeling by the body, head bowed as if in prayer. She pulls him to his feet, tears streaming from her eyes.

'This way,' she says, starting to move across the square towards the Ministry of Agriculture. 'The building will give us cover.'

They haven't gone more than a few feet when Márton's hand jerks out of hers and his body lurches to the side, crashing onto the cobbles.

'Papa! No!' Katalin screams.

In her confusion it takes her a moment to realise that her father has been shot. A crimson patch of blood is spreading over his shoulder, staining his coat. His eyes are closed and he's lying motionless. She drops to the ground beside him, frantic with despair. 'Papa, don't die! Please don't die!' She presses a hand to the wound to try and stem the flow of blood. His eyes flicker open. Thank God, he's still alive. 'Over here!' she shouts when she sees white-coated medical workers running across the square with a stretcher. 'Help us!'

*

Tamás is dizzy with horror at the sight unfolding below him. The square is strewn with bodies, too many to count. They lie there, their blood staining the cobblestones. Did he hit any himself? He doesn't know because he fired blindly, in fear that Vajda would shoot him if he didn't. Medical workers have arrived and are running across the square in their white coats like fools. Don't they know that a white coat and a red cross armband won't protect them? It's not body-armour.

'Got him!' shouts Gábor. 'Did you see that? I got that old fellow right in the shoulder?'

Tamás looks to where Gábor is pointing and his stomach lurches so much that he falls to his knees, clutching the edge of the parapet. He thinks he might throw up. Even from this height, he recognises Katalin and her father, Márton Bakos. Márton is lying on the ground, blood pouring from a wound, and she's shouting for help.

'Get up!' Gábor kicks him in the side with his boot. 'Don't let Vajda see you acting like a chicken.'

'Fuck you!' shouts Tamás. 'And fuck Vajda!'

For a moment, even Gábor looks disconcerted. 'Hey, steady on. We're only doing our jobs.'

'This isn't what I signed up for.'

'What did you expect then? That you'd get to sit behind a desk all day? We're keeping law and order here.'

Tamás isn't going to hang around listening to Gábor justify what just happened. He throws down his weapon and pushes his way past a stunned Gábor. He's not the only one abandoning his position. Vajda has lost control of his men and they're leaving in droves. Down below, the square is almost empty, only the dead and dying still lying where they fell.

He runs down the stairs, taking them two at a time. At the bottom he finds a scene of pandemonium. All around him AVO officers are darting in different directions, the fear visible in the whites of their eyes. No one seems to know what to do or where to go. Which way now? He recoils at the idea of escaping across the square, the scene of so much carnage. And he doesn't want to expose himself to people who by now must be looking for revenge. There has to be another way out.

Someone shouts that there's a truck waiting for them round the side of the building. They surge in that direction and, after a moment's hesitation, Tamás follows. But as soon as they are outside, a mob of angry protesters rushes forward, shooting. The AVO officers at the front, those who were most eager to escape, fall to the ground. Those immediately behind them, trip over the fallen bodies. From his position at the back, Tamás sees it all unfolding in front of him as if in slow motion. Then he turns and runs in the opposite direction. He doesn't know where he's going. All he knows is that he has to get away from here as quickly as possible.

*

The hospital is chaotic, the wounded being carried in on stretchers or helped by their friends. Katalin sits on the floor next to her father who is propped up against a wall where the ambulance men left him. She can tell he's in pain from the way his mouth is drawn in a tight line. He needs to get the wound seen to before it goes septic. He's already lost so much blood and his face is taut and grey. She holds his hand and waits for someone to help him.

Angry rumours are flying around that between one hundred and two hundred people were killed at Parliament Square. Katalin can't get her head around such a large number of deaths. All she can think about is the young man who died at her feet asking for help. She regrets that she couldn't do more for him.

Doctors, nurses and porters are rushing around, tending to the casualties and a harassed-looking woman with a clipboard is trying vainly to impose order. Around her Katalin sees a catalogue of human misery – gunshot wounds, shrapnel wounds, burns, missing eyes, torn off limbs. Ordinary Hungarians who until a couple of days ago were simply getting on with their lives as best they could are now sprawled on the floor, suffering injuries which will scar them for the rest of their lives. And they're only the ones who are still breathing.

Her greatest fear is that she'll see Zoltán here amongst the wounded and dying. He didn't come home last night. Wherever he is, she just prays he's safe.

'Katalin!' She jumps at the sound of a familiar voice

calling her name. Róza is making her way towards them, stepping over the legs of a young woman lying on the floor. 'What are you doing here?'

Katalin throws her arms around her, overcome with happiness at seeing her best friend alive and well, although she can't help noticing the dark rings under her eyes. Róza's usually bouncy red hair is tied back in a limp ponytail.

'It's Papa. He was shot at Parliament Square.'

'Let me see.' Róza crouches down beside Márton and checks his pulse. His eyes are closed and he barely seems to know where he is anymore. 'He's lost a lot of blood. We have to get that wound checked out. Can you help me lift him?'

'Just tell me what to do,' says Katalin, relieved that help has arrived at last. If she can just get her father home in one piece then she'll insist that he stays there until the trouble is over.

*

Tamás runs for his life. Chaos and destruction are all around him. In his haste he almost trips over a dead Russian who has been left lying in the road, his bullet-ridden body sprinkled in white lime. Why don't they clear the damn corpses away? He's barely recovered from the shock of the dead Russian when he sees something even worse. An AVO informer is swinging from a tree by his ankles, his bloody torso stripped bare and beaten while his lifeless fingertips trail on the ground. His mouth has been stuffed with banknotes. Otherwise respectable-looking women with shopping bags on their arms spit at the dangling corpse as they walk past. Tamás spins away in a daze, sickened by what he has just seen. What has happened to people? He should have kept hold of his weapon, he sees that now. It's too dangerous to be out on the streets, unarmed.

He collapses into an alleyway, gasping for breath, sweat pouring off him. He bends over with his hands on his knees and tries to suck air into his burning lungs. He wipes a drool of saliva from his mouth and stands up, trying to work out his location. Nothing looks the same anymore, there's so much destruction everywhere. But there's a street sign still visible on the blasted stonework, even if the windows have been blown out and the building gutted by fire. He's not far from his apartment now. If he can just avoid being shot at or lynched for another ten minutes, then he'll be back home.

He has no idea how his mother is coping with all of this. He hasn't been home since Tuesday when all the trouble erupted.

He's never been particularly close to his mother. After his father died in the war, she turned in on herself, as if her quotient of feeling had been used up. He's spent a lifetime trying to get her to notice him, to pay him some attention. He joined the Secret Police hoping it would make her proud and it did for a while, maybe because he reminded her of her war-hero husband. Would she be proud if she could see him now, running for his life?

He peers out from the alleyway to check that the coast is clear, then he makes a run for it. Just two blocks to go, and then a left turn.

He stops short. This isn't his street, he must have got confused. He looks around for a familiar landmark and sees the café on the corner, its shutters pulled down, the door barred. This is his street, but what in God's name has happened to it? He walks down the middle of the road, staring at the shelled buildings and piles of rubble. He stops in front of an apartment block that has had its front blown off, exposing the insides of the rooms like a doll's house. Looking up, he recognises his own sitting room and bedroom. There is no sign of any life.

He backs away from the only place he's ever called home. It's nothing more than a skeleton now, its flesh ripped clean away. Where can he go? He ran from Parliament Square, wanting to leave the AVO and have nothing more to do with any of them. Now he realises the AVO is the only family he's got left.

*

Katalin and her father hitch a lift back to their apartment with a truckload of students distributing weapons and ammunition to freedom fighters situated around the city. She helps him up the stairs and into his favourite reading chair in the living room.

Márton lets out a sigh. 'I suppose this means my fighting days are over.' He taps his bandaged shoulder with his good hand. It's just like him to make light of his injuries.

'Sit still. I'll fetch you a glass of Pálinka.' Róza recommended it as a painkiller. The hospital is running low on essential medicines.

She pours him a generous measure and watches as he takes a sip. 'That's better,' he says, closing his eyes.

The bullet caused a nasty flesh wound to Márton's shoulder, but hadn't lodged there, thankfully. Róza cleaned the area with alcohol, stitched him up, applied a dressing and put his arm in a sling.

'I won't be able to sleep on my side,' he says. 'You know, when I was locked in the cells in Andrássy Avenue, I had to sleep on my back with my palms facing upwards all the time. It wasn't very comfortable at first, but it's surprising what you get used to.'

Katalin takes his good hand and gives it a squeeze. He has hardly ever talked about his time in custody or at the labour camp, saying it's in the past and he would prefer to get on with his life. But she's sure the memory of it is still all too real for him.

The apartment door opens and she runs into the hallway. Zoltán is standing there. His face is scratched and he's covered in dirt, but he's alive and he's here now and that's all that matters. She runs into his arms and he holds her tight against his chest. He smells of petrol.

'I heard about the shooting at Parliament Square,' he says. 'I thought you might have been there, so I wanted to make sure you're all right. Where are the children?' He looks anxiously round the apartment which is unnaturally quiet.

'Don't worry, they're safe with Petra,' says Katalin. 'But Papa and I were both at the square. Papa was shot in the shoulder. It was awful. I thought...' She lets her voice trail away, unable to say she thought he might die. Instead she says, 'But he was more fortunate than some.' She thinks of the young man who died in her arms. Has Zoltán witnessed similar things? She feels sure he must have.

'Where is he now?' asks Zoltán.

'Through here.' She takes his hand and leads him into the living room. As they enter the room Márton starts to rise from his chair in greeting.

'Don't get up,' says Zoltán, clasping his father-in-law's good hand.

'How is the fight?' asks Márton. 'Are we winning?'

Whilst Katalin pours him a glass of Pálinka, Zoltán pulls up a chair next to his father-in-law and talks enthusiastically about the progress they're making at the Corvin Circle.

'We've secured a strong defensive location, and we're organised into fighting groups. We must have destroyed at least a dozen tanks by now. And we have a good supply of ammunition from the barracks. So far it's going well.'

Márton listens attentively, nodding his head. Katalin is pleased to see that Zoltán's optimism is distracting him from his own discomfort. Hope is better than any medicine.

'And what about Sándor and András?' asks Márton. 'How are they?'

'Sándor is fighting alongside me, and András and Anna

are working in the first aid station in the nearby school. They've set up a makeshift canteen in the basement of the school. The fighters sleep in the cinema.'

'That's very good,' says Márton, suppressing a yawn. 'Very good indeed. Now if you'll both excuse me, I think I could do with a lie down. I can only take so much excitement in one day.'

Katalin helps him to his feet and walks him to his bedroom. She gives her father a gentle hug, careful not to put any pressure on his injured shoulder and kisses him on his cheek.

When she returns to the living room Zoltán has taken off his coat and is waiting for her. She runs into his arms and he holds her tight.

'If it wasn't for the children, I'd come with you,' she says. 'But I can't leave them with Petra all the time.'

'I know.' He strokes her hair. 'But they need you here, and your father needs you. And I need to know that you're safe.'

'I should probably go and fetch them,' she says. 'Petra will be wondering what's happened to us and if she's heard about the shooting at Parliament Square she'll be worried sick.'

'Another half an hour won't hurt, will it?' asks Zoltán, cupping her face in his hands.

'I suppose not. I...'

'Shh, no more talking.' He puts a finger to her lips and leads her to their bedroom. 'I've missed you.'

'I've missed you too.'

As they fall onto the bed, Katalin lets the feel of their entwined bodies blot out the horrors of the morning.

CHAPTER 14

Friday, 26 October 1956

The attack begins at dawn. Zoltán is up already, unable to sleep properly on the floor of the cinema, his mind filled with thoughts of Katalin and the children. It took every last ounce of willpower to tear himself out of his wife's arms yesterday and return to the Corvin cinema. In the war Sándor and he toiled side by side, digging trenches to hold off the advancing Red Army. And they will fight side by side again for their country's freedom. He shakes Sándor who is lying on his back, snoring like a pig.

'Four Russian tanks are on their way from Boráros Square,' he shouts. 'Wake up. We have to man the anti-tank gun.'

The 76 calibre gun was captured yesterday from a Soviet truck. It took six of them to drag the heavy weapon across the street and set it up on the steps of the Corvin Cinema. It was Zoltán's idea to attach a cable to the trigger, passing the ends of the cable into the cinema's ticket booth so that the gun could be operated from inside the building.

Sándor comes to with a grunt and a snort. For a

moment he looks as if he doesn't know where he is, then he jumps to his feet, ready for action. 'Lead the way.'

Armed with an array of weapons purloined from the nearby army barracks and from captured Russian vehicles, the members of the Corvin Circle run to their assigned positions – doorways along Üllői Avenue, upper storey windows on József Boulevard. In the space of forty-eight hours, this rag-tag bunch of civilians and volunteers – many of them still in their teens – have organised themselves into a formidable fighting force, with the agility and ingenuity to launch surprise attacks on unsuspecting Russian tanks. Bandi has put Zoltán and Sándor in charge of the anti-tank gun on account of their strong working relationship.

Sándor takes up his position on the cinema steps, partially shielded by a statue. Zoltán is in the ticket booth, ready to fire the anti-tank gun, the most powerful weapon that the freedom fighters have at their disposal.

Messengers out on the streets relay the news that the tanks are approaching very slowly, making frequent stops. Zoltán takes a deep breath and wipes the palms of his hands on his trousers. This is the hardest part, the waiting. In the heat of battle there isn't time to think. There isn't time to be scared. But waiting for a tank to arrive, knowing that these may be your last moments on Earth, that is when fear has the power to strike deep into your soul.

'They're nearing the intersection,' shouts a voice.

Zoltán feels his heart starting to race. He has to rely on Sándor to tell him when the tank is in the firing line.

'Get ready!' shouts Sándor. 'Fire!'

Zoltán yanks hard on the cable, the muscles in his arm and shoulder tensing with the effort. He feels the shock wave from the blast.

'Bull's eye!' shouts Sándor. 'You hit it. Ripped the caterpillar chain right off. They're stranded. The Molotov cocktails will finish them off now.'

Zoltán breathes a sigh of relief. That's one less tank on

the streets, threatening his safety and that of his friends and family.

But there's no time for the two friends to enjoy their victory. More tanks are on the way and they need to reload the gun ready for the next attack. It's going to be a long day.

*

The wounded keep arriving at the hospital and still there's no end in sight to the fighting. Exhausted from days and nights on her feet, catching a few minutes of sleep whenever she can, Róza goes to meet the ambulance bearing the latest round of casualties.

Over the last few days she's seen some horrific sights. Limbs blown off by shellfire, grisly head wounds, missing eyes, gouged intestines. But it's the fear in people's eyes that affects her the most. She wishes she could administer hope in the way she administers medical aid. She wishes she could do more.

She braces herself as the two ambulance men, István and Bálint, open the rear doors of their vehicle and gently lift out the latest casualty on a stretcher. With not enough ambulance drivers for the current situation, medical students like these two have volunteered to make up numbers. István is tall with dark springy hair that is coated in a layer of dust. His white coat is stained with blood. Bálint is six inches shorter but broader in the chest and shoulders. He too is coated in a layer of dust and blood.

Róza sucks in her breath. It's a bad case. The man has been hit in the abdomen, probably by shrapnel, and his shirt is stained a dark, crimson red. He's unconscious, his breath making a rasping sound in his exposed chest. It's a miracle he's still alive.

'This way,' she says.

The elevators are still not working. István and Bálint carry the stretcher up the stairs to the already heaving corridors. An hour ago Magda broke down in hysterics, tore up her lists and stormed out. Róza wasn't sorry to see her go, but now the organisation of the hospital is down to her and the other doctors.

'You'll have to put him here,' she tells the ambulance men. They lift the wounded man onto a trolley in a corridor which is already lined with casualties. They ran out of beds days ago. As they move him the man wakes up and lets out a cry of pain. He's going to need urgent treatment if he isn't going to die, but all the operating theatres are busy. She'll speak to her superior and do what she can to prioritise him, but Róza fears it might not be possible to save him.

She used to believe that if she did her job to the best of her ability then she'd be able to help most people. But in the last twenty-four hours that belief has been sorely tested. It's now almost at breaking point. She's been rushing from one patient to the next, cleaning wounds, bandaging limbs, trying to do the best she can. But they are running out of supplies. Stocks of anaesthetics and painkillers are perilously low. There's a growing risk of infection because of a lack of antiseptic and penicillin. There aren't enough surgeons to deal with all the urgent cases. All Róza has to offer are words of sympathy and comfort but it's not enough. The cries of the wounded are pitiful to hear. She doesn't think she'll ever get that wailing sound out of her head. And all around her people are dying.

'We'll bring the others up,' says István grimly. She wonders what horrors he's witnessed out in the streets. Do they leave people behind because they're beyond help?

Róza nods dumbly, looking at the man on the trolley. He's not going to make it. All she can do is try to make his last moments on earth as comfortable as possible.

*

It's not fair, being grounded when other kids his age – and younger! – are out on the streets fighting for their country. Tibor kicks his toes against the skirting board and gazes longingly out of the window at the street below. So much for his moment of glory in helping to bring down Stalin's statue. He's sure Géza must be out there, having loads of fun. He's probably acquired a gun by now, the lucky devil.

He can hear his mother moving around in the kitchen, opening and closing cupboards. They've been living off dry bread and an old salami sausage for days now because she's too scared to leave the apartment. She's so preoccupied with rationing out their meagre food supply, would she even notice if he slipped out? He might be able to bring back something to eat, and then she'd thank him and realise that he's not a baby anymore.

He tiptoes over to the sideboard and eases the lid off the tin where they keep what little spare money they have. He slips a couple of banknotes into his pocket then checks at the living room door to make sure that his mum is still busy in the kitchen. She has the radio on, listening to news of the latest fighting. Keeping one eye on the kitchen, he inches towards the front door. Then in one quick movement he slips out and runs down the stairs. He'll be back before she's even noticed.

The sense of freedom is intoxicating. But he senses danger too, which makes the freedom all that more exhilarating. The smell of burning which permeated the apartment is much stronger out here and a pall of smoke hangs in the air. He can hear the rumble of artillery not so far away and the crack of gunfire. There are armed groups on every street corner, defending their territory.

At the end of the road he sees an abandoned tank and heads straight for it. Children are climbing over the tank, using it as a playground. He's always wondered what it's like inside a tank. He hoists himself up onto the metal body and lowers himself down into the hatch. It's dark and claustrophobic and there's a terrible smell, like meat that has rotted. He climbs out quickly and hurries on.

Up ahead he sees a crowd of people, mostly women, standing around a truck. He goes over to investigate. A bearded man in the back of the truck is handing out turnips and potatoes.

'What do we owe you?' asks one of the women, taking her purse out of her shopping bag.

'Nothing,' says the man. 'This food has come straight from the farms. This is our contribution to the fight.' He catches sight of Tibor standing at the back. 'How many people in your household?' he asks.

'It's just me and my mum,' says Tibor. But then he remembers Katalin with the children and her father downstairs. Plus there's old Maria and her husband. Not to forget grumpy old József the caretaker. 'But there's half a dozen other people in the building too.'

'Here you go, kid,' says the farmer. He tosses Tibor a bag of potatoes and a couple of turnips. 'Make sure that gets home safely now.'

'Will do,' says Tibor grinning. 'Thanks, Mister.'

He runs straight home, glowing with pride. His mum will give him a right earful for sneaking out, but she might relent a bit when she sees he's brought them all something to eat.

*

The wounded man has died. His injuries were too bad and there was no time to save him. Róza pulls the sheet up over his face and tells one of the porters to take him down to the already overcrowded morgue.

Suddenly it's too much to bear. She leans against the wall and lets the tears flow, her professionalism ground down through the constant barrage of misery and death. Through her blurred vision she sees István and Bálint on their way back out and, in a split second decision, she runs over to them, drying her eyes with the back of her hand.

'Take me with you,' she says.

They stop and give her a quizzical look. 'We're not going on a picnic,' says István.

'I know that,' says Róza. 'But I have to get out of here, even if it's just for a few hours. Besides, if I can help people sooner, I might be able to save more lives. By the time most people get here, they've already lost too much blood.'

István and Bálint both nod their heads, acknowledging the truth in what she's saying.

'Won't you be missed here?' asks Bálint.

'I've already worked for days without a break. I think I'm owed a change of scene.'

István and Bálint look at each other as if coming to a decision, then István shrugs and says, 'All right. But this is at your own risk.'

'I understand.'

As they head towards the exit, István says, 'There are reports of fierce fighting down by the Corvin cinema. I suggest we head that way.'

Bálint is the driver. István and Róza climb into the back of the ambulance. All at once her mood lifts, so glad is she to be out of the hospital.

'Hold on tight,' grins István. 'Bálint drives like a mad man.'

The ambulance swings round a corner and Róza is almost thrown into István's lap.

'I hope he drives more carefully when he's got an ambulance full of wounded people,' she laughs. It's liberating to be outside the hospital after so long pounding the corridors, inhaling nothing but the smell of blood and death.

They take the back streets to the cinema, making frequent U-turns as they negotiate their way around barricades, burnt out tanks and corpses.

István leans forward. 'Remember, we don't pick up the Russians.'

Róza nods. It goes against her medical training to leave a wounded person lying on the ground, whatever nationality they are. But things are different now. They can't save everyone so they have to prioritise.

The ambulance lurches round a corner and comes to a sudden halt. 'Burning Russian tank up ahead,' shouts Bálint from the driver's cab. 'People lying in the street.' He kills the engine.

'Stay close to me,' says István, getting to his feet.

Bálint is already out of the ambulance and opening the rear doors. 'It looks bad,' he shouts. They climb out of the back of the ambulance to a scene of carnage. The air is thick with black smoke from the burning tank.

Casualties are lying in the street. Róza follows Bálint and István as they rush over to the nearest prone figure. It's a young man, probably early twenties. Blood is pouring out of a gunshot wound in his right thigh, staining the ground scarlet. His eyes are closed. All at once Róza's medical training kicks in. She checks for a pulse. It's still there but it's faint. He's lost a lot of blood already. If Bálint and István can carry him back to the ambulance she can bandage his leg with a tourniquet to stem the blood loss. He might need a transfusion but she can't do that out here in the street.

István and Bálint lift him onto a stretcher and carry him back to the ambulance. Róza gets to work, cutting off his trouser leg and wrapping the wounded thigh as tightly as she can. The man's eyes flicker open and he tries to speak.

'Just lie still,' says Róza. 'You're going to be all right.'

'Thank you,' croaks the man. 'What's your name?'

'Róza. What's yours?'

'Otto.'

He looks as if he's about to say something else but Róza hears István calling her name. 'I'm sorry, I have to go.'

She leaves Otto in the ambulance and hurries over to

where István is kneeling by the prone figure of a young girl. She's in a bad way with a wound to the head.

'She's still alive,' says István. 'But only just.'

'We have to get her to the hospital. I can't do anything for her out here.'

'Help me lift her onto the stretcher.'

István takes the girl's shoulders and Róza lifts her feet. She weighs practically nothing. They lay her on the bloodied stretcher and carry her to the ambulance. Bálint is helping a man with a shoulder wound into the ambulance.

As soon as everyone is ready, Bálint starts the engine and the ambulance bumps and jolts its way back to the hospital. Róza sits on the floor and holds onto the girl with the head wound to stop her rolling off the stretcher whenever the ambulance takes a corner at speed.

Bálint brakes sharply in front of the hospital doors and István pushes open the rear doors. Otto gives her a weak smile as they carry him into the hospital. He'll make it, she thinks. It's a small achievement, but it makes up for the young man who died earlier.

They spend the whole morning driving backwards and forwards between the Corvin cinema and the hospital. Róza loses count of the number of tourniquets that she ties to prevent blood loss. For the first time in days, she feels as if she's making a real difference.

After they've delivered their fifth or sixth consignment of wounded fighters to the hospital, Bálint produces some bread, salami, onion and paprika from the front of the ambulance. The three of them stand in a huddle, beside the ambulance, sharing the food in silence. There is no need to speak. They have all seen too much in a short space of time. This simple meal of bread and salami is possibly the tastiest meal she's ever eaten. As soon as they've finished they get back into the ambulance and set off to fetch more wounded fighters.

CHAPTER 15

Saturday, 27 October 1956 - Monday, 29 October 1956

The city is a graveyard full of unburied bodies. Zoltán trudges through the devastated streets, past smouldering buildings, stepping on broken glass, rubble, spent cartridges, and other detritus of battle. He's exhausted from the fighting of the previous day, barely more alive than the corpses that lie in his path.

By yesterday evening, the area around the Corvin cinema resembled a tank scrapyard, the stench of burning oil polluting the air, scorched Russian bodies littering the streets. He wants to get out of these clothes which reek of smoke and sweat and blood, and change into something clean. Most of all he wants to feel Katalin's arms around him and for her to tell him that everything is going to be all right. But will life ever go back to normal after all that's happened? After the things he's done?

Now, as he makes his way home, he can see that the fighting wasn't just confined to the area around the cinema, but has spread across much of the city. Bodies of fallen Hungarian freedom fighters and civilians bear small bouquets of flowers and, sometimes, their names written on a piece of cardboard. By contrast, the bodies of AVO informers display a portrait of Stalin or Rákosi to show where, in life, their true loyalties lay. The bodies of dead Russians have been hastily sprinkled in quicklime. They will be picked up and disposed of last.

Zoltán climbs the stairs to the apartment and gratefully falls into the arms of his wife who is there to meet him. She doesn't ask him how he is, for which he's grateful. No doubt she can see the state he's in for herself.

'Take those clothes off,' says Katalin. 'I'll run you a bath.'

Five minutes later he closes his eyes and sinks under the hot water, drowning out the terrible things he's witnessed over the last couple of days. When he comes up for air, Katalin is perched on the side of the bath, holding a bar of soap in her hands.

'Let me wash your back for you,' she says.

He leans forwards and lets her scrub him clean, easing away the tension in his neck and shoulders which has built up from almost constant firing of the tank gun.

'Where's Sándor?' she asks.

Zoltán leans back in the water to rinse his back. 'He said he was going to the hospital to see Róza.'

'Ah,' says Katalin with a smile on her lips. 'I might have guessed.'

Over the course of the weekend they are joined by András and Anna, taking a break from manning the first aid station and the canteen at the Práter Street School. Sándor also pops his head in to say that Róza is doing fine, working with a couple of ambulance guys. Katalin, Zoltán and Márton spend most of their time gathered around the radio, listening to the latest reports.

It seems that Imre Nagy, the new Prime Minister, is starting to get to grips with the situation. On Sunday he acknowledges that the uprising came about because people loathed the atrocities of the former regime. The new government must give the people what they demand. As a result, the AVO is going to be disbanded and replaced with a new police; the emblem of Kossuth – Hungary's Coat of Arms – will replace the Soviet star on the Hungarian flag; the anniversary of the 1848 Revolution, March the fifteenth, will be a national holiday once more, and, most importantly, Soviet troops will leave the country. There must be an immediate ceasefire, but in return there will be a general amnesty. It all seems too good to be true.

*

Márton holds in his hands a thick manila folder with his name written on the front cover and an official AVO stamp. He's surprised at how heavy it is, at how much material the Secret Police have collected on him. It may contain the reasons for his arrest and internment in the labour camp. The question now is whether or not to open the file and read the contents.

A lull in the fighting means that he and András have been able to join the long queue of people at the AVO headquarters on Andrássy Avenue, all searching for the truth. Ever since his release Márton has avoided this part of town, preferring a lengthy detour to the prospect of walking past the building where he was imprisoned in the basement. He wasn't sure if he wanted to come today, but András persuaded him. The boy is desperate to know why he was sent to the labour camp. And who can blame him? Hundreds of other people have had the same idea. The truth matters.

Entering the building, Márton broke out in a cold sweat, terrified he was going to run into Vajda, stomping around giving orders. He saw himself being dragged back down to the stinking cellars in the basement, locked into one of those tiny cells, left to rot. He almost didn't make it through the front door and had to lean on András for support.

But the AVO have fled – like rats from a sinking ship –

and the building is now in the hands of armed freedom fighters. There are signs of fighting everywhere. Broken windows, overturned desks and chairs, walls riddled with bullet holes, anti-AVO graffiti. Márton hopes that someone will photograph the cellars and publish the images for all to see. The truth about this place needs to come out, but he's not the man to do it. It would break him to set foot once more in that cesspit.

They're in an upstairs room that was used for storing files. The atmosphere in the room is sober. A small group of freedom fighters have taken charge of sorting through the masses of paperwork, helping people to find what they are looking for. The young student who handed over Márton's file did so with a solemnity that he found touching.

But now that he has the folder in his hands, he doesn't know if he wants to open it. Whatever the AVO have written about him, it will all be lies. He was falsely accused on trumped up charges. The only thing that could possibly be of interest would be the name of the person or persons who informed on him. It's not that he hasn't given this question much thought over the years, but if he finds out the answer now, what is he going to do with the information? Take retribution? There comes a point when the revenge has to stop, otherwise you end up in a never-ending spiral of hate.

He glances across at András who has opened his folder and is avidly devouring the contents, his eyes scanning from left to right in wide-eyed disbelief. He turns over the sheet of paper and his hand flies to his mouth.

'What is it, son?' asks Márton gently.

András shakes his head. 'I always thought it was her father who denounced me,' he says. 'But it was Hanna herself, you know, the girl I was going out with. Her father had nothing to do with it.'

'I'm sorry to hear that,' says Márton.

'I wish I'd never come here now,' says András. He

scrunches the piece of paper into a ball and throws it on the floor.

'Come on, let's go home.' Márton leads András away. He still has his own unopened file tucked under his arm. He'll decide what to do with it later.

*

Freedom at last! Now that the fighting has mostly died down, Petra can't come up with good enough reasons for keeping Tibor at home, especially not after his last excursion provided everyone in the building with enough potatoes for two days.

'Off you go then,' she says. 'But don't be late back.'

'I won't.' Tibor suspects she's glad to get him out from under her feet for a couple of hours. He heads straight round to Géza's apartment. He finds his friend out in the street with a group of boys from school.

'Hey,' says Géza, his face lighting up. 'Thought we'd never see you again.'

'So what's happening?' asks Tibor.

'You got here just in time. We're all off to Buda to check out the houses where the Party bosses like Rákosi used to live. Wanna come?'

'You bet,' says Tibor.

They catch a tram across the Danube and walk up Rose Hill. It feels good to be outside, with his friends again, swapping stories about how many burnt out tanks they've seen and how many dead bodies they've counted, each trying to outdo the other.

They arrive at a villa set in its own grounds. There's even a swimming pool in the garden. A couple of armed freedom fighters are sitting by the front door, smoking.

'Is this Rákosi's place?' asks Tibor, looking up in awe at the huge house.

'*Was* Rákosi's place,' says one of the freedom fighters. 'But not anymore. The bastard has fled.'

'Can we go in?'

'Be our guests.'

Tibor, Géza and the other boys troop inside the big house. Some of the boys run straight up the staircase saying they're going to have a pillow fight in the bedroom. But Tibor stands in the hallway, looking around in amazement. There are so many doors leading off the hallway, he doesn't know which way to go first. He follows Géza into a room that turns out to be a lounge.

'This is the life,' says Géza, throwing himself onto a comfortable sofa and sticking his feet up on the armrests.

Tibor wanders around the room, noting with a pang of jealousy the brand new radio-phonograph and Rákosi's extensive collection of records. There are even two pianos. What on earth did Rákosi want with two pianos?

He opens a drawer in a writing desk and finds a box of cigars.

'Catch!' He tosses one of the thick brown cigar across the room where it lands with a thump on Géza's chest.

'Hey, watch it!' says Géza, sitting up.

'There's a whole box full of cigars here,' says Tibor. He tries to read the foreign label. 'I think they're from Holland.'

'Where did the old devil get Dutch cigars from?'

'Party members had access to special shops,' says Tibor, knowingly. He's heard his mum complain about such things. 'They didn't have to queue for bread like the rest of us.'

Géza jumps off the sofa and opens the doors to a cabinet. 'Whoa! Look at all this booze.'

The shelves are stocked with bottles of French wine, champagne and liqueurs. He picks up a bottle of Pálinka.

'Ever tried this stuff?'

Tibor shakes his head. His mum would have a fit if she caught him drinking Pálinka.

Géza unscrews the lid and takes a swig straight from the bottle. Then he passes it to Tibor. As Tibor lifts the bottle to his lips, he inhales the waves of alcoholic fumes.

'Go on,' says Géza. 'It won't kill you.'

Tibor knocks back a mouthful, nearly choking as the liquid burns the back of his throat and makes his eyes water. 'Jesus! How do grown-ups drink this stuff?'

'Come on,' says Géza, 'let's check out the rest of the house.'

In the kitchen they find lots of shiny new appliances, not at all like the ones Tibor's mother has to put up with. She's always complaining that Hungarian washing machines don't last five minutes and she often resorts to doing the laundry by hand. Upstairs the other boys have trashed the luxurious bedrooms with their pillow fights.

Tibor sits on the top of the stairs with his head in his hands. The revolution makes so much more sense to him now. In a communist society everyone was supposed to be equal, but it was all just a sham. Those in power had wealth and comfort whilst everyone else had virtually nothing. When he gets home he'll give his mum the biggest hug ever.

CHAPTER 16

Tuesday, 30 October 1956

With nowhere else to call home, Tamás has been holed up for the last five days at the Communist Party Headquarters in Republic Square, and he's not the only one. Other AVO officers have taken refuge there too, whilst the world they used to own is now in the hands of rank amateurs who patrol the streets with their stolen rifles and submachine guns. No one dares leave the building. They fear for their lives.

He stares glumly out of the top-floor window at the leafless trees and burnt-out cars. The Russians have been all but defeated, and by whom? By these so-called insurgents who are roaming freely around the square, smoking and talking. Some of them have stopped to chat to a group of women queueing outside a grocery shop. They share a joke. Laughter. They are the heroes of the hour, this ramshackle army of men and women who until a week ago had never held a weapon in their hands. Now look at them! Students, factory workers, office clerks, old men, children even. The Secret Police, on the other hand, are reviled and hated, hunted down like wild animals.

Everything that Tamás understood about the world has been turned upside down. The attacks against the AVO have been vicious. He has seen things which will haunt his dreams for the rest of his life, however long or short that may be.

His comrades pace up and down or sit with their feet propped on the long mahogany table, cradling their submachine guns, waiting. A portrait of Rákosi gazes down from the wall behind them. There's an air of expectancy and impatience. Nerves are frayed. Tensions are running high. It will only take a tiny spark to set them off. And then God knows what will happen.

Gábor joins him at the window and scowls at the insurgents in the square below. Tamás can feel the anger coming off him in waves.

'Bloody hooligans,' says Gábor. 'We should go out there and take back control.' That morning he proudly showed Tamás a coat that he'd stolen from a fallen freedom fighter. It's a good quality trench coat. He called it a souvenir of war.

'You wouldn't last five seconds out there,' calls one of the older men from the table. 'They'd gun you down as soon as you stepped outside.'

'Just let them try. I bet I can shoot straighter than that lot.'

'They don't need to shoot straight. There are more of them.'

Tamás ignores the argument and turns back to the window. He agrees with the man at the table, but there's nothing to be gained by antagonising Gábor in this already volatile environment. They're under siege and there's nothing to do but wait.

*

Petra has been queueing outside the grocery store for ages already, but she doesn't mind because the mood in

Republic Square is relaxed, happy even. Now that the fighting has died down, it's safe to venture outside. She hasn't enjoyed being cooped up in the apartment all this time, with Tibor driving her up the wall. She nearly had a heart attack when he gave her the slip and went out in the middle of all that anarchy. The fact that he returned half an hour later with a bag of potatoes and a couple of turnips only went partway to calming her frayed nerves. That boy will be the death of her.

The women in the queue are friendly, everyone keen to talk about the events of the past week. A pair of handsome young freedom fighters stroll past, their rifles slung over their shoulders. It seems to Petra that everyone on the streets is armed these days.

'Well done men!' says a short woman in a brown headscarf. 'You've done us all proud.'

They acknowledge the praise with a nod of the head. 'And how are you ladies coping?' asks one of the freedom fighters.

The woman in the headscarf pulls herself up to her full height. 'We're doing all right, thank you. We're survivors, aren't we ladies?' She encourages the other women to join in. There are murmurs of agreement.

Then everyone starts telling stories about how their sons and daughters helped in the fight.

'My grandson used my frying pans to stop a tank, can you believe it?' chuckles one elderly lady with no teeth. 'Turned upside down on the road, they look like land mines.' That raises a laugh. 'Then his older brother got the tank with a Molotov cocktail. You never saw anything like it!' She mimes a huge explosion with her knobbly hands.

It seems the children across the city have taken great delight in devising new and cunning ways to immobilise tanks. Silk bales soaked in oil and spread out on the ground caused the caterpillar tracks to lose their grip; jam smeared on glass viewing panels made it impossible for the Russians to see where they were going.

'My son helped bring down Stalin's statue,' says Petra proudly, completely forgetting how furious she was with him for staying out late without permission. 'And he's only fourteen, well just turned fifteen.'

'It's some of the children who've made the biggest contribution,' says the woman in the headscarf.

'And the biggest sacrifice,' says another woman in a subdued tone.

Everyone falls silent for a moment. No doubt they all know someone who has been injured or killed. The queue shuffles forward a few inches. It's still a slow and tiring business, shopping for food.

A truck pulls into the square and stops outside the Communist Party Headquarters.

'What's going on over there?' asks the woman in the brown headscarf.

The women watch the driver get out of the cab, open the rear doors and start to unload a supply of fresh meat which he carries into the building.

'Did you see that?' asks the toothless grandmother who sacrificed her frying pans in the fight against the Russians. 'They're getting supplies of fresh meat whilst we have to queue for hours for a scrap of dried sausage. It's outrageous.'

'It's a bloody disgrace,' says Petra, feeling a sudden surge of indignation. If she had a weapon, she might just be tempted to use it.

'Let's put a stop to it,' says the woman in the headscarf.

'Agreed,' says one of the freedom fighters to his companion. 'They're not going to get away with this.'

*

Tamás has been watching the delivery of meat to Party Headquarters. About time too. Their supplies were running perilously low. It was getting to the point where their choice was to starve inside the building or risk being lynched outside.

But why did the driver have to park right in front of the building in full view of all those women queueing up for their rations? Couldn't he have had the sense to use a back door? Tamás can see that the women have alerted the insurgents and now groups of angry people are storming across the square. It doesn't take much to get this lot fired up. God help us, he thinks, is this going to be the spark that ignites the fuse? A delivery of meat?

He can't see what has happened to the van driver. Is he inside the building? The shouting outside has brought other AVO officers to the windows to see what is going on. The room grows silent as everyone watches and waits.

With no warning, an explosion rocks the stairwell of the building. One of the insurgents must have thrown a hand grenade inside. A burst of gunfire from outside shatters the windows and Tamás ducks down. This is it, then.

At that moment, Vajda walks into the room from wherever he's been hobnobbing with other senior Party figures.

'What are you lot waiting for?' shouts Vajda. 'Don't just sit there. Let them have it! Show them what you're made of! Fire back!'

The men scramble for their weapons and take up position at the windows.

'About bloody time,' says Gábor, crouching down beside Tamás and pointing his submachine gun through the broken window. He pulls his finger on the trigger and lets off a magazine of bullets into the crowd, not caring where they strike. He turns to Tamás. 'Get shooting, you moron.'

*

Sitting by the open rear doors of the ambulance, Róza is sharing a moment of respite with István and Bálint.

They've become good mates in the short time they've been working together. They're chatting about their plans for the future – István wants to be a surgeon one day – when they hear the unmistakable sound of gunfire in Republic Square, just round the corner from the hospital. It's been quieter these last few days and it seemed that the worst of the fighting was over, but something has triggered this new skirmish.

They don't need to say anything to each other. Working as a team whilst dodging shells and bullets, they've learnt to communicate with very few words, just a look and a nod. There's no question of them not going to Republic Square to see what they can do to help. It's what they've been trained to do.

They jump into the ambulance and Bálint drives at speed the few hundred yards round the corner into the square. When Róza jumps down from the back of the ambulance the first thing she sees is women with shopping bags running every which way, screaming, amidst the gunfire.

She grabs the arm of a freedom fighter who is carrying a rifle. 'What's going on?'

'AVO in the Communist Party Headquarters,' he shouts, pointing to the building on the edge of the square. 'They're shooting at us, the bastards.' He runs off to join in the battle.

'Bloody hell,' says István. 'This is bad.'

*

Sándor takes the call at the Corvin cinema informing the Corvinists that fighting has broken out in Republic Square and that the freedom fighters there urgently need reinforcements. AVO men entrenched at Party Headquarters are firing at anything in the square that moves.

'We'll be there as soon as we can,' he says. He puts the

phone down and hurries off in search of Bandi.

Zoltán has gone home to spend some time with his family, but Sándor has stayed on at the cinema, helping to deal with the last remaining outbursts, mainly directed at the Secret Police. He shares Bandi's view that AVO men who are guilty of crimes should be arrested and tried, and not face mob justice at the hands of angry citizens. But it's difficult to control a crowd intent on vengeance. If the reports of AVO shooting at crowds in Republic Square are true, then there are going to be some very ugly reprisals.

It doesn't take long for the Corvinists to mobilise their forces and soon a convoy of armoured vehicles – one bearing the anti-tank gun – is on its way to Republic Square.

Riding in the front vehicle with Bandi, Sándor can't help feeling a sense of pride about what they've achieved in the past ten days. They've taken on the Russians and they've won. Now it's just a question of dealing with the handful of hard-line AVO that don't know the game is up. Once, he thought he would spend the rest of his life working in that awful factory, but his role with the Corvin Circle has taught him that he's capable of so much more. In the hours spent waiting for Russian tanks to trundle past so that he could blitz them with the anti-tank gun, he came to an important decision. When this is all over he's going to ask Róza to marry him. He's made up his mind and he shouldn't put it off any longer. If there's one thing he's learned it's that life is not a rehearsal for something else. You only get one shot at living and you have to grab opportunities as they appear.

The convoy rounds the corner into the square and he can see at a glance that this is more than just a spat involving a few hardened AVO. It's already turning into a bloodbath.

*

Tamás picks up his weapon and aims it out of the window. He doesn't want to do this anymore. He doesn't want to be here in this room, crouching next to Gábor, shooting at other Hungarians. But if he goes outside the insurgents will lynch him. He's seen it happen. They'll string him up from a tree by his ankles, douse him in petrol and set fire to him. So what other choice does he have but to shoot? He chose this line of work. Now he must stand alongside his comrades and fight until the last man is left standing. He pulls the trigger but he aims high, above the heads of the angry crowd.

The room shakes with the sound of gunfire. Plaster falls from the ceiling, lights shatter, the portrait of Rákosi cracks and falls to the floor. A shriek by the window cuts across the racket. Someone has been hit. There's a commotion whilst comrades drag the wounded man back from the window. He lies on the floor near the table, clutching his upper arm. We can't win this, thinks Tamás. The number of insurgents in the square is growing all the time, the sound of gunfire drawing them in like wasps attracted to overripe fruit. The AVO numbers are limited and they're already one man down.

Gábor turns to him, opens his mouth to speak, and then freezes as a bullet slices into his temple. For a second he looks startled, then he collapses on top of Tamás, spraying him in red blood. Tamás screams in horror, drops his weapon and pushes Gábor's limp body off him. The insurgents are firing directly at them now from the building opposite.

Tamás can't take any more of this. For one crazy moment he thinks of flinging himself from the window. All around him the room is in chaos. Wounded men are groaning. The dead ones lie silent, getting in everyone's way. More AVO appear from elsewhere in the building. They take up places at the windows and the shooting continues.

But still the insurgents keep coming. And now they're

armed with Molotov cocktails. They toss them in through the ground floor windows. A series of mini explosions rocks the building and black smoke billows into the square. And then through the smoke and chaos Tamás makes out the lumbering shape of an armoured vehicle carrying an anti-tank gun. Oh my God, he thinks, we're done for.

*

Róza and her colleagues pick their way around the edge of the square, hoping against hope that their white coats and red-cross armbands will shield them from flying bullets. There are already a couple of dozen bodies lying in front of the Communist Party Headquarters. Unless they can get closer they can't see who is already dead and who is still in with a chance.

'Go that way,' says István, pointing. 'We need to get under the cover of the building.'

'Medical workers coming through,' shouts Bálint.

The insurgents hold their fire for a moment to let Róza and her team approach the fallen, but there's no corresponding ceasefire from the building.

'Get back,' shouts István. 'It's too dangerous.'

But Róza is already running towards a man lying on the ground calling for help. From the way he's clutching his right thigh, his hand covered in blood, it looks as if he's been shot in the leg. He makes eye contact with her and his eyes light up with hope at the sight of her white uniform. He manages a thin smile in a face drained of colour. She smiles back. This is what she does – she brings hope to people. She gives them the strength to go on. The man reaches out to her with his other hand. All they have to do is roll him onto the stretcher and they can have him out of here in no time. They'll save his leg. They'll save his life.

She sees the shock in the wounded man's eyes before she feels the pain in her own body. For a moment, time stands still and the battle around her is caught in a freeze-frame. All is silent and she's floating in space. Then the ground comes up and smacks her in the face. She tries to draw breath but she can't. In the second before she dies, her medical training kicks in and she knows that she has been shot in the heart. There is no more hope left in her.

*

Tamás has the unnerving sensation that the barrel of the anti-tank gun is pointing directly at him. He ducks to the floor, his hands over his head, as a shell explodes into the building. The floor above them has been hit. God knows how many casualties there are. The other AVO officers who are still alive run for cover beneath the conference table as the ceiling cracks and chunks of plaster drop to the floor. The dust is blinding, the taste bitter.

Through the bangs and crashes, he can just make out the voices of his comrades.

'We have to get out of here.'

'They'll lynch us if we leave.'

'If the building collapses we'll be crushed to death.'

'Better to try and make a run for it.'

They're preparing to evacuate and Tamás doesn't want to be left behind.

He takes one last look at Gábor's immobile form. The bullet caught him square in the temple so that one side of his head exploded. The eyes which stare vacantly into space are covered in a film of pink plaster dust. Tamás recoils at the thought of closing them. The others are already leaving the room and he hurries to catch them up, trying not to trip over the bodies of the dead.

It's pandemonium on the stairwell. AVO are running in all directions. Those trying to go down are met by others fleeing upwards. Shouts fill the air.

'Go back up!'

'The insurgents are in the building!'

'There's no way out!'

'Isn't there a back door?'

'Where?'

'Over here!'

Tamás stops, realising what a fool he's been. He pushes his way through the panicking officers and runs back to the conference room. Gábor is where he left him, although there's even more debris covering him now. But it's not Gábor he wants. It's his coat. Where the hell is that damn coat he was going on about, the one he took from the dead rebel? He looks around the destroyed room, kicking aside lumps of plaster. And then he sees it, rolled up in the corner where Gábor put it for safe keeping. No one else has noticed it, which was Gábor's intention. With shaking fingers, Tamás rips off his blue AVO shirt and dons the trench coat. It's filthy from all the falling plaster but that doesn't matter. It makes him look as if he's been in a battle, which he has. He buttons it up to the collar to hide the fact that he's not wearing a shirt underneath and buckles the belt. Then he picks up a discarded submachine gun and makes his way cautiously to the door.

The stairwell has cleared and he starts to make his way downstairs, one step at a time. At the first turning in the stairs he nearly drops his weapon in fright when he sees a group of freedom fighters coming up from the floor below.

'Anyone up there?' asks the leader of the group.

His mouth is dry with terror and for a moment he just stares at them like an idiot. Why don't they shoot him or drag him outside for a lynching? But then he realises that they think he's one of them. Gábor's coat is doing its job. He finds his voice and points to the room he just left. 'No, that room's empty. The bastards got away.'

'Right, this way then.' The insurgents head back downstairs. Tamás follows. He'll be safe if he sticks with them. If he can just make it to the ground floor then he can slip away in the chaos that is still raging outside.

They're held up by a commotion at the door. Insurgents are holding a group of six or seven AVO officers who failed to get away, dragging them outside. If he hadn't gone back for the coat, he would have been one of them. But he mustn't let his comrades see him now. If they think he's gone over to the other side, they'll denounce him and then he's as good as mincemeat.

His AVO comrades are taken outside and Tamás almost buckles at the knees when he hears the gunshots. The men are being shot at point blank range.

Someone slaps him on the back. 'They're getting what they deserve, eh?'

'Yes,' croaks Tamás.

When no one is looking, he moves away from the building, desperate to get out of this hell-hole. He stops short when he sees a crowd clustered around one of the trees. Gut-churning cries of terror are coming from the centre of the group. He knows he should run but he's frozen to the spot. He recognises the voice that is pleading to be spared. It belongs to a man that he once looked to for recognition and promotion. He received neither.

The crowd parts just enough for him to see Vajda's flabby body, stripped naked, being hoisted upside down by his ankles. Whilst housewives spit and hurl insults at him, the insurgents douse him in petrol and set him alight.

At the sight of his boss burning like a pig, Tamás turns and flees.

*

The square is a scene of devastation and the air is pungent with the stink of burning flesh, but at least the shooting has stopped. Sándor jumps down from the armoured vehicle and joins the survivors in helping to pick up the casualties. There are plenty of walking wounded who would appreciate a lift to the hospital. They can stop off there on their way back to the Corvin Cinema. He might see if Róza can spare five minutes.

He helps a dozen or so people into the back of a truck, then he sees two white-coated medical workers carrying a stretcher across the square. They are walking slowly, their shoulders and heads bowed, as if the load they bear is too heavy for them. He runs towards them with the idea of letting them know that he'll be taking a batch of wounded people to the hospital and to see if he can give them a hand. He's got nothing but admiration for these medical students who have been risking life and limb to save their fellow citizens.

As he approaches he hears one of them sobbing. It's only then that he looks down at the figure on the stretcher and his heart leaps into his mouth. The red hair has come free from its white cap and is blowing in the breeze. A limp hand has fallen from the stretcher, the fingernails trailing along the ground.

'Róza!' The cry issues from his mouth before he's even aware that he's spoken.

The medical workers stop and look at him.

'We couldn't save her,' says the one who is sobbing. 'We tried our best.'

Sándor lifts her hand and places it across her chest where a dark red stain has spread over her white coat. Her eyes are closed and her beautiful face is unmarked. He bends down and kisses the lifeless lips. Then he staggers away, tears streaming down his face.

*

Tamás runs blindly through the streets. He is gasping for breath and has a stitch in his side, but he has to get away from the square. He can't comprehend so much horror. The sight of Vajda's pink, flabby body being strung up and set alight is too much for him. The stink of burning flesh seems to be clinging to him, following him.

He turns a corner and almost runs straight into another

charred corpse hanging upside down from a makeshift scaffold. This one is unrecognisable, the blackened flesh like old, cracked leather. It looks as if it's been hanging there for days. Under the body is a pile of money that would buy enough food for a banquet, but no one has taken it. It's tainted. Blood money. He lurches into an alleyway and is violently sick.

He ventures back into the street. People are walking past the burnt corpse as if it's perfectly normal to have such a grotesque thing hanging in the street. It's clear to him that anarchy is now the order of the day and it's every man for himself. He thrusts his hands into the pockets of his coat and tries to walk at a normal pace so as not to draw attention to himself. Every so often he comes across the body of a fallen Russian soldier lying on the ground, sprinkled in lime.

On one of the main boulevards he sees a row of Russian tanks laboriously making its way out of the city. The pavements are lined with people booing and jeering. Tamás joins in with some half-hearted boos.

'We beat the bastards,' says a jubilant young man standing next to him.

'We did,' says Tamás. 'We beat them.'

*

Wednesday, 31 October 1956 - Friday, 2 November 1956

Like a trail of giant cockroaches, Soviet tanks crawl out of the city, their guns silent. Hungarians line the streets, jeering, or just watching in silence, too stunned by the events of the past days to feel any real emotion yet. It will take a long time for the wounds to heal.

Katalin stays indoors, mourning the loss of her dearest friend. Róza's death has cast a dark and painful shadow over the revolution. She is reminded once more of her childhood friend, Liesl, who perished at the hands of the

Nazis. And what did she, Katalin, do to save Liesl or Róza? Was there anything she could have done?

On the first of November, she sits with her father and they listen to the radio as Imre Nagy, the Prime Minister, declares Hungary's neutrality from the Warsaw Pact.

'That is something, at least,' says Márton. 'If the Soviets invade again then America will have no reason not to intervene.'

'Do you think it's likely that the Soviets will come back?'

Márton shrugs. 'Who can tell? At this point, anything could happen.'

Katalin knows this to be the case. They appear to have won, but their victory feels fragile and it has come at such a high cost. She doesn't want Róza to have died in vain.

The doorbell rings and she wonders who it can be. She's not expecting anyone. When she opens the door she is surprised to find Professor Károly Novák standing on the landing. After she was dismissed so unceremoniously from the Novák's house four years ago, she never expected to see him or his wife again.

Professor Novák removes his hat and holds it in front of him in a gesture of respect. 'I'm sorry to bother you, Katalin, but I was wondering if your father was at home.'

She is tempted to tell Professor Novák that her father is out, when Márton calls from the living room, 'Who is it, dear?' The next moment he appears in the hallway.

Katalin looks from one to the other as the two former colleagues lock eyes. In Professor Novák's eyes she thinks she sees humility, maybe even remorse. In her father's eyes she sees surprise, then delight.

'Márton,' says Professor Novák. 'It's been such a long time. I just…I just wanted to see how you are. If you'd rather I went away…'

'Of course not,' says Márton. 'Come in. It's good to see you.'

Katalin stands aside and Professor Novák enters the

apartment. 'I won't stay long.'

'Long enough to have a drink, I hope,' says Márton.

Katalin takes their visitor's coat as Márton guides him through to the living room.

'I'll make coffee,' she says. When she brings the coffee through ten minutes later she finds them sitting comfortably, discussing the uprising. She puts the tray down on a table and leaves them to it. She's pleased at the thought of her father renewing his old acquaintances.

The next day brings freezing rain and a driving wind but on Saturday the day dawns bright and clear. The light dusting of snow that fell overnight glitters in the sunlight. It's still bitterly cold, but there's a freshness in the air, as if it's time to make a new start. Zoltán persuades her to leave the apartment for the first time in days. It will do her good to get outside, he says.

Muffled in scarves and winter hats, they join the hundreds of other people strolling arm in arm around their battered but beautiful city. Hardly anyone is carrying a weapon. The corpses have been cleared from the streets and the flower sellers and roast chestnut vendors have returned. Katalin and Zoltán buy a bag of roasted chestnuts to share as they walk along the bank of the Danube, watching the sun set behind the hills of Buda. For the first time in days she feels a glimmer of hope that things will get better. They've fought and they've won. The dead haven't died in vain. They will be remembered and honoured. Life will go on.

PART THREE
NOVEMBER 1956

CHAPTER 17

Sunday, 4 November 1956

The rumble of thunder invades her dreams.

Katalin is awake at once. It's still dark outside, not yet dawn. Suddenly a bright flash of light illuminates the window and she sees Zoltán standing there, silhouetted against a reddish afterglow. He's already dressed. She slips out of bed and joins him.

'What is it?' she asks, fearing she already knows the answer.

'They're back.' He doesn't have to say who. 'And this time it sounds like they mean business.'

'So they lied to us.'

'Yes,' he says as if he has expected this all along. 'They lied.'

She jumps as a series of explosions light up the sky, shaking the apartment. It's not thunder and lightning but the rumble and firing of Russian tanks on the streets. They couldn't have gone far when they left the city to have made such a speedy return. She hears her father's door open. The noise has woken him too.

Zoltán gently pulls her away from the window where

she is transfixed by the scarlet sky. 'Get dressed. We should get the children dressed too. We need to be prepared.'

She throws on yesterday's clothes which she left on the bedroom chair last night, then helps Zoltán dress a sleepy Lajos and a grisly Eva who is unhappy at being woken up. When they go through to the sitting room, Márton is tuning the dial on the radio, a look of grim resignation on his face. András is standing at the window watching the sky light up with explosions. They gather round the radio to listen to the voice of Hungary's new Prime Minister who hasn't yet been in the job a fortnight.

This is Imre Nagy speaking. Today at daybreak Soviet forces attacked the capital with the obvious intention of overthrowing the legal Hungarian democratic government. Our troops are fighting. The Government is in its place. I notify the people of our country and the entire world of this fact.

'It's over,' says Márton, shaking his head. 'They will crush the revolution and clamp down hard with an iron fist. There will be no more talk of democracy. Hungarians have died in vain.'

Katalin thinks of Róza giving her life to try and save others. It was all so pointless, she wants to scream.

The insistent ringing of the doorbell startles them all as if the Russians are on the landing.

'I'll get it,' says Zoltán. Katalin follows him into the hallway carrying Eva in her arms, Lajos clinging to her leg. The bangs are frightening the children.

It's József, the caretaker, still wearing the same moth-eaten cardigan he was wearing on that fateful day four years ago when her father was arrested. But this time he isn't accompanied by a group of AVO thugs. Behind him, supporting each other, are the elderly couple, Maria and her husband Milan, from across the landing. Petra and Tibor are making their bleary-eyed way down the stairs.

'We're under attack,' says József. 'We must take shelter in the basement. It's the only safe place in the building.'

Katalin recoils at the thought of hiding in the basement like they did during the siege of Budapest at the end of the war. She avoids the place as much as she can, fearful of reawakening the ghosts of memories that lurk in the dark recesses behind the coal bunkers. She recalls the smell of sweat and human waste. And sheltering down there didn't stop her mother from being killed.

But József is right. If the Russians have returned with the intention of overthrowing the revolution, then the fighting will be fierce. They can expect no mercy. She looks at Zoltán. She can see from the look of determination on his face that he has no intention of hiding in any basement. But there's her father and the children to think of.

'It is my duty to ensure the safety of everyone in this building,' says József, smacking his lips together. There's no hint of Pálinka on his breath. It's too early even for him to have had a sip yet.

Zoltán leans close and says in an urgent whisper, 'Do what he says. Take your father and the children downstairs.'

'What are you going to do?'

'I'm going back to the Corvin Cinema. Sándor will be there. I have to fight alongside him.'

She wants to tell him to take shelter in the basement with everyone else, but that's not the sort of person Zoltán is. He won't put his own safety before what he believes in. 'At least take some food with you,' she says, masking her anxiety behind a display of practicality. She goes into the kitchen and returns with a half loaf of bread and a whole salami sausage which she presses into his hands as if he's about to go on a picnic. He puts on his trench coat and stashes the food into the deep pockets. Then he picks up his rifle and slings the strap over his shoulder.

'I'm coming with you,' says András.

Márton shakes both their hands. 'Take care.'

Katalin has to choke back a sob. Those are the words her father spoke to her before the ÁVO took him away.

'You too,' says Zoltán, embracing his father-in-law. He takes Katalin's face in his hands and kisses her tenderly on the lips. Then he's gone.

For a moment she is too stunned to move. She gives herself a shake. Keep busy, that's the thing to do. She goes into the kitchen and starts to put together a basket of food. She tells Lajos to fetch his favourite toys and also his sister's cuddly bear. They're going on a big adventure and she needs him to be a big, brave boy, just like their upstairs neighbour Tibor. Can he do that for her? Lajos looks at her with his big brown eyes and nods his head. Yes, he'll be brave.

*

The shutters are down and the café will remain closed today. And for the foreseeable future.

Feri switches on the radio and hears the traitor János Kadar proclaiming the formation of a new Hungarian Revolutionary Worker-Peasant government.

In the interests of our people, our working class and our country, we requested the Soviet army to help the nation in destroying the dark reactionary forces and restoring order and calm in the country.

Kádár has been General Secretary of the Party for a matter of days but he's already shown his true colours by betraying the Prime Minister, Imre Nagy, and defecting to the Soviets.

Feri turns off the radio in disgust. The hard-line communists are trying to seize back power and they have called on their friends in Moscow to help them destroy the revolution. Just let them try, thinks Feri. Just let them try.

If he gets out of this alive he's going to try and escape

across the border. He's always wanted to go back to Paris. He has dreamed of running a little café in Montmartre where people will read newspapers published by a free press and discuss works of literature. There will be an atmosphere of open debate and his customers will be free to laugh and criticise the government. He will play French music on the radio and serve hot, buttery croissants to locals and tourists. He will introduce a few Hungarian delicacies to the menu as well. He'll need to brush up his French which has grown rusty.

He goes to the back of the café and uncovers a box of empty bottles. He's kept them just in case. He also has a supply of Russian vodka that he never drinks and a collection of old rags. He'll spend the morning manufacturing Molotov cocktails and when the tanks come, he'll be ready for them. By God, he'll be ready.

*

Zoltán and András run to the cinema, through streets still battle-scarred and wounded from the first round of fighting. What chance does the city have of surviving this new attack? It's already half on its knees. All it needs is for the Soviets to stamp their boots and grind them into the dust. Maybe he should have stayed in the basement with Katalin and the children. Is he just being foolhardy, trying to be a hero?

His spirits rise when he sees groups of armed freedom fighters taking up positions on street corners. Teams of men and women are tearing up the cobbles and overturning trams to build barricades across road junctions. The Hungarians are not going to take this assault lying down. They will stand and fight to the last man.

'Surely the Americans will help us now,' says András, gasping for breath. 'They promised on *Radio Free Europe* that they would.'

'Don't count on it,' says Zoltán. 'Israel has invaded Egypt. The West won't be interested in a little country like Hungary when their interests in the Suez Canal are under threat. We're on our own, I fear.'

The air around the cinema is already thick with smoke, the sound of shellfire deafening. They are under attack but Zoltán can't see where the shells are coming from.

Sándor is on the steps of the cinema, preparing the anti-tank gun. From the expression of grim determination on his face, it looks to Zoltán as if grief for Róza has been temporarily replaced with anger at the Russians. He just hopes his friend doesn't try anything reckless.

Bandi runs over to greet them. 'We've got trouble in Kisfaludy Street.' He points behind the cinema. 'A Russian tank is firing at us. Already about fifteen dead. Most of the men were sleeping in the Práter Street School when the tank approached and now they can't get through because it's blocking their way. We can't get close enough to destroy it with Molotov cocktails.'

'Then we need to use the anti-tank gun against them,' says Sándor. 'Don't just stand there. Give me a hand turning this damn thing around.'

*

Whilst Zoltán, Sándor and Bandi are manoeuvring the heavy weapon into a new position, András spots a couple of teenage boys, one dark, the other fair, hanging around, carrying a box of homemade Molotov cocktails. They've come to join in the fight.

He doesn't bother asking them their names or why they aren't hiding somewhere safe. Maybe they don't have homes left to go to. They want to help and he admires their courage. 'See that building over there?' He points to the apartment block on the north side of the cinema. 'Do you reckon we can get inside and find a way to look out over Kisfaludy Street?'

'Sure we can,' says the dark-haired boy, his eyes lighting up at the suggestion. His friend nods his head in agreement.

'Come on, then,' says András. 'Bring your bottles and follow me. I've got a job for you.'

*

'Hold Grandpa's hand,' Katalin tells her son, 'and be careful. Some of the steps are uneven.' She clutches Eva to her chest, a basket of provisions over her arm, and follows her father and Lajos down the into the cellar. Behind her, Petra and Tibor help the old couple, Maria and Milan, to navigate the worn treads. József is already down there, setting up oil lamps.

The cellar is cold and dank and smells of coal. Each family stores their firewood and coal supplies down here, but there is a small space in the centre where they can congregate. Katalin is surprised to see that József has brought stools and benches, and even a paraffin stove. Those who lived through the war are prepared for events like this. She places her basket of food supplies next to the stove.

'I hope we don't have to stay down here too long,' says Petra. 'I get claustrophobic in small spaces.' In the yellow light of the oil lamp, Katalin can see a sheen of sweat on Petra's forehead, despite the chilliness of the air.

'Can you take Eva for a moment whilst I sort out the food supplies?' Katalin transfers the baby into Petra's arms. 'She's grouchy at having been woken up so early.' If Petra has someone else's problems to focus on, she thinks, she'll forget about her own anxieties. It seems to do the trick because Petra sits down on one of the stools, making cooing noises to the baby, her own worries forgotten for the moment.

The rumble of a tank in the street outside causes everyone to fall silent.

'We should chuck petrol bombs at the tanks from an upstairs window,' says Tibor, miming the action. 'We could blow them up and the Russians inside would turn to toast.'

'Sit down!' says Petra sharply. 'You are not throwing petrol bombs, and you are not leaving this cellar until I say so. Do I make myself perfectly clear?'

'Yes, Mum.' Tibor sits down, looking glum.

Another round of firing outside, and Lajos starts to cry.

Márton, who is sitting quietly on one of the benches, says, 'Come here, child, sit on my lap.' Lajos clambers onto his Grandpa's lap, sucking his thumb. 'Now then, did I ever tell you the story of St George and the Dragon?'

Lajos shakes his head.

'Well, once upon a time, in a country called England there was a very brave man and his name was St George.'

Whilst her father recites the familiar story, Katalin lets her mind drift. The idea of going to England has always seemed like an impossible dream. But what is going to be left of their country after this fighting? What is going to be left of her family? If they survive, is it possible that they could escape?

*

An explosion rocks the building and Tamás is jolted from his hiding place by falling rubble and shattering glass. Since escaping from the Communist Party Headquarters five days ago, he's been living a hand-to-mouth existence in abandoned apartments, raiding kitchen cupboards for scraps of food, and dressing himself in clothes left behind by people who have fled or been killed.

Now the empty building in which he's been sheltering for the last two nights no longer feels safe. This morning a group of insurgents moved into the ground floor with their crates of petrol bombs and the building is now a target for Soviet reprisals. One more blast and the whole building will be destroyed, and Tamás with it. He flees down the stairs as fast as he can and finds a way out the back, stepping over the bodies of two dead Hungarians.

Once again he finds himself out on the streets with hellfire raging around him. He's so tired of scurrying from place to place in fear of his life. He doesn't know who he's more afraid of – vengeful Hungarian lynch mobs or Soviet tanks. Maybe he should just lie down in the path of a tank and all his troubles would be over. He'd hardly feel a thing.

He roams the streets mindlessly but when he looks about him he sees that his feet have brought him to the street where, it seems to him, all his problems started. He gazes up at the building where Katalin and Márton Bakos live and remembers that day, so long ago now, when Vajda ordered him to join the team that was going to arrest an academic by the name of Professor Bakos. In those days he was so sure of the communist cause and his part in it that he didn't question anything, certainly not his boss Vajda. But there was something about Márton Bakos, the way he maintained a quiet dignity despite the degradations of the cells and the treatment he endured at 60 Andrássy Avenue, that sowed the first seeds of doubt in Tamás's mind, although he didn't realise it at the time.

If he asks for Márton's forgiveness will he receive it? Will Márton remember the times Tamás let him sleep when he was supposed to be writing his life story?

*

It's a newer tank than the old second-world-war T-34s, many of which were destroyed by the freedom fighters in the early days of the uprising. This is one of the Soviet Union's new T-54 models, a highly engineered killing machine. And it's doing what it was designed to do. Zoltán feels utter despair as he takes in the bodies lying in Kisfaludy Street, too many to count, and the buildings with their fronts ripped off, exposing the devastated rooms inside. All testament to the tank's destructive power.

'Further over to the left,' shouts Sándor as they heave the anti-tank gun into position by the corner of a building.

'Point it at the bastards.'

Sándor seems to be driven by a manic energy, as if he's single-handedly going to face down the might of Soviet aggression. Zoltán understands that for Sándor the fight is now personal as much as anything else. He knows he would feel the same if anything happened to Katalin and the children.

The tank discharges a shell at the building opposite and they run for cover as a shower of masonry crashes to earth, throwing up a blinding cloud of dust and debris. When Zoltán is able to see again he realises that Sándor is already manning the anti-tank gun, winding the rope attached to the trigger around his hand.

But the Russians must have spotted him, because the tank is swivelling its gun in his direction.

'Get back!' shouts Zoltán.

But Sándor doesn't hear him, or chooses to ignore him. As he prepares to pull the trigger, the tank fires again, hitting the metal shield of the anti-tank gun, blowing it into hundreds of lethal pieces of jagged metal. Zoltán throws up his arms to protect his head from flying shrapnel. When he dares to lift his eyes, his first thought is for his best friend. But Sándor has vanished.

*

The inner courtyard of the four-storey apartment block is deserted. The residents, András guesses, have either fled or are hiding in the basement. A blast from Kisfaludy Street rocks the ground they're standing on, bringing home to them the urgency of their mission.

'Over there,' shouts András, pointing to an open door in the corner of the building.

The electricity is out, shrouding the stairwell in semi-darkness.

'Up to the top floor,' he says to the two boys. 'Let's see if we can get into one of the apartments.'

The teenagers nod their understanding and start to mount the stairs, the petrol-filled bottles clanking against one another in the box.

'Careful in the dark,' says András, following behind. 'You don't want to trip and drop that lot.'

They're younger and fitter than him – they haven't spent months of their lives on a labour camp breaking rocks – and they soon disappear round the bend in the stairs, leaving him to catch up.

A fresh round of firing in Kisfaludy Street causes the plaster in the ceiling to crack, and a shower of dust descends on him. Dear God, it feels as if they're trying to destroy the building. He hurries to catch up with the boys.

On the top landing there are two doors. One is locked, but the other is ajar, as if the tenants left in too much of a hurry to worry about their personal possessions. András pushes it open with his foot and the teenagers follow him inside.

From the living room window they can see the tank in the street below, but it's about twenty yards off to their left.

The fair-haired boy calls from the hallway. 'There's a hatch into the attic. If we go up into the roof space, we might be able to get through to the neighbouring building and get closer to the tank.'

'That's a terrific idea,' says András, patting the boy on the back. 'Fetch that chair and help me up.'

*

Time drags. It feels to Katalin as if they've been in the cellar for days, but it's only been a matter of hours so far. The blasts and explosions outside make it sound as if the world is ending.

She has politely declined to share the bottle of Pálinka which József brought down to the basement, preferring to keep a clear head. The old couple, Maria and Milan, have both had a generous slug and are now dozing peacefully propped up beside a coal bunker. Tibor is telling Lajos stories about Superman, and Eva is sleeping in Petra's arms.

Katalin kneels by her father's feet. He has a faraway look in his eye, as if his mind is elsewhere.

'What are you thinking?' she asks.

He strokes her hair with his hand. 'I was remembering the last time we hid down here.'

She knows what he means. She's been having the same thoughts too. How her mother looked after everyone, making sure they were all right, that everyone had enough food to eat – although that was a daily struggle – and how she kept their spirits up by singing songs. She was always so cheerful, even in the midst of the darkest days. In fact, Katalin only recalls one time when she saw her mother rattled. It was just before the war started – Katalin must have been eight or nine – and they'd gone to the Lukács thermal baths in Buda. Katalin loved splashing in the warm water and demonstrating her aquatic skills. After an hour in the water, they were heading back to the changing rooms, their wet hair plastered to their heads, when they ran into Ilona Novák, emerging from a cubicle, her dark hair piled dramatically on top of her head, a towelling bath robe hugging her shapely figure. Eva caught hold of Katalin's hand.

'Eva, what a surprise,' said Ilona, her shrill voice echoing off the hard tiled surfaces of the baths. 'And Katalin too. My, hasn't she grown since I last saw you. How are you both?'

'We're well, thank you.'

'And Márton, how is he?'

Eva's hand tightened on Katalin's, crushing her fingers. 'He's busy at the university.'

'Of course.'

Ilona smiled and Katalin waited for her mother to say something else, maybe ask after Ilona's husband but the silence stretched awkwardly. Finally Eva said, 'We should go. Katalin will be getting cold.' Eva dragged Katalin away to fetch their clothes without another word being exchanged between the adults.

The following week when Katalin asked if they could go swimming again Eva said she was too tired. They never went again.

*

'Sándor!' Zoltán staggers into the smoke, shouting frantically for his friend. What the hell happened to him? He was standing right here, behind the anti-tank gun, and now it's as if he's been obliterated. Heedless of his own safety, he stumbles like a blind man with his arms outstretched, through the cloud of dust. He almost trips over a figure lying on the ground. 'Sándor!' The blast must have thrown him backwards. He grabs Sándor under the arms, dragging his limp body out of the line of fire.

Bandi runs over to help. 'Is he dead?'

'I don't know,' gasps Zoltán. 'But he's knocked out and his leg's a bloody mess. Help me carry him to the school.'

Bandi takes the ankles and Zoltán lifts Sándor under his arms. Sándor lets out a groan and Zoltán almost weeps for joy. He's still alive. There's hope yet.

Together they carry him as quickly as they can to the first aid station in the school where Anna is single-handedly manning the fort. Blood is pouring thickly from a gash to Sándor's right thigh where a piece of shrapnel has embedded itself.

If Anna is shocked by the sight of Sándor in this state, she does her best not to let it show. Zoltán is grateful to her, because he's barely managing to hold it together himself. What he needs right now is for everyone to do their best for Sándor.

Anna instructs them to lay Sándor down on a row of desks which have been pushed together to form a makeshift operating table. Wasting no time, she rips open his trouser leg, exposing the wound in all its horrific detail. The flesh of the right thigh has been shredded, revealing splinters of shattered bone.

'Bloody hell,' says Bandi, making a gagging sound in his throat.

Even to Zoltán's untrained eye, it's obvious that the leg can't be saved. But what about Sándor's life? That's all that matters now.

'Give me your belt,' says Anna. 'I need something to tie tight around the top of his thigh to stem the flow of blood.'

In a daze, Zoltán obeys, pulling his belt out of his trousers and handing it to her. Anna ties the leather strap around Sándor's thigh as tightly as she can, ignoring the blood that is staining her hands and clothes.

'We need to get him to the hospital immediately,' she says, 'otherwise he's almost certain to bleed to death. He's already lost so much blood.' She puts two fingers on his neck. 'His pulse is erratic.' She looks around helplessly at their dwindling stocks of bandages and splints. Zoltán understands. She can only patch people up, not perform life-saving operations.

'No one can get to the hospital at the moment,' says Bandi. 'The fighting out there is too intense. The ambulances can't get through. It's chaos.'

'Then I'll carry him there myself,' says Zoltán, preparing to pick up the prone figure of his friend.

'Don't be a fool.' Bandi grabs his wrist.

Zoltán pulls his arm free. 'You can't stop me.'

'I can and I will.' Bandi steps in front of him, blocking his path. 'There's a raging battle going on out there. If you try to take him to the hospital you'll both end up dead and as the commander of the Corvin Circle I can't allow that to happen.'

*

Katalin tries to distract herself by organising the cooking of lunch. They all have to eat. She and Petra crouch by the paraffin stove and sort through their ingredients, deciding what to cook. A shell explodes on the street right outside and the flame on the paraffin stove flickers, threatening to go out. They'll need to watch they don't gas themselves in this confined space.

They heat up lentils and beans with a little lard, stirring in slices of smoked bacon and sausage. Katalin remembers her mother being inventive with whatever was to hand in the war when fierce battles raged outside in the street. But when the food supplies started to run out there were days when they had virtually nothing. Until…No, she mustn't think about that time now or she'll fall to pieces. She stirs the stew and tries to focus on the present situation, on her family and neighbours who need feeding. But now that her memory has been stirred, the thought she is trying to suppress refuses to go away. It demands her attention. She stares into the pot but all she sees is her mother preparing to go out in search of food. As the siege dragged on and food supplies ran perilously low, abandoned horses from German cavalry units became their only source of meat. It was on a Tuesday, she remembers, when a neighbour from across the street reported a freshly dead horse not far from their apartment. 'I won't be long,' said Eva, tying a scarf around her hair. 'A good piece of horse meat will last us all week.' Katalin never knew precisely what happened to her mother, other than that she was killed by a stray bullet on her way to the horse. Friends carried her home on a door used as a stretcher. Maria's husband, Milan, made a coffin out of an old chest of drawers.

Katalin can no longer see what she is doing as tears well up in eyes, clouding her vision. She rises to her feet and staggers away from the stove. She doesn't want Lajos to see her upset.

A hand on her shoulder makes her turn around. It's József, offering her the bottle of Pálinka. This time she takes the bottle and has a sip. 'Courage, girl,' says József. 'Have courage. Like your mother.'

Katalin nods her thanks.

When she returns to the stove, Petra says she thinks the stew is ready to be served. They ladle the mixture into bowls and pass them around.

For a few minutes the only sounds are those of chewing and swallowing. Not a drop of the stew goes to waste.

'That was delicious,' says Márton when they've finished. 'Best lentil and bean stew I've ever eaten.'

'It was yummy,' says Tibor, and everyone agrees.

Katalin smiles at them all, pleased to have brought a brief moment of comfort to this terrible day.

Then little Eva lets out a wail and Katalin picks her up, wrinkling her nose. The baby needs a new nappy and she's forgotten to bring any with her.

'Don't worry, I'll go,' says her father, getting to his feet. 'You stay here. I won't be long.'

*

For an hour or more Tamás has been circling the block, too scared to go inside and present himself to Márton Bakos. Márton would be justified in sending him away. But he keeps coming back to the building's double doors. He's got nowhere else to go. What has he got to lose?

He pushes open the door, expecting to be shooed away by that grizzled old caretaker, but József is nowhere to be seen. In fact there's a deathly silence about the place, as if all the residents have disappeared.

He climbs the stairs to the Bakos apartment, his boots echoing in the empty stairwell. He presses the bell. Just a quick short ring, not like the way Vajda held the button down for ages until Márton opened the door.

There's no answer.

In some ways he's relieved. If they had answered they

might have turned him away. And justifiably so. Probably out of the habits he's picked up over the last few days, he tries the door handle anyway and finds the door unlocked.

'Hello?'

Silence.

He steps inside, closing the door behind him.

The apartment is just how he remembered it. He stands on the threshold of the living room and sees that the books have been replaced on the bookshelves, although there are gaps where the foreign language titles are still missing. The pictures have been rehung on the wall and the piano music has been tidied away.

He goes to Katalin's room but from the shirt and tie hanging on the back of a wooden chair, he supposes this must be Márton's room now. He crosses the hallway and opens the door to what was Márton's room. Besides the double bed, there's a child's bed under the window and a baby's cot. This must be where she sleeps now with her husband and children.

On top of the chest of drawers is the violin case which he failed to open when they searched the apartment. He walks over to it and runs his fingers over the lock. He could open it now, but he's sure that all he would find inside is a violin, quite harmless.

He shouldn't be here. He'll go to the kitchen and see if they've left any food, then he'll go somewhere else. Just then he hears the front door opening and closing. There are footsteps in the hallway. He looks around, but there's nowhere to hide.

*

Márton closes the door behind him. He's surprised to find it unlocked, but then they left in such a hurry this morning. He'll lock it before he goes back to the cellar. You can't be too careful. A group of hungry Russians could easily break in and help themselves to whatever they fancy. In the war they went around demanding that people hand over their wristwatches, as if they didn't have any timepieces in the Soviet Union. He shakes his head at the memory. Now, where does Katalin keep Eva's things? Ah, yes, he remembers. In the chest of drawers in the bedroom. Best be quick and get back down to the basement. He pushes open the door and walks in.

The shock of seeing a figure lurking by the wardrobe is so great that for a moment he isn't able to utter a sound. Is the man armed? Márton doesn't have anything with which to defend himself. He assumes the intruder must be because almost everyone is these days.

'Who are you?' he asks brusquely, trying to inject a note of aggression into his voice to mask his fear. 'There's nothing of value here.'

The intruder steps forwards, showing his face properly for the first time. 'Please don't hurt me. I'm not armed.'

Márton blinks in surprise and realises it's the boy from Andrássy Avenue. What was his name? Tamás, that was it. He was the junior AVO officer who was involved in his arrest and who patrolled the cellars, opening and closing the spy holes with such needless force. Even at the time he knew it was just a ploy to intimidate the prisoners and he tried not to let the noise of clanking spy holes bother him. But now Tamás is the one who is frightened. This is what communism has done to them. They've all been living in a state of perpetual fear and it's hard to shake it off.

'What are you doing here?' he asks more gently. Now that he's got over his initial shock, he can see that Tamás is no longer wearing his AVO uniform but a jumbled set of clothes – a check shirt, a brown jumper, an old trench coat – that look as if they have been chosen at random from different people's wardrobes.

'The door was unlocked. I've been living rough for days and I…I just wanted to…' His voice starts to break up.

'It's all right,' says Márton. 'Take your time.' The boy

has obviously suffered some kind of trauma.

Suddenly Tamás crumples. He drops onto the edge of the bed, his head in his hands. His shoulders shake and he lets out a great heaving sob. Taken aback, Márton sits next to him and pats him on the back.

'I'm…I'm so sorry,' splutters Tamás between sobs. 'For everything.'

'I know,' says Márton. He passes Tamás a clean handkerchief and waits whilst he wipes his eyes and blows his nose.

'Can you ever forgive me?'

This is a question which Márton has wrestled with over the years since his release from the labour camp. What would he do if he were to come face to face with Vajda? Who is ultimately to blame for what he suffered? It's an impossible question to answer, so in the end he says, 'You were doing your job in a corrupt system. Of all the guards at Andrássy Avenue, you were my favourite.'

Tamás gives him a weak smile. 'Thank you.'

'Now,' says Márton, standing up, 'I came in here to fetch a clean nappy for my granddaughter. Katalin will send out a search party if I'm not back soon.' He opens the top drawer and takes out half a dozen clean towelling nappies, just in case.

'Where is everyone?' asks Tamás.

'We're sheltering in the basement. It's not really safe to be upstairs with all this fighting going on.' As if to prove his point, a blast from outside shakes the building and they both duck down. 'Will you come with me?'

Tamás nods his head and a tear trickles down his face.

*

Feri is ready for them. Lining the counter top is a row of Molotov cocktails, as carefully prepared as one of his famous coffees. He loads the bottles into an empty crate and carries it to an upstairs window overlooking the street.

Down below are the carcases of burnt out cars and an overturned tram. There is also a bunch of flowers marking the spot where a freedom fighter died, and an open suitcase overflowing with money people have donated to help those widowed or orphaned by the fighting.

He opens the window to its full height and waits. When all this is over he'll go to Paris. He'll climb the Eiffel Tower before he's too old for such a thing. He'll visit Notre Dame and Sacré Coeur. He'll stroll around the Louvre and the many art galleries and afterwards he'll drink coffee in Montmartre. In the spring he'll enjoy long walks along the banks of the Seine. Maybe he'll even fall in love.

He is jerked out of his daydream by a rumbling that sounds like an earthquake. He leans out of the window and sees a convoy of three tanks lumbering down the street, firing indiscriminately at buildings and people. The bottles in the crate clink together as the floorboards pick up the vibrations of the caterpillar tracks on the cobbles. It feels as if every bone in his body is rattling in sympathy.

With a deep breath he picks up one of the bottles. In his other hand he holds a cigarette lighter. As the gun of the first tank draws level with his café, he lights the rag in the bottle and hurls it with all his strength at the vehicle, aiming for the engine grille at the back. He's heard you have to douse the engine in burning petrol to bring the tank to a standstill. The bottle explodes in a ball of flame – not a bad shot for a first attempt. But the tank is still moving forwards, like a creature from prehistoric times.

He picks up a second bottle. As he prepares to light the rag, the tank turns its gun on him. He throws the bottle at the same instant the tank fires.

As the building explodes around him and Feri falls to earth in an avalanche of stone and rubble, he fancies he hears a choir of angels singing the Marseillaise.

*

The attic roof is so steeply pitched that there's only room for András and the two boys to stand up in the very centre. The smoke and dust outside prevent much light getting through the tiny windows.

'This must be the last attic,' says András. They've had to knock down two fire walls to reach the attic at the very end of the block. By his reckoning they should be directly above the tank now. Close enough to hit it.

He prises open the sky light in the roof. The hinges, which probably haven't been used in years, howl in protest. He sticks his head out of the window, but all he can see at this angle is the grey slate roof sloping away before him. If he's going to hit the tank, he'll have to lean out further than that. Otherwise there's the risk that a Molotov cocktail will simply land in the gutter and blow the top off the building, sending them all skywards. He contemplates the two boys. Between the pair of them, they're probably strong enough to take his weight.

Another blast from the tank rocks the building and he comes to a decision.

'All right, boys, this is what we're going to do.' They look at him expectantly. Oh God, he thinks, please let this work. 'I'm going to lean out of the window with a bottle in my hands and you're going to hold me by the ankles. As soon as I've thrown the bottle, you're going to haul me back inside. Have you got that?'

They nod their heads vigorously. 'Sure, we can do that.'

He removes his jacket and prepares to lower himself out of the window. 'Remember, hold on tight and don't let go.'

'We won't, Mister. Promise.'

Bottle in one hand, lighter in the other, he eases himself out of the window onto the slate roof. The wind whips his hair and he is reminded of the mountainside at Recsk and of the day a landslide threatened to kill him. He shouts at the boys to grab his ankles. He feels their strong grips holding him tight, then he lowers himself further down the roof until he can see over the gutter into the street below. The tank is swivelling its gun, preparing to fire another round. He lights the bottle and throws it at the tank, directly above the engine grille.

'Now!' he shouts and suddenly he's being hauled backwards by his ankles. He lands on the attic floor with a bump.

An explosion in the street below rips the tiles off the roof above them and András sees the clouds scudding across the sky.

*

Zoltán sits on the floor with his back against the schoolroom wall, Sándor's head resting in his lap. He can't take his friend to the hospital but he isn't going to leave him alone. He's done with fighting. Look where it's got them.

'We had some good times, didn't we?' says Sándor. Anna has made him as comfortable as she can and given him something for the pain, but Zoltán suspects Sándor's present nostalgic mood has more to do with the half bottle of Pálinka which Bandi gave them, telling them to finish it off.

'We did,' says Zoltán, taking a sip and holding the neck of the bottle to Sándor's dry lips.

'Remember when we used to pick apples in old Ferenc's orchard and you fell from the tree?' says Sándor.

Zoltán had forgotten, but he remembers now. It was a simpler, more innocent time, before the war, before the communists, when their families still owned vineyards north of Budapest.

'Tell Csaba Elek from me that...' Sándor's voice falls so low that Zoltán can't hear what he wants him to say to the Party Secretary at the factory.

'What should I tell him?'

'Tell him he's a jerk.'

'Right, will do.'

They both fall silent for a moment. Zoltán takes the bottle of Pálinka and tilts it to Sándor's lips before taking a gulp himself. It's nearly all gone. Outside there are more bangs and explosions. Zoltán is so used to them now, he almost doesn't notice.

Suddenly Sándor says, 'You've got a pretty wife. And two great kids.'

'I know,' says Zoltán, his throat tightening.

'When you get out of here,' says Sándor, 'you should go to…go to…'merica.' His voice is starting to slur.

'America, you reckon?' asks Zoltán. 'What have they got there, then?' He wants to keep Sándor talking for as long as possible. He's still clinging to the ever-decreasing hope that the fighting will ease and they'll be able to get him to the hospital before it's too late.

'They got…they got…' His voice is no more than a croak.

'Tell me,' says Zoltán leaning his face close to Sándor's.

Sándor smiles and his eyes roll into the back of his head. As he draws his last breath, a cry goes up from outside that the tank has been destroyed.

CHAPTER 18

Zoltán doesn't see the point anymore. All around him the battle rages on, but it's clearly a lost cause. This time the Russians have come prepared and they're not going to give up until every last Hungarian freedom fighter has surrendered or been killed.

Out of loyalty to Bandi, he soldiers on as part of the Corvin Circle for another day, but without his best friend by his side, he's lost heart. Their dreams of a better life have been crushed under the caterpillar tracks of the T-54 tanks. Blown to smithereens by the mortar shells. It's time to think about self preservation and the safety of his family. It's time to think about escape.

He abandons his post on the corner of Üllői Avenue and goes in search of András and Anna in the first aid station at the Práter Street school. Outside the main entrance, piles of rubble have grown. He inhales a sickly sweet smell of rotting meat and recoils sharply at the sight of a dismembered leg sticking up out of the pile of debris, a boot still attached to the foot. He has no idea whose leg it is. Gagging, he pushes open the door and stumbles inside.

Sándor's body was taken away by Red Cross workers

the previous evening during a brief lull in the fighting. Now the former classroom is unusable as a first aid centre. Lumps of plaster and shards of glass litter the floor and every surface. Their medical supplies have run out. And with every passing minute their chances of being blown up rise higher and higher. They can't keep rolling the dice and hoping to be spared. Anna and András are trying to salvage what they can but it's pointless.

'We should get out of here,' says Zoltán. 'More tanks are on their way from Buda. We don't have the resources to deal with them.'

'Why did it have to end like this?' says Anna, close to tears. She brushes her hair off her face with grimy hands. Her forehead is streaked with soot. 'I wanted to do more. I wish I could have saved Sándor.'

'Hey, it's not your fault,' says András, pulling her into an embrace. 'You did the very best you could. You were incredibly brave. If it wasn't for you I would never have had the courage to get involved in the first place.'

She nods and gives him a wan smile.

'You should go home and see your family,' says András.

'Come with me,' she says. 'I'd like you to meet them.'

A blast shakes the building.

'Come on,' says Zoltán. 'Now!'

They run for the exit, ducking the flying debris.

It feels as if they're heading into Armageddon as they run through the streets full of panicking and wounded people, dodging tanks, explosions and shrapnel. Fires are burning out of control, buildings are wrecked, and the number of bodies littering the streets has risen to a level unimaginable since the war. On the corner of Erzsébet Boulevard, Zoltán says good-bye to András and Anna and carries on alone. He's sick with worry about what he'll find when he gets home, if he gets there in one piece. The sky is black with the smoke from burning fuel.

He turns into Király Street, dreading what he might

find. But the building is still standing, thank God. It's nothing short of a miracle.

*

There are ten of them sheltering in the basement now. When Márton returned with a pile of clean nappies for the baby, he calmly introduced Tamás to the group and said that he would be joining them. Katalin was surprised to say the least. She had never expected to see Tamás again, had even wondered if he had been lynched as so many Secret Police had. She found she was glad to know he was all right. She could see Petra was wary of the new arrival, but he's since made himself useful fixing the paraffin stove when it failed to light and bringing Márton's radio downstairs so they can listen to the latest government pronouncements.

They are clustered around the radio when the cellar door clatters open. Katalin looks up in alarm, but then she almost laughs with relief when she makes out, in the dim light, the figure of Zoltán coming down the stairs. She runs into his arms.

'Thank God you're safe. I've been so worried about you. Where are the others?'

'Anna has taken András to meet her family.'

'And Sándor? He's not still fighting the Russians, is he?' Her voice trails away when she sees the bleak look in her husband's eyes. The expression on his face is one of sheer wretchedness.

'Oh my God, I'm so sorry.' She doesn't know what else to say. First Róza and now Sándor. How many more losses do they have to endure?

Márton embraces his son-in-law, saying nothing. Words are useless here.

Katalin holds tight to Zoltán's hand as they cluster around the paraffin stove for warmth.

'How many tanks did you blow up?' asks Tibor, his

eyes wide.

'Tibor!' Petra glares at him and he falls silent.

Zoltán knocks back the glass of Pálinka which József offers him and wipes his mouth on the sleeve of his coat. 'We have to think about leaving Budapest and getting out of Hungary. It isn't safe for us to stay here.'

Márton nods his head. 'I agree. They are saying on the radio that Imre Nagy has been arrested and the hardliner János Kádár has seized power. The AVO will show no mercy to anyone who fought in the uprising.'

'Where would we go?' asks Katalin.

'Austria,' says Zoltán. 'That's the route to freedom.'

Austria. The name alone conjures visions of mountain pastures and idyllic villages. When Katalin imagined escaping, it seemed like an impossible dream. But now Zoltán is talking about it as a reality. A necessity, in fact. Could they really do it? With the children in tow? But the alternative might be imprisonment, even execution.

'I don't know,' says Petra, hugging herself tight. 'It all seems far too risky to me.'

'Don't worry, Mum,' says Tibor taking her hand. 'I'll make sure we get to Austria safely.'

Ah, thinks, Katalin, the eternal optimism of the young. But then her father speaks, his voice strong and clear.

'András and I once made it out of the labour camp at Recsk. I'm sure we can make it across the border to Austria.'

*

The AVO driver opens the rear door of the black Pobeda and Ilona steps out, pulling her fur coat tight against the frosty air. A gust of wind blows a flurry of autumn leaves across her path and she shivers, tucking her hands deep inside her cuffs. The driver has brought her to a large, old house in the country, just outside Budapest. The house has a red-tiled roof, blue shutters at the leaded windows and a climbing rose around the front door. At this time of year the thorny branches are bare, but she imagines it must be delightful in the summer. Quite the idyllic little hideaway.

'This way, if you please.' The driver opens the front door and steps aside for her to pass. She enters the wood-panelled hallway where a stag's head mounted on a plaque stares at her with glazed eyes. Ilona averts her gaze from the animal and follows the driver into an elegantly furnished room on the ground floor. Her host is standing in front of a blazing log fire, his hands clasped behind his back. Her first impression is of a well dressed cadaver, he's so tall and gaunt, the black suit only serving to accentuate the pallor of his skin which is stretched taut over sunken cheekbones.

'Mrs Novák, what a pleasure to finally meet you.' He extends a bony hand. The voice is deep and sonorous.

'The pleasure is all mine, Colonel Szabó.' She takes his hand and flashes him her sweetest smile. In response the colonel's thin lips curl upwards and the deep-hooded eyes crinkle ever so slightly at the corners.

'Let me take your coat.' He helps her out of her fur and hands it to the driver who takes it away, closing the door behind him. 'Now, what can I get you to drink?'

A table beside the fireplace has been generously stocked with a selection of wine and spirits.

'A glass of red wine would be lovely,' says Ilona, making herself comfortable on the plush velvet sofa.

Whilst the colonel uncorks a bottle of burgundy and fills two large glasses, she glances around the room, admiring the oak bookcases filled with leather-bound volumes, the oil paintings in heavy gilt frames, the grand piano in the far corner, and the antique clock on the mantelpiece which ticks reassuringly. The logs in the fire crackle and pop, emitting a heady scent of pine resin. The heavy brocade curtains have been drawn against the chilly weather and the room is lit by a collection of lamps, giving a cosy feel. She starts to relax.

Colonel Szabó passes her a glass of wine and Ilona takes a sip. It's a quality vintage with a full-bodied texture and rich, fruity aroma. She takes another sip, telling herself that she definitely made the right decision in coming here today.

A few days ago, when the fighting erupted again, her husband Károly said they should escape to Austria. This time he was prepared, he told her, having made sure that the car had a full tank of petrol. But she demurred, saying they couldn't travel in the midst of all that chaos and that surely this time the Russians would sort things out once and for all. And she was proved right. Now with Imre Nagy deposed and János Kádár in power, there won't be any more trouble, she feels sure of that. And if she plays her cards right, the future could be very promising indeed.

Colonel Szabó takes an armchair next to the fire and picks up a black notebook from a side table. He turns to a bookmarked page and says, 'I have asked you here today to talk about a mutual acquaintance of ours. Professor Márton Bakos.'

She inclines her head but stays silent, waiting for the colonel to continue.

'I have been meeting on a regular basis with Professor Bakos since his release from the labour camp at Recsk. Keeping track of his whereabouts and his contacts, you understand. Standard procedure for released prisoners. I noted from his file – which has subsequently vanished from Andrássy Avenue – that your husband and Professor Bakos were colleagues at the university and that both of you were friends with the family.'

'This is correct,' says Ilona, taking a larger mouthful of wine. She remembers the musical evenings they used to hold, Eva accompanying her on the piano whilst she sang arias from Mozart's operas. Her favourite was the Countess's lament *Dove Sono* from *The Marriage of Figaro* – *Where are the beautiful moments of sweetness and pleasure?* The soaring melodic line, the passion, the tenderness…

'And during that time you also worked for the Secret Police?' The colonel's voice brings her sharply back to the present.

'I did.' Ilona nods her head. It was such a difficult time back in the early fifties. People were being arrested on the flimsiest of pretexts. It was essential to make sure you weren't caught yourself. Back in '52, the Secret Police wanted the names of dissident academics at the university. She knew her husband was having doubts about the regime, doubts that could have landed him – and her for that matter! – in serious trouble. So she decided to set up a decoy – an idea purloined from *The Marriage of Figaro* in fact. She gave the authorities the name of Márton Bakos, the only man to have spurned her affections, the only man who wasn't charmed by her, who only had eyes for his wife. Károly never knew.

'You could be of help to us again,' says the colonel, holding her gaze.

'What is it you want to know?'

'How much do you know about the part played by Márton Bakos's family in the uprising?'

A surprising amount, thinks Ilona, smiling to herself. Károly told her all about their activities after he visited Márton during the lull in the fighting, before the Russians returned.

'More wine?' asks the colonel.

'Please.' She holds out her glass. She might as well indulge herself if she's going to be here a while.

*

If András had any concerns about meeting Anna's family and what they would think of him, he needn't have worried. Her parents' joy at seeing their daughter return home safe and sound is soon extended to him as they welcome him into their tiny, but homely apartment.

'I hope my daughter didn't put you in too much

danger,' says Anna's father, a jolly man in his mid fifties with silver-grey hair and a firm handshake. 'She always was a bit of a tearaway.'

'Stop it, Papa,' says Anna, patting him playfully on the arm.

'You will stay for tea won't you, dear?' asks Anna's mother, as she takes András's coat. She's a shorter, older version of Anna, but he can see where Anna gets her radiant smile from.

'That's very kind of you, Mrs Benedek.'

'Please, call me Geerte. And my husband's name is Madzar. Kristóf and Tóni, Anna's brothers, will be home soon and then we'll eat. Anna, why don't you give me a hand in the kitchen, then András and your father can get to know one another.'

Anna gives him a wink as her mother ushers her into the kitchen.

'Beer?' asks Madzar, inviting András to join him in the living room.

'Thank you,' says András, accepting the proffered bottle.

'Now, tell me exactly what the pair of you have been getting up to. Anna's been very cagey about it all. I think she didn't want to worry her mother.'

Madzar listens intently as András explains the workings of the Corvin Circle and the first aid station at the Práter Street school. He leaves out the most painful events though, preferring not to mention Sándor just yet. He's relating the story of how he and a couple of teenagers hit a tank with a Molotov cocktail from an attic window, when the front door bursts open and there are loud voices and laughter in the hallway.

'That'll be Anna's brothers,' says Madzar. 'They never could do anything quietly, those two.'

Anna appears then, flanked by two young men who tower over her. András rises to his feet, wondering what these two will make of him. He gets the impression they are protective of their little sister.

Anna steps forwards. 'András, meet Kristóf and Tóni.'

Kristóf pumps András's hand. 'Glad to finally meet you.' Tóni does likewise.

'So,' says Kristóf. 'We hear you were in the Corvin Circle. Very impressive. We were both involved in the fighting at Móricz Zsigmond Square in Buda.'

For the next half hour, András and the brothers swap stories of tank battles and casualties. It appears that the fighting in Buda was every bit as fierce as that in Pest.

'The city's been destroyed,' says Tóni. 'All such a bloody waste.'

Geerte walks into the room and claps her hands together. 'All right, that's enough talk of fighting. Food is on the table. Let's sit down and eat.'

They enjoy a simple meal of bread, cheese and cold meats. András is touched at how they have welcomed him into their home.

When they've finished eating, Geerte serves coffee and the conversation soon turns to a discussion of the current situation.

'It's not safe here anymore,' says Kristóf, the older of the brothers. 'Tóni and I were talking about going to Austria, before they clamp down hard on the borders. Now is a good time, whilst the political situation is still chaotic.'

Geerte looks longingly at her children. 'You must do whatever you think best,' she says. 'But Madzar and I will stay here. There's no question of us leaving, what with my elderly parents...' Her voice trails off and András can see she is struggling to hold herself together. Madzar lays a hand on his wife's.

'I know this is hard,' says Kristóf, 'but those of us who fought in the uprising are in danger if we stay. There will be reprisals.'

András feels Anna's hand on his thigh under the table. He knows what she's thinking – they should escape too.

'What about you, András?' asks Geerte. 'Do you have family in Budapest?'

'My parents both died,' says András. 'But I have an adopted family that I live with.' He thinks of Márton as his father now.

'What plans do you have for escaping, son?' asks Madzar, turning to Kristóf.

'Tóni and I know a man with a truck,' says Kristóf. 'He's prepared to drive us close to the Austrian border. From there we'd have to cross on foot.' He looks at his sister across the table. 'There's room for you in the truck, and for András too. You don't have to decide right this minute. But a decision in the next twenty-four hours would be good.'

Geerte gasps. Clearly she hadn't thought their departure would be so soon.

After they've cleared the table and helped Geerte with the washing up, Anna draws András aside, saying they need to talk. She takes him into her room and closes the door.

'What are we going to do?'

'What do you want to do?' he asks, stroking a strand of hair off her face.

She looks at him with her clear blue eyes. 'I want to go with Kristóf and Tóni, but only if you'll come with me.'

András's heart floods with love. 'Of course I'll come with you. Wherever you go, I'll be there.'

She throws her arms around him and they kiss, long and passionately.

'But first,' he says, pulling away. 'I need to go home, pack a few things and say goodbye to Márton.' The thought of saying goodbye to the man who kept him going through that terrible time at the labour camp almost breaks his heart. But he knows Márton will understand. He's always telling András to think about his plans for the future, and András's future is here, with Anna. 'I'll go now. But I promise I'll come straight back in the morning.'

'We'll be waiting for you,' says Anna. 'Don't be late.'

*

Márton kneels at his wife's grave and lays a bunch of flowers by the headstone. He's never stopped loving her. He just wishes they could have had more time together. He used to come to the cemetery at least once a week, to sit and talk to her, but today will be the last time. Tomorrow he must say goodbye to Budapest. They will leave for Austria, if they get that far, and then who knows where? They will be refugees, at the mercy of others. Katalin helps him to his feet and they stand for a few moments in silent contemplation. A few drops of rain start to fall and Katalin says they should go home. They need to get ready for their journey.

They make their way arm-in-arm through the damaged streets, passing people with dazed expressions on their faces. Everyone has lost someone in this tragedy. When they arrive home, he is pleased to see that András is back. Despite the terrible defeat the country has suffered, the boy looks happier than he has ever seen him and he wonders if it has anything to do with that pretty, young girlfriend of his. He invites András to join him for a drink.

Over a glass of Pálinka Márton explains their plan to take the train to Sopron tomorrow, close to the Austrian border.

'You're more than welcome to join us,' he says. 'Unless you have other plans, that is.'

'That's what I wanted to talk to you about,' says András. 'You see, I met Anna's family yesterday, and her brothers are planning to escape in the back of a truck. Anna wants to go with them, and…'

'And you want to go with her,' says Márton, finishing the sentence for him.

András nods. 'I don't want you to think that I'm ungrateful for everything you've done for me. On the contrary, I wouldn't be alive now if you hadn't looked after me in the labour camp.'

Márton lays his hand on András's arm. 'But your place now is to be with the woman you love.' He thinks of his wife Eva and of how he'd have followed her to the ends of the earth. 'Of course you must go with Anna and her brothers. I wouldn't have it any other way.'

András's face breaks into a smile. 'Thank you. I knew you'd understand. Anna's expecting me by midday tomorrow so I'll see you all off first.'

'I'd like that,' says Márton.

*

The next morning Katalin bundles the children into triple layers of clothes, despite Lajos's protests that he's too hot. The rest of their things she stuffs into a small suitcase along with a change of clothes for herself.

'It'll only be for a little while,' she tells her son, although she doesn't know that. How long will it take for them to escape to Austria, assuming they make it at all? She rips a bed sheet into strips and fashions a sling so that she can strap Eva to her front. Zoltán is in the kitchen packing a rucksack with as much food as he can carry. She glances around the room to see if there's anything important she's forgotten. Her eyes light on her violin. She hasn't played it for so long now, she's getting rusty. She opens the lid and runs her finger along the polished grain of the maple wood. The strings need tuning.

On an impulse she lifts the violin to her chin and turns the pegs until the strings are all sounding in perfect fifths. Then she loses herself in one of her favourite pieces, her fingers remembering where to position themselves. As the last note drifts away, she hears a voice behind her.

'That was beautiful.' Tamás is standing in the doorway, looking slightly lost. He's wearing an old shirt and pair of trousers that used to belong to her father.

'I didn't know you were there.'

'What is the name of that piece?'

'*Liebesleid* by Fritz Kreisler. It means *Love's Sorrow*.' She puts the violin back in its case and shuts the lid.

'You're not leaving your violin behind, are you?' asks Tamás.

'I can't take it with me,' she says, sadly. 'I'll have my hands full with the children and the suitcase.'

'I'll carry it for you,' he says, stepping into the room. 'If you trust me with it, that is?'

Tamás has no other possessions in this world, so has nothing to pack himself. Since her father took him in two days ago, he's shown himself to be kind and loyal. Katalin understands that he just wants to be accepted.

'All right,' she says. 'Here you go.' She passes him the precious violin.

'I'll take care of it.'

'I know.' And maybe one day she'll feel able to play the companion piece, *Love's Joy*.

Katalin goes into the living room where she finds her father taking a last, wistful look at his remaining books, the ones the AVO didn't take with them. He never got the others back.

'Are you nearly ready, Papa?'

He turns from the bookcase with a sigh and nods. Then he picks up the photograph of himself and his wife on their honeymoon, looks at it with shining eyes and slips it inside his jacket pocket.

'We shouldn't be so attached to things, should we? What really matters is in here.' He taps his heart.

'It's time to leave,' says Zoltán, sticking his head around the door.

Whilst Márton goes to fetch his coat, Katalin looks around the room one last time to make sure they haven't forgotten anything important. Her mother's piano will have to be left behind. József has promised to try and find a good home for it. On the table next to her father's reading chair, she notices a manila folder peeking out from under a pile of newspapers. She pulls it out and sees that it's her father's AVO file, the one he collected from Andrássy Avenue with András. András read his file and discovered something which upset him. Katalin is not sure if her father ever read his. Zoltán is gathering everyone together in the hallway, but she just wants a moment to look inside the file. She has always wondered who was responsible for denouncing him. Whose lies sent him to the labour camp? She flicks through the pages quickly, furtively. They are mostly typed transcripts of conversations, proving that his work telephone was bugged, just as he thought. And then she sees a name that suddenly makes sense of everything. Ilona Novák. The woman with the beautiful voice was really singing for the Secret Police.

'Katalin, are your ready?' Zoltán is calling for her from the hallway.

'Coming.' She drops the hateful file and hurries into the hallway where everyone is waiting for her. Discovering the truth has hardened her resolve to escape from this city, from this country. If she ever sees Ilona again she will be tempted to kill her with her bare hands.

With Zoltán's help she straps little Eva into the makeshift sling. Then she takes Lajos by the hand. 'Come on,' she says. 'We're going on a big adventure.'

They all bid András a fond farewell, promising to make contact once they are across the border, then they leave.

It's like walking through a post-apocalyptic city. Damaged buildings line the route; burnt-out tanks and overturned trams impede their progress. Feri's café has been reduced to rubble. There's been no word from the jovial café owner since the tanks came back and they all fear the worst.

The train station is heaving with the mass of people. Everyone is pushing, jostling, shouting. Lost children cry out. Desperate parents yell frantically. Katalin is terrified that Lajos's tiny hand will slip out of hers so she lifts him onto Zoltán's shoulders. They must all stick together whatever happens.

The train for the border town of Sopron is already on the platform, belching out thick clouds of grey steam. The press of people carries them towards the train, almost without them having to move their feet.

'What about tickets?' shouts Katalin over the din.

'No time,' replies Zoltán. 'No one's bothering. We don't want to miss the train.'

They squeeze into the last carriage moments before the doors slam and the train jolts forward. The jam-packed passengers are thrown against one another. Every inch of available space is taken. There's no hope of finding a seat.

Pressed up against her neighbour – a man in a heavy winter overcoat – Katalin does a quick head count of their party to make sure everyone is there: Zoltán and Lajos, her father and Tamás, Petra and Tibor, and little Eva strapped to her chest and sleeping soundly, at least for the time being. All present and correct. The teacher in her relaxes. The train is moving and they are on their way.

*

The apartment is so quiet with everyone gone. It almost broke András's heart to say goodbye, but Márton assured him they would meet up again once they had escaped. Suddenly he feels a deep sense of foreboding. He knows only too well how escapes can go horribly wrong. Does Márton really believe they will see each other again, or was he just being his usual optimistic self? Without his friend and mentor by his side, András feels vulnerable, like the young student he was at the time of his arrest. But you're not that same young student, he tells himself. Anna is waiting for you, so get a move on.

He packs the book that Márton gave him as a parting gift into a canvas shoulder bag and puts some clothes in on top. He plans to travel light in case of trouble. He takes one last look around the apartment that has been his home for the last few years and then steps outside, closing the door behind him.

Once he's outside and striding down the street, his mood lifts. This is the start of the rest of his life and he intends to make the most of it. When they get to Austria, he'll ask Anna to marry him. And then they'll have to think about where they want to live. Could they go to America or Canada? He hopes to finish his studies and find work as an engineer.

He's busy pondering the possibilities when a sleek, black car drives past and comes to a stop twenty yards ahead. He doesn't react until two men in black overcoats jump out and start walking towards him. Suddenly, he realises the danger he's in. His stomach muscles clench and his heart thuds against his ribcage. He knows what those men are. The Secret Police. He looks left and right for an alleyway to run down, anywhere to hide, but the tall apartment blocks on either side offer no means of escape. He turns to run back the way he has just come, but the men have caught up with him by now. They take an arm each and march him towards the waiting car. They are both bigger and stronger than he is and resistance is useless. They bundle him into the back of the car where he falls into the footwell behind the front passenger seat. Before he has time to get his bearings, the car pulls away from the curb and speeds down the street.

'Good day, András,' says a deep voice. A thin, hollow-cheeked man in a black coat is sitting in the corner of the back seat. 'My name is Colonel Szabó and you are under arrest for your part in the uprising.'

*

An eerie silence has fallen on the packed carriage. No one dares say too much in case there are AVO men on board.

Old habits die hard. When she can see past the shoulders of those standing around her, Katalin peers out of the window at the mud-brown fields and the dull afternoon light which will soon fade to dusk.

At each stop a few people alight but even more clamber on board, cramming themselves into the tiniest of spaces. There are rumours that the stations up ahead are swarming with Secret Police. Katalin feels sick with worry. If they're caught trying to escape they'll go to prison. She's putting her children's lives at risk.

The train rumbles through the countryside, but is it taking them to safety or leading them into danger?

After almost three hours they are close to the last stop before the border. An urgent whispered message is passed down the carriage that the driver will slow down before the station so that people can jump off the train. That way they can avoid the AVO who are lying in wait on the platform.

Jump off! Katalin looks in alarm at Zoltán. How are they going to jump off with a baby, a small child and her father in tow? It's madness. Petra looks as if she might cry. Only Tibor is grinning at the thought of jumping off a moving train. And even if they do manage to jump off without injuring themselves, can they still avoid arrest?

As promised, the train slows to a crawl and everyone starts to stir. This is the moment of truth. Katalin feels a rush of cold air on her face as someone opens the door and it bangs against the side of the carriage. Then those closest to the door start to jump.

'It's all right,' says Zoltán. 'We're moving at a walking pace. I'll go first with Lajos. Then you can help your father down and pass Eva to me.'

There's a press of people behind them, keen to get off the train whilst they still have a chance.

Before Katalin can protest, Zoltán scoops Lajos into his arms and leaps from the train. And then he is striding alongside to help Márton climb down. With her father safely on terra firma, Katalin unstraps Eva from the sling and hands her to Zoltán. Then she takes a deep breath and jumps, rolling onto the muddy grass. When she stands up she's amazed to see that she's still in one piece. Tamás has jumped too and is still holding her violin case under his arm.

Petra and Tibor have exited from the other side of the train. When the train disappears, they cross over the tracks to join the others.

'That was brilliant,' says Tibor.

Petra shakes her head but Katalin sees that she is smiling.

There must be a few hundred people milling around along the length of the railway track. Some of them have already started to head across the fields, fanning out in a wide arc.

'Wait until the crowds have dispersed,' says Zoltán. 'It will be better if we don't travel with a large group. We'll be less conspicuous.' He takes a map and compass out of his rucksack and waits for the needle to settle. 'That way is west. The road to freedom.'

It's already dusk when they set out across the fields, avoiding the roads. So far, so good, thinks Katalin. But there's still a long way to go.

*

They have locked him in a prison cell. It's cold and dark, the only light from a tiny barred window high in the wall. András sits on the hard wooden bed, his head in his hands. All he can think about is Anna and how he's failed her. He's terrified that she'll wait for him and put herself in danger. He hopes that her brothers will persuade her to leave anyway.

He listens to the footsteps and shouts in the corridor. It sounds as if they are rounding up as many freedom fighters as they can find and throwing them into the cells.

Brave, young men and women who fought for their country's freedom right across the city. Thousands more on the run. He hopes with all his heart that Márton and his family made it onto the train and that they manage to cross the border safely. His own situation looks dire, so all he can do is hope and pray for his friends.

The cell door slams open and Colonel Szabó enters. His tall, cadaver-like frame fills the tiny cell. He looks down at András from beneath his hooded eyelids.

'Your fate depends on how useful you can be,' says the colonel. 'Give me the names of your fellow insurgents and you could walk out of here a free man.'

András doesn't believe him. And even if he did, he would never supply this man with the names of those he fought with in the Corvin Circle.

'Where has Márton Bakos gone? Where is his son-in-law, Zoltán Dobos?'

András's head jerks up at the mention of Márton and Zoltán.

'Their apartment is empty,' says the colonel. 'The traitors have fled.'

'I don't know where they are,' says András, which is true in a way. He has no idea if they are still on the train or walking across fields or what.

'What about your girlfriend? Anna is her name, isn't it?'

At the mention of Anna, András jumps to his feet, ready to punch this evil man. Colonel Szabó puts out a hand to stall him. 'Think about it. You could be out of here if you give me the information I require.'

'I have nothing to tell you,' says András. If his silence ensures the safety of those he loves, then he will never breathe a word about their whereabouts.

Colonel Szabó turns on his heel and leaves the cell. The door is slammed shut and bolted behind him.

*

It's hard going, tramping across the muddy, ploughed fields in the freezing cold, a biting wind searing the skin off their faces. For long stretches Márton imagines he's still at Recsk, trudging back to the camp after a gruelling day at the quarry, every muscle in his body aching from carrying such heavy loads. He hears Béla's voice in his head saying the quarry is too steep, and the barked orders of the guards, and he sees himself lying down on his bunk bed, too exhausted to even take off his boots. But then he hears a whimper from little Eva tucked snuggly against Katalin's chest, and sees his tiny grandson asleep on Zoltán's shoulders, and he's jolted back to the present moment. He's fleeing his homeland – he'll probably never see it again in his lifetime – and he feels an overwhelming sorrow.

Darkness has fallen now and they are travelling by the light of the moon. Every now and again they pause so that Zoltán can check the compass with a small flashlight. But he doesn't keep the light on for long in case a border guard spots it. They keep an eye out for watchtowers and try to stay as quiet as possible.

'It shouldn't be much further now,' says Zoltán. 'Maybe a couple of miles.' But it's impossible to be sure, thinks Márton. They can't see anything and it feels as if they are walking in a wilderness.

They sit on the freezing ground and share their provisions of food. No one says much because they are all too exhausted. It's too cold to sit there for long so as soon as they've finished eating they continue on their way.

They've gone about another mile when the ground underfoot starts to become swampy. Mud sucks at Márton's shoes and with his next step his foot sinks into the ground up to his ankle. He almost loses his balance as he pulls his foot free with a squelching sound. The others are having the same problem trying to stay upright in the boggy ground. He is on the point of suggesting they turn back and try a detour when Zoltán points at something in the distance.

'Look, what's that light over there?'

Márton strains his eyes into the distance. He can just make out a tiny gleam on the horizon. Maybe it's a village, maybe it's a watchtower. From this distance they have no way of knowing.

They trudge on through the mire, walking in pairs for support in the marshy ground. Márton is touched to see Tamás offer him his arm to lean on.

After half an hour of sinking sometimes knee deep into the swamp, they come to the edge of a fast-flowing river, swollen with the recent heavy rain.

'Look,' says Zoltán triumphantly. The light which was no more than a speck earlier is now clearly visible. They are looking at the lights of a small village. An Austrian village.

But it's on the other side of the river which is churning at their feet, a barrier as effective as any barbed wire fence.

Márton sinks to his knees in the mud, exhausted from hours of walking through the night. He doesn't think he has the strength to go on. He should lie down here and let the others go. They're all younger and fitter than he is, he is only holding them up. He's about to tell them to go on without him when a bright flare lights up the sky and the silence is split by the sound of machine-gun fire.

*

Anna stands at the window of her parents' apartment, anxiously scanning the street for any sign of András. It's already hours after he promised he would be here and darkness has fallen. Maybe she should go and look for him.

Kristóf enters the room and comes to stand beside her. 'The truck is ready to leave. We need to go.'

'But he said he would be here,' she wails.

'I'm sorry,' says Kristóf. He puts his hands on her

shoulders and turns her to look at him. 'We can't wait any longer. If they are rounding up freedom fighters then every moment we delay puts us in more danger.'

Anna bites her lower lip, her eyes brimming with tears. 'But I love him. And he loves me. He wouldn't just let me down. Something must have happened to him.'

'If that is the case, then all the more reason for you to leave now, whilst you still can. If András truly loves you then he will want you to be safe. He won't want you to stay in Budapest waiting for him. If he was going to come he would have been here by now.'

Her heart is breaking, but Anna nods her head, absorbing the truth of her brother's words.

'Come and say goodbye to Mama and Papa. Then we really must leave.'

With her eyes full of tears, she lets Kristóf lead her away from the window.

*

'Everyone down!' hisses Zoltán.

Katalin crouches down in the mud, trying to make herself invisible. The children have been blessedly quiet so far, but at the sound of the machine-gun fire, Lajos starts to cry. Eva wakes from her slumbering position against Katalin's breast and lets out a piercing wail.

In desperation Katalin sticks her little finger into her daughter's mouth in an effort to pacify her whilst Zoltán tries to calm Lajos but the little boy is deaf to all entreaties to be quiet.

As soon as Katalin takes her finger from Eva's mouth so that she can hug her son, the baby starts wailing again. It's hopeless.

Zoltán is rummaging in the rucksack and eventually pulls out a squashed bar of chocolate.

'Look what I found,' he says, breaking off a piece and holding it out to his son.

At first Lajos is too distraught to notice the chocolate and continues to cry, loud hacking sobs that fill the night air. Zoltán puts the piece of chocolate into Lajos's mouth and slowly the boy's cries lessen.

'Pass me Eva's bottle,' says Katalin. It's the only way to calm her down. She stuffs the teat into Eva's open mouth and silence descends. This is the last of the milk. There will be no more food now until they are in Austria. If they get that far.

'Did you see what was on the horizon?' she says in a low voice. When the flare lit up the sky, she saw the vertical outline of a watchtower, less than two hundred yards away. Proof that they are right on the border and are in grave danger of being caught.

'Yes,' says Zoltán. 'We can't go any further. We have to cross here.'

Katalin contemplates the water. It's maybe ten or twelve yards across, but how deep is it?

As if he's read her thoughts, Tibor says, 'I'm going to test it out.'

'No!' says Petra. 'It's too dangerous.'

'Sitting here is dangerous,' says Tibor. 'Besides, I'm fifteen now. You can't stop me.'

Before Petra can say anything else, Tibor wades into the water.

Katalin puts a hand on Petra's shoulder. 'Don't worry. He's a good boy. He won't do anything stupid.'

'I can't see him,' says Petra. 'Where is he?'

Katalin peers into the darkness, but she can barely make out Tibor's upper body above the level of the water. If Tibor drowns she'll never forgive herself for persuading Petra to come with them. But then there's a splashing sound and he is climbing back out of the water.

'I got over halfway,' he says, 'and it only came up as far as my chest. Look.' He points to his sodden clothes. He's shaking with cold, but he's proved that they can cross the river if they try. Petra hugs him to her.

'Come on, Mum, hold onto me,' says Tibor. 'It'll be all right.' He jumps into the water and pulls her with him.

'Can you manage with Eva?' asks Zoltán. 'I'll take Lajos on my shoulders.'

'I think so,' says Katalin. It's her father she's worried about though. He hasn't spoken for some time. It's as if he's given up hope. 'What about you, Papa?'

'I'll take care of Professor Bakos,' says Tamás.

She watches as her father and his former captor plunge into the water and start to wade across. Now it's only her, Zoltán and the children.

'You go in front,' says Zoltán, 'so I can keep an eye on you.'

Katalin gasps as the icy water cuts through her clothes, cramping her leg muscles, freezing her to the bone. Eva howls in protest even though the water hasn't yet reached her. She forces herself to keep moving. The current tugs at her legs and she dare not turn around to look at Zoltán in case she loses her balance and falls beneath the surface.

Suddenly darkest night becomes brightest day as the searchlight picks them out. She and Zoltán are not yet on Austrian soil and they are fair game for the border guards. She is terrified for the safety of her children. The air crackles with a round of machine-gun fire. Katalin screams, losing her footing on the rocky river bed. Suddenly Zoltán is beside her, gripping her upper arm.

'Don't worry, I've got you. We're nearly there.'

The water starts to recede from her chest when a shot rings out and Zoltán's grip on her arm loosens. He falls backwards, splashing into the water. Lajos slips from his father's shoulders and screams as he disappears beneath the surface.

Katalin is beside herself. She can't see Zoltán anymore. If she tries to search for Lajos then Eva, who is strapped to her chest, will drown. It's an impossible dilemma for a mother, having to choose one child over the over. Suddenly someone jumps into the water from the opposite bank, disappears beneath the surface and comes up shouting.

'I have him! Lajos is here!'

Katalin is crying tears of despair and joy. Tibor has rescued her son. She knows he's alive because she can hear him screaming. His cries are music to her ears.

Strong arms reach down and pull her out of the river. It might be Tamás but she's too exhausted to notice properly. At least her father and Petra have made it across too. She gives Eva to Márton to hold and returns to the water's edge to search for Zoltán. Where is he?

She screams his name, no longer caring if the border guards can hear her. But there is only silence and blackness. And then in the light of a flare that illuminates the whole sky, he emerges godlike from the water, her tall, brave husband. He's staggering, clutching his right arm where he must have been shot. She reaches out to him but there's another clatter of machine-gun fire and he is hit in the back. He disappears under the surface of the water and his body floats away in the current.

CHAPTER 19

Six months later.

The sun is dazzling after months being shut in a cold, dark cell. András turns his face skyward and feels the warm rays caressing his pallid skin.

'Move it!' The guards push him across the prison yard. His legs are unused to exercise and his hands are tied behind his back, causing him to stumble through lack of balance.

His captors have beaten and tortured him, but he has told Colonel Szabó nothing about former members of the Corvin Circle. He has fully admitted his own role, proud of the part he played, just sorry that they weren't ultimately successful.

'Climb the steps!' orders one of the guards.

He hopes that Márton, Katalin and Zoltán, and especially Anna are far away by now, in another country where they can live their lives in freedom.

On legs that threaten to give way, he ascends the scaffold. He looks up at the startlingly blue sky and sees a bird hovering overhead. He's almost glad that his suffering will soon be over, but he wants to enjoy this last moment of being alive.

'Stand there!'

They shove him into position. He glances one last time at the bird before a black hood is pulled roughly over his head. Then he feels the rope being placed around his neck.

May they live in peace, he thinks, as the trap door opens beneath his feet.

*

'Is that England?' In the last six months Lajos has grown into a chatty toddler who never stops asking questions.

'Yes, it is,' says Katalin. She holds Eva tight in her arms as the famous white cliffs of Dover come ever nearer. She's heard about these cliffs from her father so many times but she always expected that she would see them for the first time with Zoltán by her side.

'Do you remember who lives in England?' Márton asks his grandson.

'St George,' shouts Lajos. 'And the dragon,' he adds in a quieter voice.

'But remember the dragon is dead,' says Márton. 'St George killed him, so there's no reason to be afraid. This is going to be our new home. We'll be safe here.'

Safe, thinks Katalin. But what is safety without the man she loves?

After their escape into Austria they arrived at the village of Schattendorf, soaking, frozen and in a state of shock. They spent a week in the village at a camp run by the Red Cross. She has little memory of those days, so grief-stricken was she by Zoltán's death. She has a vague recollection of Petra encouraging her to eat soup and nursing her back to life.

They left Schattendorf and transferred to a refugee camp just outside Vienna where Márton and the others set about making arrangements for their futures whilst she cared for the children. Anna and her brothers turned up at the camp, having escaped Hungary in the back of a truck. But Anna was distraught because András never showed up on the day they were due to leave. There's been no news of him since and Katalin fears the worst. She knows Márton blames himself for not insisting that András travel with them on the train.

Anna and her brothers were the first to leave Austria, embarking on a new life in Canada. Katalin remembers the tearful farewells and the promises to stay in touch. She hopes Anna will find love in her new home. Tamás and Tibor struck up a friendship and Petra, who is never happier than when she has someone to mother, took the older boy under her wing. The three of them sailed for America two weeks ago amidst more heart-wrenching goodbyes. Katalin doesn't think she'll ever get over so much loss.

The white cliffs are getting closer now, and seagulls circle overhead, crying out a raucous welcome. Márton puts an arm around her shoulders.

'When your mother died, I thought my life was over,' he says. 'But you gave me something to live for.'

'I miss him so much,' says Katalin, her eyes filling with tears.

'I know you do.'

'Mummy, mummy.' Lajos is tugging at the sleeve of her coat. 'Can I have a sword like St George?'

Katalin looks down at her son, his face full of hope and excitement.

'Of course you can,' she says. 'You're going to grow up big and strong and brave, just like St George.' And just like your father, she thinks, smiling to herself.

THANK YOU FOR READING

I hope you enjoyed this book. If you did, then I would
be very grateful if you would please take a moment to
leave a review at the retailer where you bought it, or on
Goodreads. Thank you.

JOIN MY MAILING LIST

If you would like to receive news about new books,
promotions and giveaways, please join my mailing list via
the link on my website. Thank you.
http://margaritamorris.com

OTHER BOOKS BY MARGARITA

Oranges for Christmas
The Sleeping Angel
Scarborough Fair
Scarborough Ball
Scarborough Rock

ABOUT THE AUTHOR

Margarita Morris was born in Harrogate, North
Yorkshire. She studied Modern Languages at Jesus
College, Oxford and worked in computing for eleven
years. She lives in Oxfordshire with her husband and
two sons.

SELECT BIBLIOGRAPHY

I am indebted to the authors of the following books:

Enemies of the People - My Family's Journey to America by Kati Márton, Simon & Schuster, 2009

Journey to a Revolution - A Personal Memoir and History of the Hungarian Revolution of 1956 by Michael Korda, Harper Perennial, 2007

Twelve Days: Revolution: Revolution 1956 - How the Hungarians Tried to Topple their Soviet Masters by Victor Sebestyen, Weidenfeld & Nicolson, 2007

Corvin Circle 1956 by Gergely Pongrátz, online

Molotov Cocktails by Anna Mandoki, Amazon Media

Cry Hungary! Uprising 1956 by Reg Gadney, London, 1986

My Happy Days in Hell by George Faludy, Penguin, 2010

The Undefeated by George Paloczi-Horváth, Eland Publishing, 2012

Budapest 1900 - A Historical Portrait of a City and its Culture by John Lukacs, Grove Press, 1988

Vanished by the Danube - Peace, War, Revolution, and Flight to the West by Charles Farkas, Excelsior Editions, 2013

CPSIA information can be obtained
at www.ICGtesting.com
Printed in the USA
LVHW092022290819
629406LV00005B/647/P